"Hide"

First published 2020 by Nick Harper. All characters and events are fictional and any resemblance to real people or places is coincidental.

Please enjoy this book. Look for Nick Harper's other works on Amazon or go to nickharperbooks.com for updates, previews and more information. The author is grateful for any reviews on Amazon or Goodreads.

Ben,
may your soul rest forever
in a glass jar

enjoy!

HIDE

A NOVEL

NICK HARPER

4

CHAPTER ONE
THE HEARSE

1
1993

The deer froze as something lurched out of the shadows, fat and bloated and moaning. She turned her wide, brown eyes up from the frosted grass and they glistened in the moonlight as she watched, peering into the dark of the forest as the thing moved. Wet grass still half-chewed in the deer's mouth, she tensed her muscles and waited.

It wasn't coming for her, not yet.

For a few seconds, the black, swollen shape was still. It stood amongst the clawed branches of dead, stripped trees, hunched over. A sloppy, wet sound echoed about the crippled trunks around them as it chewed something. Strings of flesh hung from its chin. The deer watched, frozen in place, as the thing ate. At its feet, something whimpered and twitched on the ground.

The beast stopped chewing, stood for a moment. Its

body was dark and featureless and the deer understood why she hadn't seen the thing before; in that moment of stillness, of silence, it almost faded completely into the shadows, framed by the tall, slanted pines and the brittle birch trunks.

As the deer watched, the dark shape raised a black, deformed snout.

It sniffed.

The deer's entire body rippled with fright. A wave of cold passed through the clearing. The beast paused, head lifted, nose wet and twitching. The breeze had changed direction and it had caught a scent. *Her* scent. The thing's jaw shifted – all narrow spines and slivers of shining saliva – and it smiled. It dropped whatever slippery, shining mess it had been holding in its claws and its shoulders twisted. It turned its head towards the doe and a pair of yellow, glaring eyes narrowed in the dark.

Powerful, muscular thighs dug the deer's hind legs into the earth and she bolted. Already she could hear it coming after her. Branches tore and cracked under lumbering feet as the thing burst out of the shadows. The ground trembled with every heavy, powerful stride it took, particles of black earth shuddering over the foliage. A great oak trunk rose up before the doe and she pivoted left, twisting her whole body around the tree. Her hooves carried her swiftly over cracked soil and dried, dead leaves and fallen lengths of branch that jutted up from the ground like daggers. Dew had fallen over the ground in the later hours of the day, and beads of frost melted away under the pelt of her cloven feet.

The deer ducked under an overturned tree, wrenched from the ground by the latest storm in a tangle of twisted roots. The ground was damp and slippery and the deer spun around, digging her hooves into the filth. She dove for the base of the tree and pressed her back to the coiled mass of rotting wood, ears flattening against the side of her head as she listened.

There. Thundering towards her, the thing's heavy feet churned up swathes of black murk and loam as it charged after its prey. Then it was dead above her and it pulled the shadows with it as it pounced. The tree splintered and cracked under its weight and a knot of thick, twisted claws swiped for her face and caught her snout. Warmth dripped down into her mouth and the deer recoiled. The dead tree groaned above her and rotten clutches of wood fell away and splintered beneath the creature's weight. The beast stumbled over the fallen birch and the deer sprung out from the shelter of the roots, slipping between its claws. She tore back in the direction she had come from, carving a path through the trees. Erratically she zigzagged about slender, crooked trunks, navigating the maze of broken, dead things as easily as in daylight. Behind her the thing let out a deep, hungry moan from the pit of its stomach. The deer glanced over her shoulder and caught a blur of shadow tumbling between the trees; her eyes widened. It had latched onto the scent of her blood now, and as much as she ran, as much as she twisted herself about the labyrinth of the forest, it wouldn't let up the hunt.

Suddenly the deer lost her footing and slid down a steep bank, bleating in panic as the ground turned to mulch and uneven, slippery nothing beneath her. The cold smacked her in the stomach as she plunged into the stream. She swung her hooves, thrashing madly in the water. She found a footing in the chaos of the stream, but the ground was loose and corroded and already she was sinking into the thick of the riverbed. Cold seared the deer's flesh and clamped down on her lungs and she stretched her neck up in a desperate attempt to keep her head above the water. Her spindly legs skittered over the riverbed and the stream rushed about her, thick and loud and cold enough to mask the earthy scent of the forest and mute her senses.

Flat, smooth pebbles crumbled away beneath her feet. Tilted slabs of rock cut into her hooves as the deer forced herself forward, thrusting deeper into the stream, eyes wide and round and wet as she headed for the opposite bank. She stumbled awkwardly, numb with cold and fear. Then the ground sloped up, out of the river, and she crashed onto dry land in a wave of ice-cold, black water that spattered the bank as she clambered wildly out of the stream.

She darted forward, shaking off the ice water that

clung to her brown-white fur. With one furtive glance back at the glittering, black crevice of the stream, the deer plunged into the dark. Behind the farthest row of thin, dead trees, she caught a glimpse of some dim, burnt light. The deer was hesitant; the light didn't seem natural, didn't seem right. But it was close, and it was a safer bet than whatever had chased her through the forest.

The beast crashed into the stream behind her, heavy and chaotic, splashing in the cold and the dark as a loud, low rumble poured out of its shadowy maw. The deer ran, bucking towards the light at the edge of the forest. She ducked beneath another fallen tree and leapt wildly over a second, smacking the ground with her shins as she came back down. She hurtled forwards, heading with reckless abandon towards that sombre, burning glow.

A shadow rose up before her and a thick, clawed arm swiped madly at her flank. The deer screamed, terrified, staggered off to one side as blood pooled over her sodden rump. The beast grabbed for her throat and she keeled forward, kicking out behind her, slipping out of the thing's hungered grasp. She was closer, now, to that light, close enough that she just might –

Earth turned to tarmac beneath the deer's hooves and she skidded over the new, smooth surface, came to a panting halt. Her eyes turned upward, toward the unnatural light she had been chasing. It hung, suspended on the top of a narrow, grey pole slick with moonlight, encased in a round, faded ball and humming above her head. More of them stood at regular intervals along the edge of the forest.

Streetlights.

The deer didn't have time to puzzle over the light globes; a rumbling behind her turned to a terrible, mangled grinding and then to a screech and the deer whirled around.

Her eyes widened as she saw it. Too late.

2

'I just don't see why we have to bring him!'

Philip Drake flexed his knuckles on the wheel, eyes drifting across to the woman in the passenger seat. Outside, a hollow wind pulled at the crooked branches of the trees at the side of the road, tearing brittle leaves from them in a callous display of brutality. The sky had darkened a little over three hours into the drive, blackening above the motorway as they sat, fuming, in a thirty-mile queue of red lights and blaring horns. Now, as they plunged into the depths of the forest, darkness smothered the little car like a blanket.

'We've been through this, Phil,' Elizabeth hissed, tugging at her hair in the rearview mirror. Behind her Edward Drake was slumped forward in the backseat, straining against the vinyl belt across his chest. His head lolled onto a drooping shoulder, eyelashes twitching as he slept. The boy's tousled, black hair fell over his tilted face, covering his eyes. He'd been sound since the motorway. 'Look,' Elizabeth continued, turning to her husband, 'Granny hasn't seen Eddie since he was a baby. I can't keep telling her that he's ill, or... on a school trip, or whatever. She's not an idiot.'

'No, she's a voodoo wackjob,' Philip scowled He shook his head. 'It's bad enough that *we* have to go see her, but Eddie? He's a *kid*, Liz. He's eight years old. I don't want that old hag teaching our son to read tea leaves or, I don't know... glue googly eyes on pheasant bones.'

'Pheasant bones?' Elizabeth echoed.

'I'm not a witch,' Philip shrugged. 'I don't know *where* they glue their googly eyes, but I bet it's not teddy bears.'

Leaves fluttered over the tarmac, glowing like embers in the headlight beams.

'It's not like we'll have to worry about it now, anyway,' Elizabeth said, folding her arms. She shifted her weight in the seat. Orange streetlights threw dull shadows over the tarmac. 'Phil, we're gonna have to find a hotel or something for tonight. This forest goes on for dozens of miles. It'll be impossible to find her house in the dark. Do you even know where we are?'

Philip frowned, glancing at the map pinned to the dashboard. The pages were crumpled, edges frayed and bent in. He had marked the path in red. 'I think so,' he said. 'I mean… yeah, I think so.'

'You sure?'

'Absolutely not.'

Elizabeth sighed.

'Look,' Philip said, 'not that I don't want to find your mother's place, but maybe a hotel would be a good idea. Get our bearings, try again in the morning.'

Elizabeth watched as the trees blurred past them, hazy fragments of grey and black rising up from the ground at the edge of the road. 'If not for that hold-up we'd be there by now...'

'Thank *fuck* for the hold-up, then,' Philip murmured.

'Phil! Watch it while Eddie's in the car!'

'What?'

'Watch your language,' Elizabeth scowled. 'You're setting a bad example.'

'He's asleep,' Philip said, eyes sliding up to the rearview mirror. 'He can't –'

The deer stepped out of nowhere. Pale fur glowed a hazy white in the glare of the streetlamp. Round, wide eyes glittered as it opened its mouth and bleated –

Philip stamped the brake into the floor and cried out, yanking the wheel off to the right. Elizabeth was thrust forward in her seat and she grabbed at something solid; needles of pain jabbed her fingertips as she dug her nails in. In the backseat Eddie's eyes snapped open and he yelped as the car veered off to the other side of the road, swinging wildly over the faded markings on the tarmac. The deer bucked, twisting its entire body around and kicking up with its hind legs, and Elizabeth screamed as the rump of the thing clipped the front of the car. She gripped tighter, gasping as the thing in her hand moved. It jerked upward and she realised it was Philip's thigh, suddenly off the brake and twisted in some involuntary convulsion, and they spun out of control, tyres screeching over tarmac as sparks flew up around the wheels.

Crack!

The bonnet crumpled around a lamppost, pushing it back into the trees. The orange bulb flickered, throwing wild, dancing shadows over the road, illuminating a twisted wreck of scrap metal and plastic and glass. Elizabeth barely registered the smoke filtering into her lungs. She heard a wailing from the backseat – Eddie was awake and he was terrified.

A wisp of black poured out from beneath the bonnet as the car lay still.

All at once, the world stopped spinning.

3
NOW

Matthew Kramer sat at the edge of the world and raised the bottle to his lips as the ocean wind swirled around him. He tilted his head back and drank. A tiny spot of crimson ran over the back of his hand and dropped onto the tattered sleeve of an old, moth-eaten overcoat. Pale moonlight brushed the bloody curves of his knuckles. Patches of red, cracked skin shone in the moonlight, still wet and raw.

Kramer closed his eyes and let the ocean breeze wash over him. His legs dangled over the edge of the cliff, swinging softly. Below him, the sea attacked a narrow crescent of beach, biting at the sand with vicious, crashing teeth. The water was wild and black and it smacked the base of the cliff with such force that Kramer wondered if it might crumble away beneath him.

Usually, this was the calmest spot on the island. Not tonight.

A storm was coming.

Kramer set the near-empty bottle down beside him; foam crackled at its rim as it toppled onto its side in the long, dry grass. Slowly the man leaned forward, eyes narrowed and dark, the same dull grey as the clouds above his head. He could see all of the beach from up here. From the strip of sand that held back the ocean to a ring of shiny, black rocks jutting up from the waves - the *Devil's Crown* - and across to a crude ramp that drew the beach up to the top of the cliff.

Something fluttered across the sand and Kramer blinked, leaning forwards. He considered calling out, but whatever was down there disappeared before he could open his mouth. *You're imagining things,* he thought. *There's nobody down there.*

Still, he shuddered.

'You're out late, detective.'

Kramer looked over his shoulder. The world swam around his head and he winced. His head throbbed and he blinked away the faded spots that danced before his eyes.

Debbie stood in the grass behind him, hands in her pockets.

Kramer smiled. 'What are you doing out here?' he said quietly, slurring his words a little. 'You should be asleep, Deb.'

Even now, even out here, Debbie Martin's hair was tied up neatly behind her head, a spiralling bun of golden-yellow threatening to pull apart in the wind. One strand had come loose and it fluttered across her forehead. Her eyes were bright, but she looked tired. A thick parka jacket was wrapped tight around her. Striped pyjama bottoms were tucked into heavy, brown boots. She spoke calmly, her voice a flight of warmth on the air. 'You're on duty in five hours, Matt. How much have you had?'

Kramer turned back to the sea, shaking his head. He reached up with a red-knuckled hand, pushing matted, sand-brown tangles out of his eyes. He didn't answer.

Debbie's eyes moved over Kramer's back and she

clocked the mess of empty bottles around him. Her gaze flickered to the man's sleeve, on a splash of red there. Just a speck, barely even that, but enough for her to notice. She stepped forward and nodded to a spot on the ground beside him. 'May I?'

Kramer nodded, reaching for the bottle that he'd laid there. He took it to his lips and drained the last of it; sweet, cold whiskey burned the back of his throat as it slid down towards his gut. He patted the ground, slipping the empty bottle into the shadows behind him and letting it fall into the dirt and the clay.

Cautiously, Debbie sat.

For a while the two of them said nothing. They looked out over the black scape of the sea, watching as a little grey smudge curved towards them on the waves. The boat was a small, narrow thing, top deck awash with floodlights. The round-cornered windows were all barred.

New arrivals.

Cain's End was a small island, barely three miles long and bent in the middle. Ragged and unrestrained, it looked form above like the jawbone of some long-dead beast. The northern half of the island was scattered with the terraced houses that made up the village, criss-crossed with a winding network of dirt tracks and flat, tarmac roads. The southern half was wild and torn-up with a thick pine forest that threw itself over the ground and descended into a chaotic jumble of rocks and caves and low, broken cliffs.

Deep within the forest, sheltered from the sun and the rain and the relentless wind that battered the island from all sides, the decaying wreck of the asylum was wrapped in barbed wire and tall, stone walls. Black River Asylum was the island's dirty little secret, taking the desperate, unhinged dregs of society from the mainland and hiding them away from the rest of the world.

'You know,' Kramer said, 'I miss the days when it was our job to round up all the crazy bastards that escaped that place.'

'What?' Debbie frowned.

'Back before they locked down the security. Remember when that strangler got out and tried to garrotte some poor fucker? And that old woman who practically managed to hijack a ferry off the island? And me and you, Deb, we stopped them. Remember that?'

'You *miss* that?' Debbie said, incredulous.

'Last time I got to do my job,' Kramer said. 'Last time I really got to be a detective. I mean, what the fuck else have we got to do out here, Debbie, in this *shithole?* Nothing ever happens here. Ever. I wish...'

He trailed off. The boat had disappeared in the shadows behind the pier and Kramer could hear yelling from the jetty. He leaned forward to look and something flickered in the corner of his vision, down on the beach. His eyes shifted. There was nothing there.

'Is that why you're angry, Matt?'

Kramer frowned, turning his head. 'Hm?'

Debbie gestured. 'Give me your hand.'

'What for?'

'Just give it to me.'

Kramer held out his palm, grey and calloused in the moonlight.

Slowly Debbie took it, turning it over in her own. She ran her fingertips over his broken knuckles, tracing a gentle path over the red, open blisters. Kramer's hand twitched.

'You have to stop doing this, Matt,' Debbie whispered.

'It's nothing,' Kramer said, pulling his hand away. He watched as the boat reappeared in a splash of white in the distance, lit by the fizzing bulbs of the floodlights on its top deck. It bobbed wildly as black-clad figures hopped onto the pier, unravelling coils of rope and calling to each other through the dark. The old arcade at the end of the pier was silent, a derelict mess of white, fluttering tape and boarded-up windows. The old neon lights had been turned off for years.

'Did Charlie send you out here?' Kramer said after a moment.

Debbie shook her head. 'She didn't need to.'

'How did you know I'd be out here?'

'Matt, I always know. And I know why you're really angry. I know it's going to keep getting worse until

Charlotte's birthday. How long is it now?'

'Three days,' Kramer said.

'Three days, then. Matt, I know you feel helpless about this whole thing, about this secret you've been keeping for so long. But you have to do this, okay? You have to tell her. And I know that's what's really making you angry, I know you think she'll...' She paused. Her eyes dropped to Kramer's knuckles and she swallowed. 'Well, whatever you think is going to happen, you have to *tell* her.'

'I will. When she's sixteen, that's what I've always said. She deserves to know.'

'Then you need to stop this, Matt,' Debbie pleaded, laying her hand on his knee. 'Not for me. For her. Whatever happens in three days, she's your daughter. Do you remember why you came to Cain's End?'

'To look after her.'

'Right. And you can't look after her if you're out here every night getting pissed up, can you? However difficult this is for you - and I know it's difficult - you don't need to keep doing this. I'm here for you, you know. And I know you're not going to want to hear this, but I believe with all my heart that some up there is looking out for you too.'

'God?' Kramer cocked an eyebrow.

'Maybe.'

'I don't think God's been paying much attention to Cain's End lately, Deb.'

'So do something good,' she shrugged. 'Catch his attention.'

Kramer looked at her, losing himself a little in her face. There was something there, tonight, that he didn't usually notice. Something beyond the kind, gentle shine in her eyes. Something deeper.

Silently, Debbie reached for his hand and held it. For a while the two of them watched the pier as black-padded guards hooked a narrow, steel ramp to the edge of the jetty and ushered a string of half a dozen men and women up off the boat. White, baggy clothes flapped in the wind.

'I can't tell you what to do, Matt,' Debbie said. 'Get up off your arse or give up and stay down. But don't you dare drag that girl into the dirt with you.'

4

'It's going to be okay,' Elizabeth sobbed through choked-up gasps. In the seat beside her, Philip was silent. 'Eddie, it's going to be –'

Something heavy slammed into the back of the car and the whole thing rocked against the bent-up spine of the lamppost. The engine was still running, somehow, and a horrific grinding sound sputtered out from the broken belly of the vehicle. Elizabeth whirled round in her seat and reached for Eddie with a trembling hand -

Suddenly the car wrenched itself free of the lamppost

and twisted around, pulled by some impossible force, strong enough to drag them across the road. It swung the car like a flat, burning baseball bat and Elizabeth caught sight of the deer through the rear window, laying crimson and hollow in the road. Then the car was tumbling over onto its side and the deer's body vanished in a jagged blur of movement. A deep, burning amber seared her vision, and then the car was on its roof. The windscreen exploded in a shower of glass dust and splintered pieces flew out into the car, scratching her face, tearing jagged gashes over her arms. Something smacked her belly and she screamed as warmth spread over her and her head cracked against the ceiling of the car. Eddie tumbled out of his seatbelt, screaming as he crashed into the framework. Philip slumped a little further over the wheel, his broken neck twisting as his skull pushed up against the top of the car, cracking and splintering and fracturing in Elizabeth's ears. She blinked furiously as something dripped onto her chin.

Something moved beyond the broken windscreen. It lumbered away from them, white-feathered fur caught between its bloody teeth. The engine shuddered and cut out in a horrible sputter of stinking oil and smoke.

The car fell silent.

Embers floated into the air at the side of the road and Elizabeth watched them drift up into the dark. Her vision was hazy and clouded with red. Somewhere in the black sea of the dashboard, warning lights flashed.

'Eddie...' Elizabeth whispered. Blood bubbled over her lips. 'Eddie, get out... get out of the car. Go...' She tried to turn her head, but she couldn't move. Numbness spread over her chest and her arms and held her in place. '*Eddie...*'

The boy moved in the corner of her eye and Elizabeth turned her eyes up to the cracked glass of the rearview mirror. Eddie tried to sit up, but he was twisted up against the roof of the car, moaning as a bloody string of drool peeled over his chin. One of his legs was caught in the seatbelt that had thrown him loose.

'Get out...' Elizabeth moaned up at the mirror. 'Please... run.' A hot, intense pain sheared her gut and she looked toward her torso, pressing at it with shaking fingers. Something thick and warm stuck to her palm. 'Oh, god...'

A broken, curved piece of glass burst out of her stomach in a mess of red and purple. Strings of blood drizzled over the glass, oozed over it like paint. A thin, sheared coil of something crimson and slippery twisted itself around the shard like a rubbery, lumpen snake and Elizabeth shrieked as she realised what she was looking at.

The world stopped moving.

Dried, dead leaves hung in the air above the road, suspended in the dark. Shadows lingered all around the broken frame of the car. Eddie's tortured moaning had stopped. Every sound was muffled, every smell – the fresh, bitter scent of the leather car seats, the wet, tripe-like smell of her own intestines – faded away, as if Elizabeth's senses had given up on her. Even the pounding of her heart slowed right down, so far that she could barely hear it at all.

Slowly, resisting the urge to cry out in agony, Elizabeth Drake turned her head. It hurt to move her neck but she twisted around as far as she could and looked into the road.

The deer's mangled carcass was nowhere to be seen. A bloody smear was all that was left, a dark splash in the flickering orange light. The beast was gone.

A tall, slender man stood in the middle of the road, shoulders askew so that one arm hung just a little lower than the other. A wrinkled, jet-black jacket pressed down against his ribcage, buttoned over a dark, silken shirt. Ink-black trousers wrapped around his impossibly thin legs like a second, shadowy skin. Polished brogues grinned up from the tarmac.

Slowly, the black-suited man started walking towards the car. Something screamed at Elizabeth from the very back of her mind and she yelled over the thumping of blood in her ears: '*Eddie get out the car right now get out get out get OUT -*'

A shadow fell over the car and Elizabeth stopped screaming.

The dark figure knelt slowly, crouching outside the upturned passenger window. Neck bent up against the ceiling, Elizabeth struggled with her seatbelt, wrestling against the buckle with bloody hands. It was jammed in place and she fumbled desperately, wide eyes on the window. Her hands froze on the buckle and she cursed.

'Oh, *shit*...'

Shadows twisted over the glass as a long, crooked finger reached for the window. The man's skin was yellow. His finger was bent up and wrinkled and ended in a filthy, cracked nail. Red dust lingered in the folds of his skin.

He touched the glass.

Blood and fire rained down around Elizabeth and she *shrieked*. The window shattered with the black-suited man's touch and fragments of glass shot in every direction. Shards erupted around her, buried themselves in her face, her eyes, her heaving chest. Something wrenched against the back of her seat. She couldn't move.

'*Edward Drake get OUT OF THIS FUCKING CAR RIGHT NOW* –'

The black-suited man leaned down and for the first time, Elizabeth saw his face. Behind her, Eddie was screaming, hoarse and terrified. The dark figure outside the window smiled.

Elizabeth swallowed.

One half of the man's skull was so horribly mutilated that the skin had folded into layers and layers of bubbling, raw mess, wet and sticky with pus. The skin on the other side had almost completely peeled away, sick and raw around a bulging, popping eyeball round with lust and animal hunger. Where the remnants of his skin clung to him it was yellow, burned and broken and sickening to behold. His flesh was wrinkled and repulsive and he smelled, stronger than the petrol and the fire that had crept up from the mess of the engine, he smelled like tobacco and *shit* –

Elizabeth Drake heard sirens in the distance, but they were too late. Her lungs filled up with blood and a surge of incontinence ripped her guts apart. Crimson flew over her lips and she let out one last, horrific screech as the man with the yellow face grinned down through the shattered screen and reached for her heart.

5

Charlotte Kramer was asleep when her dad came home.

Her eyes snapped open at the sound of footsteps, crunching heavily over the gravel on the front drive. The girl reached for a digital clock on the bedside table and turned it round, groaning as the time blinked up at her. Almost one in the morning. She listened as her father fumbled rabidly with the door. This was the fourth night in a row that he'd come home after midnight. He'd never tried particularly hard to mask his drinking habit, but at least it had been less... *regular* before.

He seemed different, the last few days. Like he was hiding something from her.

The door opened with a *click* and Kramer stumbled into the front hall. There was a faint *thwump* downstairs as he dropped his coat, then his footsteps faded as he crossed the hallway. Charlotte closed her eyes as she tracked the man's movements – he passed quickly into the kitchen, and a soft trickle told the girl that he was pouring himself another drink. She cursed under her breath. 'Go to sleep,' she whispered. 'Just go to *sleep, dad...*'

The footsteps grew louder again, and she listened intently as he moved along the hallway. After a moment Kramer turned and stepped into the living room. Charlotte waited – *one, two, three* – then flinched at a sudden burst of noise. Downstairs, Kramer swore, blundered about the room until he found the television remote and the sound from the screen faded into a soft haze. 'Better,' Charlotte heard him mumble.

She smiled. The man was doing an awful job of keeping quiet, but at least he was *trying*.

He always tried.

Charlotte laid still for a few minutes, sandy hair in her face. Her eyes closed. One ear pressed to the mattress, she listened to the faint sounds of the television in the living room. She couldn't make out much, but the mattress seemed to hum a little with every sound, vibrating against the side of her face. It was oddly calming - hypnotic, almost - and before too long the girl had fallen asleep again. The cold, hazy drift of unconsciousness caught her and she slipped into the dark and the silent, writhing shadows.

Charlotte stood at the edge of the forest, bare feet sunk into the earth. The dirt dug cold fingers into the gaps between her toes, holding her in place. She peered through the trees.

'Hello?' she called. Something moved, off to her right, but she couldn't turn her head, couldn't look in the direction of the noise. Her eyes were fixed on something up ahead, obscured by the curled, gnarled claws of the tall pines at the treeline.

Burning, flickering lights seeped out into the night through greasy windows and Charlotte frowned.

Who would live all the way out here?

'Help me...' Charlotte whispered, and suddenly she was stumbling toward the crooked house, knees aching as she dragged something behind her, something limp and heavy...

Slowly, the front door of the old house opened and someone stepped out onto the sagging porch, beckoning her forward. An old woman, so narrow that the light seemed to twist around her waist and flare about her wispy, grey hair. Charlotte fell to her knees in the foliage and sobbed. 'Please...'

Something moved behind her. Shadows twisted

around the trees and something lunged toward her face
-

Charlotte kicked out wildly, yelped as her foot hit the bedpost. Something crashed outside her room and she frowned. Breathing heavy, she looked around her. Sweating, stuck to the sheets.

'Dad?' she yelled.

Nothing.

'*Shit*,' Charlotte murmured. 'Shit, not *again*.' Already she was out of bed, fighting with the sheets that had wrapped themselves around her ankles and her wrists. She stumbled over the floor, almost falling, and for a second she could see the forest floor rushing up to meet her face, shadows moving in the dead leaves –

'Fuck off,' Charlotte snapped, steadying herself. 'You're just a... just a stupid dream.'

But what if it's not just a dream?

'Dad?' Charlotte called, shaking off the thought as she staggered for the door.

What if she's real?

Charlotte pushed the door open, stepped out of her bedroom and onto the landing.

There, on the stairs. Halfway up, fingers of one hand wrapped round the banister.

'Oh, shit,' Charlotte breathed. 'Dad…'

'I'm alright, sweetie,' her father said quietly. His head was lowered, face hidden in the shadows. His eyes were dark.

'Dad...'

Charlotte saw it then, a spot of red at Kramer's temple. A smear of it along the rail of the banister. 'Charlie, go to bed,' he said. 'I just need... a minute.'

What if she's here?

'Shut up, dad,' Charlotte said, crossing to the top of the stairs, taking them quickly until she was crouched by his side. She wrapped an arm around his neck, grabbed his arm and pushed up until he was on his knees. Tilted his head back. 'Just a scratch,' she whispered, squinting at the mark on his forehead. 'You're going to be okay.'

She clocked the man's eyes, barely open. Grey and empty, red-rimmed from lack of sleep. Wet with tears. 'Charlie...' he whispered.

'Yeah, it's alright, dad,' she said softly. 'You fell, that's all. It's alright. I'm here. Come on, let's get you upstairs, get you into bed.'

'Charlie, I'm sorry.'

'It's okay. Come on, dad, help me out. Can you get up?'

Kramer looked her in the eyes, and Charlotte swallowed. There was a look there that she had very rarely seen on his face, one that made her wish she'd stayed in bed, one that made her wish she could return to that dream, that terrible nightmare...

'Charlie... I am so, so *sorry.*'

'Dad, stop it. Just... let's go. Nearly there, weren't

you? Let's get you to your room, at least.'

She tried to ignore that look in his eyes, tried to focus on the scratch at his temple. She pressed her fingertips to it, wiped a thick, dark bead of blood away before it could drizzle down into her father's eye. 'You go to bed, get changed,' she said. 'I'll get you a plaster –'

'Charlie,' Kramer hissed, and the girl froze. Looked him in the eyes. '*Stop*,' he said. 'I'm fine. Just... go to your room. I can do this.'

'I know you can, dad,' the girl said. Her gaze shifted to the hand gripping the banister and she noted the battered knuckles, the blood that had pooled in the scratches and scars there. 'But you don't have to. Let me help you.'

'You're a good kid, Charlie.'

'I know,' Charlotte said, and she pulled the man up onto his feet, grimacing as the stale smell of beer wafted over her. 'Come on, stupid.'

Carefully, she walked her father up the stairs.

6

Edward Drake screamed as blood splashed his face. He fumbled blindly for the door, wrapping his fingers around the handle. Quickly, he pulled.

It was jammed.

Eddie froze. His mother had stopped screaming. Somewhere in the distance, muted by the heavy pounding of his blood, flames crackled in the dark. Eddie grunted as he yanked on the doorhandle, whole body rippling with tremors. 'Open!' he sobbed, tears streaming down his face. His cheeks were hot, throat dry and coarse.

He coughed, gripping the handle as he stared out the window.

There was something out there, in the shadows at the edge of the road.

Eddie shrank back from the window, one hand over his mouth. He watched as the thing moved, shifting over the tarmac, getting closer to the car with every second...

Eddie shut his eyes, swallowing a ragged scream back into his throat. The darkness behind his eyelids was quiet and hot. His mouth felt dry. His lungs were stinging. But if he couldn't see the thing, it couldn't see him. All he had to do was stay perfectly still, and it would leave. *One,* he counted, breaths trembling over his fingers. *Two...*

His eyes snapped open.

Eddie shrieked, recoiled from the glass. One wild, bulging eye stared at him through the window while the other wandered madly about, narrowed and dark and stricken with thin, spiralling red capillaries. Pus peeled over the raw layers of the man's yellow face as he smiled. Thin lips pulled back over crooked, flat teeth. His throat was torn-up and savaged, pale folds stuffed into the collar of his black shirt. He reached for the window with a darkened, yellow palm...

The glass shattered and now Eddie was screaming, scrambling backward, pounding with his fists on the back of his mother's seat. 'Help me!' he yelled, eyes burning as he looked up, watched as tendrils of glowing orange flame licked the edges of the overturned car bonnet.

Yellow hands grabbed Eddie's shirt and pulled him away from the front of the car, dragged him over the twisted metal of the ceiling. Glass cut at the eight-year-old's back, shredding the fabric of his shirt as the yellow man yanked him out onto the road, onto the burning black tarmac. Eddie screwed his eyes shut again, hiding his face with trembling, tear-stained fists. 'Please don't hurt me please please please *please*...'

He trailed off. Slowly, Eddie lowered his fists and looked. Yellow Face stood above him, towering over him in a wrinkled scaffold of black velvet and burned features. Tall and slender and horrible, but not hurting him.

Just watching.

Slowly, the yellow-skinned man smiled.

'No,' he said, and his voice seeped out from a shrivelled, hollow chest like rusted metal scraping over a slick, wet rock. Black fabric shivered over his chest as he breathed, rasping, shallow breaths. His smile grew wider. 'Not yet, you jammy fucker. Not yet.'

And then he turned and began to walk away.

Eddie saw something, then, that he hadn't before. Flickering in the glow of the flames at the edge of the road, something was parked on the tarmac thirty feet from the overturned wreck; a pale, chrome-grilled hearse, dead and silent. The hearse was a sick, pallid white and long, round-cornered windows glinted along its side. There was a coffin in the back, half-hidden by the flitting folds of lurid, pink curtains behind the windows.

Yellow Face raised a crooked hand as he reached the hearse and the thing's engine roared to life. Headlight beams cracked and threw dazzling tunnels of white light into the trees and for a moment Eddie was blinded.

When the afterglow had faded, the hearse was gone, and so was the yellow-skinned man. Eddie sobbed, slumping onto the tarmac, curled in a ball beside the bloody wreck of his parents' car, and he *howled*.

7

'Alright, come forward!' Sarah called into the wind. A slim, black tablet glowed in her hands, throwing pale shadows over her face. Beneath her feet, the wooden slats of the pier moaned quietly.

In front of her, something moved in the glow of the floodlights. A dark shape stepped forward; a padded, black jacket was wrapped around the guard's shoulders, obscuring the stab-proof vest strapped to him. He took the first inmate by the arm, gripping it tight. The lower half of his face was hidden behind a black windcheater. Quickly he marched the woman forward and Sarah's eyes moved to the inmate's face. Head bowed into the wind, the woman's hair was wild and orange and seemed to hum with static as it tossed about her pasty scalp. She was dressed in the same white t-shirt and joggers as all the inmates, her wrists bound in front of her by a thick, leather band.

The guard stopped a few feet from Sarah and held his arm out across the inmate's chest. *No further.*

'Your name?' Sarah said, glancing down at the tablet.

The wild-haired woman looked up. Her eyes were wide and frightened. 'I'm... Lissa. Lissa Harding. I have a family. Please... I have a son. *Cats.* I want to see my cats again.'

A pang of guilt struck Sarah in the belly and she shook her head. She had to ignore it. She always did. 'Lissa Harding. Please advance to the transport at the end of the pier. The guards will escort you up to Black River Asylum. Thank you.' She raised her head as the guard marched the wild-haired woman past her and looked towards the boat and the gleaming, silver ramp connecting it with the pier. 'Next!'

The second inmate was a tall, black man, bald-headed and covered in tattoos. They spread over his neck and his bare arms, circling the top of his head like the art of a madman. The rabid scrawls across his skin seemed to melt into the dark and his pupils shrunk to tiny, dull beads as he approached. The guards beside him seemed insignificant in the big, tattooed man's presence.

'Name?' Sarah asked.

'Pete,' said the tattooed man. His voice was a low rumble. Sarah scanned the list on her tablet screen, frowning. *Pete...*

'Peter Knapton?

'Right.'

'Thank you. Move along, Damian will take you up to the transport.'

The guard nodded and walked Peter along the pier, footsteps fading into the tumbling of the waves.

Sarah looked up, opening her mouth to call out again. Her eyes locked onto the face of the next inmate and she paused. His expression was empty of emotion, blank and soulless, but something glittered in his eyes, something dark and unfeeling and hungry.

'Next,' Sarah croaked. Her voice was lost in the wind and she tried again, almost shouting to be heard. 'Next!'

The third inmate stepped forward, movements fluid and controlled as if he was completely oblivious to the guard pushing him along. He barely shivered in the cold, even as the wind dug at his arms. His chest and shoulders bulged beneath a clinging, white t-shirt that rippled across a flat, hard torso. His arms were thick, hands clasped together in front of his gut. His hair was jet-black, swept back from his forehead in a mess of thick, greasy strands and his jaw was coated in a dark layer of stubble. His throat was exposed, and three long, pale scars ran crisp and jagged from the base of his jaw to the top of his chest.

'Name,' Sarah said quietly.

For a long time, the man said nothing. Then he looked towards the island, nodding in the direction of the cliffs. 'Tell me something,' he said, in a voice as thick and dark as the ocean beneath them. 'How many people?'

Sarah frowned, glancing at the guard for an explanation.

He shrugged. *No idea.*

'What do you mean?' Sarah said.

'On the island,' the inmate said. A thin, black scar of a mouth opened across his unshaved jaw as he spoke. 'How many people on the island?'

'That's not important,' Sarah said. 'Tell me your name.'

'How many?' he said again.

Sarah paused. 'About nine hundred. Nine-fifty, maybe. Now tell me your name.'

The inmate looked into her eyes and Sarah's heart skipped a couple of beats and shot up into her mouth. 'It will follow me here,' the man said.

'Your *name,*' Sarah insisted.

'Do as the lady says, mate,' the guard murmured,

reaching for a shining, black baton clipped to his belt. 'We haven't got all night.'

The inmate's eyes dropped to the baton and he smiled, a hollow, narrow smile. He turned his eyes back up to Sarah's and his jaw set. The smile disappeared. 'It will follow me here,' he repeated. 'It will *kill them all.*'

'That's enough,' said the guard, unclipping the baton.

'What do you mean?' Sarah whispered, keeping her eyes on the inmate as she raised a hand in the guard's direction, shaking her head.

The inmate said nothing. Suddenly Sarah felt truly cold, cold to her bones. She shuddered. 'Tell me your name,' Sarah said quietly. 'Just that. Only that. *Tell me your name.*'

The man looked across the island and for a moment the floodlights behind him flickered. Shadows fell over his face. 'Edward Drake,' he said slowly. 'My name is *Edward Drake.*'

CHAPTER TWO
SHADOWS

1
NOW

The monitor on Dr. Hayley King's desk was cracked. She gazed at the screen absent-mindedly, tracking the line of the crack with dull, tired eyes. Cautiously she leant forward, gingerly touching the very tip of the crack. A discoloured clutter of pixels spat beneath her thumb as she traced it over the fracture, a crooked smile that stretched from one corner of the screen to the other. Hayley reclined, rubbing glass dust off the pad of her thumb. It sprinkled the desk soundlessly.

The doctor grimaced at her reflection in the screen, cut in half by that splintered grin. She looked exhausted. The brown dye in her hair was growing out and the greying roots were visible even in the hazy depths of the monitor. Her eyes were a dim, pale green, ringed with the grey lines of another sleepless night. A grey blazer hung open at her throat, fluttering over a pale silk shirt in the draft from a fan above her head. It spun lazily, dragging thin strings of cobweb in a slow, hypnotic circle.

'Shouldn't you be at home?'

Hayley looked up, blinking. The door had opened and light filtered into the office, obscured by the silhouette of a woman in the corridor. She smiled over at Hayley and crossed the room, setting a glass of water on the corner of the desk. 'Thought you might still be here,' said the newcomer. Blonde hair trickled over her shoulders. 'You know, we've got security guards for that.'

'Hm?' Hayley's brow wrinkled with confusion.

'You don't have to keep an eye on the feeds all the time,' the younger woman said, nodding towards the computer. Her arms folded across a taut, blue nurse's blouse. 'You know nothing's going to happen, Hayley.'

Hayley smiled weakly. 'Monitor's broken,' she said. 'Couldn't watch if I wanted to, Emma.'

Emma Green frowned. 'Can I take a look?'

Hayley nodded, stepping out of her chair.

Emma slid around the desk and bent over the monitor, fumbling with a button beneath the thing. 'It's just turned off,' she said, jabbing the button and holding it in until the display lit up. She turned back to Hayley, looking into the doctor's eyes with the same concerned expression she reserved, mostly, for her patients. 'God, how long have you been in this room? You need to go home. You need to *sleep*.'

Hayley shook her head. Her eyes dropped to the computer. 'But... it's cracked.'

Emma stood straight, hands moving to her hips. A pale strand of hair fell in front of her ear, framing a pretty face. She smiled sadly, eyes never leaving Hayley's. 'I can get someone to fix the screen, love, but the computer still works fine. See?'

The monitor whirred to life, humming softly. The screen flickered.

'Thank you,' Hayley said quietly. She winced.

'When did you last eat?' Emma said. 'I didn't see you in the canteen today.'

'I don't...' Hayley started. She trailed off. She couldn't remember the last time she'd left the office.

'Go home, doc,' Emma said. She took a step closer to Hayley, smiling. She smelled like old wine and fabric softener. Closer now, Emma could taste the caffeine on the older woman's breath. 'The new patients are settling in. You don't need to meet any of them till the morning, Hayley.'

'What time is it?'

Emma glanced up at a silent, digital clock on the wall. Red digits glowed in the dim light of the office. 'Nearly one,' she said. 'I'm heading home, if you want a lift back into the village/'

'Your shift's finished?'

Emma grinned. A hand moved to Hayley's waist. 'Don't tell me you were just waiting for me,' she said.

Hayley tried to return the smile, but it faltered. 'Maybe a lift back to mine would be nice,' she said, reaching for the water on her desk. She drank quickly, emptying half the glass. 'I can't sleep in this office.'

Emma nodded. The nurse moved her hand back up to Hayley's cheek, stroking the woman's soft, pale skin with her thumb. 'Good decision,' she said quietly. 'Look, I just need to get my coat and sign out, but I'll be as quick as I can, okay? I'll meet you in the car park in five minutes.'

'Fie minutes,' Hayley echoed. 'Thank you, Emma.'

Tentatively, Hayley laid a hand on Emma's chest, closed her eyes as the nurse's bosom heaved beneath her palm. She could feel Emma's heartbeat through the crisp, blue material of her uniform.

'You okay?' Emma said softly, wrapping her arms around Hayley's waist.

Hayley nodded. 'I'm sorry,' she murmured. 'I'm just... I'm a mess. You shouldn't have to keep looking out for me.'

'It's alright,' Emma told her. 'My husband was a mess, too, remember? I'm used to it.'

Hayley smiled. 'Your husband was the reason you ended up here. I don't want to be the reason you leave.'

'Whole different kind of mess,' Emma breathed, and they kissed.

Hayley pulled Emma's body up against hers and a gentle warmth slipped between their lips as they melted together. Hayley smiled into the kiss, palm trembling on Emma's fluttering chest as the nurse's heartbeat quickened. The kiss lasted longer, this time, stirring something in Hayley's gut that shivered and swelled and grew with every second.

'See you in five,' Emma murmured, pulling away.

'Hope you can remember the way back to my place,' Hayley said. She pressed her forehead to Emma's, closing her eyes. This, right now, was the way it was meant to be. 'I don't know if I can think straight enough to give you directions.'

'Oh, you're coming back to mine,' Emma said. They kissed again, quickly, and she stepped away and turned for the door.

Hayley smiled after the nurse as she disappeared into the corridor. For a moment she stood, resting the heels of her hands on the edge of the desk. Her own heart was quivering madly in her chest. She closed her eyes and exhaled. Christ, they couldn't keep doing this. It wasn't professional.

'Oh, fuck professionalism,' Hayley whispered to herself, sinking back into her chair.

Quickly, she signed into the computer and loaded up the computers. The screen flitted in a hazy, static confusion of black-and-white, but the picture was clear enough. The corridor outside her office was well-lit, splashed with the glare of fluorescent bulbs and gas lamps set into the walls.

Hayley pressed a button on the keyboard and a new image slid into place on the screen. Shafts of light gleamed in the dark, bouncing off the hoods of cars and trucks and the rings of a tall, iron fence. She pressed the button again and another corridor, deeper in the building, flickered on the cracked monitor.

Two figures walked into frame before Hayley could switch cameras a third time; Hayley watched as one of them, dressed in the black, padded shirt and trousers of a guard, thumbed a keypad on the wall. A door beside him opened and the guard ushered his ward inside. A tall, black-haired man disappeared through the door and it closed behind him.

Hayley sighed. 'I'll be seeing you tomorrow morning, I guess,' she said. She leaned across to turn off the computer.

A shadow flickered across the screen.

Hayley froze in her seat. She watched as the picture shifted, waiting for the shadow to reappear as a cool, numbing silence swept over her chest.

Nothing.

Narrowing her eyes, Hayley rewound the tape. She watched as, in reverse, the door opened out into the corridor and the black-haired man shuffled backwards out of his cell. Hayley froze the image, played the video forward again. She watched intently, her brow furrowed in an inquisitive frown.

There.

Hayley hit pause, just as the shadow passed across the camera lens. That was all it was, she realised. Just a shadow. A flare of the camera. A trick of the light, caught on tape.

Just a ghost in the machine.

But for a single moment, for the tiniest fraction of a second, Hayley could have sworn it was *grinning* at her.

2

The cliff dragged itself up from the sand in a chaotic mess of thick, red clay and crumbling flint, stricken with black veins and the remnants of ancient, broken fossils. Thirty feet up, it splintered and crashed forward in a twisted display of tangled grass and filtered moonlight. At the base of the cliff, the sand stretched around towards an old, black cave mouth. Bitten by a white-tipped wash of saltwater, the beach was stained a pale, blotchy red by the clay that seeped through in thin rivers and streams.

Something moved in the dark.

It was shapeless, at first. No more than a whisper in shifting particles of sand beneath the cliff, a crackle of blood on the wind. It barely cast a shadow on the ground, just a wisp of nothing in the dust, and yet whatever thingless form it held was enough to conceal a jumble of emotion; feelings it couldn't control, screaming rage and bitter, empty silence that it could neither quell nor wake.

For a while, the thing waited. Everything was new, in this place, and some strangled part of the shadow's consciousness was afraid, but it found an unfamiliar sort of pleasure in that fear. It relished the cold skin of the clay, the crisp, fickle levity of the sand. The bite of the waves and the wind that drew itself up the cliff face in sweeping curves and spirals.

The night was ling and dark, and the thing grew tired of sand. Guided by anguish and lust and avarice, compelled by some insatiable, unappeasable hunger, the thing dug shadowy fingers into the cliff face and slipped silently above the ledge.

Slowly it moved toward the north of the island, drawn to the chatter and the dull snap of streetlights. It lingered at the edge of the village, latching on to the smell of beer and sweat and old, stale brick dust. Tall, fleshy shapes stumbled out of doorways talking and laughing as they marched about their little island like they had nowhere else to go. The thing felt a cold familiarity when it saw them. It could almost taste the meat on their bones, the sweat and lust on their breath.

Oh, it was so *hungry*...

The thing stalked the village for a while, filtering through the shadows and the dark, passing beneath streetlights in a blur of grey and dark, ink-blot brown.

Something lurched towards it, loud and shining as it screamed over the tarmac. Curved edges gleamed in the moonlight as two bright, glaring beams shot out of its twisted grille of a mouth. The great metal beast roared as it tore down the street and the thing reeled back into the shadows, fearful. After a moment it turned away from the village and back towards the cliffs.

The moon drifted across a starless sky and the waves rose and swelled. The thing smelled them before it saw them and it listened as they approached the clifftop; a young couple, barely into adulthood, drunken and amorous and secretive. Two bundles of flesh wrapped in cloth ad leather and fabric.

They settled at the top of the cliff and sat, rumps perched precariously on the crumbling, red clay. Their legs hung over the ledge like thick, dangling ropes of meat. Long grass danced around them in a wild breeze that arced up from the sea.

The thing watched them for a while, listening to the man's voice and the young woman's wild, shrill giggle.

Quietly, it imitated, whispering into the wind, shaping its voice until it became *hers.* A perfect copy of the girl's high-pitched trill echoed in the thing's throat and broke out into the darkness, a stolen thing that it relished in taking.

The girl seemed to hear it, and for a moment she stopped laughing. Her companion tried to speak, but she silenced him. Listening to the wind. 'Shh,' she whispered.

Shh...

The thing faded into the shadows, silent and invisible. The clay was cold and the wind rippled over its skinless back.

'What is it?' the man hissed, pushing hair out of his eyes as he peered over the ledge.

The girl shook her head. 'I thought... never mind.'

The shadow could sense her heartbeat, a muffled thumping on the breeze, and it listened, closing in on that sound until even the rumble of the sea was drowned out. The thing found something, in the pulsing, throbbing rhythm of her heart; flashes of old, harboured memories and fragmented images. It explored, digging further, pushing forward into the girl's thoughts until it found something buried. A nightmare from her childhood, bloody and forgotten. A skeletal creature walked on all fours towards her, long spines shivering on its back and its hunched, grey shoulders. Its limbs were long and slender and bony claws dragged over the ground as it moved. It was a creature born of her imagination, a leprous abomination spat out of the mind of a terrified little child.

It was *perfect.*

The thing focused, shifting in the dark. Gradually a form built itself out of the shadows, dark bones drenched in blood and bandaged in a thick, mucus-covered skin. The thing flexed its new limbs, digging long, knotted claws into the sand. It found a face in the deepest echoes of the girl's terrible dream, a broken, diseased mask of bone and peeling, grey-brown flesh. It was broken and blind and featureless, save for a twisted, savage maw filled with spines and splintered teeth.

The thing smiled.

After a while, the couple came down to the beach, keeping their backs to the cliff as they moved drunkenly down the old ramp. It was worn so badly by the weathering of years and the weight of thousands of footsteps that one edge crumbled into the sea and the rocks below. Black and slippery and gleaming in the moonlight, the Devil's Crown was half-buried in the water, a ring of jagged points as dark as the sky above.

Giggling, the couple crept to the bottom of the cliff. The man led his companion by the hand, grinning in the dark. She was just as eager, and they shuffled with unsteady feet towards a spot on the beach completely sheltered from the moonlight and laid down together in the sand.

For a while, hidden in the shadows, the thing watched them with its new, eyeless face. It was patient.

Eventually, they grew tired of conversation, and the girl climbd on top of her partner, straddling his midsection with a drunken wobble. The thng crept closer, entranced by the sight of their slim bodies writhing in the dark. The sea washed forward onto the shore and mirrored their movements slow and hypnotic.

Waves rippled as the couple's bodies intertwined and trembled in the sand. After a while the girl began to make a new sound, a low, soft bleat that pushed out of her mouth with every twist of her hips.

The thing copied her. Hidden in the shadows, its mouth opened and it moaned in harmony with the girl. The perfect echo.

The couple stopped their wild movements and the girl looked up into the shadows, eyes wide and shining in the moonlight. There was a shape, pressed against the cliff, and she fowned...

'What's wrong?' the man grunted. His skin reeked of urgency. 'It's okay, there's no one there. We're -'

The thing struck, bursting from the face of the cliff. A black shape hurtling through the sand, driven wild by the shrieking ghosts of emotion inside its belly. It screeched, and the primal sound that escaped its gut was one of pure, agonised hunger.

The girl screamed, clambering off her lover. Sand blew up in grey clouds of dust at her feet. The man turned, sluggish. Shadowy claws plunged into his open mouth and tore it apart, shredding his lips and cheeks in a shower of red. The thing grabbed his head and wrenched open the man's jaw with a sickening *crack,* yanking his chin down with a bent claw and shoving its arm into his throat. A deep, crimson mist sprayed out of the man's head as it burst open and the thing scooped chunks of wet, pulsing brain out of his skull and tossed

49

them into the sand. The girl had abandone her companion and she ran, skirts wet and tangled around her ankles. She staggered into the sea, splashing madly in the waves, driven by a mad, broken desire to flee.

The thing watched her run. Without eyes, all it saw was her shape, a hazy, red-tinged mess of shadow stumbling in the water. It could almost taste the heat between her legs, the fear in her chest, and it dug desperately into the caverns of the man's corpse and rummaging inside. Its claws twisted around slippery trails of intestine and it fed, biting and shredding in a manic, lustful fury. Strings and tendons snapped in the thing's teeth and it buried its snout in the man's opened chest, clamping its jaws around his still-beating heart. The palpitating muscle popped inside its mouth and slid down its throat, purple juices flowing over its tongue. The shadowy creature bit at the man's neck, tearing away writhing, slippery tubes and shredded flesh with careless abandon. It swallowed, gulping down great, stinking clumps of meat.

Finally, it was finished with him.

The girl sobbed madly as she waded deeper into the water, slowed by the cold sway of the waves. She pushed forward, beating at the black, glittering thrust of the sea as it pooled up to her belly.

The thing left the bloody carcass of the man in the sand, moving slowly towards the ocean. It stalked the girl on all fours, borrowing the gait of the thing it had seen in her long-forgotten dream. Its movements were awkward and half-learned and it reeled as the waves lashed at its feet, but it crept steadily forwards on slender, bent-up limbs, undeterred by the cold or the bitter sting of the salt. Waves washed over the thing's bloody skin and it let them cleanse it, never taking its eyes off the fleeting prey.

It didn't take the thing long to catch up with her, cutting through the waves like a brown-grey eel in the dark. The girl tried to run, stumbling over loose sand and wet, crushed rocks. She stumbled, catching her toe on something sharp on the bed of the sea. Tight, bony claws wrapped around her thigh and yanked her beneath the waves. She shrieked, bobbing to the surface, kicking and lashing out at the thing as it dragged her back to shore. It pulled her to the Devil's Crown and threw her wet body up against the rocks and she could smell blood on its breath. It looked into her eyes and for a second she stopped screaming.

'Oh, god...' she moaned. 'Oh, my god...'

The creature smiled.

'You're not real. God, you're not fucking *real*...'

The thing smashed the back of her skull against the tip of a jagged boulder and she screamed, hoarse and ragged. The noise cut out abruptly as the creature slammed her down again and again, pounding the limp mess of her body over the rocks. Waves splashed over them in a frenzy of froth and cool saltwater as the girl's head became slippery and warm and collapsed inward with every crash of bone on bloody, barnacle-encrusted rock until it was slopping about like a pulpy, soaked slab of meat. Her eyes rolled back into their sockets and blood poured from her in rivers.

The thing stopped beating in her head only when it was absolutely sure the job was done.

It moved over her body, taking pleasure in the curves of the carcass. It moved its grey tongue over her still form, tracing lines over her battered skull with its claws. It slid its hands over her skin and savoured in the warmth of her pooling blood. Quickly it moved to her hips and spread her bare legs over the rock and it had its terrible, silent way with the corpse, quieting the sensation in its gut that had been burning there since it had first seen her. The skin of the girl's back peeled over the rocks as her body slid upward and her head lolled back over the crest of the boulder. When the creature was finished it plunged a black fist into her abdomen and dug around inside her, pulling free anything it could find. it spread the slops and scraps over the sand and devoured anything worth taking. Its tongue slithered over shining coils of muscle and sinew glistened between its teeth as it feasted.

When its hunger had been satiated, the thing abandoned the meaty carcasses, shredded and pulled apart in the sand. It felt bloated. Satisifed. It caught a glimpse of its reflection in the blood-infused water at the edge of the beach, a blurry silhouette tinged with red and black and flashing, searing white. Slowly, a pair of wet, narrow slits opened above its mouth, glaring a dim, burnt amber.

Something prickled and the spines on the thing's shoulders trembled. It turned slowly and looked up from the water, ignoring the cold brush of salt as the waves washed over its ankles.

It was not alone.

An old, white hearse was parked on the clifftop, thin tyres dug into the swaying grass. A long window across the side of the car was cracked and smeared with blood. Pink curtains behind the window fluttered softly.

There was a pale shadow leaning on the bonnet. Wisps of black hair drifted in the wind.

Slowly, the man with the yellow face waved a slender, long-fingered hand. His features flickered and shadows twisted around him as he stood, turning back to the driver's side of the hearse and climbing in.

The creature turned away from the cliff and slunk back into the shadows.

Despite everything, it couldn't help but be afraid.

3

1993

Rain spattered Oliver's forehead as he walked, loose

gravel shifting and crunching beneath his boots. The sky had opened as he stepped out of the car; he'd left it on the road, afraid to bring it any closer to the house. Around him, twisted shapes dug great, scathing coils of black out of the sky, trees bent and misshapen and bloody.

Something howled, deep within the forest. Oliver swallowed and kept walking.

The house appeared in front of him, breaking free of the ground like the old, twisted roots pushing up out of the earth behind. Eerie orange lights flickered behind windows caked in dried muck and filth and coated in dust. A couple of the windows on the upper floors were cracked, taped over or boarded with splintered planks. The roof slanted down, sagging as if the sky was trying to stamp the old house back down into the dirt. The walls sloped a little too, cracked and sinking into the soft murk at the corner of the building so that it stood entirely crooked. Wonky, wooden slats were clapped together, dark gaps between them filled in with grey stone and flint. Oliver felt like there should be ivy, writhing, dark tendrils of the stuff crawling over the narrow building, but nothing grew here. Even the grass at the very edges of the forest that behind him was dry and brown. The trees were all dead, stripped bare. Nothing lived, save for the things in the dark that moaned and called to each other. Oliver had passed a bloody wreck of bones and fur on his way through the woods, shortly after he'd left the car; it could have been a badger, but it was impossible to tell.

Whatever had eaten it had stripped the face off its bones and crushed the skull in like a tin can.

Oliver paused as he neared the porch and turned his head. He had to squint through the dark, through the slanting rain that drizzled all around him, but he could still see the car, edges and curves glimmering silver in the moonlight. Already, something up in the treetops had shat on the bonnet. Oliver couldn't hear any birdsong.

He should turn back. He should get back to the car and *go...*

No, he thought. *You haven't come all this way to turn around now.* He was here for *her,* for Rose. His Rose. His beautiful, shining daughter.

Still, he shouldn't have left so quickly. He hadn't even stopped by the hospital to say goodbye...

Oliver stepped up onto the porch, sheltered from the swelling rain by a sweeping panel of roof above his head. He shuddered, pulling a thick, green coat around him, swiping the rain off his damp hair. He shuddered as rain hammered on the porch roof, suddenly heavy and pelting. 'You've come this far,' Oliver murmured, 'do what you have to do.'

Slowly, he reached forward. The door was old and warped, set into a red frame that had long faded so that, in the moonlight, it was a pale rose colour. The door itself was stained dark and smeared with something black that drizzled into the knots in the wood. Oliver curled his trembling hand into a fist, raised it to knock -

Rain pelted the backs of his ankles and a burst of wind pushed him forward and for a second, just inches from the door, he could *smell* something, something that had been hidden from him before, beneath the damp and the dark and the thick, earthy scent of the forest.

The door smelled like blood.

Oliver steadied himself, laying a palm on the frame, and his eyes crossed the wood, taking it all in. That deep, black stain...

He shook his head. 'I'll find another way,' he said, taking a step back. 'Rose, I promise I will find *something...*'

Quickly, Oliver turned around, stepping down onto the gravel. Stuffing his hands into the pockets of his old coat he started walking, back to the forest and the shining silhouette of the car. He would find another way...

The door groaned open behind him. Shadows on the gravel curled away from his feet as a shaft of flickering, burnt firelight threw itself onto the ground. Oliver froze.

Keep walking, he thought. His legs didn't move. *There's another way. Get out of here. This was a mistake...*

For a moment Oliver closed his eyes, let the rain wash over him. His hair had fallen down over his face and damp strings tracked jagged lines down his cheeks and his throat. The rain was all he could hear; the constant pounding of water on gravel and the dead bark of the trees and the whisper of the wind. Then there was a voice, low and rasping and coarse, the voice of an old woman:

'*Come,* Oliver.'

Run.

Oliver turned around. He couldn't help himself. He *wanted* to run, to get in the car and drive out of the forest and away from here. Every fibre of his being screeched for him to leave this awful place, this crooked, ancient house.

She stood in the doorway, a silhouette in the glow from the hallway, slender and dark and tall. One arm was raised, a hand outstretched. A thin, bony finger bent inward, gesturing Oliver forward.

Run. Get back to the car and go. Leave. Just leave. Run -

He walked towards the porch and stepped up onto the raised, wooden plinth. The smell of blood had gone now, and in its place there was a new aroma, the pleasant tang of charcoal and smoke and rum, slipping down his throat and laying soft and sweet and hot in his belly.

It's not too late. Run.

Oliver stepped inside, and the door slammed shut behind him.

4

The shower was running when Hayley woke up.

She lay still for a while, listening to the hammering of water in the tray, muffled by the closed bathroom door. Hayley couldn't help but smile as she ground dust from her eyes, pulled the sheets just a little tighter to her throat. She could still smell Emma on the pillow beneath her head. She kept her eyes closed and sighed.

This was the third time Hayley had spent the night in Emma Green's bed, and the first time it felt like she was really supposed to be here. The first time they had slept together, Hayley was new to the island and her job at the asylum. She had been afraid. Alone. Emma had been *there*. Hayley was disgusted, now, to think that she had been so crude. That she had *used* the girl, for... for what? A distraction?

The second time had been an apology.

The two of them grew close, down at the asylum, surrounded by a constantly-changing cycle of guards and patients and doctors. Eventually Cain's End started to look like Hayley's new home, and Black River Asylum looked more and more like her new *life*. Emma became a friend, and for a few months that was all. Then, that second night, she became something more.

Tonight hadn't been distracting. It hadn't been repentant. Tonight had been *right*. Hayley reached forward, her eyes still closed. After a moment or two she found her glasses on the bedside cabinet and slid them onto her nose, pushing thin hair out of her face. She rolled onto her back and finally, cautiously, opened her eyes.

The ceiling was a pure, dazzling white. The room was sparsely decorated, every piece of furniture square moulded and functional. It was homely, Hayley supposed, in its own way. There was a candle, on the windowsill, burned halfway down. The scent of the thing still wafted about the room.

Hayley's head fell back against the pillow. She had no idea what the time was, she realised, but her next shift couldn't be too far away.

The shower stopped running. Hayley listened to the soft slap of bare, wet feet on the bathroom tiles, the running of the tap as Emma brushed her teeth.

After a minute or two, the bathroom door opened.

'You know, you don't have to come in to work today,' Emma said. She spoke softly, sweetly.

Hayley turned, pulling the sheets with her. She propped herself up on a tired elbow and her eyes moved over the figure in the doorway.

Emma was wrapped in a crisp, white towel that clung to her curves and came apart at her waist so a long sliver of thigh was showing. She stood with her arms folded, wet shoulders shining as her hair dripped onto the carpet. She smiled. 'You could call in sick,' she continued. 'Stay here, get some sleep.'

Hayley shook her head. 'I'd love to,' she said quietly. 'But?'

'I have to go in,' Hayley said. 'The new inmates... you know. God, I've got to meet them all. Then there's all the paperwork. Besides, Karl saw me leave with you. They'll start talking if I don't come back.'

'Security guards talk,' Emma grinned. 'But fair enough. Look, how about this - stay here for now, get some rest. Your shift doesn't start for a couple of hours, right? If you insist on coming in, at least let me come pick you up. I'll just come back with the car when it's time. Sound good?'

Hayley paused. She knew that, despite all of Emma's kindness, she was burdening the young woman. But god, she was *exhausted...*

'Sounds good,' she said quietly. 'But you don't have to pick me up. I'll walk in, maybe the fresh air will clear my head a little.'

'You sure?' Emma raised an eyebrow. 'You know, I don't think they'll miss me for the ten minutes it takes to come back here and get you.'

'I'm sure. You've done plenty for me, Emma. You've been so kind to me. Thank you.'

Emma stepped forward, leaned over the bed and kissed Hayley deeply. 'Anything,' she murmured.

Hayley closed her eyes, pulling herself up into the kiss. Wet fingers ran through her hair and she groaned.

'How long do you have?'

Emma pulled away from the kiss. The towel had fallen away and it lay in a damp bundle on the floor. 'Long enough,' she whispered, and smiling, she knelt by the side of the bed and pulled Hayley towards her.

5

Hayley liked to walk the long way around, when she had the time.

She passed a young couple as she left the village. A scruffy terrier yapped at their feet as Hayley moved past them. She kept her head down, bowed against the wind. Cain's End seemed almost silent, apart from the relentless barking of the little dog - usually there were kids running about this part of the village, screaming on their way to the new arcade on the high street. School had started up again, Hayley supposed, for the last time before summer. Still, it was eerily quiet.

Soon enough, Hayley found herself on the narrow, stone pathway that led to the clifftops. It wound through dry, wind-stripped fields and crops of clipped, rough grass fresh from grazing. The cows had been moved, now, to the other side of the island, and already the grass was starting to push its way back up through the earth.

At least now she could walk through the field without being watched. Creed's cows weren't exactly threatening, but there was something about the way they looked at her when she had occasion to pass through their midst. Something ominous, like they knew more than they were letting on.

The clifftop reared up before her and Hayley stood for a while, looking out over the sea with her hands in her pockets. A dark scarf fluttered around her throat as brown hair peeled back from her face. She squinted out to the horizon, watched as the waves rose and swallowed themselves. The sun filtered through low, grey clouds and glittered over the surface of the water. Mist whispered as it trailed low, pale blankets over the water. It looked like it was going to rain again.

'No place like home,' Hayley said to herself, murmuring beneath the folds of the scarf. She closed her eyes, let the wind brush over her face. She had hated this place, when she first transferred. She had despised the isolation, the cold. The wind.

Cain's End was growing on her.

Hayley sighed, turned away from the sea and kept walking. The ground at the edge of the island was uneven and rocky and she stumbled a couple of times, sticking close to the top of the cliff, wary that the earth could give way any time but knowing that as long as she could see the forest, she was on course. She still managed to get lost sometimes, even after six months.

The walk was pleasant, though, and it gave her time to think. Silence, save for the wash of the sea and a whisper on the wind. She fancied she might be able to hear kids playing, down in the schoolyard, but it was likely her overwrought imagination. After all, half a mile separated her now from the village. Black River Asylum crept a little closer with every forward step, obscured by a wall of trees but visible through them in blurs and splashes of grey.

Hayley frowned. She could smell something on the wind.

She shook her head, kept her eyes down. It was nothing. One foot in front of the other, she tracked a steady line over the earth. There was a vague pathway here, along the clifftop, but it faded and broke away every thirty feet or so, replaced by a brittle plateau of stone and cracked soil.

There. Something metallic, almost indiscernible but stronger here.

Hayley stopped, glancing furtively about her. She was alone. Behind her, the pathway curved back through the fields and towards the village. To her right, the ragged clifftop and the ocean. And directly in front of her now, the ramp that led down to the beach. Slowly she abandoned the path and moved towards it, grimacing as the smell grew stronger. It was coming from down there, on the sand.

Hayley stood at the edge of the cliff and looked down.

Her hand shot up to her mouth and she cried out into her palm. 'Oh, god...'

Hayley took a step back, snapping her eyes shut. It smelled like copper and smouldering, frayed wires, like meat that had been left out in the sun to rot and decay and curdle.

Before she could stop herself, Hayley was doubled over. Bile rose up in her throat and forced itself out. She couldn't remove her hand in time and flecks of vomit spattered her fingers; the rest splashed the floor and clung to the longer blades of grass in thick, yellow beads.

'Oh, fuck,' Hayley said, sinking to her knees. She could barely bring herself to open her eyes as she wiped her lips on the back of her sleeve. She shook her head. 'No,' she murmured. 'No, no, no, it isn't real. It can't be real, oh, *no...*'

She had to take another look. Had to make sure she hadn't imagined it. After a minute she crawled forwards, careful to avoid the vomit on the ground. Tentatively, she moved to the ledge. Flakes of clay and soil crumbled away beneath her hands. A shard of flint buried in the earth came free and tumbled down into the sand.

Slowly, Hayley leant forward. Looked down.

'Oh, what happened to you?' she breathed.

Hayley turned away from the edge, reaching into the pocket of her coat to pull out a slim, rubber-encased mobile. She dialled quickly. Cain's End was a small place, and the police department had an extension that was easy enough to memorise. Christ, she could list *thirty* phone numbers off the top of her head if anyone asked her to. Whatever she lacked in any other department, she more than made up for with numbers.

'Hello?' came a man's voice from the other end of the telephone. 'Police. This is detective Kramer.'

'Hi,' Hayley said quickly. 'I'm down by the... there's been... oh, god. I don't know... look, I'm on the cliffs. Overlooking the beach. There's something *down there,* in the sand. It's... how quickly can you be here?' She turned back to face the beach as Kramer spoke, took one last look over the edge of the cliff. 'I don't know what to do... I don't... can you? Okay. Okay, I'll... okay. Just hurry.'

Hayley hung up and swallowed. She wished she had just gone with Emma in the car. She had never seen a damn thing like this. 'Oh, you poor girl...'

Hayley moved to the top of the ramp, sliding the phone back into her pocket. Something drew her forward, something dark and inexplicable, and she took paced, slow steps down the ramp, back pressed to the cliff face. Her eyes never left the carnage in the sand. The smell grew more potent with every step and she grimaced, pulling the scarf up so that it covered the lower half of her face.

The ocean bit and chewed at the edge of the beach, tore at the sand in lines and swirls of white foam. It seemed angry, today. Hayley reached, again, for the mobile, dialled another number. She stared at the mess on the sand as she held the phone to her ear, waited. It rang out, passed to voicemail.

'Hey, Emma,' Hayley said quietly. 'Listen, I'm going to be a little bit late to work. Just letting you know so you don't... not that you would... I mean, so you don't worry. Or anything. Just in case.' She laughed nervously, winced as the horrific aroma wafted into her throat. 'I'll explain later. And... thank you for last night.'

Hayley cut the phone and turned away from the dreadful mess in the sand. Her eyes moved to the cliff face and tracked upward, over the dried clay and the slithers and black veins that ran up to the jagged edge above.

Halfway up the cliff, something had dug three rough, jagged scars in the clay. A little further up, a similar mark. And another, near the top. It looked like...

'No...' Hayley breathed.

It looked like something had climbed its way up to the top of the cliff.

But it wasn't the strange marks that had Hayley's attention.

There was something else. It was everywhere. It had soaked into the sand, smeared the black rocks that made the Devil's Crown. There were great lashings of the stuff over the boulders and it pooled into the sea in faded, crimson clouds.

But Hayley couldn't understand how the blood had

spattered the *very top of the cliff.*

6

Nana Death led Oliver through the house to a living room crammed with nightmares. Dread strangled his bowels and churned his gut until he felt s though he might throw up on the ragged, stained carpet. He reached out a hand, leant on the doorframe as his eyes flitted between the terrible things in the room and he opened his mouth to speak.

'What is all this?' Oliver said quietly, stepping into the living room. A broad, marble fireplace was lit on the far wall. Fat, full flames cracked and spat embers onto the floorboards, trapped in a twisted, ornately-carved frame.

The old woman didn't answer. She stood behind him, watching as Oliver looked around the room. A moth-eaten, black dress clung to her slender frame, long-sleeved and sewn from tattered, shining feathers and leathery so thin it could've been torn straight from the wings of a jet-black bat. There was a ruff of feathers around her neck that shimmered purple and red and gold as it splashed over her shoulders. It was torn and ragged and plucked. A small splash of red dribbled along one of the feathers.

The mantelpiece was littered with tokens and trinkets and things Oliver would not dare to name. A cracked monocle glinted in the shadows beside a fat, wooden sculpture with a painted face. Tiny, pewter statues faced each other down from opposite ends of the marble shelf. A square, scratched canvas hung above the fireplace. It was blank, save for a horizontal strip of crimson that spread like blood across its middle. Lined up beneath the painting, watching him with empty, soulless eyes, were a set of four skulls. Cracked and blistered and brittle but *alive* somehow. The first was painted a gleaming, bone-white, wet and glossy despite the coat of dust over it; the second was coated in a crimson so dark it could have been blood; the third, a black so deep that its hollow eye-sockets were almost invisible. The fourth was a pale, sickly green.

The colour of Death.

Slowly, Oliver took a step forward. Beneath him, the rug shifted and the floorboards squealed, uneasy. He tilted his eyes to the right; a collection of masks hung on the wall around a faded window, tacked to the wood and plaster with long, bent copper nails. Some had been given ugly, painted faces, tribal screams frozen in splashes of red and deep, sqeeping sea-green. Most of them carried furious expressions, full of hatred and anger and bloodlust. A couple were carved out of rough, ice-blue stone. One, halfway up the wall, was completely emotionless, a featureless, white oval broken by two narrow slits halfway down, angled in a little to form a shallow *V*.

The old woman stepped past him, moved slowly to the fireplace. She barely lifted her feet, Oliver noticed, and she seemed to float over the rotting floorboards and the thin rug that concealed them. There were two worn, stained armchairs in front of the fire, one either side, twisted a little so they faced each other. The old woman turned her head to look back at Oliver, gesturing towards one of the chairs. 'Sit,' she rasped. 'That is, if you're quite ready to do business?'

Oliver nodded, crossing the room. He kept his eyes off the woman as he moved.

Nana Death. That was what they called her, round here. She had a name, of course, but even those who knew it were afraid to say it out loud. Perhaps it was too terrible to speak; perhaps it was simply a name, but acknowledging it would make her *human,* and that could not be allowed. Nana Death was anything but.

'Do we have to do this in here?' Oliver said, settling into the armchair. The fabric was tired and peeled beneath his rump; there was a stain, behind his head, that he decided not to think about. 'Don't you have an office or something? Or - I don't know - a kitchen?'

Nana smiled. It was a terrible smile, all yellow teeth strung together with thick, drooping saliva and what was left of her corroded gums. Narrow, wet lips peeled back into her withered face in what looked to Oliver like a snarl. 'Oh, we could go to the kitchen,' the old woman said slowly, 'but I'm afraid we might wake the baby, and

I couldn't *bear* to have her screaming when I turn on the oven.'

Oliver froze. His mouth opened a little to say something, but there were no words.

This is a mistake. Get out, he thought, eyes darting frantically to the door. It was painted white, a grim, dirty paint that had faded far quicker than the coat that covered the skull on the mantelpiece. 'I...'

'Oh, calm yourself,' Nana said, almost scolding. 'There's really nothing to be afraid of, Oliver.'

'So... you were joking, then?'

Slowly, Nana eased herself into the second armchair. It wasn't a snarl, Oliver realised, torn back in her face, but a smile. Perhaps she had looked pleasant, a long time ago, even attractive, but age had stripped her of any beauty and torn holes in her skin. But she din't look so wicked anymore, not in this light at least. Just old. Oliver wondered why he had been so afraid. *She's just an old woman.* Just...

'Shall we discuss, then, why you came?' she said, and Oliver remembered his fear. He was right to be frightened, here, in this crooked house.

'You know my name,' Oliver realised, cocking an eyebrow.

'Oh, I know a great many things. Names are rather insignificant, though, don't you think? Now, if you'd like to *discuss...*'

'Do you know why I'm here, too?'

'Of course.'

'Then what is there to discuss?'

Nana leaned forward a little, eyes flickering in the firelight. The flames glistened in the black pits of her pupils. For the first time Oliver took a poper look at the old woman's face; it was thin, misshapen, cheeks hollowed out and pulled in so that Oliver could see the outline of her skull beyond that withered, peeling skin. Her hair was thin and white and spread back from her forehead in a wild crow's nest of braids and wisps that knotted together in a loose, tangled bun. The lines in her face were clear and crisp and splintered around the corners of her eyes and mouth, travelling down to her throat, where they disappeared beneath the shining feather scarf around her neck.

'I would hate,' Nana said slowly, 'for you to regret your decision. It isn't too late, Oliver. You can turn back. I believe you left your car close by?'

'I did. I... I didn't want to walk too far through the forest.'

'A sensible decision,' Nana smiled. 'Those woods are dark and full of monsters, and they would *love* a pretty boy like you...'

Something shifted in Oliver's gut as the old woman licked her lips.

'All I'm saying, Oliver, is that you can still go home. You can go to your wife. Your daughter. Perhaps, if you simply allowed the continuation of her treatment -'

'No,' Oliver said. 'The treatment isn't working. It... it's making her *worse*.'

'I see,' Nana said, as if this was news to her. But there was something in her eyes, a cold, harsh *knowing,* like there was nothing Oliver could tell her she didn't already know. 'And her condition... is it incurable?'

'It's terminal. Please... you have to help me. She's only six years old. She has so much *left* to live for. Her whole life.'

Nana leant back. Calmly she reached into a mangled, tin pot on the arm of the chair and drew out a narrow cigarette. She never took her eyes off of Oliver as she dipped the end of the cigarrete into the fire and plucked a bead of glowing, amber light from the flames. She looked the man over, scrutinising him; Oliver was thin, narrow-shouldered. Unshaven. He looked like he hadn't slept in days. His eyes sagged, drooping as he watched Nana poke the cigarette into her teeth and draw a long, ragged breath. Her gaze dropped, fell to Oliver's left hand. He was scratching at the arm of his chair, digging his fingernails into the fabric, peeling away the old, tired leather a little more with every scrape, digging deeper, *deeper...*

'You are aware of the cost, Oliver?'

The man nodded, swallowing a little. A speck of red dripped from the nail of his index finger, soaked into the carpet.

Nana smiled, watched as Oliver kept scratching, kept

digging. 'And will you be sharing the cost with another? Or are you here to pay in full?'

Oliver paused. Tentative. His knee twitched as he spoke. 'My wife...' he started, 'she wants to pay half. She wanted to come with me. I... I couldn't allow that. You understand. She doesn't know I'm here. I had to do this on my own. For our daughter.'

'You must care for her very much,' Nana said.

'Of course I care for her!' Oliver snapped. He blinked. Shook his head. 'I'm sorry. Look, I... I have to ask, Nana. You understand.'

'I do. Please,' she said, as a narrow wisp of smoke rose from her tongue, 'ask.'

'Will I... will I die?'

Nana Death looked up at an old clock above the door. The hands were bent and twisted around each other like serpents, gold and flaking and corrupt over the ivory face of the instrument. It hadn't worked for decades. Still, it ticked...

'The payment will take much from you,' Nana said. 'There is a... *physical* toll. Some cannot handle it, Oliver. Some die. *Most* die. There have been very few cases where a client has survived. And those that *do*...'

Oliver nodded, took a deep breath. 'But my little girl...'

'Your daughter will be fine.'

'You're sure,' Oliver said. 'It'll work.'

'It never fails,' said the old woman. 'Now, Oliver, all

I need from you is a yes. Just say yes, and it will all be over.'

'Just say yes,' Oliver repeated. His eyes shifted to the fire.

'Your daughter will be okay. I will take my payment. The deal will be made, Oliver. All I need is a *yes*.'

Oliver paused. He could die. If he didn't, he'd never be the same. This would change him. He wouldn't be Oliver Baines anymore, not once the deal was made. He'd be nothing more than a shell, an empty husk with the face of Oliver Baines, but his daughter would be okay...

Do it for her. Do it for Rose.

'Alright,' Oliver said. Slowly, he nodded his head -

Nana raised a hand. A bent, bony finger stopped Oliver before he could say anything. 'One moment,' the old woman said. 'It seems we have a visitor.'

Oliver frowned. 'I don't hear -'

Someone knocked at the front door. Oliver cried out, jumping out of his skin, but Nana was expecting the arrival. She smiled faintly, stood from her armchair. Bowed a little. 'If you'll excuse me, Oliver. I won't be a minute. Think on my offer. Think on our deal.' Firelight crackled over her twisted face.

Oliver turned his head as she left the room, watched the old woman leave.

After a few seconds, his eyes turned back to the flames in the fireplace. He could see her face in the flames, his darling girl. His Rosie. With clear, narrow tubes streaming out of her nose as she convulsed in the hospital bed, screaming as her bones cracked and her lungs threw blood up over her tongue -

'*Yes,*' Oliver whispered.

For a while, nothing happened. Oliver waited. He hadn't expected to feel anything - a tingle, perhaps, or a slight heat in his chest, and then it would all be over. But he didn't feel a damn thing. He frowned. Maybe it hadn't worked, maybe he should say it again. Maybe Nana Death had to be in the room for it to happen.

Maybe it wasn't too late to change his mind.

Take it back, he thought. *Get out of here.*

Oliver opened his mouth.

Then he whimpered, crying out weakly as a shearing pain tore through his chest and cracked his ribs open and something wrenched itself from the depths of his body, drifting out of his mouth in a string of blood and vomit and shadow.

Something important.

It smiled as it left him.

Oliver gasped, choked up on something tight and hot in his throat. His body was rocked by a fit of violent convulsions and he gripped the arm of the chair so tight that his nails bent and snapped, leaving bloody patches of raw, wet skin at the end of his fingers. His chest heaved and sunk inward and his mouth opened wide in an agonised, breathless scream as his eyes bulged and threatened to pop in his skull. A drizzle of blood ran over his bottom lip as his guts churned and a second wave of vomit pushed up his throat, fell back down into his belly in a mess of bloody spittle. Finally his head was thrown back and the muscles in his throat recoiled and writhed and tore at his windpipe, crushing the vertebrae that held his skull in place and twisting them apart with a hollow, distorted *crunch*.

Oliver was dead before his head hit the back of the armchair.

7

The forest grew thicker around them with every mile they drove. Thin, spindly trees turned into hunched, lurching coils and great oak archways that bent and dragged over the dirt road. Martha Price glanced up into the rearview mirror, threw an uneasy smile at the boy in the back of the police car.

The boy did not smile back.

'Nearly there,' Martha said quietly, turning her attention back to the road. The battered old car's headlights were on full beam, pushing wide shafts of dazzling, white light into the dark. Rain slanted through the glare of the lights, glistening, obscuring any clear view of the path that would lead them to the middle of the woods.

Something howled outside.

Martha flinched, pressed her foot a little harder onto the accelerator. She had heard stories about these forests. About the *things* that lived in the dark between the trees. Stories to stop the kids coming out to the woods at night. Stories to bring in the tourists. Martha had heard the stories when she first transferred to the station here, never thought to give them any credibility. But now, with the trees all around her and the moon fat and full in the sky...

Martha turned her head a little as they curved along a skew in the road. Rain hammered on the roof of the car. The boy in the backseat had been silent all the way out here. He stared out of the window, eyes calm and still. Black hair fell over his forehead.

Nobody had been able to get the boy talking so far. What little the police had gathered about the crash, they had gleaned from the carnage on the road. It had been a struggle, understandably, to get the kid back into a car. Martha had only been called in to prove that a woman's touch was what the situation needed. She shrugged it off. It was the nineties, she thought. What else could she do? Still, even though she managed to convince the boy that it was a good idea to get in the police car, that nothing bad was going to happen to him, she couldn't get him to open his mouth.

Edward Drake was in shock.

'Everything okay?' Martha asked, but the boy didn't reply.

He might talk, in time, but for now he needed to rest. To eat. He hadn't touched any of the sandwiches they'd offered him at the station, hadn't drunk the water. Christ, he hadn't even looked Martha in the eyes, not once. Still, she couldn't blame him. She had seen the photographs of the crash. She had seen Drake's mother, bent up around a curved slither of glass that poked out of her belly, shining with blood.

'Stupid question,' she murmured after a while. Something slid into view, hazy beyond the slanting rain, on the side of the road. Something gleaming and silver. Martha frowned, touched the brake gently. It was a car, bigger than hers, newer, parked at the edge of the dirt road beneath the trees. Beside the vehicle, leading off into the forest, a ragged track led off the road towards a narrow pathway, and beyond that...

Martha pulled in behind the silver car, cut the engine. 'Looks like the place,' she said, leaning across to look out the passenger window. A shiver ran over her spine, curled around her waist. The windscreen wipers had halted with the engine and in seconds the window was awash with rain, a sliding sheet of grey that obscured any view of the forest. But the image of the crooked house hung before Martha's eyes like the glow of a fading lightbulb, all slanting walls and broken windows, flickering lights and cracked, stained flint.

She unbuckled her seatbelt, turned to face the boy. 'Have you been to your granny's before?' Martha said.

He looked at her, blinked. Still, his mouth was closed. He didn't answer.

'Look, I know this is rough,' Martha tried. 'I can't tell you I know how it feels, but I know it's *hard*. If you don't want to talk to me, or anyone, I get that. But I promise you I'm here, if you decide you *do* want to. And your grandmother – if she agrees to look after you – she's going to do her best to make things better. Okay?'

The boy said nothing and turned back to the window.

Something flickered across the glass, a shadow, but Martha barely noticed. Her eyes were on the child, on his face, on the features that were frozen in some expressionless, silent display. A pang of guilt slid up her throat and she swallowed. Surely there must have been another relative for the kid, an aunt or an uncle. Somewhere else, somewhere that wasn't this damn forest.

'Alright, I'm going to head inside,' Martha said. 'I don't think we can take the car any closer, so you stay here, alright? There's a radio on the dash. If you need me you just press this button,' she pointed, 'and tell me what's up. I'll come right out. Alright, Edward?'

Nothing.

'Okay,' Martha sighed. She leant for the car door, moved her hand to open it.

'Eddie,' said the boy. Timid, so quiet that Martha almost couldn't hear him. She looked up into the rearview, caught his eye.

Martha smiled. 'Eddie,' she said, and she stepped out of the car and into the dark.

CHAPTER THREE
SECRETS

1
NOW

Debbie was already at the station by the time Kramer came in. She glanced up from her desk and winked across at him. 'You made it, then,' she said.

Kramer grunted in response and crossed the room to his own desk, slumped down into his seat. The room was small and soulless; the walls were a shade of beige that he fancied was exactly halfway between brown and white, the carpet a dark, threatening blue that he felt could start lapping at his ankles any minute. His satchel dropped to the floor as he reached around a bulky computer monitor to switch it on. He caught Debbie's eye as he moved; she looked away.

'You look different,' he said quietly, keeping his eyes on his partner as he leant back again. 'No ponytail today?'

Debbie smiled, shrugging a little. A narrow, wooden cross hung around her neck, dipped beneath the collar of her uniform - a pale, grey blouse just a couple of shades lighter than her trousers. 'Ran out of hairbands,' she said.

'You look nice.'

Debbie raised an eyebrow.

'I'm sorry,' Kramer raised his hands, 'long night, ignore me.'

'No, it's fine,' she smiled. 'Just didn't realise we were doing compliments so early in the morning.'

'Got any for me?'

'Not a single one,' Debbie said. 'Christ, Matt, you look *awful*.'

Kramer nodded. 'Fair enough. Like I said, long night.'

'Charlotte okay?' Debbie stood from her desk, then, abandoning a pile of papers as she stepped across to the seat across from Kramer and perched herself in it. Her hair swayed about her face as she moved. It looked darker now that it was down, closer to a hazy bronze than blonde.

'She's good. Woke her up again, can't imagine she's having the best day at school.'

Debbie leant forward. 'You're still going to tell her, aren't you? Remember, we talked about this. Two days now, Matt.'

Kramer hesitated. There was a pen in his hand, and

he tapped it impatiently on the corner of the desk. 'You know, Roberts'll be *pissed* if he finds out I let you sit in his chair.'

'Then don't tell him,' Debbie grinned. Her eyes darted to the pen in Kramer's hand. He stopped tapping. She held her gaze, focused on the cracks that ran over his knuckles. They had dried up overnight, but they wouldn't heal properly for weeks. 'You can do it, you know,' she said. 'Charlotte, I mean. You can tell her.'

'She'll hate me, Deb.'

'As if she ever could. She *loves* you, Matt. Telling her the truth isn't going to change that.'

Kramer leaned forward, hands clasped together. His knuckles *burned.* 'Deb, it's going to ruin everything. And she's got exams coming up. She's going to do so well. Maybe if I just wait until after...'

He trailed off when he saw the look in Debbie's face.

Slowly, Debbie laid a hand on Kramer's knee. 'You're going to be fine. *She's* going to be fine. It won't change a thing, Matt. Whatever happens, she will always be your daughter. And if you ever need me, I'm always here. If you need company, or... I don't know, if you want me to just say a prayer for you, or something. I'm always here.'

The phone rang. Debbie's hand flinched on Kramer's leg and she pulled it back, clearing her throat. Kramer turned, reaching for the handset.

'Hello?' Kramer said. 'Police. This is detective

Kramer.'

Debbie watched Kramer's face quietly as he listened. All she could hear from the other end of the phone was some kind of unintelligible babble, but she could see enough in his eyes to know that something had happened. Something out of the ordinary.

'Calm down,' Kramer was saying. 'Listen... hey, listen. It's okay. Stay calm. I'll be along in five minutes to check it out. Stay where you are. No, listen... *listen* to me. I will be there soon. Just stay put. That's... yeah, stay there.' He flashed his eyes at Debbie. She was already standing, reaching for the coat she'd laid on the edge of her desk.

Kramer hung up. 'Something on the beach,' he said. 'By the Devil's Crown. You coming?'

Debbie glanced around the empty office, pulling on her coat. 'Think I'm staying here while you go do all the fun stuff?'

'Should've known better,' Kramer nodded, turning. They crossed the room together, and he pushed open the door, stood aside as Debbie passed through.

'You know, you still have to tell her,' Debbie said as they made their way to the parking lot.

'Oh, I know,' Kramer murmured. 'One thing at a time.'

2

Charlotte Kramer hugged her rucksack to her chest, almost tripping over her laces as she stepped out into the corridor. Something knocked into her back, pushing her forward, and before she could duck aside she was trapped in a sluggish throng of heavy boots and hoodies and armfuls of books and papers. The bell was still ringing in her ears and Charlotte kept her head down, eyes on the ground. Somewhere, a locker door slammed shut.

The corridor broke off into two and she turned a corner, stumbling through a cluster of teenagers gathered at the edges of the hall and spilling into the middle. A group of older kids shoved her aside, heading to the canteen. Charlotte wasn't hungry. A green-painted door at the end of the corridor led out onto the playing field. If she could just find somewhere to sit, for a while...

Charlotte fought her way to the door, gripping the folds of her rucksack tight as she held it close. She raised a knee to shove the door open and stepped outside -

The wind bit at her face, pushed her back. She frowned. This wasn't the playing field.

Charlotte turned her face up to the sky. Moonlight filtered in through the treetops, shooting holes in the canopy of dead, black leaves above her head. Branches cracked under her shoes as she walked.

'Hello?' she called. Firelight crackled in the shadows, torn apart by dust and thickets and brambles. Charlotte pressed towards it, entranced.

Something moved behind her.

Charlotte flinched, slinging the rucksack over one shoulder as she broke through the trees and came to a small glade in the middle of the forest. The ground was flat and wet here and she was surrounded by thin, tall trunks. Off to one side, she could hear a thick, damp bubbling. She dipped her head, glancing through the trees; the light fell differently there, moving and rippling as though it were landing on the wet surface of a pond.

Something reared up from the murk and Charlotte's eyes widened and she was running, turning back to the firelight ahead and following it through the trees. The edges of the glade closed around her and she was in the thick of the woods again, running and ducking beneath hanging branches, crying out as thorns and spines tugged at her clothes and scratched her face, and then it loomed up out of the dark in front of her.

The crooked house.

Charlotte stopped. There was something in her hands, something cold and fleshy. Blood drooled through her fingers like sand.

The front door of the old, derelict building opened with a squeal. There she was. The old woman from

Charlotte's nightmares. Slender and terrible, the witch stepped forward, her haggard face hidden in the shadows. Even in the dark, Charlotte could see the whites of the old woman's narrowed eyes as she raised a hand, curling a long, crooked finger...

'Am I boring you, Charlie?'

Charlotte snapped awake and raised her head, almost falling off her chair in her stunned surprise. 'What?' she murmured. Someone laughed behind her.

Oh god, she thought. *Not again...*

At the front of the classroom, Mr Crawford folded his arms and glared at her. 'Hang behind after class, Charlie. I think we need to have a little word.'

Then Crawford forgot about her and turned back to the class, and within seconds he was deep into the same rambling monologue that had sent the girl to sleep in the first place, jabbing flaky fingers at the whiteboard on the wall behind him.

Quickly, Charlotte grabbed the pen that had fallen onto her desk and started scribbling in the corner of her notebook. If only she could draw the house, while its image was fresh in her mind, then she wouldn't forget...

No.

Charlotte scratched out the drawing and squeezed her eyes shut, gripping the pen with white knuckles.

No, she *wanted* to forget.

Hurriedly, she closed the book and turned it over on her desk. The cover was a mess of fragmented, scrawled doodles: thin, snake-like creatures; shadowy figures without eyes, without faces.

And in the lower corner of the book, a drawing she'd forgotten about; an old, white hearse with a shadow in the driver's seat and a long, black coffin in the back.

3

'Is that her?' Debbie peered through the windscreen, nodding towards the woman at the cliff's edge. 'The woman who called us?'

Kramer shrugged, pulling the car off to the left as he slowed to a stop. 'I guess so,' he said. 'She look familiar to you?'

Debbie shook her head. The woman was in her late thirties, at a guess, with dyed brown hair and a stuffy coat wrapped around her shoulders. Beneath it, Debbie caught a glimpse of what looked like a white-fabric uniform. She raised her eyebrow. 'Looks like she works down at Black River.'

'Great,' Kramer grunted, yanking up the handbrake as he cut the engine. 'Last time I spoke to someone from the asylum he tried to psycho-analyse me. I'm not messing about with all that again.'

'They're not all like that, you know,' Debbie said, pushing open the passenger door. 'Besides, she looks pretty distracted.'

Kramer stepped out of the car and slammed his door,

wincing as the noise sent echoes bouncing about the inside of his skull.

Debbie grinned at him across the bonnet. 'Still hungover?'

'I don't *get* hungover,' Kramer lied. 'It's just brain freeze, from... the wind.'

'Nice one,' Debbie said.

'Shut up.'

Behind them, the woman had started moving towards the car. 'Are you police?' she called.

Kramer turned. He was about to open his mouth, point to the red-tinted bulb on the roof of the battered old car and ask the brown-haired woman who the hell *else* they might be. He stopped himself.

Christ, this woman looked *terrified*.

'Yeah,' Debbie said. 'We're the police. Can you tell us what's happened?'

The woman gestured towards the clifftop, to the ramp that led down to the sea. 'I don't know what to tell you,' she said. 'I don't... I don't think I can describe it. Have a look.'

Kramer was hesitant. 'Down on the beach?' he said.

The woman nodded. 'I was just... I was walking along, and... oh, god, I'm a suspect. Oh, I shouldn't have called this in. Are you... do you arrest me now? I have to get to work...'

'Calm down,' Debbie said, raising her hands. 'We're not going to arrest you. We might need to take you to the station, ask a few questions. Depends what's happened down there. Can you tell me your name?'

The woman nodded. 'Hayley,' she said quickly. 'Hayley King.'

'Alright, Hayley,' Kramer said. 'Shall we have a look?'

She shook her head. 'I'm not... I've seen enough.'

'That's alright,' he said, nodding towards the car. 'Deb, you look after her for a minute. I'll go take a look, see what's going on.'

Debbie nodded.

Slowly, Kramer walked toward the cliff edge. The wind battered him, growing stronger as he neared the clifftop. He pressed on, dark tie flailing about his throat in a mad dance. There was a bitter taste on the air and he grimaced. He recognised that smell...

'Oh, shit,' he murmured. He stopped, stood at the edge of the cliff and looked down.

'What is it?' Debbie called.

Kramer didn't answer. For a second he couldn't move, frozen to the spot. He had never seen anything like it. Even back on the mainland, before he'd moved out to Cain's End, he had never seen anything like this.

'Matt!' Debbie yelled. 'What's down there?'

Kramer took a step back, shook his head. He couldn't take his eyes off the sand, off the blood...

'*Matt!*'

'Oh, *shit,*' Kramer whispered. He turned away from

the cliff, walked back towards the car. He could feel Debbie's eyes on him, raised his head. 'Murder,' he said calmly. 'Double. Two victims, male and female. I think so, anyway.'

Debbie's eyes widened. 'Murder? Wait... what do you mean, you *think* so?'

'You'll see,' Kramer said. 'Deb, we're going to need to cut off the beach. This... fuck me, this is bad.' He turned to Hayley, squinted across at her through the wind that stung his eyes. 'Listen, it looks old. A few hours old, at least. We'll have to get forensics to double check, but as long as you've got an alibi for last night, I think you're in the clear. Were you with anyone, until this morning?'

Hayley paused. 'Yes,' she said quietly, after a moment.

Kramer nodded. 'Can you give me his name?'

Hayley looked from Kramer to Debbie, hesitant. 'Emma,' she whispered. '*Her* name. Her name is Emma Green. I was with her until a couple of hours ago.'

Kramer nodded, glanced across at Debbie. 'Get this woman to work,' he said quickly. 'Meantime, I'll stick around here, get the beach closed down, call in forensics.'

'Alright,' Debbie said. 'And Emma Green?'

Kramer looked at Hayley. 'Does she work with you, down at the asylum?'

Hayley nodded.

'See if you can find her while you're there, Deb. Make sure that alibi checks out. Then get back here, fast as you can. Sound okay?'

Debbie smiled grimly. 'Got it.' She turned, beckoned Debbie into the police car. 'Oh, and Matt,' she said, casting one last look his way. 'Don't go down there by yourself. Not till I get back, alright?'

Kramer raised his hand in a mock-salute and Debbie climbed into the driver's seat.

The police car pulled away and Kramer watched them go, peering through the mist that had rolled in off the sea. After a few moments the car had disappeared, and he was alone.

Kramer turned back to the cliff and exhaled.

'Sorry, Deb,' he said quietly, and he began heading towards the ramp.

4

The sand shifted under Kramer's feet as he moved. His overcoat fluttered about the shirt and tie of his detective's uniform, exposing a broad frame as it peeled back from his shoulders. The hand over his mouth did little to mute the sickly smell of the carnage before him, but it remained nonetheless. The bristles of his unshaven jaw pricked his palm.

'Christ,' he mumbled.

The girl's body was the first Kramer had seen from

above the ledge. It was spread over the beach, pieces of it as far out as the Devil's Crown. The dead girl's blood was painted over the rocks in vast, terrible swathes. Smudged and smeared in whorls and manic patterns too narrow to have been drawn with fingers. The tide had abandoned the jagged stone circle and a feeble swill of grey water lapped at the heels of the boulders. Scraps and thin, pale sheets of skin clung to the granite, flapping a little in the wind, slapping the rocks wetly. The girl's back had been torn almost completely off by whatever had dragged her over the rocks.

Her torso laid at the edge of the sand and bobbed as the shallow waves drew onto the sand, shifting in the murk and the foam. The water pulled away red and thick. Even now that the blood had started to dry, it was plentiful. It trickled from the torn-open cavity in the belly of her carcass, from the savaged stumps of her legs and her left arm. The right was still attached, but it was so bent and scarred that it was nothing more than an unhinged mess of tendons and raw flesh.

Kramer could barely look at the girl's discarded legs, or what was left of them. The missing arm, too, had been tossed to one side, mangled and broken. Hunks of flesh were missing everywhere and in places even the bones had been snapped and removed. Organs spilled out onto the sand, where the blood had dried and darkened. Some of them were torn apart, some popped and opened up by whatever cruel hands had done this.

The girl's head was missing.

Kramer walked a little way along the sand, keeping close to the cliff face. The second body had been treated in much the same way as the first, although his head was still attached to his throat. Rabid fingers had torn out one of his eyes and peeled away all the flesh of his jaw. His teeth hung raw and wet from bloody, exposed gums in a morbid scream. His throat was shredded, his chest opened up like the girl's. His heart had been taken. Bits of him had been removed and strewn over the beach, mixed with the girl's organs in a macabre jumble of grey and red.

The pieces looked *chewed.*

'Fucking hell,' Kramer whispered. This didn't look like a murder, not anymore. This was a *massacre*. He would have considered a wild animal, except Cain's End didn't *have* wild animals. Not the kind that could do this, anyway.

Kramer tore his eyes away from the man's grizzled body. Blood swirled over the sand and led around the cliff, disappearing behind a crag in the clay-streaked wall that dipped off to the right. Beyond that were the caves, a network of tunnels abandoned since the remnants of some crippled smuggling operation left the island decades ago. Kramer moved forward, following the crimson trail in the dust -

Something flickered in front of him. A shadow.

Kramer froze.

'Hello?' he called. Kramer stepped over the dead man's twisted leg, glancing over his shoulder. His eyes moved to the top of the cliff - no sign of forensics yet.

He was on his own.

Slowly, Kramer pressed his back to the cliff; even in low tide, this part of the beach was so narrow that the low waves poked at his toes. He followed the trail of blood around until he could see the cave entrance, a screaming maw of black, ragged rock dug out of the cliff. Here the ground fell away; the floor of the cave had been broken down and brushed over until all that was left was a strip of wet, black rock just wide enough for a man to stand if he was careful.

Shallow water lapped at Kramer's ankles as the ground shifted beneath him. Twisting himself around the cliff face he moved into the cave, ducking beneath a lurch of grey that dripped with slick, white saltwater.

It was quiet, inside the cave. The wash of the waves was muted by a wall of wind behind him, but Kramer's footsteps echoed as he moved further into the dark. Grappling with his mobile he flicked the screen upwards, throwing a flimsy square of light into the shadows.

Kramer stopped.

The wall opposite him was scratched and scarred and red.

Blood dripped from the ceiling, drooled over every crevice and bulge in the rock. In places, it had been drawn into crude shapes; there, close to the ground, half washed away by the swell of the water, it formed a crimson, branching structure that looked like a great oak tree, splintering into jagged branches and roots. Level with his eyes, a pair of bloody, faceless figures raised their arms in some twisted prayer. Kramer swung the phone across and cast the pale beam of light over the entire wall. Something twisted in the pit of his stomach.

Fear.

There were words, too, in the midst of the rough, nonsense drawings. Words like *hurt* and *burning* and *hatred* and strings of gory, furious expletives. And in the middle of it all, red and dripping, a question:

WHO IS EDWARD DRAKE?

CHAPTER FOUR
BLACK RIVER

1
1993

Martha knew, even before she reached the front door of the crooked house, that this was a mistake. Thick gobs of rain spat down from the sky as it rumbled, threatening to open up above her head. Behind her, the forest echoed with the strangled scream of some poor creature caught in a trap.

This was no place for a child.

Martha paused on the porch, blinking the rain out of her eyes. She pulled soaked hair back from her forehead, glancing up. She would have to change when she got back to the station; the rain had seeped into her blouse and laid heavy on her cold skin. It was getting worse.

Slowly, Martha raised her fist to rap on the door. It was rough and splintered beneath a thick, dark stain.

The whole house gave her the creeps. The firelight behind the windows, the cracked flint and ragged slats of wood that made up the slanting walls. The building should have been torn down by the wind years ago. The fact that it was still standing was either a miracle or... something else.

Martha knocked

She wasn't waiting long. The door opened and flickering, orange light crashed onto the porch, obscured by the silhouette of an old, withered woman.

Martha swallowed, looked up into the woman's face. 'Hello,' she said. Her voice was little more than a croak. She coughed, tried again. 'Sorry. Hello. Are you... there's something I need to tell you.'

You sound like an idiot, she thought. *Tell her you're police. Tell her about the kid.*

Martha opened her mouth, but nothing came.

Slowly, the old woman raised an eyebrow. The lines of her forehead pulled back. Her lips peeled away into a cold, hard smile.

She narrowed her eyes, and the smile disappeared. 'They're dead,' she said, 'aren't they?' Her voice was like rusted metal.

Martha froze. Goosebumps popped up on her arms. 'How did you...'

'*Magic,*' the old woman whispered. Her face stayed perfectly still. Rain hammered on the roof of the porch, but Martha barely noticed. Inexplicably, she was terrified. Had the old woman really just...

'I'm sorry,' Martha frowned. 'Was that a *joke?*'

The old woman straightened her back and suddenly she was six inches taller, staring down at Martha with empty, scolding eyes. 'I'm afraid I lose a grip on my sense of humour, when I'm... saddened.'

Martha nodded cautiously. There was a funny smell, she noticed, now that the door had opened. She couldn't place it, but it was strong. Getting stronger. 'Look, did someone call ahead? I'm sorry, I know this is terrible, but... how did you know what happened?'

Cigarette smoke. That was it. Tobacco, laced with fruit and spices and dripping with old, bitter rum.

'Yes,' said the old woman. 'Someone called ahead.' She paused for a minute, as if deciding what to say next. She tilted her head, just a little. 'It was a car crash. A real *tragedy.*'

Something else, beyond the smoke. Something *filthy.*

'I'm sorry,' Martha said. 'Your daughter, your son-in-law... they both passed, I'm afraid. I know how hard this is to hear, but -'

'Is he in the car?'

Martha frowned. 'Excuse me?'

'The boy,' the old woman rasped. 'Is he in the car?'

'Eddie? Yeah, he's... listen, I have to ask... the kid, you're his closest relation by blood. Automatically, that means you're our first choice for...'

'Bring him in,' said the old woman.

'I'm sorry?'

'I assume there is a lot of paperwork.'

Martha hesitated. 'A fair amount,' she nodded.

'Well, he can't spend all evening in the car, can he? Bring the boy indoors, he can sit in the kitchen while we figure everything out.'

'You're sure?' Martha said, half-hoping the old woman would reconsider. 'I mean, it's so sudden. Do you want a little time to think it over?'

'What is there to think about?' the old woman said. 'The child needs a guardian. What kind of grandmother would I be if I declined?'

Martha said nothing.

'Bring him in. I have a little clearing up to do, it should only take a moment.' The old woman turned, silhouette twisting in the light from the hallway, and the door closed behind her.

Martha stood, for a moment, grimacing as her chest heaved. She exhaled, finally aware that her breathing had become shallow and ragged in the last few moments. Her heart was pounding.

The tobacco smell lingered, even after the door had closed.

2

Debbie shuddered as she pulled the battered police car up to the asylum gates. Rows of trees disappeared behind them rusted, iron bars twisted up from the ground. The narrow dirt road that wound through the forest became a flat, wide strip of tarmac.

'How do we get in?' Debbie said. The gates were tall and spiked; a sheet of wire mesh was laid over the bars to make even the three-inch gaps between them impassible. Debbie noted a pair of spotlights trained directly on the gates, a manned guard tower beyond the thick stone wall in which they were set. A wide, flat bolt laid heavily across the bars and held the gates closed. Every now and then the wind pushed, just a little, on the gates and they strained against the bar with a horrible, metal-on-metal squeal.

Hayley nodded towards an electronic panel in the wall. 'We type in the code,' she explained. 'Karl - the guy up there, in the tower - buzzes us through. Nice and easy.'

'Sounds good,' Debbie nodded, glancing up at the guard tower as she pulled up the handbrake. 'Would you do us the honours?'

Hayley unbuckled her seatbelt and pushed open the door, flinching as a shifting breeze rolled into the car. She stepped out onto the tarmac and Hayley watched as she reached for the control panel, jabbing keys with the pad of her thumb.

Metal ground over metal as the hefty bolt slid open and the gates parted with a mechanical whir. Debbie drove forward slowly, pausing once she was beyond the wall to let Hayley catch up and climb back into the car. The gates shuddered to a jerky close behind them as they followed a wide, flat path towards the building. A man nodded down at them from the guard tower, but his face was muted by a greasy layer of glass.

'Tight security,' Debbie murmured as they drove. The asylum rose up before them in a towering mass of red brick and cracked mortar. The roof was slanted and grey, the windows - what few of them were littered about the place - were tiny, barred squares.

'Has to be,' Hayley agreed. 'Used to be a little more slack when it was first set up. The village wasn't here back then, I guess, so nobody really cared if anyone got out. Island as small as this, they'd be easy to find. If they managed to get *off* the island, they'd drown before they ever reached the mainland.'

'Nice system,' Debbie said, turning the car into a space near the front door.

'Then they decided that the staff deserved living quarters *outside* the hospital, so they built a compound a little way out the forest. Then they hired more staff, and the compound turned into a village, and then...'

'People started worrying a little more.'

'A little.'

Debbie cut the engine. 'Shall we?'

Hayley paused. Her eyes shifted to the dashboard and she exhaled.

'Something wrong?' Debbie frowned.

'Listen,' Hayley said slowly. She looked across at Debbie, smiling weakly. 'I don't want... I know you have to talk to Emma, get my story straight about last night. But...'

'You're not ready for people to know,' Debbie said. She nodded. 'I get that. Don't worry, I'll keep it quiet.'

'Thank you,' Hayley said. Her gaze shifted to the cross hung around Debbie's throat and she shook her head. 'Shouldn't you be... you know.'

'Depends who you ask,' Debbie said. 'Me? I don't think a loving God would give a shit who you sleep with, and I certainly don't think he'd let me hold it against you.'

'You're kind,' Hayley said.

'I know,' Debbie grinned. 'You ready?'

Hayley nodded quickly and they stepped out of the car.

'You know, you shouldn't be afraid, though,' Debbie said, calling a little louder above the wind. 'People won't see you any differently. And if they do...'

'They're not worth my time,' Hayley said. 'I know.' She turned her eyes to the ground as they stepped towards the front door. The car locked with a timid bleep behind them. 'It's just that... never mind. It's complicated.'

'Fair enough,' Debbie said. 'As long as you're both happy.' She glanced up as they neared the door; a faded, bronze plaque hung beneath another keypad, engraved with the name *Black River Asylum: Institution and Asylum for the Mentally Unwell.*

Hayley stepped forward, keyed in the code for the door. Four digits - a different combination to the one she had tapped in at the gates, Debbie noticed.

'God, how do you *remember* all these?'

'You get used to it,' Hayley said. The door clicked open and they stepped inside.

The hallway was far less depressing than Debbie had imagined, all thick, red carpet and faded walls. She had been expecting drab, grey tiles and swinging, crackling bulbs. This was worse, somehow. It looked... *inviting.* 'Who thought it would be a good idea to make this place look like a hotel?' Debbie said.

Hayley shrugged. 'You get used to that too, I guess.'

Debbie's eyes tracked the high walls as she looked about the entrance hall. Fluorescent bulbs hung from the ceiling, set into simplistic, plastic chandeliers. Framed photographs were strung up along the corridor. 'It's creepy,' she said quietly.

'Damn right it's creepy,' Hayley said. '*All* hotels are creepy.'

'Interesting view. Listen, Hayley, I can take you home if you need. Point me in the direction of Emma Green and I'll give you a lift. You don't have to be here, if you're not ready. What you've seen this morning...'

'I'm ready,' Hayley nodded. 'I think it'll do me good to get to wor. Distract myself.'

'Of course. But if you need anything...'

'I'll be fine,' Hayley smiled. 'But thank you. Emma should be in the medical suite, if she's not with an inmate. If she isn't there, one of the nurses will tell you where to find her.'

'Thank you,' Debbie said. She glanced down the hall. 'Where's medical?'

'Keep walking down past reception,' Hayley nodded. 'First door on the left, third on the right. This place is a maze.'

'Let me guess, you get used to it?'

'Oh, never,' Hayley grinned. 'It's *impossible.*'

Debbie smiled. 'Good meeting you, Hayley. You gonna be okay?'

'I'll do my best. Not every day you see... *that*. But I'll be fine. Just you catch whatever sick bastard did that, yeah? You and your partner.'

'We'll get him,' Debbie said. 'Don't you worry.'

'Good luck.'

Debbie gave a little wave, started to walk off the way Hayley had told her. Her footsteps were silent on the carpet. Above her head, a fluorescent light flickered softly. 'Oh!' she called, turning back for a moment. 'Don't be afraid, Hayley King. Remember that. You and Emma... be happy. Whatever that takes. Whether you keep it to yourselves or decide to tell the world, just be *happy.*'

Hayley smiled.

Debbie disappeared down the hall and turned a corner. Her footsteps faded as she moved further into the asylum.

Hayley was alone. She shivered, closed her eyes for a moment. She could still *see* them. The images were imprinted on the backs of her eyelids, burned into her brain by some gory, blood-stained brand. Bodies in the sand, torn apart and twisted and mangled. She stood on the clifftop and watched as the tide came in, washing up a severed leg in a rise of white foam. The girl's shoe was still on her foot and the laces were spattered a dull, faded red...

'It's okay,' Hayley whispered to herself. 'You're okay. Don't be afraid.'

She opened her eyes. The hotel-lobby hallway was silent. Nothing moved. Still, she couldn't help feeling like someone was watching her.

3

Eddie sat on a low kitchen stool, head bowed a little, peering up through the mess of black fringe that had fallen into his face. Across the room from him, Nana - she had told him to call her that - stood over a rough, wooden counter, poring over a wad of bright yellow papers. Beside her, the policewoman stood with one hand on her hip, the other on the edge of the counter. She seemed quieter than she had been in the car. Every now and then Eddie would catch her staring at the old woman with narrowed eyes, suspicious. The paperwork was done, mostly, in silence, the odd word exchanged purely out of necessity.

As the two women worked, Eddie looked about him. The kitchen was as crooked as the outside of the house; the walls were tiled, but the glossy, black-and-white slabs had cracked and peeled apart to reveal a mess of crumbling, red clay. The counters were uneven and warped, the only instruments a battered, black stove and a faded enamel basin. The floor was a patchwork of dusty, varnished bricks, some so broken up by constant wear that they were little more than fragments and chunks of stone.

Slowly, Eddie turned on his stool. With his back to Martha and his grandmother he looked through the open kitchen doorway, an arch of twisted wood and red-stained stone. The other side of the hallway, a white door stood in a pale, faded frame. A bent handle cast a curled, clawed shadow over the wood. Despite the fire burning behind the door, it bristled with a numb, dark coldness. A dull kind of energy seeped into the air, drawing Eddie off his rump, onto his feet. His footsteps were silent, even on the broken bricks of the floor, and then over that blood-red carpet, and he reached up, fingers trembling. The numb sensation was stronger now that he was closer to the door. Colder. Eddie's palm settled on the handle.

He pushed. The hinges screamed as the old, white door opened...

'Eddie?' Martha called behind him. Eddie turned. The two women were staring at him. They watched quietly as he stood there; the policewoman with an intense kind of curiosity, Nana with a cool, burning anger.

Eddie swallowed.

'That room's not been cleaned out yet,' Nana said, with that thick, rasping voice. 'Close the door, boy.'

Eddie turned back to the door. He could see it all, through the crack he had made; a thin shaft of firelight illuminated the masks on the wall, the skulls lined up along the mantelpiece, and he pushed, just a little further...

Suddenly Nana was behind him, one hand on his shoulder while the other reached above his head for the handle and yanked the door shut. Eddie turned up his head and for a moment he saw it in her eyes, the same thing that he had seen in that room.

Death.

'Come,' Nana hissed. 'Back to the kitchen, now.'

Eddie followed her, stealing one last glance at the white door. He had *seen* it, before she closed the door. Slumped in front of the fireplace, head lolling back on the crest of an old, tattered armchair.

Eddie's father had been right. He wasn't safe here.

Martha smiled at the boy as he returned to his stool,

but there was nothing she could do. Not now. Eddie's lip quivered as Nana moved back to the papers on the counter, spreading them on the wooden surface. He watched as the old woman turned to Martha and held out her hand.

'Pen?' Nana rasped.

Martha nodded silently, reaching into the top pocket of her blouse. She pulled out a black biro and handed it to the old woman.

Nana took one last look at Eddie and smiled. 'You're home now, child.'

Eddie's breath hitched in his throat as the old woman turned back to the papers and started to sign. The pen shifted over rough pape with a harsh scratching and Eddie winced. Suddenly the sound was all he could hear, louder than the crackling of the flames and the pounding in his chest. His throat was dry.

Martha frowned, moved over to him. Quietly, she knelt down before the boy and laid a hand on his knee. 'Eddie,' she said, her voice barely more than a whisper, 'is everything okay?'

Eddie opened his mouth, but nothing came out. The scratching had stopped. He looked into Martha's eyes, shook his head as slightly as possible. Nana was listening. She would know if he said anything. She would know if he *moved.*

'Eddie, talk to me,' Martha said. 'If you don't want to stay here...'

Eddie blinked. He tried to shake his head again, but his skull drooped, heavy. The muscles in his neck tightened at the base of his skull and *squeezed*. He couldn't move. He tried to open his mouth, to stand -

Eddie *couldn't move.*

The pen started scratching again. Eddie's eyes shifted to the back of Nana's head and he swallowed. It was all he could do.

Martha looked desperate. 'Eddie,' she tried again. 'Please, say something.'

'The boy isn't going to talk,' Nana called. 'He's in shock. He needs time.'

'He *has* to talk,' Martha hissed quietly, without turning her head. Her eyes were pleading. 'Eddie, you have to talk to me. If there's anything you need to tell me, you need to do it *now.*'

Eddie *wanted* to tell her. He wanted to tell her that he was afraid, that he didn't trust his grandmother. He wanted to tell her to open the white door and see what was on the other side.

He couldn't breathe.

Something cold and clinging clamped down on the boy's lungs, tightened around them. Eddie's windpipe twisted about in his throat and he strained his head, tilted it upward, trying to catch his breath -

There. The vice around his lungs opened up. Air flowed into them and he opened his mouth to speak.

Get me out, he wanted to say. *Open the door. Look.*

Get me out of here.

'No,' he whispered. 'Everything's fine.'

Get me out! screamed the voice in his head. *You have to see what's in there!*

'I'm just tired,' Eddie said. His eyes widened. *No!* he tried to say. *She's...*

The scratching had stopped.

'There we go,' Nana said. She turned around, and her pupils were small and sunken pits. She looked into Eddie's eyes, smiled a little. She winked.

She's not letting me speak! yelled the voice.

'There we go,' Eddie echoed.

Why can't I speak? What are you doing to me?

'Thank you, Nana,' Eddie said. The muscles in his mouth and his cheeks twisted, pulled upward, and his lips broke into a forced, quivering smile. 'I suppose that's it, then.'

No!

'I'm home.'

For a moment, Martha looked... disappointed. She stood slowly, reached into her pocket. Keeping her eyes on the boy, she spoke slowly. There was something on his face, an anguished pain that shone through like desperation in his eyes. 'Do you mind if I speak to him for a moment?'

'Not at all,' Nana rasped. 'I shall see to my business in the living room. Do see yourself out when you're finished with him.' She turned her head back to Eddie, smiled.

It was not a pleasant smile. 'Do come through when you're ready, child.'

Eddie opened his mouth, but something in his throat closed up and pushed down the words. Eddie's tongue twisted around itself and he almost gagged.

Nana stepped out of the kitchen. Eddie listened as she opened the white door nd it squealed, dragging itself over the sagging floorboards of the hallway. The old woman's clipped, harsh footsteps faded beneath the crackling of the fire. The door closed.

Quickly, Martha pulled something out of her pocket and handed it to the boy. He took the card silently, gripped it between trembling fingers. Crisp, black print on white paper. A name. A string of digits.

'It's going to be okay,' Martha said softly, running her hand through his hair. 'Eddie, everything's going to be okay. They'll send someone out in a couple of weeks to make sure you're alright. I'll make sure they keep me informed. In the meantime,' she said, nodding toward the card in his hand, 'that's my extension. If you ever need me, or *anyone,* call that number and I'll be here as soon as I can. Don't you ever lose that card, okay?'

'Never,' Eddie whispered.

Martha smiled weakly. 'Nana's going to look after you,' she said. She didn't sound convinced. 'Call me if you need. Day or night. Just *call* me. Look after yourself, Eddie.'

Eddie nodded again. It was all he could manage.

Martha turned, reluctant, stepping out into the hallway.

Eddie shut his eyes, listening as the front door opened and rain slammed into the wood, thousands of bullets smacking the front of the house in a barrage of shining lead. The door closed. Eddie blinked a single tear out of the corner of his eye. Silently, he bowed his head and exhaled.

'Come,' Nana called from the living room.

Eddie stood on shaking legs, slipping the card into the pocket of his trousers. She couldn't see it. She couldn't find it. No, he had to keep it safe. And when Nana was asleep, when she couldn't stop him, he would find a telephone and call that number. He'd ask Martha to come back for him.

He'd *beg,* if he had to.

Slowly, Eddie pushed open the white door and crossed into the living room.

Nana sat in an armchair by the fire, arms folded in her lap. Opposite her, the dead man's head lolled against the back of the chair he'd died in.

'Did you kill him?' Eddie whispered.

'Don't be silly,' Nana said, smiling sweetly. Blood drizzled over the corpse's bottom lip. 'I gave him exactly what he wanted.'

'Are you a witch?'

Nana leaned forwards in the chair. Her eyes were

wild. She looked different, in the firelight. The frail, aged facade was gone. She was young, here. Powerful. The wrinkles were still there, on her face, drawn down her slender throat, but her eyes *burned*. 'I'm your grandmother,' she hissed.

'You're not a witch,' Eddie whispered. 'You're the *Devil*.'

There was that smile again, a thin, harsh line that split her withered face in two. She didn't answer. Instead, she raised her hand, palm facing upwards, fingers curled into long, thin claws.

'Give me the card,' she said.

Fuck!

Eddie blinked. 'I don't...'

How did she know?

Before he could stop himself, Eddie was reaching into his pocket. His arm felt numb, heavy, moving almost completely on its own. 'No...' he whispered, staring down at his arm with horrified, wide eyes. He could do nothing. His fingers wrapped around the card and he pulled it free of his trousers, held it out towards the old woman.

No! No, don't let her have it!

'Thank you,' Nana said, plucking the card from his fingers. Slowly, she leant back in her chair, looked it over. The smile never shrunk, never faded. The glimmer in her eyes was dark and red and shining.

Nana Death stood up from her chair and stepped over

to the fire.

'No!' Eddie yelled, but it was too late. The card floated down into the flames and caught alight, glowing hot and white at one corner before crumpling and shrivelling into a scrap of singed, black nothing.

Embers floated into the living room, and Eddie sobbed.

'That's enough, child,' Nana said. She turned, and her narrow smile was sickly. 'You're *home* now, remember?'

4

Blue tape fluttered in the wind, strung up along the edge of the cliff. Matthew Kramer clambered to the top of the sand-hewn ramp and ducked beneath the barrier, already reaching for the mobile in his grey overcoat. He glanced down toward the beach as he dialled.

Below him, the sand was covered in a twisted network of tracks and footprints. The forensics team had only arrived ten minutes ago, but already they had bagged up most of the smaller pieces; chunks of flesh and samples of blood, slithers of organ and stained, damp clay. He watched as two white-suited figures moved over the beach. Pale, baggy suits zipped up to their throats flapped about their bulky frames. Blue latex gloves clung to their hands. Sunlight glinted off their suits as it scraped through the clouds. On the horizon, it was cut up by a slanted sheen of rainwater.

The storm hadn't reached them yet, but it was coming.

'Charlie,' Kramer said, speaking loud enough that he could be heard over the wind. The phone had rang through to voicemail - she was still in school, would be for a few more hours. 'Hey, love, I'm just calling to let you know something's happened on the beach. Stay away from the cliffs today, alright? Get straight home when you finish school. I'm sorry, I know how this sounds. It's just... it's not safe out here, right now. Get home, lock the door. I've got my keys, I'll see you tonight.'

He paused, took a breath. He caught a flash of light in the corner of his eye and glanced towards the Devil's Crown; one of the forensics guys was photographing the rocks, and with every flash of the camera a glint of white bounced off the blood splashed over the stones. Kramer watched as the white suit stood up, looping the camera about his neck, and scraped a sheet of bubbling, bloody skin off the rock. Quickly, he bagged it up and carried it to a blue tarp laid down by the cliff face.

'Let me know when you get this,' Kramer said. 'I'll explain everything later.' He hung up the phone and scrolled through to his speed dial, found Debbie's number at the top of the list.

He swallowed. He lifted the phone to his ear and rapped the pads of his fingers on the back of the little device. His knuckles stung. His gut burned with a sick, fearful anger and he pushed it down. Whoever had done this - or *whatever,* he thought, remembering the bite marks on the discarded organs, the shredded flesh in the sand - it was up to him and Debbie to figure out. And if it was a wild animal, then they'd work that out too. But god, if a *person* had done this...

Kramer's fist clenched at his side and he gritted his teeth.

'Hey, Matt,' came Debbie's voice over the phone, muffled a little by the crackling speaker.

Kramer turned away from the cliff, eyes shifting to the ground. His fist loosened and he shoved his free hand into the pocket of his coat. 'Hey,' he said. 'How are you getting on?'

'I'm down at Black River,' Debbie said. 'Emma Green's here with me. Nice girl.'

'Does the doctor's story check out?'

'Yeah, they were together.'

'Good to hear. Listen, Deb, I found something, down on the beach -'

'Matt, I told you not to go down there!'

'You did, yeah.'

Kramer paused as Debbie sighed on the other end of the line. 'What did you find, Matt?'

'Nothing much on the bodies. Jamie and the forensics guys are on the beach now, we'll see what they find. But I went across to the caves, Deb. I thought I saw something move, so I followed it.'

'You're an idiot.'

'I know,' Kramer agreed.

'Find anything in there?'

'Plenty. A message. Bunch of random crap written on the walls, couple of drawings. All done in red. I've asked one of Jamie's lot to take a look, but I'm betting it's not paint. The way these bodies were torn apart, it's not like our killer was short of material.'

'Nasty. Fucking hell, Matt.'

'There's something really wrong here, Debbie,' Kramer said quietly. 'I've just got this feeling. Like there's something... out of the ordinary going on.'

'Well, it's a double homicide,' Debbie said. 'Does that seem ordinary, for Cain's End?'

'A double murder that looks like an animal attack,' Kramer countered. 'Twenty feet from a bloody, *handwritten* message. Does any part of that seem right to you?'

'Of course not,' Debbie said. 'Maybe we should be thinking *pet,* rather than wild animal. Maybe the owner's involved too. You know, the guy sets his dog on the victims, leaves a message for the police to throw them off.'

Kramer shook his head. 'Not that kind of message, Deb. This wasn't meant for us to see. It's like whatever left it was trying to figure something out. Trying to figure *itself* out.'

'What did it say?'

'Nothing. Just a bunch of psycho ramble. The only

118

part that made any sense was a question. "Who is Edward Drake?"'

'Who *is* Edward Drake?' Debbie said.

'Not a clue. But whatever wrote this, it wants to know as badly as we do.'

'Matt... why do you keep saying that?'

Kramer frowned. 'What?'

'You keep saying "whatever". Not "whoever". You keep calling the murderer "it". I mean, you know that message wasn't left by an animal, right? You know we're looking for a man?'

Kramer opened his mouth to reply, but he had nothing to say. He turned back to the clifftop, stared out over the ocean. One of the white suits was beckoning him down to the beach. He nodded, heading toward the ramp.

'I told you,' he said quietly, 'I've got a feeling.'

5

Debbie slid the phone back into her pocket and smiled across the room. Emma Green was stood beside a plain, grey desk, arms folded over the chets of her nurse's uniform.

'Sorry about that,' Debbie said. 'My partner.'

Emma shook her head. 'It's alright.'

'Alright,' Debbie smiled. 'Well, I'll get out of your hair. I've taken up plenty of your time already.'

Emma opened her mouth, as if she was about to say something. Then she closed it again.

'Everything okay?' Debbie said.

'I just... sorry, I couldn't help but overhear,' Emma said. 'You mentioned Edward Drake?'

'Yeah,' Debbie frowned. 'Why, do you know who he is?'

Emma nodded. 'He's an inmate.'

'What, here?'

'He arrived last night. I saw his name on the list.'

Debbie froze. 'Last night? That's a hell of a coincidence.'

The nurse shook her head. 'But he can't have had anything to do with what happened. We've got a security feed in his room. In every room. No sound, but we'll have a visual record of his being here. And there's no way he could have gotten out, not without setting off a dozen different alarms and alerting every guard in the building.'

'I think I'm going to need to see that security feed, Miss Green.'

Emma paused. 'I don't know if I can... do you need a warrant for that?'

'Ideally,' Debbie said. She stepped forward a little, hands in her pockets. 'If you were unwilling to pass the tapes over, I'd have to get a warrant. But I *would* get one. The only difference would be that our investigation would be put on hold for twenty-four hours, give or take. The paperwork doesn't take too long to process, but it would slow us down. And that means the murderer is running free for one more day than he could be. Do you understand?'

'I'll find the recording,' Emma said. 'There's a monitor in Hayley's office, that's closest.'

'Okay,' Debbie smiled. 'Thank you.'

'Follow me,' the nurse said, moving toward the door. They stepped out into the corridor and Debbie followed the young woman a little way. Their footsteps were almost silent on the faded carpet. The hotel theme was interrupted by flashes of hospital-white; the doors, all along the corridor, were framed in steel and locked with a number of heavy, electronically-sealed bolts; the ceiling was a flat, stark shade of grey. And there was a faded, disinfectant smell all around them, a clinical odour in the air.

'I don't know how you can work here,' Debbie said.

In front of her, Emma stopped at a white door with a frosted-glass window set into its upper half. Quickly, she tapped four digits into a keypad beside the door and pushed it open. 'Me neither,' she said, 'but you get used to it.'

Debbie frowned. 'Everyone seems to think so,' she said quietly.

The next corridor was much the same, and twisted about the side of the building before turning off to the right. The maze was ridiculously complex and Debbie wondered how Emma could find her way to the office, let alone to any of the identical cells. She noticed, as they walked, that each one was marked by a number, printed in black above the upper bolt. A narrow slit at eye level was covered with a metal plate, the kind that could be slid upward to allow an opening.

Debbie moved, without thinking, to the nearest door. Emma's quiet footsteps faded even further into silence and for a moment Debbie was alone, every sound muted by the pounding of her heart, the thickening of her blood. She reached for the metal plate, touched the edge with her fingertips. She *pushed -*

'I wouldn't,' Emma said from the end of the corridor.

Debbie jumped, recoiled. Her hand fell to her side. She turned her head, saw the nurse standing with her hands on her hips, head cocked a little.

'Who's in there?' Debbie said.

'It doesn't matter,' Emma shook her head. Debbie caught a flash of expression on the young woman's face. Disgust. 'They're all the same, up here.'

'What do you mean?'

'Rapists. Murderers, molesters, criminals. The worst of the worst. Do you know why they send these people out here, to Cain's End? Because they want to *forget* about them. They send them here to die where they won't make a lot of noise. Nobody in this building would *hesitate* to hurt you, if you gave them a chance.'

'But you help them, don't you? They're here so you

122

can make them better.'

Emma smiled sadly. 'They're here so we can *try.* But a lot of the time, it's just not possible. We get our resources from the mainland. Our funding. And how much do you think they're willing to spend on a bunch of throwaways?'

Debbie nodded. 'I get it,' she said quietly.

'This way,' Emma said, and they kept moving.

Before long they came to the office and stepped inside. A clock ticked loudly on one wall. Quickly, Emma moved around a wooden desk in the middle of the room and started tapping buttons on a bulky, white keyboard.

Debbie followed the nurse around and glanced down toward a square, white-framed monitor on the desk. The screen was cracked.

A black-and-white image flickered on the screen, hazy with lines of static that rolled up and down, pulled this way and that by some invisible pulley within the machine. The room on the screen was filled with round tables and chairs; along one wall, a row of coffee machines and cutlery tables was set before a rectangular opening, through which Debbie could just make out the blurry setting of a kitchen.

'Staff canteen,' Emma murmured. 'That's not what you want to see. Hang on...'

She tapped a button and the image changed. The corridor they had just left flickered for a moment, replaced after a few seconds with a shot of the car park outside.

'Ugh,' Emma grunted. 'Sorry, this system is ancient. Let me just...'

She started typing and the screen split into four, then to sixteen. On every section of the screen the image was almost exactly the same; a small, square room, barely furnished, flickering and empty. In each one, a man or woman in a white t-shirt and white bottoms sat or stood or laid or huddled. In a few, the inmates paced their cells. In more than a couple, they pounded on the doors. The screen panned out further and Debbie lost count.

'God, how many of them are there?'

'Two hundred rooms,' Emma said quietly, 'One-hundred and twenty full. Give or take.'

'That's...'

'Over ten per cent of the population of the island,' Emma said. 'And they all want to kill the other ninety per cent. Now you know why security's so damn high. Okay, here we go.'

She selected an image and scrolled inward until it filled the entire monitor screen.

Edward Drake sat in a corner of the foam-padded cell, hands in his lap. He was perched on the edge of a fat, square mattress, velcroed to the floor. Where Hayley had seen a desk or a low, plastic chair in some of the other cells, Drake's was empty. The floor was a patchwork of white mats. A pile of blankets in one corner was folded neatly. Drake hadn't touched them.

The man was broad-built, and even hunched over he looked tall. Black, tangled hair cast a shadow over his face. He sat perfectly still, and Debbie wondered for a second whether the video was paused. Her eyes darted to a timestamp in the corner of the screen. The seconds ticked by as she watched.

'So this is right now,' Emma said. 'If we track back...'

The timestamp started to roll backwards. Drake moved in reverse, standing awkwardly from the bed and moving to the door. He took an empty plate from the hatch and carried it back to the bed, sitting down with it. Debbie watched as he spat food onto the plate, and after a few seconds it was full. His steps were strange and jerky as he stood up again and slid the plate back out of sight. For a few moments he paced the cell, walking backwards and turning as he reached the wall, repeating this a few times. It might have been funny, Debbie thought, if he wasn't the only suspect in a double homicide.

'Here we are,' Emma said, 'this is about five o'clock this morning.'

'Matt said the bodies were a few hours old,' Debbie said. 'I need to know he was here the whole night.'

The video tracked back further. Four o'clock, then three. Drake paced, and sat, and moved between the corners of the room. Never once did he lay down.

'Not much of a sleeper, then,' Debbie said.

'First night here,' Emma shrugged. 'Even murderers get scared.'

Debbie stood straight. 'Edward Drake is a murderer?'

'Well, why did you think he was here? I told you, this isn't a place for nice guys.' She paused fo a minute before continuing. 'I've seen his file. He's a strange one. Apparently he can't feel pain - the medical examiners who handed him over to us couldn't find any physical damage in his nervous system, but he just doesn't *feel* it. Doesn't feel anything. Beyond psychopathic. Oh, Edward Drake is a killer.'

Debbie's eyes fell to the screen and she watched as the footage skipped, played forwards again. Drake sat, again, at the edge of the bed, hands over his head, whole body hunched over. 'Well, he's not our killer,' Debbie murmured. 'Looks like he was here all night. I'm going to need you to send a copy of this to...'

She trailed off.

On the screen, Drake had reared up and his head was tilted back, mouth open. His body tore up in a writhing, horrific convulsion and he kicked out with his leg as he gripped the mattress with white-knuckled fists.

Even without audio, Debbie could tell he was screaming. 'When is this?' she said quietly.

'Timestamp says just after one o'clock this morning.'

Debbie nodded. Beside her, Emma tapped a couple of buttons. The image went live again.

The door of Drake's cell opened.

Debbie frowned. 'Is this happening now?'

'Right now,' Emma breathed.

A shadow passed beneath the camera as a figure stepped into the room.

'Is that...'

'Oh my god,' Emma said. 'It's Hayley.'

'What's she doing in there?'

On the screen, Edward Drake looked up as Hayley crossed the room, stepped towards him. 'She's profiling,' Emma said. 'She has to do this with all the new inmates, talk to them, set up a profile for them...'

'You have to get her out of there,' Debbie said.

Edward Drake shifted where he was sat. It was difficult to pinpoint the expression on his face, but Debbie could swear the man was *smiling*.

'Now,' Debbie said. 'Get her out of there *now.*'

CHAPTER FIVE
EDWARD DRAKE

1
NOW

Hayley closed the door behind her, stepping forward into Edward Drake's cell.

Drake looked up as she entered. His eyes were blank.

'Good morning, Mr Drake,' Hayley smiled.

Drake said nothing.

That's okay, Hayley thought. *Give him time.* The clipboard trembled in her hands, and she stilled herself. 'Now, I'll keep this short,' she said. 'I'm Doctor King, I'll be conducting what we call a psychological profile. Just a few questions, okay? Then I'll leave you in peace.'

Edward Drake nodded a little. His expression was stoic and firm, his eyes narrowed and dark. A greasy, tangled mess of black hung over his forehead, a shade darker than the layer of stubble that coated his chin and thick, scarred throat. He was muscular, beneath the baggy white shirt and trousers, and Hayley knew that if he stood from the edge of the mattress he would tower above her. Big hands dangled in his lap, calloused and tanned.

'Edward - do you mind if I call you Edward?'

Drake's eyes narrowed a little further. He opened his mouth, and Hayley caught a glimpse of pointed, shining teeth. 'I prefer Eddie,' he said quietly, his voice almost a growl. It was low and rough and rasping, as though he hadn't said more than three words in a week.

'Eddie, then,' Hayley said. 'Before I go any further with this, Eddie, are you able to tell me where you are?'

'Yes.'

'Will you?'

Eddie smiled. It was an empty smile, no more than a thin, meaningless crack across his unshaven jaw. 'I am in a prison, on an island. I do not know the name of the island.'

'The island is called Cain's End,' Hayley said. She paused. 'Are you aware that this isn't a prison, Eddie?'

'Yes.'

'So why call it one?'

'Can I get out?'

Hayley hesitated. The clipboard hovered in her hand. There was a pen tacked to it, but she hadn't removed the lid yet. 'Would you like to get out, Eddie?' she asked.

The inmate's reply was instant. '*Yes,*' he said.

'Why is that?' Hayley said. She backed up to the wall,

sat down on the padded floor with the clipboard in her lap, legs crossed. She took the lid off of the pen. If there was a chair in Eddie's cell, she would have sat there, but she couldn't stand over him any more. There was something about the way he looked up at her, like he knew what she was thinking. What she was *feeling*.

There was something cold in his eyes, something dead and rotting, like something was *missing*.

'It's out there,' Eddie said suddenly. 'It's *here*. On the island.'

Hayley frowned. 'Excuse me?'

'It followed me here. I knew that it would.'

'What followed you, Eddie?'

Eddie's face didn't change, he didn't blink.

'Let's get back to *you,* shall we?' Hayley said.

The man smiled. His hands shifted, as if he were playing Cat's Cradle with an invisible rubber band. Dark shadows passed over his fingers as they moved and curled over each other. 'Tell me about the island,' he said.

'I'd rather talk about you, Eddie.'

'No, you wouldn't,' Eddie said. He leant back a little, so that the back of his head rested on the padding of the wall behind him. His eyes drifted up to the ceiling, and Hayley caught a glimpse of something on his throat. A scar - no, a set of scars, three of them, three jagged lines that ran parallel to each other, crossing his neck and spreading to his left shoulder. 'Tell me about the island,'

Eddie said again.

Hayley set down the clipboard, folded her arms. 'Alright,' she said. 'I'll bite. What do you want to know, Eddie?'

'You told me the island is called Cain's End,' Eddie said. 'Tell me why.'

'I don't know,' Hayley said, shaking her head. 'It's a translation from the Spanish, I think. *Muerto del Hermanos*.'

'"Death of the Brother,"' Eddie said. 'Interesting.'

'Why is that?'

Eddie shrugged. 'Cain was the killer,' he said. '*Abel* was the brother who died.'

'I see. Where did you learn Spanish?'

'Somewhere,' Eddie murmured. 'My father, I think. He was a businessman. He was always... going places.'

'When did your parents die, Eddie?'

'Nineteen ninety-three,' he said calmly. 'I was eight years old.' There was no movement in the man's face, no feeling in his dull expression. Usually there would be something - a subtle tic, or a tell, or the slightest flash of emotion - but there was *nothing*.

'And you saw it happen?'

Eddie tilted his head forward, looking Hayley dead in the eyes as he spoke. 'Yes.'

'And how did that make you feel, Eddie?'

'I don't remember.'

'Is that because you don't *want* to remember?'

'You tell me.'

Hayley paused. 'Let's move on,' she said. 'Let's talk about your grandmother. How was the relationship there?'

'My turn,' Eddie said. 'You've asked your questions. Tell me something.'

'Fair enough,' Hayley said.

'Why are you here?'

'Excuse me?'

'On Cain's End. On this little island. What brought you here?'

'I...' Hayley trailed off. Eddie didn't have to know the truth. He wouldn't know if she was lying. Still, she couldn't help but feel pressed to tell him. The silence in his eyes was compelling, somehow. 'I... I don't know what to tell you. There was a job going, and I took it.'

'There's more to your story than that,' Eddie said.

'Yes.'

He smiled. 'You hurt somebody.'

'Yes.'

'Who?'

'You had your question,' Hayley said quietly. 'My turn. The relationship with your grandmother. Tell me about that. What was she like?'

'She was complicated.'

'Was she a nice lady?'

'No.'

'Did she... *hurt* you, in any way?'

Eddie smiled grimly. It never reached his eyes. 'You know,' he said, 'you can just ask me why I did it.'

Hayley grimaced. 'Excuse me?'

'You want to know, don't you?' Eddie said. 'You want to know why I did it. So why not just *ask* me?'

Hayley tightened her grip on the pen, swallowing nervously. Her gut twisted up and she asked. 'Alright then, Eddie, tell me. Why did you *kill* her?'

2

'I don't understand!' Emma said, panting as they hurried down the corridor. 'Eddie was in here the whole night, it's not *possible!*'

Debbie shook her head. Her legs ached. 'His name was at the scene. Written in *blood.* And he's already killed. Whatever connection he has to this, we have to get Hayley away from him.'

'Up here,' Emma breathed, nodding towards a staircase at the end of the hall.

They moved to the stairs and took them quickly, two at a time, turning back on themselves halfway up and coming out onto another, identical corridor. The carpet was the same faded red, the bulbs the same flickering, fluorescent white. The metal doors were spaced apart at equal intervals and set into thicker, black frames. Three heavy-duty bolts on each kept them locked.

Debbie passed a door on her left, glanced up at the

number printed on it in thick, white legend. Thirty-nine. The next, on her right, was thirty-eight.

'Up here,' Emma said, moving quickly along the corridor.

A guard stood outside one of the doors, head tilted back, arms folded. He turned his eyes, looking across at the two women as they approached. 'Everything okay?'

'Is Hayley in there?' Debbie said.

The guard nodded.

'Get her out,' Emma said.

He frowned. 'I don't...'

'Get her *out.*'

The guard turned quickly, punching numbers into the keypad with a gloved hand. 'Time to go, doctor!' he called. The bolts slid across and the door opened. Emma reached it first, moved to step inside -

Hayley came out and the two bumped into each other. 'What's going on?' Hayley said.

'You're fine,' Emma breathed. 'You're okay.'

She wrapped her arms around the woman and held her for a moment, then seemed to remember they weren't alone. 'Sorry,' she mumbled, stepping back. She brushed down her uniform, gathering her breath, and Hayley turned. Behind them, the door to room thirty-one closed.

'What's happening?' Hayley said.

Debbie shook her head. 'We have reason to believe that Edward Drake might be involved in the... you

134

know,' she said, glancing toward the guard, 'what you saw this morning.'

Hayley frowned. 'How can he be involved?' she said, turning back to Emma. 'He was here. There's no way he could have got out last night. Have you been through the security tapes?'

The nurse nodded. 'He was here.'

'But his name was at the scene,' Debbie interrupted. 'However he's linked to this, he *is* linked to it. I'm just asking you to be careful around him until we know what's going on.'

'I have to do my job,' Hayley said, gesturing towards the closed door. 'I was getting somewhere with him. I could have started to *help* him, with more time.'

Debbie stepped forward. 'I understand that,' she said. 'Look, I just want you to be safe. Two people are dead, and it has *something* to do with the man in that cell. He is *connected* to this.'

The guard raised an eyebrow, turned to Hayley. 'Two people... what? What's happened?'

There was silence, then, for a moment.

'On the beach,' Hayley said slowly. 'This morning. They were... torn apart.'

'And that's information that can't go beyond these walls, okay?' Debbie said, looking across at the guard. 'We'll release an official statement later on, but we don't want to scare people.'

'People *should* be scared,' Hayley said. 'I saw what

happened down there. What was left of those people.'

'Then you'll know to leave Edward Drake alone until this is all over, yeah? Just until we know what's going on.'

Hayley hesitated. 'What are you going to tell everyone?'

'What they need to know,' Debbie said. 'At the minute we don't know what we're looking for. When we know more, we'll be able to warn people. For now we're closing off the area, and we're trying to keep the island as safe as possible. But we will do everything we can to stop this going any further.'

'No one else dies?'

'No one else dies. Not on our watch.'

Hayley paused. Nodded. 'Okay.'

'Alright, good,' Debbie said. 'Now, I'm going to head back to the beach. Can you three keep this quiet, until the police release a statement this afternoon?'

The guard said nothing. Silently, he nodded.

Emma laid a hand on Hayley's arm. 'Yeah, we'll keep quiet,' she said.

Hayley nodded her head.

'Thank you,' Debbie said. 'One more thing, before I go.'

Hayley raised an eyebrow.

Debbie nodded towards the door to cell thirty-one. 'I'm going to need any information you have on Edward Drake,' she said. 'Files, medical records, anything. I need to know who this guy is.'

3

'How many?' Eddie asked quietly. His voice sunk in the cool air of the cell, buffeted by padding. There was no echo, nowhere for the sound to travel. He leaned against the wall, closing his eyes as he tilted his skull upward.

Hayley had left the room, but Edward Drake was not alone.

The figure stepped forward a little from the shadows in the corner of the room. He didn't answer, but Eddie could hear he breathing, hoarse and ragged, like the act was a struggle for his shrivelled lungs.

'Answer me,' Eddie said. 'How many?'

The newcomer paused. He smelled like old smoke and smeared dogshit. Finally, he spoke. 'Why do you ask?' he said. His voice was familiar, throaty and thick with the hoarse cadence of a chain-smoker.

'Why not?' Eddie asked. Even with his eyes closed, he could tell his companion was pacing the room. The thing's footsteps were silent, but the smell followed it, trickling over paticles of dust on the air.

'Do you care?' the figure asked, after a moment. He moved closer to Eddie and the smell grew stronger. 'I know you, kid. Do you give a single *fuck* how many?'

Eddie considered. 'No,' he said eventually.

'Then why do you ask?'

Eddie turned, opened his eyes. He stared the thing in the face and scowled. 'It's here,' he said. 'On the island. I know it is. I can *feel* it.'

'Yes,' the newcomer said. His breath was stale and hot.

'And it's killed already?'

'Yes.'

'So tell me *how many.*'

The man with the yellow face stood in the corner of Eddie's cell, hands stuffed in the pockets of his black suit. He hadn't changed in twenty-six years, hadn't aged a single day. His face was still the horrifying, burned mess that it had been that night, the first night Eddie had seen him. His skin was the same pus-yellow, wrinkled and scarred and peeling around one bulging eye. His hair was as black as Eddie's and sprouted from a bubbling, wet scalp in tufts and stringy clumps.

He smiled. 'Two,' he growled. 'A man and his whore.'

'Their names?'

'It played with the girl first, of course.'

'Tell me their names.'

Yellow Face smiled. 'It stripped the skin off their fucking *bones,* Eddie. It shoved its snout into their guts and chewed the shit out of their bowels -'

Eddie shook his head. 'Enough. Tell me their names.'

'Oh, fuck off,' Yellow Face scolded. 'You're always spoiling my fun. You think their names matter, Eddie?

You think the dead give a shit whether you know their names or not? Do *you* give a shit whether you know their names or not?'

'No,' Eddie said quietly. 'I suppose not.'

He paused, for a while. The yellow-skinned man stepped over to the cell door, apparently distracted by something there. He pressed the side of his face to the metal, listening. His bloodshot, rolling eyeball throbbed as his eyelids drew together. A tiny, black pupil swum in a pool of milk-white fluid. 'Shh...' he whispered.

'I need to get out of here,' Eddie said. 'Is that why you're here? To help me out?'

Yellow Face turned to him, frowning a little. 'Help you out? The fuck do you think I am, kid? I'm not here out the goodness of my little black heart, you know. I've got things to do.'

Eddie hesitated. 'You saved me,' he said. 'When I was a child. You pulled me out of the car. I remember...'

'All part of the plan,' Yellow Face grinned. 'Just like this,' he said, looking around the cell. 'You're here for a reason, kid. And you'll get out when it's time.'

'What plan?'

The nightmare man closed his eyes again and pressed a palm to the surface of the door. 'Why do you want to get out of here, anyway? Nice place, this. Lovely building. And the *nurses*...'

'It's out there,' Eddie said. 'It has *killed*.'

Yellow Face cocked an eyebrow. The skin above his

eye cracked open and a thin trickle of pus ran down into his eyeball. He blinked it away. 'You want to stop it?'

'It's mine,' Eddie said. 'I want it *back*.'

Yellow Face peeled his features from the door, opened his eyes. 'Ooh, talking of nurses...' he said. He turned his face, smiling wickedly at Eddie as he stood straight and slid his hands back into his pockets. 'Someone's coming. Listen, kid, whatever plans you're dreaming up in here, forget them.'

Suddenly the yellow-skinned man's face darkened. His bulging eye narrowed as the other drooped in his skull. His teeth gritted as a bitter kind of fury flashed over his grim smile. 'Don't fuck me over, kid. I pulled you from that car for a reason. You know you shat yourself, right? I dragged your shit-covered arse out of that car and saved your pathetic fucking life and I'll tell you something,' he snarled, stepping forwards, 'I could snap my fucking fingers and send you right back there. I could twist your spine into a fucking circle and drag your brains down through your windpipe and your slimy little intestines until you're shitting out pink goo, and I wouldn't have to *touch* you. You know why I'm not doing that right now?'

Eddie said nothing.

'Because you're important,' Yellow Face said, clapping a hand on Eddie's arm. The nightmare man smiled. 'Don't fuck me over, kid.' And then, with no ceremony at all, no puff of smoke or flash of light, the yellow-skinned figure disappeared. It was like he'd never been there at all.

Well, Eddie supposed, he never *had*.

He heard something then, outside the door. Black-gloved thumbs tapped a number into the keypad in the wall and an electronic beep echoed through the metal. Three bolts slid across simultaneously and the door opened with a squeal. A woman stepped into the cell - not Hayley, Eddie saw, but a younger woman, in a nurse's uniform. She was blonde, pretty. Twenties.

She smiled at him.

Eddie glanced over the woman's shoulder, caught sight of a man in the corridor, standing by. A black uniform was wrapped around him, velcroed up his side, padded over his back and chest. A thick, brown beard grew over dark skin.

There was a gun strapped to the guard's belt.

'You don't trust me,' Eddie said.

The nurse smiled, looking back towards the guard. 'Just a precaution,' she said. 'Give us a wave, Tony.'

The black-clad guard nodded, raised his hand. He waggled his fingers and turned away.

Eddie's attention shifted back to the nurse as she leant forward, passing him a plastic cup half-filled with water. He took it, looked down at her other hand. In her palm were two small, white capsules.

'Breakfast,' Eddie murmured, taking the pills in his hand.

The nurse stood straight, watched as Eddie pushed the tablets between his lips and raised the plastic cup to his mouth.

He looked her dead in the eyes as he drank.

She winced.

Eddie's eyes flickered to the nurse's lapel; pinned to the blue material was a slim, bronze badge, and engraved upon it a name. *Emma.*

'Thank you,' Eddie said, handing her the empty cup.

Emma nodded a little, turning to leave. She stepped through the door and it closed. After a second the bolts slid back across with a hiss and two pairs of muffled footsteps retreated back into the corridor.

Finally, Eddie was alone.

Slowly, he reached up into his mouth with a thick thumb and index finger, pushed them into the cavity of his cheek. Carefully he pulled out the pills and bent down to lay them on the floor. In one fluid movement he lifted up the edge of his mattress and pushed the capsules underneath.

Eddie stood straight, turning his face to the locked door.

A flat pool of wet, sticky pus drizzled slowly down the metal. Flecks of yellow skin bubbled in the mess.

'You naughty fucker,' the nightmare man said from the corner of the room, and Eddie closed his eyes.

Yellow Face grinned. 'Don't you want your dinner?'

'Don't you want your dinner?'

Eddie twitched as Nana spoke, looking up from his dinner.

The old woman sat at the opposite end of the kitchen table, her narrow figure hunched over a mug of thick, dark coffee. Her eyes shifted to the boy's plate, still full. He gripped a fork in his hand - the prongs were clean. He hadn't taken a single mouthful.

Eddie had seen Nana eat, once; he had looked on from the hallway as she bent over a slab of meat and tore through the gristle with her crooked teeth. The meat was pink and fleshy and Eddie was certain she hadn't cooked it. Nana never ate with him. She served up his dinner, and she sat with her coffee, and she watched. She wouldn't take her eyes off the boy until he finished every scrap.

'I'm not hungry,' Eddie said quietly. The fork jerked in his hand as an involuntary spasm wracked his arm. He shuddered. 'Can I eat later?'

Nana shook her head. Withered lips pouted as she sipped her coffee. Eddie could smell it from his end of the table. It didn't smell like the coffee his mum used to drink, back when...

'Eat,' Nana said, jolting him from the memory.

Eddie blinked. Reluctantly, he dipped his fork to the

plate and pricked a chunk of white, fatty flesh from the black gravy that swilled over his meal. Nana had told him the meat was chicken. Eddie had never tasted chicken like this.

'Go on,' Nana whispered, leaning forward.

Eddie lifted the fork to his mouth. A drop of gravy fell from the prongs as he plucked the meat from them and chewed.

'How is it?'

'It's nice,' Eddie lied. He was reluctant to swallow, and his words were muffled by a string of meat that pulled on his teeth as it twisted around his tongue. 'Thank you.'

Nana smiled. Yellow teeth flashed in the flickering light of a black chandelier on the ceiling. Eerie shadows fell over the warped table as the chandelier threw tiny, white lights into Nana's pupils, lights that rose and fell with every breath and with the crackle of the tiny flames.

'Do you still miss them?' the old woman said suddenly.

Eddie froze. The squeal of his fork on the cracked ceramic plate stopped. Silence. The question was a trick. It had to be.

She's going to hit me again.

Still, he couldn't lie. He could never lie to her. She had made sure of that. Eddie looked up from the plate and swallowed. 'Yes,' he whispered. 'I miss them.'

144

Nana's eyes darkened. 'You're nearly ten now, boy. Don't you think it's time to grow up?'

'I...'

Nana's face changed. She smiled. 'Go on,' she said, nodding towards his plate. 'Eat up.'

Eddie shook his head. 'I don't want to.'

'Excuse me?' Nana said. Slowly, she lowered her mug to the table. A wet, pink tongue slithered over her lips as she leaned in, narrowing her eyes. 'What did you say, child?'

'I don't want to eat,' Eddie said, suddenly spurred on by an inexplicable flight of confidence. 'And I don't want to forget about my mum and dad. You never let me talk about them. You never even let me go see them, at the cemetery. And when I *do* talk about them... you...'

He trailed off.

Nana cocked an eyebrow. 'Yes?'

'You hurt me,' Eddie whispered.

'Oh, no,' Nana said. 'I could never... oh, *Eddie.*' She clutched at her chest, as though a great pain threatened her heart. 'How could you say such a thing? I would *never* hurt you...'

'But you...' Eddie started, 'you...'

'Go on,' Nana whispered.

Eddie bowed his head. 'I'm sorry.'

'That's okay,' Nana smiled. Her face softened. Slowly, the old woman stood from her chair and stepped around the table. For a moment Eddie's whole body tensed up, then Nana laid a hand on his shoulder and he relaxed.

'It's okay,' she said again, quietly. Her hand moved to the back of his head, fingers wrapped up in his thick, black hair, stroking it softly, tousling it as she spoke. 'Shall I tell you why I don't like to talk about your parents, Eddie?'

Eddie said nothing. Nana's fingers brushed his scalp as she tousled his hair. She was gentle, comforting. For a moment - for the first time since he had arrived here - Eddie felt *safe*.

Then Nana yanked his head back and Eddie cried out as shards of pain rocked the base of his scalp. The old woman leaned down, grabbing Eddie's chin with her free hand, and a cracked, dirty fingernail slid over his lip. 'Because they're *dead,* Eddie,' Nana hissed. Flecks of spittle landed on the boy's cheek and her breath, hot and thick with coffee, stung his eyes. 'What's dead should be forgotten, don't you agree?'

Eddie couldn't move, couldn't speak. He tried to nod, to open his mouth, but the grip on his hair was too tight. 'I...'

Nana slammed the boy's face down into the plate of meat on the table. His nose smacked the ceramic with a *crack* and Eddie screamed as the plate shattered. Slivers of pain ran down his cheeks and shot up his nose and forehead. Warmth spread over his face but he couldn't tell if it was the gravy on the broken plate or his own blood. He tried to speak, to ask her to stop...

'What's dead should be *forgotten*,' Nana repeated, letting go of Eddie's hair.

The boy tried to raise his head, but his vision was blurry and clogged with red and he slipped, tumbling off his chair and onto the floor. His hands moved to his head and he breathed heavy and ragged, whimpering into his elbows as he trembled.

'Get up,' Nana hissed. Eddie didn't move, and the old woman's shadow fell over him. She grabbed the back of his shirt and yanked him off the ground. 'I said, get *up!*'

Eddie scrambled to his knees, shaking his head. 'I've seen it...' he sobbed. 'I've seen you *do* it...'

Nana scowled down at him. 'What have you seen, child?'

Eddie looked up, and his eyes were wide. 'I've seen you bring people back to life.'

Nana glared. Her face was a narrow mask of hatred and fury. The lines around her eyes seemed to deepen in the flickering light from the black chandelier as she opened her thin lips and whispered. 'You've seen *nothing*,' she spat. 'Magic has a cost, Edward. Magic that *powerful* has a cost you couldn't imagine. Pay a price that high and you *die.*'

'No...'

Eddie's voice sunk back into his throat as a wrinkled, bony hand wrapped around his neck and squeezed. Nana shoved him back onto the ground and jabbed her

147

toe into his groin, ground her heel in the tender space between his legs. Eddie cried out, but she wouldn't let up, stamping his crotch down until the ache had spread to his stomach. Then there was a sliver of plate in her hand, curved and white and shining in the light from the chandelier, and Eddie screamed as the sharpened ceramic piece curved down towards his face -

Nana stopped. The shard fell to the ground and she smiled. 'You want to see magic, child? Let me *show* you.'

She pulled him by the hair, dragging him out into the hallway and over the carpets as he kicked out and thrashed against her furious grip. He tried to wriggle free and Nana threw him into the living room.

'No!' Eddie cried. 'I don't want to be in here!'

'Shut your fucking mouth,' Nana spat, slamming the white door behind them. 'Sit by the fire.'

Eddie didn't move.

'*Sit by the fucking fire!*' Nana shrieked, and Eddie crawled over the carpet toward the blood-stained armchair. He looked up into the eyes of a dead, limp woman and his breath hitched in his throat.

'Who is she?' Eddie whispered.

'Her name was Harriet,' Nana said. 'She asked me for a favour. She asked me to return her dead husband to her, boy.'

'You did it,' Eddie breathed. 'You brought him back.'

Above him, Harriet's chest was in bloody ribbons.

148

Like something had torn its way out of her.

'I did,' Nana said. 'Not quite the same as he was before, but close enough.'

'You could...'

'Look at her!' Nana said, shoving Eddie towards the dead woman.

Her hair was black and ragged, her face frozen in a drooping, sorry smile. Her eyes were cold.

'She paid the price,' Nana whispered. 'It killed her. It kills most people. Do you understand?'

'But her husband...'

'Coming back from Hell bears its own cost,' Nana said quietly.

Then she plucked a hair from his head. Eddie cried out, raising a hand to his scalp, but Nana was already moving toward the fire. Wordlessly she reached down with her free hand and grabbed a rusted pair of old, brass scissors from a stand in the fireplace.

Eddie frowned as the old woman lifted the scissors to the single strand of hair she had torn from him and cut the hair in half.

Slowly, the two halves floated to the carpet.

'I don't understand,' Eddie said.

'You will,' Nana whispered.

Then a surge of pain tore across Eddie's belly and the boy screamed, clutching at his gut. He writhed on the ground and lifted up his shirt, eyes wide and round. He stared.

The cut was little more than a shallow, discoloured line at first, a thin band of pink across his belly that was barely deep enough to draw blood. But as he watched, the cut grew longer and wider and deeper and the pain worsened as a river of crimson formed in the gash in his flesh and flowed out of him, drizzling down over the lower half of his torso. It spread, carving a string of blood across his belly and around his sides until the two ends of the scar connected in the middle of his back, forming a perfect belt of red around him.

'Stop!' Eddie screamed. The pain was unbearable. 'Please, please make it stop!'

'Forget them,' Nana whispered.

'*Make it stop!*'

Slowly, the old woman crouched before him. The scissors dangled from her wrinkled fingers, glinting wildly in the firelight. 'Say you'll forget them,' she hissed.

Eddie shook his head vigorously, laying his palms over the spreading cut on his torso. Blood pooled between his fingers and his hands came away sticky and red as Nana leaned over and yanked another hair from his scalp, ignoring the boy's cries.

Nana stood straight, stepping back to the fire. 'Say you'll forget them,' she muttered.

'I don't want to!' Eddie screamed. A damp, wet heat bubbled inside his belly. If the scar grew any deeper it would reach his intestines, tear him apart completely.

But he couldn't forget. He *couldn't*.

Nana Death reached out her hand and held the black hair above the crackling flames in the fireplace. Eddie felt his blood grow warmer. He shook his head. 'No...'

'*Say you'll forget them!*' Nana yelled, and she pushed her arm into the fire. 'Say it, or I *burn* you!'

'I'll forget them!' Eddie yelled, eyes screwed shut, arms wrapped around his belly in a futile attempt to push back the pain.

Nana smiled. Calmly, she retracted her arm. The black sleeve of her dress was unburned. Her skin was untouched.

She let go of the hair and it dropped to the floor, unscathed.

'There's a good boy,' Nana whispered. 'Now, let's get that cut looked at, shall we?'

5

Martha was sitting at her desk when a woman walked into the station.

She looked thirty-ish, Martha thought, maybe a little older - it was hard to tell. Lines had formed around the edges of her eyes, red-rimmed from exhaustion. Her pupils flared as she clutched at a handbag by her waist. She glanced about the station, lost. 'Hello?' the woman said. A couple of officers glanced up, but nobody stood to help her. She might have been pretty, if not for the ragged mess of her hair and the blouse which clearly hadn't been changed in a couple of days.

Maybe then one of you chauvinistic pricks would help her out, Martha thought. She sighed, standing up from her desk.

The woman flinched as Martha approached. Her eyes widened a little.

'It's alright,' Martha said. 'Can I help you?'

The woman gripped her bag a little tighter. Her tousled hair was wiry and thin, greying a little at her temples, and it had been pulled back to reveal a scalp scratched and peeled away with nerves. Her fingers trembled.

Martha laid a hand on the woman's arm, guided her to the desk. 'Here,' she gestured. 'Sit. Can I get you a drink?'

The woman shook her head, settling into a chair one side of Martha's desk.

Martha slid into the seat across from her and smiled again. 'Can you tell me your name?'

'Elizabeth,' the woman croaked. Her throat rose and fell with every breath. She pulled a faded blue coat tighter around her chest and her eyes darted about the room. It was like she was just *waiting* for someone to storm in and take her away.

She looked afraid.

'It's okay,' Martha said. 'Elizabeth? It's okay. You're *safe* here. Can you tell me what's going on?'

152

'She'll find me,' Elizabeth whispered. Suddenly her eyes were locked on Martha's and they spread with fear, shining in the dim light of the station. She grabbed Martha's sleeve, digging her fingers into the material. Her fingers were blotchy with red and white and old, dampened bruises. 'She'll *find* me,' the woman hissed. 'Please, I need you to help me.'

'I'll do what I can,' Martha said. She looked up. Nobody was paying them any attention. She thought about calling somebody over, but they all knew what was going on. They just didn't *want* to help. 'Can you tell me what's going on? Is somebody after you?'

'It's...' Elizabeth stopped, trailed off. Somewhere in the station, a phone was ringing. The place smelled like coffee and fresh paint - the back wall had been patched up more than two weeks ago, but the aroma lingered - and Elizabeth sniffed. 'She'll find me...'

Martha leant forward, laying her hand gently on the woman's wrist. 'Please,' she said. 'I need you to tell me what's going on. Who are you talking about?'

'It's... it's *Rose.*'

'Okay,' Martha nodded. 'There's something. Now, can you tell me who Rose is?'

Elizabeth flinched at the name. 'She's my daughter.'

Martha frowned. 'Are you... *scared* of your daughter?'

Elizabeth blinked. 'She's different. Please, I need you to believe me. Please... she's not the same, not anymore.

153

Not since...'

'It's okay,' Martha said again. 'Take it nice and slow. Elizabeth, I'm going to need you to stay calm for me. Whatever's going on, you're safe here.'

'She was ill,' Elizabeth whispered. 'She was *sick*. She was going to *die*. We had no choice...'

'Elizabeth?' Martha glanced about her, trying to catch somebody's attention. She had a feeling this wasn't something she knew how to deal with. She caught the eye of an officer across the room, nodded him over. Quickly, he looked away.

For fuck's sake, Martha thought. She turned back to the woman at her desk, smiling fleetingly. 'Elizabeth, I'm going to need a little more than this. What happened?'

'I told him we should both go,' Elizabeth continued, staring at a spot on the wall just beyond Martha's shoulder. 'My Oliver. I said we should go and fix it together. For our daughter. Our Rose. He didn't listen to me, stupid... oh, but he never listened to me. He went without me...'

'Where did he go?' Martha said. 'To see a doctor? Elizabeth, I'm confused...'

'It *worked*,' Elizabeth hissed suddenly. 'She was cured. He did it. God, it worked... but then it didn't.' Her eyes snapped to Martha and she leant forward and gripped the edge of the desk with both hands. 'Please, I need you to take her away. I need you to *lock her up.*

She's not my daughter, not anymore, she's... please, she's *changed...*'

'Wait,' Martha said. She remembered. 'Is your daughter *Rose Turner?* I remember the papers, a couple of years ago... you two were on the news. You and your daughter. The *miracle girl.*'

'It wasn't a miracle,' Elizabeth shook her head. 'It was *witchcraft.* We heard the rumours, about that old woman in the forest... we never thought anything of it. Not until... but when we heard what she could *do...*'

'Elizabeth, I need you to focus on *facts.* Start from the beginning. What happened?'

'These *are* the facts,' Elizabeth protested. 'Oliver went to her house, while I was with Rose at the hospital. He never said anything, never said goodbye. I guess he was worried I would come with him... that I'd want to share the cost. I *know* that's what he did. And it worked. Rose was cured. She got *better.*'

Martha nodded. 'You said she's not your daughter anymore, Elizabeth. Can you tell me what you meant by that?'

'She *changed.* She stopped eating, she stopped sleeping... she stopped calling me *mummy.* She disappears, sometimes. At night. I'll go into her room and she'll be gone. Her bed's just empty. And then she comes back and her *feet...* god, they're covered in mud and filth and *blood,* and...'

'Elizabeth, what happened to your husband? What

155

happened to Oliver?'

Elizabeth's eyes darkened. 'That old hag *killed* him,' she hissed. 'She killed my husband and turned my daughter into a... into a monster. I'm so scared...'

'Okay,' Martha said. 'It's okay. Can you tell me where this old woman lives?'

She paused.

We heard the rumours, about that old woman in the forest...

'Wait...' Martha said. 'This house... did you go there? Did you see it?'

'We stopped by a couple of weeks before... before Ollie left. We didn't go in. Yes, I saw it.'

'Old, crooked-looking house,' Martha said. 'Firelight behind the windows.'

'That's it,' Elizabeth swallowed.

'And the roof...'

'Like it was all about to cave in,' Elizabeth finished. 'That's the place.'

'That's her,' Martha whispered. 'That's his grandmother. Oh, god. I left him there...'

'I don't understand,' Elizabeth said, shaking her head. 'What are you talking about?'

Martha sat back in her chair and ran a hand through her hair. 'Elizabeth... oh, Elizabeth, I made a mistake. Listen,' she said, standing up from the chair, 'if you want to stay here for a little while, that's okay. I'll send out an officer to check up on your daughter, make sure she's alright.'

'Where are you going?'

Martha paused. 'I have to go back to that house,' she said. 'I left something there.' She stepped forward. Suddenly Elizabeth's hand was on her arm, fingers wrapped around her wrist. The woman squeezed.

'You can't go there,' she whispered. 'She'll kill you.'

'Who is she?' Martha said.

'She's Death,' Elizabeth hissed. 'She is Death, and her friends are all the devils in Hell.'

CHAPTER SIX
SKIN

1
NOW

The shadow tracked the smell of meat to the other side of the island. Salt and sweat drifted on the breeze, but the creature focused on the scent, pushing towards it over the rocks and the dirt. It slunk through long, swaying grass and dipped through the shadows, moving silently. It could hear children, somewhere on the island.

For a moment it was tempted. But their smell was faint, muted - trapped behind layers of concrete and rusted iron fences. The creature caught a wisp of blood; a grazed knee. A child sobbed wildly and his tears splashed the ground. The creature sniffed. Its horrible face twisted up in a gruesome snarl.

Someone passed, sweating heavily and wrapped in lurid, neon cloth. The creature thought about going after her, but she wouldn't hear it coming. The shadow could hear the faint slap of wire cables against the woman's chest as she ran. A tinny whine bounced around the insides of her ears. Music. She wouldn't hear it coming. There would be no chase. No hunt. She wouldn't see the creature until it was upon her, and there was no thrill in that.

The shadow let her go and moved on through the grass. Its form shifted and changed as it crept forward, switching from thick, indiscernible shadow to black-grey flesh and back again. An aura of cloudy, sifting murk surrounded the creature, drifting over its skin. Its claws dug into the earth and gouged out clumps of dirt as it walked. It sniffed again, latching onto the scent of leather and manure. Its lips pulled back and tore its face into a chaotic mask of splintered, bony teeth.

The smell grew stronger as the creature reached a field far from the clifftop. It hadn't yet strayed this far from the clifftop, least of all in daylight, but it was too excited to stay away from that smell, too hungry not to follow it here. There were no thoughts in its skull, the skull it had borrowed from the nightmare of a little girl; all that drove it forward was emotion, a soupy network of feelings and senses and sensations. Untethered from logic and reason and coherent thinking, it didn't care that it might be discovered. That it might be interrupted.

A wire fence burst up from the ground, a wall of thin mesh and grey, steel string. It bristled with an electric hum. Every few seconds, a loud *crack* sent pulses of energy rippling over the wire.

The creature paused. It reached for the fence with a dark, bony claw and curled it around a link in the fence, pulling the metal wire taut.

Bzzz

The creature reeled back as electricity surged through it. Black, shadowy blood tingled in stringy veins that snapped and twisted around its bones. For a fraction of a second it lost hold of the form it had created, and in that moment it was a swirling cloud of nothing, burnt ash and shadow writhing and squirming in the air. It convulsed, tearing back into reality with a shearing of bone and rippling flesh. Slender limbs dug into the ground, held it steady. The creature bowed its head, strings of drool peeling from bloody lips. The screaming in its skull was louder now.

The creature had never felt pain like this.

It smiled.

The creature looked up, peering through the buzzing wire mesh; even without eyes in its nightmare of a face, it could see them. Just smudges and shapes beyond the fence, dark and pulsing as the lumbered over the ground. Slow, heavy beasts, heads lowered as they chewed and spat over the grass. The creature watched as they moved, savouring the leathery smell that rose above the crackle of the fence and drifted through the links in the wire. Some of the animals laid lazily on the ground, massive, square bodies lapping up what little sunlight broke through the clouds and the breeze. The creature listened as they moaned and called to one another.

They couldn't smell it, not like it could smell them, but they seemed to understand that they were being watched.

The creature reached up and laid its bony, grey talons on the wire. It knew to expect the shock this time and its muscles tensed as a wave of electricity pulsed through its blood.

Bzzz

Again.

The creature grinned as black blood oozed over its teeth. It gripped the wire tight as the shocks grew more intense, more painful, sending shivers of pain through its limbs and long, mutilated body, burning up into the top of its skull. The creature shuddered with a primal kind of arousal and reared forward with its free arm, wrapping the claws of its twisted hand around the wire and pulling, tearing...

The creature's body rocked and twisted and convulsed with every second that passed but it relished the agony, loved the feeling of hurt. Blood pounded in its ears, tingling and spasming with electricity, and it tore the fence apart, shredding the mesh as its spiny teeth ground into its gums.

The fence opened up. A wide, jagged gash appeared

in the mesh and the creature passed through, savouring the murmur of electricity over its flesh as every broken link in the barrier passed across its skin.

The creature burst into the field and lunged, bounding through the swaying grass in long, wild strides. In seconds it was in the midst of the herd and it lunged toward the closest cow, a magnificent, brown-skinned beast with its massive head lowered into the ground, jaws turning side-to-side as it chewed.

The animal looked up.

Terrible, serrated claws plunged into the cow's throat and it bellowed, a terrible scream of agony and pure, uneasy fear. Bloody leather fell away and the cow's oesophagus was exposed, a fat, shining string of purple and red that trembled in its opened throat. The creature wrapped its claws around the slippery pipe and yanked downward - the cow's head shot upwards as its throat was torn down into the grass and its spine cracked. The great beast's legs jerked as it crumpled to the ground and the creature curled its body over the back of the beast and sunk its jaws deep into the cow's back. Bones split and crunched between its teeth and muscles popped open in a mess of dark, spurting blood.

The thundering of hooves drew the creature's attention away from its first victim and it glared up, its teeth stained red, tongue flicking gobs of spittle and blood into the ground. The shadow leapt into the thick of the panicking herd and latched onto a slow, black cow, digging its claws into the beast's rump and dragging the animal back as it bleated –

The cow fell with a *thwump,* sinking into the grass as streams of crimson burst out of the jagged tear in its backside. The creature didn't stop to feed, didn't stop to make sure the animal was truly dead, no, it was too excited for that. Surges of adrenaline and pure, ecstatic pleasure peeled out from its brain and every atom of its being trembled with the thrill of the hunt, the rapturous freedom of the kill. The creature coiled its body and leapt up, turning in the air and landing on the shoulders of a huge, black-and-white bull, latching on to its prey and wrapping its limbs around the beast's neck. Rippling leather covered thick, bunched muscles.

The bull's flesh was harder to tear, tougher. The creature's spiny teeth did little to pierce the animal's skin and it grinned, opened its mouth wider. Wind rushed past it and trickled over its skin as it clung to the back of the lumbering bull, pressing its claws into the animal's shoulder and clutching at thick hide. Blood streamed over the creature's skin as the bull dove wildly left and right, trying to shake off its attacker. The creature's teeth slid back into its gums, cracking and re-forming into something worse, something altogether new. The thing's maw broke open in a shower of saliva and skin and the creature's new teeth ruptured its jaws, jutting from a shadowy skull in a contorted maze of ivory and bone. Thicker, sharper, *stronger.* It lowered its head and sunk its new fangs into the beast's neck; the bull's throat erupted and blood pooled around the creature's jaws, flowed over a silver, flickering tongue. The creature bit down, tore at the bull's spine and wrenched it free -

Crack!

The bull tumbled in a mess of bloody leather and twisted limbs, spine sagging inward as it crashed into the ground. The creature was flung into the grass. It looked up, into the throng of the staggering herd, saw something new, beyond the mass of fur and flesh, something bleeding smoke into the air.

The shotgun fired again and a spray of pellets caught the creature's hide. It screamed. This was a new pain, a warm, thick pain that stung its rump and threatened to drag it to the ground. This was *agony*.

The thing's eyes widened as it caught a glimpse of silver coming toward it and it ducked off to one side, flattened itself into the ground in a confused web of slender limbs and torn, broken skin. The bullet tore past and the creature ran, away from the cows and the weapon that had torn a hole in its side. The shadowy monster scanned the fence wildly, searching for the hole it had dug in the wire. There, in a chaotic knot of buzzing metal, was the opening. The creature dove forward.

Crack!

Pain seared its hind leg and the creature's rump

shattered. It screamed, tearing through the hole in the fence.

Coward.

The creature ran into the tall, dancing grass of the field beyond the fence and it didn't stop running until it reached the other side of the island.

The shadowy thing dropped, suddenly, to the ground. It glanced down at its leg. The flesh had been stripped away and the bone was cracked. Blood flowed into the grass, thick and dark and rotten.

It had to keep going. Keep running.

It had to find somewhere to hide.

2

Charlotte Kramer sat at the front of the classroom, perched on a desk six feet from Mr Crawford's whiteboard. Her legs dangled over the ledge of the desk and she swung them back and forth, waiting impatiently. The teacher was hunched over his computer, frowning above a pair of square, wire-rimmed lenses balanced on his nose.

Charlotte gazed wistfully at the door, catching sight of a couple of kids running down the corridor. Her eyes darted up to the clock above the board; if Crawford didn't hurry this along, she'd miss lunch. Again.

'I won't be a moment, Charlie,' Crawford murmured, eyes glued to the screen.

'That's okay,' Charlotte said quietly. And then, under her breath, quiet enough that he wouldn't hear, 'It's not like I've got anything better to do.'

Crawford clicked frantically, brow furrowed over the monitor. 'Stupid thing,' he said. Shaking his head, he stood straight, apparently abandoning whatever he'd been obsessing over. The man poked his glasses a little further up at his nose and looked across at Charlotte, smiling. 'Now, why did I ask you to stay behind?'

Charlotte blinked. *You're not serious.* 'I fell asleep...' she said slowly.

'Oh, of course,' Crawford said, stepping around to the front of his desk. He leaned back against the wood and shrugged, folding his arms over his chest. 'Any particular reason you think it's okay to sleep in my lessons?'

Charlotte shook her head. 'No,' she said. 'I'm sorry...'

'I mean, that's... what, the third time in the last couple of weeks? Well, the third time *I've* caught you. Do you think it's acceptable?'

'No,' Charlotte repeated.

The teacher frowned. Perhaps he had been expecting Charlotte to argue. Perhaps he was still considering a punishment. Eventually, he spoke. His tone was more serious now. 'Are you getting enough sleep at home, Charlie?'

'Yes,' she lied. 'Everything's fine.'

'I only ask because... well, it's a stressful time for

everyone,' Crawford said. His glasses had slid back down his nose and he pushed them up again. The hairs on the back of his palm were lighter, Charlotte realised, than those that made up the thinning mess atop his head. Almost grey, in fact. She wondered, for a second, if Crawford dyed his hair. God, what if it was a *wig?*

'Are you listening to me?'

Charlotte started, blinking. 'Sorry?'

'I said, it's a stressful time. Exams coming up, the end of school... and it's your sixteenth in a couple of days, am I right?'

'Day after tomorrow,' Charlotte nodded.

'Exactly. So, perhaps you need to consider taking some measures to *de-stress.* If everything going on is meaning you're losing sleep at home, you know, if you're *overthinking* things...'

'I'm fine,' Charlotte said. Her eyes moved again to the clock, and she grimaced. 'Look, is it okay if I go? I didn't bring any lunch, and the canteen's only going to be open for another ten...'

She stopped. There was something in Crawford's eyes, she noticed, that she hadn't seen before. Something she didn't like.

'You lost a little time in my lesson,' Crawford said quietly. 'I think it's only fair that you make up that time, don't you?'

Charlotte nodded slowly. *Stop looking at me like that.*

'Now, let's see your book,' Crawford said, reaching out a weathered palm. A waft of aftershave rose up with the movement, dampened by a sticky, tobacco smell that seemed to cling to the man's clothes. 'Figure out how much work you've missed, shall we?'

Charlotte reached into the rucksack she'd laid by her feet and pulled out her notebook, handed it over. Crawford flicked through the pages, licking his index finger every now and then. About halfway through the book, he paused. Looked up.

'Is this supposed to be me?' he said, turning the book so that Charlotte could see it.

The girl's eyes widened. 'Oh, no,' she said, shaking her head. 'No, that's... that's not you. No, that's something I saw in a...' She swallowed, unable to finish. 'It's not you,' she said, 'I promise.'

The drawing was spread across two pages, scratched into the paper in a mess of black biro. It was a man, but it wasn't Mr Crawford. In place of the teacher's tweed jacket and pale, green shirt was a black suit, filled in with rough lines and blotches of ink. The dark figure's face was a nightmare of scars and crooked, black lips and one bulging, bloodshot eye, framed with wisps of black hair in patches and clumps atop a smooth, round scalp.

The man's face had been coloured in with yellow felt tip.

'Well, I should hope it *isn't* me,' Crawford said,

turning pages until he came to the last one Charlotte had written upon. 'Doesn't look like you missed too much, actually. You'll need to catch up with someone else, perhaps, just jot down any notes you didn't get today. But no more of this, alright?' He closed the book and handed it back to her, stepping forward a little. 'And no more doodling in your workbook.'

'No more,' Charlotte echoed, slipping the book back into her rucksack. She had almost forgotten about the yellow man from her nightmares, but now the image burned behind her eyes, all wrinkled, pus-stained skin and black velvet, and she shuddered.

'Is that a promise?' Crawford said, leaning his hands on the girl's desk.

Charlotte nodded. 'Yes.'

'Good,' Crawford said, and he laid a hand over the top of hers.

Charlotte's eyes flickered down to the man's fingers and she pulled back, frowning.

'Sorry,' Crawford murmured, 'I didn't mean to...'

'Can I go now?'

The teacher nodded and Charlotte scrambled out of her chair, headed for the door. She stepped out into the corridor and exhaled, let it fall closed behind her. She stumbled a little way down the hall and leant against the wall, screwing her eyes shut. Her head pounded. Her breath started to catch in her throat. *Not now,* she thought, shaking her head. *Fuck, not now.*

'Pervert, isn't he?' came a voice from beside her.

Charlotte's eyes snapped open and she turned, startled. 'Darcy? How come you're not with the others?'

Darcy Jones raised an eyebrow, a grim smile forming on her dark-skinned face. 'What, and leave you with Creepy Crawford? I know what he's *like,* Charlie.'

Charlotte smiled weakly. 'It's fine,' she said.

'Come on,' Darcy said, nodding towards the food hall. 'Let's go find everyone and get you some food.'

Charlotte nodded and they started down the empty corridor. 'I can't believe we've still got six weeks left of that guy,' she said. 'God, he just makes me... ugh, I don't know. He makes me so uncomfortable.'

'Six weeks?' Darcy cocked an eyebrow. 'Somebody's counting.'

'God, aren't we all? Month and a half more of this, then I am *out* of here.'

Darcy grinned. 'You know, if you don't feel up to facing Crawford right now, you should come with us tomorrow.'

Charlotte frowned. 'Hmm?'

'You know, *tomorrow*. The arcade?'

Charlotte laughed, shaking her head. 'Darcy, we can't just skip a day of school to go piss about down the end of the pier. Well, you lot can. But be careful – isn't that place meant to be, like, a complete death trap?'

'Sparrow found a way in,' Darcy said as they neared the doors. 'Said it's not that bad inside. And all the old machines are still there, apparently. Couple of places where the boards have come away, but as long as we've got light we'll be fine. What do you think?'

'I've *told* you what I think. We're a class of *twelve,* Darcy. I think Crawford's gonna notice if four of us don't show up in the morning.'

'So what? You said it yourself. Six weeks left.'

Charlotte paused.

'And it's not like your dad'll care,' Darcy shrugged. 'I swear, he lets you get away with *anything.*'

'You'd be surprised,' Charlotte murmured.

'What's that supposed to mean?'

They stopped, at the doors to the canteen, and Charlotte shrugged. 'Nothing.'

'No, what? Is everything okay?'

'Yeah, yeah. Everything's fine, Darce. Just, you know. He's police. He gets... *overprotective.*'

'I get you,' Darcy said, reaching for the door.

'It's more than that,' Charlotte said quietly.

Darcy's hand fell away from the doorhandle and she frowned. Charlotte's face had darkened. Her eyes were on the floor. Beyond the door, Darcy heard a swell of excited chatter. Lunch was almost over. 'What's going on, Charlie?'

'It's just... it's nothing.'

'Charlie.'

Charlotte looked up. 'He's just so *angry* all the time,' she said. 'He's so nice to me, don't get me wrong. Like, all the time. I think he still feels like he has to do mum's job as well as his own.'

'But?'

'But I think he's finally realising that mum's *gone,* Darce. She's been gone since I was born. Now that it's coming up to my sixteenth, I think... I think he's struggling. He gets so argumentative, now. Little things annoy him. And sometimes... sometimes he'll go for a walk, at night, or real early in the morning, and when he comes back his knuckles are all red and bleeding, like he's... like he's gone out and found something to punch.'

Darcy said nothing.

'I'm sorry,' Charlotte smiled. 'Oversharing, right?'

'As long as everything's okay.'

'Everything's okay. I know he'd never hurt me. I know he's just... having a rough time. I just wish he'd tell me what's going on, you know?'

'Oh, I get that,' Darcy said. 'Now, let's get you some food before the bell rings. You can tell me more about this tomorrow morning. You know,' she said, flashing Charlotte a cheeky grin, 'at the arcade.'

'I'll think about it,' Charlotte grumbled.

Darcy pushed the door open and they stepped into the canteen. 'You better,' she said, and Charlotte shook her head.

'I'll *think* about it.'

3

'So what are forensics saying about this?' Debbie said, nodding towards the white suits on the beach.

Kramer stepped forward and stood beside her, hands deep in the pockets of his coat. He shook his head, eyes on the sand. Tangled hair whipped about his stony face in the breeze. 'Not much, so far,' he said. 'No ID on either victim, must have been washed away.'

'Or taken.'

'Or taken,' Kramer agreed. 'You'd think it'd be easier to identify them both, place as small as Cain's End.'

'You'd think so,' Debbie murmured. The cross around her neck swayed a little in the wind and she reached up, touching it uneasily. She slid the necklace down into her blouse and it pressed, cold, against her chest.

Two unzipped body bags laid on the sand. Black material fluttered around two piles of bloody mess. Smaller, clear plastic bags surrounded the canvas-wrapped carcasses, filled with slippery organs and scraps of skin. Each one was labelled. 'They're going to run DNA on both,' Kramer said, 'see if they can find anything. Might not be entirely necessary, though.'

Debbie frowned. 'How come?'

'Had a call, about ten minutes before you got back from the asylum.' He turned his head. 'What took you so long, by the way?'

'Turns out that name on the cave wall - Edward Drake - he's a patient down there. A psychopath.

'I hate that place,' Kramer murmured. 'Did you pick up any files?'

'In the car,' Debbie said, nodding. 'So, this call?'

'Scared mother. Said her daughter went out last night with the boyfriend, never came back.'

'Crap.'

'Yeah, that's the one.'

Debbie exhaled. 'Any chance it's *not* these two?'

At the base of the cliff, white-gloved hands zipped up the bodybags. One of the forensics guys shot Kramer a thumbs-up and he returned it with a grim nod. *Ready,* the look said. *Bring them up.* As he and Debbie watched, the forensics team started lifting the bags onto the back of a steel-plated trolley, wheels half-dug into the sand. In moments they were ready to pull it back up the ramp.

'The mother said the two of them went out after the last ferry left,' Kramer continued.

'Meaning?'

'Meaning they're definitely still on the island,' Kramer said. 'And it's a small island.'

'What about the blood in the cave?' Debie said. 'Is it...'

'Jamie's lot are going to run some tests,' Kramer said. He nodded to the ramp as a man in white, flapping canvas dragged the trolley up on squeaking, rusted wheels. Jamie shot them a nod and pulled the trolley towards a waiting truck at the top of the cliff. 'Based on volume,' Kramer said, 'it looks like it's the girl's. She had about half as much left in her as her friend.'

Debbie looked up at him. Kramer stood straight, a good few inches taller than her, but he looked for all the world as though a great weight were dragging him to the ground. The man stared out into the sea, lost in some terrible thought that Debbie daren't question. 'You okay?' she said.

'Couple of hours ago, worst thing I had to worry about was my daughter's birthday. Christ, last night I was complaining we never had anything to do.'

'Things change,' Debbie said quietly.

Beside her, Kramer took a hand from his pocket and rubbed his jaw, grimacing. His knuckles looked even worse today than they had last night. Debbie said nothing. For a moment, they stood in silence, watching as the forensics guys wrapped up the last of their work. Then Kramer spoke. 'I don't know how you do it, Deb.'

Debbie blinked. 'Excuse me?'

'I tried it once, you know,' Kramer said. 'Religion. Faith. But if there's a God, Debbie, he lets shit things happen to good people. I don't know how you can just... *believe*.'

'I get it, Matt,' Debbie said, stepping forward. She laid a hand on his arm. 'The world is a shithole. I'm not blind to that. But I have to believe there's a reason for that.'

'What if the reason is just that God *hates* us?'

'Then we have to give him a reason to change his mind.'

Kramer smiled grimly. 'You're too good at this, Deb.'

'You think I don't ask myself these same questions every day? Trust me, Matt, you get snappy with the answers after a while.'

Kramer nodded.

'What is it?' Debbie said, pulling her hand away from Kramer's sleeve. He barely seemed to notice. He never did, when he was like this. Lost in thought. 'I know that face.'

'I need to take another look,' Kramer said. 'In the cave. I feel like we're *missing* something. It can't be an animal attack, not with a handwritten message, but...'

'But you can't imagine a human would be savage enough to do that to a person,' Debbie said. 'Two people.'

'Oh, I can imagine it,' Kramer said, 'but it's just not possible. The way they were torn apart... I mean, there were *bite* marks in that girl's body. None of the cuts were clean, they were all... do you know of any human strong enough to *do* that? To tear off a woman's arms? To just shred half a guy's face off his skull without any kind of tools?'

'So what are you thinking? A wild animal learned how to spell?'

'I don't know *what* I think, Deb. But we have to figure this out before anything else happens. And if the answer's down there, in that cave -'

Crack!

The bang of the shotgun rippled across the island and Kramer spun round, eyes wide.

'What the...' Debbie started, but Kramer was already heading for the car. In the distance, a narrow funnel of smoke rose up beyond the village, dissipating into the mist. A cow groaned over the echoes of the shot. Something yelped, hit by the spray of the weapon.

'It's the farm!' Debbie yelled, crossing the front of the car and yanking open her door. She clambered in, slammed the door after her. 'Creed's place, past the village.'

Kramer had already slid the car into reverse and they pulled away from the cliff edge, rearing back onto the dirt track and turning wildly. 'Basketcase should never have got a gun license,' he grunted, and the police car rumbled over the road towards the farm.

4

Emma Green dragged the razor across Eddie's face and flicked the suds of shaving cream into a ceramic basin behind her. There was a little blood, and she pressed her thumb to the line of the man's jaw. 'Sorry,' she murmured.

Eddie's expression was still, eyes calm and unfaltering. He hadn't flinched when the nurse had cut him. Didn't blink when he saw the spatter of red in the sink. He was shirtless, hands bound together behind his back with a thick, velcro strap. The muscles of his neck rippled as he turned his head, looking down at the nurse standing between him and the mirror on the wall.

'I was talking to the doctor this morning,' Eddie said slowly, tilting up his chin as Emma lifted the blade to his throat. His voice was low, and the nurse shivered a little as he spoke.

'I know,' Emma said. 'She told me she felt like she was really getting to know you, Eddie. Do you feel like that?'

'Why did she leave?' Eddie said, brushing the question aside.

'There was... something happened,' Emma said. 'We needed her help.'

'You didn't want to leave her with me.'

Emma said nothing. The razor curled smoothly down Eddie's jaw and scraped a clean, wide path across his skin. Emma peeled back the blade, drew it down from the base of his ear.

'I'm right, then,' Eddie said quietly.

'Yes.'

'So why have *you* been left with me?'

Emma froze. 'This is procedure,' she said. 'I'm just doing my job.'

'So was Dr King.'

'She was *alone* with you,' the nurse said, dipping the blade into the basin and rinsing it.

Eddie's eyes moved up in the mirror above the basin, dark and narrow beneath his straight brow. He smiled thinly at the guard standing behind him. 'Of course,' he said, and his voice seemed to drop half a tone. 'I suppose you're in safe hands.'

The guard shifted uncomfortably. Black-gloved hands twitched at his waist. A hefty, square-barrelled gun was strapped to his belt. All matte-black metal and polished mechanisms. It hadn't been used in a long time.

'That's right,' Emma said. She nodded toward the guard, never taking her eyes off Eddie's face as she dragged the razor across his throat. 'This is Karl. Say hi to Eddie, Karl.'

'Hi, Eddie.'

Edward Drake's face was still. 'Karl,' he said. 'I suppose you've heard some uncomfortable stories, in your time here.'

Karl swallowed, looking toward the nurse.

Emma nodded.

'I guess so,' Karl said, turning back to the mirror.

'Strong stomach, then,' Eddie said.

'You could say that.'

'There was a guard just like you, back at the prison,' Eddie said. 'On the mainland. He tried to *rape* me, Karl.'

Karl paused. At Eddie's throat, the razor in Emma's

hand shifted as the nurse's heartbeat quickened. 'I'm sorry to hear that,' Karl said slowly.

'I opened up his throat with a razor blade,' Eddie said.

He tilted his head back, just a little, as the razor curled up the straight of his throat. There was no movement in his eyes, even as the blade trailed over the scars on his neck.

'How did you get those?' Emma said quietly.

Eddie didn't answer.

'Do they hurt?'

'No.'

Emma paused. 'What about this?' she said, gesturing at Eddie's torso with the razor. The man's gut was toned, thick skin pulled tight around bunched, firm muscles that pressed against his flesh. His skin was a mess of bruises and long-healed cuts. In places it was so badly discoloured that it could have been mistaken for black, damp mould. A ring of puckered, red marks formed a *C* at his side, as though something with blunt, wide teeth had taken a bite out of him. A pale purple bruise spread over his left shoulder looked more recent.

But Emma wasn't pointing at these. For a moment the very tip of the razor touched the scar around Eddie's midsection. Still, the man didn't flinch.

The scar curled all the way around Edward Drake's gut, a thick, twisted line where something had cut across his belly and dragged itself around his entire body, forming a loop across his back. The scar had fused together all wrong, and in places the skin was ropey and deformed where it met over the wound. At his sides, where the flesh was thinnest, the old cut was peeled and yellow.

'That one must hurt,' Emma said. 'How did that... how did that happen to you?'

Eddie said nothing.

'I bet you did them yourself,' the guard said suddenly. 'Didn't you? Wouldn't be the first psycho in here to do something like that.'

'Karl, don't.'

'What?' Karl said. He raised his eyebrows, locking eyes with Eddie's reflection in the mirror. 'I've been here long enough. I *know* you. It's not enough, is it? Killing people. It gets boring. You're a *masochist*.'

Eddie's jaw cracked open as a thin, black smile spread across it. For a moment, he said nothing. When he opened his lips, the words were soft and deep. 'You know me?' he said.

'That's right, Eddie.'

'Karl,' Emma snapped, 'that's enough. Now, shall we get back to this?'

Eddie didn't blink. 'I know *you,* Karl.'

'*Fuck* you.'

'I know exactly who you are. And I'll tell you something.'

'Eddie, ignore him,' Emma tried. 'He's just...'

Karl raised a hand. The gun swayed at his waist as

metallic buckles clacked against each other. 'Come on, Green, let the man talk. What is it, Eddie? What do you want to tell me?'

Eddie's face darkened.

'I'm going to kill you first,' he said. 'When I get out of here, you're going to stand in my way, and I'm going to beat your face so far into your skull that your eyes burst out through your fucking ears.'

'Oh, really?' Karl said. He shifted his weight uneasily onto his right foot.

Emma took a step back. 'Eddie, shall we take you back to your room?' she said. The razor jerked in her hand as her wrist twitched. 'How about we get your shirt on and go, yeah?'

'Not because I want to kill you,' Eddie continued, ignoring her, 'but because you'll be *there.* You'll try and stop me leaving, Karl, and I'll have to kill you.'

'Eddie,' Emma said softly, 'stop it. Please. I'm sorry, but you don't get to leave until we discharge you.'

Karl smirked at the back of the room. 'That's right, Eddie.'

Emma scowled. 'Karl, stop. That's *enough.*'

'I will leave this place,' Eddie said. The scars across his throat shivered. 'Believe me. There is something out there, on this island. Something of mine. I *will* get it back.'

Karl grunted behind him. 'You so much as knock on your cell door, freak, and I shoot you dead.'

182

'Karl!' Emma glared.

'Let him talk,' Eddie said quietly. 'While he still can.'

'Both of you,' Emma said, 'stop this, now. You can measure dicks on your own time, but I've got another twenty faces to shave and I do *not* intend to spend my morning listening to you both threaten to kill each other.'

Karl grunted. 'He started it.'

'Shut the *fuck* up, Karl,' Emma snapped. She turned to Eddie. 'Now, if you're quite finished, shall we get this done?'

Slowly, Eddie tilted back his face.

'That's better,' Emma said, bringing the razor up to his neck to draw away the last traces of stubble. The scars over his throat throbbed as he swallowed, Adam's apple bobbing beneath his square chin.

Emma did it without thinking.

Blood drizzled over the razor as she pulled back her hand. The cut wasn't deep, but it was long; a shallow, crimson line across the edge of his jaw. As she watched, beads of red slid out of the slash in Eddie's skin and oozed over his neck. 'Oh, I'm so sorry,' Emma said quietly, reeling off a pad of cotton from a box on the basin to dab at the cut.

Eddie hadn't reacted at all. Almost as if he couldn't *feel* it.

5

'So you're telling me it was a *wolf?*' Kramer said. He crouched by the shredded hole in the electric fence, one hand on the grass. The opening was about tall enough for him to clamber through, if he wished, and certainly wide enough. The edges were ragged and twisted where the wire mesh had been peeled across.

Creed shook his head. 'No, I said it *looked* like a wolf. It was bigger than that. Almost as big as the cows, I'm telling you. And it *tore* through them. I couldn't... I wasn't fast enough.'

Kramer raised an eyebrow, turning around. Creed stood just a little shorter than Debbie, pot-belly exaggerated by the sagging folds of a stained, brown shirt that hung over a tattered belt. The old farmer's face was haggard and worn, his eyes narrow. His hair had nearly all abandoned him and his polished scalp gleamed in the sunlight beneath the stubborn wisps of grey that remained.

'It's alright,' Debbie said beside him, laying a hand on the man's shoulder. The shotgun shivered in the crook of his arm and the farmer blinked.

'Could you not have left that thing inside, Creed?' Kramer said, nodding down at the gun. A slender, near-invisible trail of smoke rose from the barrel.

'What if it comes back?' Creed said.

Kramer paused. 'You said you shot it, right? It's not

coming back.'

'Yeah, I got it. Right in the backside.'

'Where did it fall?' Debbie said.

Creed shook his head. 'It *didn't*. I hit it, square enough. I'm a good shot, you know. I'm *telling* you I hit the thing damn square in the arse. And it just... kept on running. Back the way it came.'

'Through here?' Kramer pointed toward the tear in the fence.

'Careful!' Creed said. His jowels trembled. 'The fence is still on. You touch it, that's one hell of a shock. Strong current, that. Custom job.'

Kramer stood straight, shaking his head. 'So you're telling me this thing tore its way through the fence while it was *turned on?*'

'Must have,' Creed shrugged. 'Fence is *always* on. Well, when the cows are in this field. When they're the other side of the island, I turn it off. Got to conserve energy, haven't you? What with all this global warming and that. I'm telling you, the fence was on. And this... *creature* just shredded it like tissue paper.'

'Can you describe it to us?' Debbie said.

Creed turned to her, shaking his head. 'It was... I don't know, it was dark. Dark-skinned. Like a shadow.'

'Like a *shadow?*' Kramer raised an eyebrow.

Creed nodded vigorously, gesturing with his hands. The shotgun swung wildly in the bend of his arm. 'At first, I thought it must be a dog, you know? They're always walking dogs past here, up to the cliffs at the far end of the island - I just thought, you know, one had got free. Then it started running at my cows and I saw it, *really* saw it, and that wasn't no dog. That was never a damned dog like I've ever seen.'

'So definitely more of a wolf, then,' Kramer said drily.

Debbie shot him a look.

'Definitely,' Creed said. 'Except... no fur. Its skin was like *hide,* you know? Like cow leather, but without the fur. Like leather when it's stripped. It kind of rippled. Like it was covered in something sticky. Like mucus. Or... you know the shit that covers a newborn calf? Like *that.* And its *face.* God, its face was fucking horrible - oh, I'm so sorry,' he stopped, turning to Debbie. 'I didn't mean to...'

Debbie shrugged it off. 'I'm used to it,' she said, nodding towards Kramer. 'This one swears like a trooper. So do I, for that matter. Now, you were describing the animal's face?'

'It was...' Creed's eyes glazed a little as he stared at the hole in the fence. 'Fuck me, it was a nightmare.'

'Okay, so we're looking for an ugly, sticky shadow,' Kramer said.

Creed glared up at him. The shotgun hung heavy at his side. 'You think this is funny?' he spat. 'You think I'd be telling you this if I wasn't shitting myself?

'Maybe we should have a look at the damage,'

Debbie said softly.

Creed turned to her. 'You mean my cows? My *dead* cows?'

Debbie nodded.

For a moment, Creed was silent. Then he pointed toward the middle of the field. 'Go on, then,' he said. 'Can't miss them.'

'Thank you.'

They stepped past him, headed for the herd. Most of the cows had moved to one corner of the field and groaned uneasily at each other as they stood.

Three big, black shapes muddied a backdrop of lush, clipped grass, spilling pools of crimson into the ground.

'Sounds like you were right, then,' Debbie said quietly as they approached the nearest of the fallen beasts. 'About a wild animal.'

'Do you think that's what he saw?' Kramer said. 'A wolf? I mean, where would it have *come* from?'

Debbie shrugged as they stopped walking. At their feet, the cow was bent up and spread out over the grass. Its insides had been pulled out and coiled around its twisted thighs, torn from a great, gaping hole in its belly.

'I don't know what else could have done this,' Debbie whispered. She looked up, and her eyes fell upon the huddled mass of cows in the far corner. 'They look terrified.'

'They should be,' Kramer said. He couldn't tear his

gaze from the mess of blood and ruptured organs dampening the ground before him. 'Whatever this thing is, it's new. A wolf might be able to do this to a cow, Deb, but it can't tear its way through an electric fence. And it can't leave handwritten messages on a cave wall. Whatever we're dealing with... it's wild, and it's hurt, and it's screaming at us.'

6

The shadow limped to the edge of the cliff and stood, for a while, slumped in the tall grass. Its flesh rippled, black and shining and bloody. Its jaws hung open. Every ragged breath drew a low, deep growl out of its belly and it snarled down at the sand, drool sliding over its narrow teeth.

The carcasses at the base of the cliff had disappeared, but the creature hardly noticed. Strings of blue tape fluttered across the top of the ramp and curled around thick, iron posts dug into the ground. Drawn back to the beach and the cave, the creature slunk under the tape and descended. Each stride sent shears of pain slicing up its thighs and into its rump. Its blood was cold and black and drizzled over its legs like thick tar, seeping out of the pepper-mill wound in the shadow's rump.

The pain would fade, soon enough. Already, the creature's skin had started to fuse back together; the reconstruction would be faster without the constant screeching in the shadow's head, without the stinging at the base of its skull, but it was difficult to concentrate. It knew that it could repair this form, in the same way that it had *created* it, but it needed quiet. It needed to still the shivering mess of pain and angst in its skull, to find the peace it needed to focus and to heal.

Slowly the shadow moved across the sand, padding lightly over crisp, bloody white. A ring of black rocks rose up from the foam to the creature's left as it reached the edge of the water. Soon, only the sharpened tips of the stones would be visible above the waves. The tide was coming in. The salt smell had grown stronger, and with it the creature tasted an earthy dullness on the air. The first signs of a storm, and a big one. The rain was coming.

The creature dug a tentative forelimb into the water, pushing its claws into the white foam at the shore. Cold washed over its skin and for a moment the screaming in its head was muffled by a numbing, cool silence. The shadow stepped forward, lowering its jaws into the water, pushing its shoulders forward as its claws sunk into the softer ground. It kept walking until it was completely submerged, ignoring the wash of stinging, salty pain that stung its wounded rear.

The shadow closed its eyes as salt covered its flesh. Above, rain bounced off the surface of the ocean, but down here, beneath the water, it was sheltered. Every sound was muffled. The light played differently, tracing warped, curling paths over the shifting sand.

Peace.

The screaming faded, just a little. Enough that the creature could focus, enough that it could raise a wall of empty, flat nothing at the front of its mind and *concentrate.*

Black mist broke into the water as blood washed off of the shadow's body. Dark skin curled and fused together, forming a thick, wiry mesh before wrapping itself tight around the pellet wound. Thick bandages of grey formed and pulled the creature's thigh back into place. Bone slid past bone with a deep, low grinding, muted by the swell of the sea.

The creature could be hurt, it realise, and *badly* hurt. The wound from the shotgun had shown that. The thing was vulnerable, to some things at least.

It could fix that.

Slowly, the thing's skin began to stretch as its body rippled and twisted with a horrible cracking sound. Muscles aligned and pushed up against its dreadful flesh, bunching together and tightening. The creature's flesh peeled, stretched so far and so thin that it came away altogether, and for a moment its shape was lost in a salt-encrusted mess of black blood and writhing, shining coils of darkness. Then its new skin broke through, even as the shredded first coat drifted slowly down into the sand. This new flesh was thicker, tougher. It forced its way through a maze of shadowy bones and *up,* spreading and contorting and lashing in great strings around the creature's limbs and cracked, spiny joints.

Brown-grey plates of armour layered over each other, sliding over the curves of the creature's body. Its skull hardened and shredded the skin of its face into a raw, red mess. It reached up with new, thicker claws and peeled away the scraps; its lips reformed, thinner, darker around a carnage of monstrous teeth and shivers of bone; narrow slits opened up beneath the outer skull that covered the thing's head and a pair of burning, yellow eyes shone through the murk of the water. Thick, harsh bumps and spines coiled over its shoulders and rump and along the broken line of its backbone.

Slowly, the shadow turned and began to step out of the water.

The moment it left the sea that horrible screaming returned to it, dreadful and loud and relentless, and a confusion of emotions and feelings and dark, deep pain riddled its body, and as the creature slunk back into the cave at the face of the cliff, it grinned.

7

Edward Drake stepped into the cell and the door closed.

Behind him, Karl's hands moved to the velcro band around Eddie's wrists and tore it off. 'You have a good day, now,' Karl hissed, leaning forward.

Eddie could smell him; thick, offensive aftershave wafted over the guard's clothes and weed lingered on his breath as it brushed Eddie's neck.

'What are you waiting for, Drake?' Karl said, stepping back. They were alone in the room. The air was thick. 'No more empty threats for me?'

Eddie turned slowly, hands dangling by his sides. There was a spot of blood at the line of his jaw and he raised his arm to wipe it away Calmly, he nodded to a space behind Karl's head. 'You haven't locked the door,' he said calmly. 'Perhaps you should.'

'Oh, so you don't get out?' Karl said. 'Wishful thinking, mate.'

'You should leave,' Eddie said quietly. 'You should...'

He froze. Something rippled across Eddie's forehead and he raised a hand to his temple, gritting his teeth. It wasn't a pain, as such, but... a *sensation*. A feeling. Like something was knocking on his head to get in. 'You should...'

Karl grinned, turning for the door. 'Aw, does little Eddie Drake have a headache? What's up there, huh? Did someone forget to take his vitamins?'

'Quiet,' Eddie whispered. The feeling in his head had turned to a throbbing and he closed his eyes. He had felt this before, recently. 'I need you to be quiet.'

'Excuse me?' Karl snapped. 'You think you can tell me what to do, now?' He turned away from the door and stepped back to Eddie, anger flashing across his face.

'Huh? You think *you* get to do that? Not today, Drake.' The guard reached out a hand, threaded his fingers through Eddie's hair. 'No, you listen to *me...*'

Suddenly Eddie reared up and barrelled forward, pressing Karl back against the wall. A thick forearm shot up to the guard's throat and pinned him there as Eddie glared, stony-faced and emotionless. 'I said be *quiet.*'

He turned away, and Karl slid down the wall, gasping for breath. Ignoring the man, Eddie moved to the mattress in the corner of the room and dropped to his knees. 'Show me,' he whispered. If he closed his eyes he could almost see it. He felt salt wash over his skin, felt calm run through his mind as the water covered him, felt the wind at the bottom of the cliff. He could feel everything. If only he could *see...*

'I'll show you something,' Karl hissed. Something clicked at the guard's hip.

Eddie turned, but he was too slow; the baton crashed into the side of his head and he tumbled onto his shoulder. For a moment his vision faltered and the throbbing in his mind turned to an intense, shrill screaming. He saw it for a moment, eyes narrowed in a vicious, spiny skull, glowing yellow beneath the shadows of the waves, face distorted by the water...

'It's here,' he breathed. 'It's really here.'

Karl shook his head. The baton was steady in his gloved hand. 'You're insane,' he spat. 'Prick.'

The guard turned away and pulled the cell door open, shooting Eddie one last, disgusted look before he stepped back out into the corridor.

The door closed and Edward Drake was alone with a pulsing warmth at the front of his skull and that image in his mind - a clear picture of the thing's face, clearer than he had ever seen before. And different now, than it had looked before. It had eyes, now, for one thing.

It had followed him here. He had known it would, of course.

And for just a second, he had seen it.

Slowly, a dark smile opened across Eddie's face. Blood ran down from the graze on his skull where the guard's nightstick had hit him, but Eddie didn't notice.

It was here. The thing had followed him to Cain's End. And if it meant killing every bastard in this place, Eddie would find it.

CHAPTER SEVEN
DEAD COWS AND ZOMBIES

1
NOW

Flies buzzed madly above a bovine carcass as Kramer slid the vibrating phone out of his pocket. He glanced at the screen and lifted it to his ear.

'Police,' he said, turning away from the corpse. The stench of the thing burned the insides of his nostrils and he exhaled, glancing up at the sky. Grey clouds rolled in over the mid-afternoon sun. 'Kramer,' he said. 'If it's bad news, I'm handing you over to my partner.'

He paused for a second, listening, then turned to Debbie and nodded her over. 'Forensics,' he said. 'It's Jamie.'

Debbie nodded. 'What have they got?'

'Alright,' Kramer said into the phone, 'I'm putting you on speaker.'

Debbie stood beside him, hands on her hips.

Behind her, a black fly picked at the cow's rolled-back eyeball and peeled wet, pink flesh from a bloody socket. Kramer grimaced as he watched. 'Go on,' he said, holding the phone between them. 'What have you got?'

'Well,' Jamie sounded disdained, even through the crackling phone speaker, 'it's not *good* news.'

'Never saw that coming,' Debbie said.

'Looks like it's the daughter of that woman who called,' the voice continued.

Kramer groaned. 'Fantastic. And the guy, was that her boyfriend?'

'Still working on that one, but that's our best guess. The mother's down here now, she hasn't given us an official ID on the body but we'll get it in time. She's in a bit of a state. Sure you can imagine.'

Debbie glanced up, saw it on Kramer's face; he could. He was a difficult man to read, most of the time, but right now the single thought running through his head was painted in the dull grey splashes of his eyes: *If that girl had been Charlotte...*

'What about the boy's parents?' Debbie said. 'Have we heard anything from them? Surely they must have noticed their son's missing by now.'

'Lived on his own, if this is the guy. You know how it is, kids that age. Cheapest place possible, you know? Worked down at the Crow's Head weekends, cleaned up at the asylum during the week.'

'So he was doing alright for himself,' Kramer said. 'You know, Jamie, you could have just lied. Told me they were a pair of scumbags.'

'Would it have helped?'

Kramer paused. 'Not really. What about time of death?'

'Definitely after midnight. Somewhere between one and two, we're thinking.'

'Narrows it down,' Kramer nodded.

Debbie frowned. 'Hang on,' she said. 'There was... when I was down at the asylum, we were looking over the security tape for Eddie's room. He was there all night, but he... no, it's crazy. Carry on.'

Kramer raised an eyebrow. 'No, go on.'

'Well, he just sat there the whole time, right? Got up a couple of times, but he was *calm*. The whole time. Completely expressionless. Christ, he didn't even look *bored*. And then... there was a moment. Just after one in the morning. He went crazy. Just started screaming. Like he was... like he was in pain. Then it stopped.'

'The hell are you saying, Deb?' Jamie's voice rose from the phone in a hiss of static, half-lost in the wind.

'I told you it was crazy,' Debbie said. 'Just a coincidence, that's all.'

Kramer shook his head. His face was still. 'He's connected. First his name on the wall, now this? Edward Drake has some sort of a connection to this.'

Debbie laughed nervously. 'Sure, Matt, but... I mean,

he was in there all night. He can't have had anything to do with what happened.'

'Maybe not physically. But he's connected, *somehow*.' Kramer raised a hand to his temple, pushed hair out of his eyes. 'Christ, this is a mess. Jamie, anything else?'

'Yeah, something. Not sure *what,* exactly, but something.'

'Go on,' Debbie said.

'I got a call from my guy at the beach a few minutes ago. He said there's something in that cave. Something else, you know, other than the blood on the walls. Sounded *messed up,* if you ask me. He didn't say what it was, just said to get someone to go check it out.'

'We'll go have a look,' Debbie nodded.

'Ah,' Jamie said. There was a pause.

'What do you mean, "ah"?' Kramer said.

'Maybe just one of you.' Jamie said. 'There's one more thing, you two.'

Kramer frowned. 'Hm?'

'Apparently a couple of kids down at the high school got wind of what happened down the beach this morning. The school's asking us questions. I'm gonna need one of you to head down there and talk to someone, get them clear on this.'

'Fuck,' Kramer murmured.

Debbie shrugged. 'Had to happen,' she said, turning to Kramer. 'You want the cave?'

For a moment Kramer paused. He should take the school. He wanted to check on Charlotte, make sure she was okay. What if she had heard what happened? God, what if she'd *seen* it, on her walk in? 'I should...' he started, but he paused. He couldn't send Debbie into that cave on her own. Oh, she could take care of herself, probably better than him, but...

'Matt?' Debbie said. 'Do you want to take the cave?'

'Sounds good,' he said quietly.

'Alright,' Jamie said. 'I'll give you a call if we find anything else.'

'Bye,' Kramer said, hanging up as he shoved the phone back into his coat. He looked down at Debbie, opened his mouth. Closed it. 'Would you...'

'Yeah, I'll let you know she's okay,' Debbie said. She smiled.

Kramer couldn't help but smile back. 'You're the best, Deb.'

Debbie leaned up and planted a kiss on his cheek. 'Be safe,' she whispered.

'I'll do my best.'

Kramer watched as she turned and headed back to where Creed was standing, over by the torn electric mesh, and he blinked.

Behind him, the cow's eyeball had caved in and the socket was little more than a blood-stained, stringy hole.

2
1995

Little had changed in the two years since Martha had last been here.

The trees seemed a little thicker, and blocked the light with a fierce, clawed sort of determination. They seemed, she thought, to have grown closer together, but she knew that was impossible. A couple had fallen, torn down by some violent storm. Martha peered through the trees toward the old, crooked house, just visible through a dug-out path in the woods. Here the trees had been ripped apart from each other, branches cracked and fallen away. A winding passage led all the way from the road to the gravel drive, broken by twisted roots and shllow rivers of swamp water.

Martha pressed on, tugging her uniform around her to brace herself against the cool wind. Shadows moved between the trees, bumping against them, colliding and twisting about each other. Martha shuddered. Black shapes watched her from the shadows.

'Just trees,' she hissed. 'Grow up, Martha. It's just *trees*.'

A branch snapped on the ground behind her and she whirled around, staring into the dark.

Nothing. Just a squirrel, or something like that. But it had sounded heavier than a squirrel, far *bigger* than a squirrel...

'Stop it,' Martha told herself. The house was so close that she couldn't help but feel like someone was watching her from within. Flickering, orange light burned beyond the grease-stained windows. Shadows scratched at the glass.

The cold bit at Martha's face as she moved through the trees, pushing with her sleeves as dangling, bent branches threatened to tear her skin. The foliage grew tighter as Martha came nearer to the gravel drive; thorns sprouted up before her and bunched into thick vines and snaking, dark trails. They coiled up from the ground as she walked and curled around her ankles, pulling her back. Like something didn't want her to *get* any closer...

Something moved in the trees. Martha froze, squinted into the dark off to her left.

A dead branch cracked loudly as something pawed through the undergrowth. Martha could see it, in the shadows, black and deformed and *twisted,* and she turned back, toward the house, pressed on, heart pounding. It was just a deer. Or a badger, maybe.

But badgers didn't *move* like that...

Behind her, the thing coughed.

Martha frowned. Slowly, she turned her head and looked.

Beyond a near row of trees, the thing limped along the forest floor, dragging something limp and heavy with it.

It paused, raised its head. Breathing heavy, it raised

a hand to its face and sputtered.

It sounded like a *child*.

'Eddie?' Martha breathed.

He was a little taller, a little thinner, but it was *him*. Barely a silhouette, but recognisable even in the dark. For a moment Eddie stood completely still and it looked like he might have heard her, but then he pushed on, into the trees, shaking it off as a whisper on the wind. He dragged the heavy-looking shape behind him, burdened by its weight.

Martha moved cautiously towards the boy, sticking to the trees. She wanted to call out to him, let him know she was there, but she was curious.

She wanted to see what he was carrying. Where he was taking it.

Eddie made a crooked line through the trees, keeping clear of the road, and before long Martha could smell burning. Not fire, but the bitter, stinging heat of steam and smoke. She heard a bubbling, over the rustle of leaves above her head, and the air grew thick and warm and humid. She saw it, then, pooling around the bottoms of the trees, black and thick over the roots and foliage on the ground.

Eddie had led her to the swamp.

The boy stopped, at the edge of the sludge, and Martha pressed her back to a thick, twisted trunk, peering through the dark.

'What are you doing, kid?' she whispered.

Eddie dropped the thing he had been pulling along with him and fell to his knees at the edge of the swamp. Murky, black filth splashed his knees. The boy whispered something to himself, something Martha couldn't hear, and when he had been speaking for a while she realised he was repeating the same words, over and over. The same few words, ringing like a chant, like a prayer. With his head bowed, shadows playing over his gaunt figure, the boy's face was hidden from her.

If Martha didn't know any better, she would say the boy was *crying.*

'Forgive me...' Eddie murmured, and he stood up.

Something moved in the water. It trailed through the murk, sliding left to right, thick, black body covered in spines and spikes. Eddie scrambled to his feet and took a staggering step back, afraid. Something rumbled, beneath the bubbling surface of the swamp. Something hungry.

Martha made to step forward, but she couldn't move. She could *see* it now...

Eddie picked up the corpse by her armpits, held the dead woman aloft. Her head lolled back against the boy's chest as he shoved her limp body into the swamp water.

The creature in the filth lashed out with wide, snapping jaws and the corpse disappeared, dragged down into the black, boiling swill. The scaly animal's thick, lumpen tail cracked against the surface of the water and bone crunched between its teeth, and then it was gone, vanished into the dark. In the distance of the swamp, something else moved. Another whip-like tail lashed violently out of the water. Something howled.

'Oh my god...' Martha breathed.

Eddie turned around.

Shit, Martha thought, but there was nothing she could do.

The boy's eyes widened. He saw her.

'Eddie...' Martha said. She stepped forward. 'What's going on?'

The child shook his head. His hands were bloody. His cheeks were hollow. Eddie opened his mouth, eyes darting towards the house. 'You shouldn't be here,' he whispered. Black swamp water dripped from his ankles. His feet were bare. The boy was so thin that his ribs were visible through the folds of a stained, white shirt. 'You need to *run.*'

'Eddie, I'm here to take you away,' Martha said, holding out a hand. 'Please, come on... we can leave now. My car's just on the other side of the road. Eddie, this place... it's not safe. Let me get you out of here.'

Eddie shook his head again. 'You can't.'

'Eddie, whatever this is,' Martha said, gesturing toward the swamp, 'whatever she's making you *do,* I don't care. I don't care what you've done. I just need you to come with me, and you'll be safe. I promise.'

'You *can't,*' Eddie said. 'She'll know...'

'She won't, Eddie. She's not going to find you.'

'If she doesn't know you're here already, she will. She's *coming for you.*'

Martha's blood ran cold. She shook her head. 'No,' she said. 'Please, Eddie, come with me. Let me get you somewhere *safe.*'

Eddie blinked. His eyes dropped to the floor. Behind him, the swamp creatures fought madly for the scraps of the carcass he had tossed into the filth. When Eddie's gaze rose to Martha's face, his eyes were dark. 'Can you kill her?'

Martha froze. 'What?'

Eddie pointed to the crooked house. 'Can you *kill* her?'

'Eddie, I can't... that's not...'

'Then there *is* nowhere safe,' he hissed.

Something cracked, behind Martha's ankles, and she grimaced.

Hot breath brushed the back of her neck.

'He's right, you know,' Nana whispered.

Before Martha could move a pair of wrinkled, slender hands had latched onto her skull. The woman's neck twisted around with a sickening *crack* and she fell to her knees, eyes wide and round and cold.

'Eddie,' she gargled as a stream of blood rose up into her throat. Her neck was bent around so far that her spine pushed against the skin at the base of her skull.

'Eddie, *run...*'

Martha's body fell forward with a *thwump.*

Quietly, Eddie choked back a sob.

Nana Death looked at him with narrowed eyes, wiping spittle from her lips with the back of her withered hand. 'You can run, if you like,' she rasped, 'or you can come back inside and finish your dinner.'

Eddie said nothing. Around him, the shadows moved and twisted, writhing about the trees. Pale, yellow eyes blinked at him from the dark and he shivered.

Nana smiled.

'You know how they love to *hunt...*'

3

Anderson cleared his throat, knocking on the front door. 'Anyone home?'

He waited for a moment, tapping the heel of his boot anxiously. *Is this what my job is now?* he thought to himself. *Checking up on the daughters of crazy ladies?*

This wasn't what he'd signed up for as a police officer. He should be on the streets, busting shifty drug deals and grabbing shiftier meat off the nearest hot dog stand. Taking names with his partner. But nowadays, Hank Anderson's partner was a woman, and Martha had told him to come here.

'What's the fucking point,' he mumbled, turning around. The kid was probably fine. *Well,* he thought, *as fine as you can be when your mum runs around telling everyone you're a psycho killer.*

Anderson's eyes dropped to a plant pot on the front step, half-hidden by the shadow that he cast on the concrete. He paused. Elizabeth had told them, down at the station, that there was a second key under the pot.

'For fuck's sake,' Anderson sighed. Well, he had driven out here. He may as well take a look.

'Hello?' Anderson called again, a little louder. 'Police! If you're in there, Rose, can you answer the door for me?'

Your nutjob mother told us you needed a little help.

Anderson stepped back from the door, moved a little way down the garden path and looked up at the house. It was a two-storey building - nice place, he thought, even if it was a little small. Set back a way from the road and boxed in by two slightly taller houses.

The front garden was rough and overgrown, littered with patches of long grass. Splashes of colour were broken into fragments by twisted, spiny weeds. Anderson's eyes passed over the front of the building and he grunted. No movement behind any of the windows. Anderson stepped back up to the door.

'Alright, I'm coming in!' he called, reaching for the plant pot. Clumps of dirt embedded themselves beneath his nails as he gripped the side of the thing and dragged it back to reveal the flat, brass key on the ground. He nudged the pot back into place and straightened up.

Quickly, he slid the key into the lock. 'Fucking fool's errand,' he murmured.

The door clicked open and Anderson stepped inside.

The hallway was dark. Quiet, too. Every sound from outside was blocked out behind him as he shut the door. He fumbled in the shadows for a light switch, found it by his head. He flicked it absent-mindedly.

After a second the light turned on, buzzing erratically as it flickered. A dull glow rippled over the hallway.

'Jesus,' Anderson said to himself, 'crazy *and* a fucking hoarder.'

The carpet was a mess of parcel-taped boxes and plastic tubs, frayed at the edges and crammed with papers and cutlery. Junk spilled over their edges and onto the floor. Anderson noticed a pile of DVDs that he might've fancied looking through, if he didn't have a bagel waiting for him back at his desk. A tall, wooden coatstand had tumbled from its place by the wall and fallen against the staircase. It slanted across the hall and cast long, rectangular shadows over the mess on the carpet. Anderson ducked beneath it as he stepped through towards the stairs.

'Hello?' he called. 'Rose?'

Nothing.

'We've got your mum down at the station, love! She asked us to come make sure you're okay. Are you about?' Anderson moved a little further down the hall, past the stairs. Stepping over a mound of filthy clothes that spilled out from the wall and spread over the floor, he crossed to a half-open door at the back of the house. He pushed it and it squealed. Beyond it, a tiny laundry room was cluttered with piles of shirts and shoes and empty, toppled baskets.

'For fuck's sake,' Anderson mumbled, turning and closing the door behind him. '*Hello!* Anyone home?'

No reply.

Anderson moved to the bottom of the stairs and curled around the banister, cupped a hand around his mouth and yelled up. 'Rose? Really appreciate an answer, if you would! Your mum's worried about you, see?'

For a moment, there was silence. And then a quiet, timid voice from the top of the stairs, a little girl's voice: 'I'm up here.'

'Thank fuck for that,' Anderson hissed under his breath. Then, louder: 'You mind if I join you up there?'

'Please,' said the voice, barely a whisper. 'Join me up here.'

Anderson took the stairs slowly, squinting up onto the landing. There was no light up there, and the shadows shifted around the top of the stairs. 'Rose, love, can you turn a light on up there? Just so I can see you, is all.'

No answer. Anderson sighed. 'Guess I'll just walk around in the fucking dark like an idiot then, shall I?' he breathed.

'Yes,' came the voice, quieter than before. Almost a whisper.

Anderson froze.

'Just walk around in the fucking dark like an idiot.'

'Jeez, your mother let you swear like that?' Anderson called up the stairs. He shivered.

'My mother lets me swear like that.'

Anderson swallowed. Quickly he reached the top of the stairs and something bumped his foot. He looked down, peering into the dark by his feet, caught the outline of something that looked like a toy car. A truck, maybe. He kicked it aside and the thing rolled away on plastic wheels, bouncing off the banister and tumbling down the first few stairs. The sound echoed. 'Rose,' Anderson said, stepping forward onto the landing, 'where are you?'

He turned his head, keeping one hand on the wall as he moved along the landing. A door to Anderson's left was slightly ajar and he pushed it open.

A slit of white pushed between two thick, cloth curtains and threw itself over a queen-sized bed, crumpled duvet stained with damp. A desk chair sat crooked under the window. There was an ottoman by the door. Thick, square shapes loomed in the corners. A tall wardrobe at the side of the room was half-buried in shadow, the other half bathed in a pale grey light. The wardrobe door was open and shapeless things spilled out onto the carpet.

'Okay, guessing this is mummy's room,' Anderson said, retreating onto the landing. His gaze stopped on another door, right at the end of the hall. Someone had drawn a flower in pink and red crayon on the wood. Fingerstrokes of green along the bottom of the door were meant to look like grass, but they had faded. 'Rose?' he said, a little louder. 'You in there?'

'I'm in here,' came the girl's voice from inside the room.

Anderson moved forward, heading for the door. His hand brushed against the knob and he twisted, pushed. The door groaned and Anderson took a cautious step inside. 'Hello?'

It was dark in here too. *Come on,* Anderson thought, slapping his hand against the wall and tracing his fingers over the plaster. *Got to be a switch somewhere.*

'Hello.'

'It's alright, Rose,' he said. 'I'm just trying to find the...'

Click.

Anderson's eyes widened. His pupils shrunk as the light burst on and the room was covered in a soft, damp glow. 'Oh, *fuck...*'

Rose sat on the floor in the middle of the room, legs crossed in front of her. The little girl was surrounded by mess. An old mattress was torn and hung off a sagging, wooden bedframe. Bunches of tattered stuffing pooled out of gashes in the casing. Behind her, moth-eaten curtains had been pulled down from a boarded-up window. The rail hung across sheets of gaffer-taped cardboard. The rest of the room was carnage.

Kid's mother was right, Anderson thought. *Oh, fuck me...*

Then he saw it.

Oh, god.

There was something in the little girl's lap.

Shit!

Teddy bears and stuffed animals littered the floor. Heads had been ripped off of fabric shoulders and strewn across the brown-stained carpet. Some of the teddies still had their soft faces attached, but button eyes had been torn from their faces. One of the little bears hung from the bedpost, a black cable-tie pulled tight around its throat.

'Mummy ran away from me,' Rose whispered, 'didn't she?'

A tiny spatter of red glistened on her pigtail.

'No...' Anderson said, taking a step back. 'No, she... your mummy just needed a little time. Did you... did you do all this?'

Rose smiled. The thing in her lap twitched.

'Rose, did you... is it still alive?'

The cat's narrow limbs had been snapped. Fresh, white bones poked out of its bloody flesh, jabbing out of the skin of its knees and shoulders where the legs had been cocked into unnatural angles. The little animal's fur was matted and wet and tangled in Rose's lap. Its mouth was open, tiny, pointed teeth bared in a frozen snarl. The cat's eyes were rolled up in its head, but it wasn't dead. Not yet.

Anderson couldn't tear his attention from the animal, couldn't help but stare as it lay in the girl's arms, convulsing every few seconds.

Rose's smile was crimson and wet and her eyes were dark. Blood drizzled over her lips. Slowly, she chewed something, never taking her eyes off the police officer in the doorway.

The cat's left ear was missing.

'I'm going to go now,' Anderson said quietly. His heart thumped against his ribs and he swallowed. 'Okay, Rose? I'm going to go and find your mother. Can you wait here?'

Rose pouted. A hair dangled over her lip. It was the same colour as the cat's bloody fur. 'Won't you stay?' the child said, lifting up the limp body of the cat and setting it down on the carpet beside her. 'I *like* you.'

Anderson took another step back onto the landing and shook his head. 'Oh, I have to *go*...'

The cat looked up at him and he opened his mouth to say something else, but stopped. His eyes fell on the little girl's face.

Slowly, Rose stood up, wiping her bloody hands on a pastel-pink dress. 'Stay,' she said. 'Play with me.'

213

Anderson raised his hands, shaking his head. 'No...'

'*Play* with me,' Rose whispered. 'I thought we could have a tea party, now that you're here. Would you like that?'

'I have to leave.' Anderson took another step back. His rump hit the banister and he almost cried out. His fingers wrapped around the rail and he gripped it tight. 'I have to *go*.'

'No,' Rose said, flashing orange-stained teeth. 'We're going to have a tea party. I'm *hungry*.'

CHAPTER EIGHT
THE DOOR

1
NOW

'Anyone about?'

Kramer's voice bounced off the cave walls as he stepped forward. He walked carefully, keeping his back to the slippery rock face behind him. The tide had almost fully come in and the floor at the cave entrance was submerged in dark, murky water. Kramer swung the torch in his hand; even in the wide shaft of light it threw out, the cave was a shifting tunnel of grey-black. He could hardly see six feet ahead of him.

'Hey!' Kramer called. 'Jamie told me you were still down here?'

The detective took another step, one hand outstretched to steady himself. Kramer was largely sheltered from the push of the wind in here, but he didn't fancy a dip in the water.

His eyes drifted up to the opposite wall as he moved. The bloody scrawl was still there - he'd asked forensics not to wash it away until they knew what was going on - but it made no more sense than it had before.

Kramer noticed things, this time around, that he hadn't the first; some of the words were spelt wrong or cut short, like whatever had written them couldn't think coherently enough to form them properly. The whole wall was a mad, enraged display of red nonsense. Even where it wasn't clear exactly what the deranged artist had been trying to paint, his *message* was clear.

Payn was spelled in big, dripping letters above the saltwater that lapped the walls. Beside that, in six-inch-tall capitals: *HUNGRY.*

Maybe this was nothing to do with the animal attack, Kramer thought. Maybe the two bodies on the beach were the victim of whatever wild creature had been set loose on the island, and this...

Well, it would be one hell of a coincidence. But whatever was going on, Matthew Kramer had never seen anything like it.

'Hello?' he called again, moving forward.

The writing grew more and more desperate as Kramer ventured farther into the cave. He swung the torch beam over the wall, pausing every now and then to read.

Stop scREeming, the killer had written.
STOP!

Kramer shuddered and kept moving. About thirty feet from the cave entrance, the ground slid up from beneath the water in a shimmering curl of flattened, smooth rock. Kramer broke away from the wall and moved more confidently over this new plateau of stone. His footsteps echoed off the walls and the dripping pillars of calcium and stone that drew down from the ceiling.

'Come on,' he called into the dark of the cavern before him. 'Did Jamie tell you I was coming? What have you found?'

He paused, waiting for a response.

Nothing.

Toward the very back of the cave, something whispered in the pitch-black that his torch beam couldn't reach. Not a human voice. Barely a voice at all. But he heard *something...*

'Hello? Hey, enough of this, alright? Whatever you've found, how about you show me and we can both get out of here?'

Nothing.

'Unbelievable,' Kramer murmured, pressing forward.

Behind him, something splashed lightly in the water.

Kramer whirled round, holding the torch high. A shallow ripple spread over the surface of the water before dissipating into the dark and the spittle at the mouth of the cave.

Kramer shook his head and turned back, carrying on along the wall. The rock seemed to pale as he broached the shadows of the cavern; it faded from a deep black to a sleek, damp grey before melting into shades of brown and white stricken with deep, red veins. Kramer's boot sunk into an inch-deep puddle as the rock dipped and he swore.

'Hello!' he yelled. 'Can you...'

He froze.

There was that sound again, deep in the shadows of the cave. The whispering. Louder now.

Closer.

For a moment Kramer thought about running, turning and getting back out into the open. What if it was in here with him? What if the wounded wolf-creature Creed had seen had a nest, and Kramer was about to step headfirst into it?

The air seemed to hum around him, tingling with the kind of electricity that he could *hear* as well as feel in the vibrations over his skin. The hair on the back of Kramer's neck stood on end and he pressed forward, sweeping the torch over the darkest parts of the cavern.

There.

Kramer moved towards an opening in the far wall, where the cave branched off into a narrow, black tunnel. Through it he saw something, a flicker of movement. A break in the shadows where the torch beam was swallowed by another light.

Kramer turned off the torch, frowning. For a second he kept his eyes on the tunnel opening.

Silence.

Then the light twisted again and the whispering turned to a hiss. A terrible light splintered the dark as the tunnel opening erupted into shafts and slivers of pure, dazzling white.

There was something *through* there. Whatever Jamie's forensics guy had seen, it was through that tunnel. And it was *glowing.*

'Oh, I really hope you're still in there,' Kramer whispered, flicking on the torch as he headed for the opening.

2

'Isn't she like, your dad's girlfriend or something?'

Charlotte shot a look at Darcy, shaking her head. 'No, they're not... shut up.'

The girls turned their attention back to the stage at the front of the assembly hall, watching as Debbie Martin stepped up onto the little platform.

Crawford sat at the back of the stage with a couple of the other teachers, arms folded across his chest. Charlotte had noticed him looking their way as she and Darcy filtered into the hall, but his gaze seemed to have shifted now. Charlotte was almost surprised to find that she was more than a little relieved.

'Hi, everyone,' Debbie said from the stage, nodding toward her audience.

It wasn't a hard task to cram the entire school into one room, but somehow the assembly hall seemed to have struggled nonetheless. Ninety-odd kids formed uneven, twisting rows across the vinyl floor and a handful of teachers sat on a single bench at the side of the hall.

On the stage, the policewoman cleared her throat. A quiet hum died down to silence as heads turned and people turned to listen.

'Okay,' Debbie said. 'Thanks to your head, first off, for gathering you all here.' She looked about as she spoke, locking eyes with a couple of kids on the back row. Immediately, they stopped whispering. Debbie rested her hands on a flat, wooden podium in front of her.

Charlotte watched as the policewoman rapped her fingers on the plinth. Whatever she was about to tell them, it was enough to make her nervous. Charlotte swallowed. What if something had happened to her dad?

No, she would know. She'd have felt something.

'I know a couple of you might have heard about what happened this morning,' Debbie continued. 'I'm here to clear some things up and just make everybody aware of what's going on.'

'What's she on about?' Darcy hissed, nudging

Charlotte with her elbow.

Charlotte shrugged. 'I guess we're about to find out,' she said quietly. They had chosen to sit right at the back of the hall, and she was glad for it. Something turned in her gut; the last time the police had been called in to talk to them all like this, someone had fallen off the clifftop and drowned.

This time, it looked worse.

Charlotte Kramer liked Debbie, despite everything. The woman was pretty much the only friend her dad had on the island, and she was nice. She had come over a couple of times, just to have a drink with Charlotte and her dad in front of the telly. She could be funny, once she had swallowed down a couple of glasses.

Right now, she looked more serious than she ever had. Debbie's eyes were dark. Her shoulders were hunched a little, tensed up.

'Do you think they found out about the arcade?' Darcy whispered.

'Don't be stupid,' Charlotte replied. 'Listen and see.'

Up on the stage, Debbie continued. 'There's been... an *incident,* on the beach. Two people...' Debbie paused. She looked around the hall. The place was silent. 'Two people have been killed. A young girl and -'

Debbie stopped, cut off by a sudden swell of chatter. Hushed whispers became murmurs and turned into discussions.

Darcy jammed her elbow into Charlotte's ribs, face

twisted with shock. 'What the fuck?' she hissed. 'Does she mean *murdered?*'

'*Shh.*'

Debbie raised a hand, kept it up until the chatter subsided. When the hall finally fell silent again, she carried on. 'I'm sorry to have to bring you news like this,' the detective said, 'but know that the police are doing everything we can to figure out what's happened and stop it from happening again.'

'What, all three of you?' someone called. A ripple of uneasy laughter shook the middle of the crowd. Debbie's face didn't change, and the laughter faded.

'We're doing everything we can,' Debbie said. 'Now, there's no reason so far to believe that this is the work of a man or woman. All the signs point toward a wild animal attack, at our best guess.'

'The hell kind of animal kills people?' Darcy whispered.

Charlotte shrugged. 'Panther?'

'What, on Cain's End? More like the Johnsons' little staffy terrier.'

'This does *not,*' Debbie said, 'mean you are unsafe, or that there's any cause for panic. However, I would recommend that until we can at least tell you more, everyone stays *away* from the cliffs and the forest down by the asylum. The beach is *absolutely* off limits. When school ends, I'd like to advise that you all head home and stay indoors until we've put an end to this. A call has gone out to everyone on the island, and a bus has been arranged for those of you who usually walk home.'

'So we have a curfew now?' came a voice from the back of the room.

'Not officially,' Debbie said, 'but I would strongly recommend that you don't stay out this evening and that you keep doors locked tonight, at the very least. When we know more, we'll pass that information on.'

'What kind of animal is it?' called another voice.

'Good question,' Debbie started. 'It... we don't know, not yet. But we are working on getting that information, and as soon as we have it we'll know how to deal with it. In that vein, if anybody *sees* anything, *tell* somebody. But in no circumstances should anyone go looking for this thing.'

She took a breath. 'Nobody else needs to die on this island.'

3

The air started to grow warmer as Kramer walked along the tunnel. Halfway along, the torch beam faltered. It flickered once, twice, then faded to a dull orange and died.

He barely noticed. His eyes were on the thing in the cavern ahead, spitting enough light into the tunnel that he almost had to squint.

At the end of the tunnel, the rock walls broke apart

and opened up on a space bigger than the cavern at the cave entrance. The ceiling here was too high for Kramer to see. The walls were painted with a criss-cross pattern of red and blue, veins that seemed to ripple and pulse in the unearthly glow of the thing in the middle of it all. The ground was worn rough here, uneven and crumbling and cracked in places.

Kramer shook his head. 'What the hell are you?' he breathed.

In the middle of the cavern, a sliver of light twisted and writhed in the air. Suspended a foot and a half above the ground, it was at least double Kramer's height and the width of a car.

Even as it shifted and shuddered, swelling and pulsing before him, it never once touched the walls of the cave. Kramer couldn't tear his eyes away from the thing, but he was afraid to look directly into it. The light hummed and whispered and *sang* as he watched, beckoning him forward, daring him to step closer.

Before he knew what he was doing, Kramer had reached out a hand.

The tips of his fingers brushed the face of the twisting, convulsing light and for a moment his flesh melted into it, disappeared into the white emptiness of the thing. A thick, muggy warmth spread over his palm as his arm vanished up to the elbow.

Kramer reeled back, yanking his hand out of the light. He could smell something, this close to the light, as if it was pushing an aroma out into the cavern. It reminded him of sulphur, of bad eggs and smouldering, hot stone.

Something whispered, the other side of the glimmering wall of light.

Kramer lifted his hand and pressed his palm to the face of the light. Breathing deeply, he pushed forward, let the dazzling face of the thing swallow his hand. There was that heat again, even stronger than the warmth he'd felt back in the tunnel. There was something through there...

Kramer exhaled and stepped forward. His arm disappeared, vanishing beyond the white, warped thing. The heat spread to his shoulder, brushed his face. This thing wasn't a wall, he realised, but a door. A gateway. And something on the other side was reaching for him.

'Christ, what the *fuck*...'

The light pulled him forward and Kramer stumbled, lost his balance, crumpling as he put his hands out to steady his fall -

The floor beneath him disappeared and he slipped, tumbling to the ground. One knee crashed into something soft beneath him and Kramer's wrists disappeared into a burned, thick powder that rose up in a cloud around him as he collapsed. Kramer scrambled to his feet, unsteady on the shifting ground. He cried out as his ankle sunk into the ground and a wave of heat passed over his face, and he looked up -

Kramer wasn't in the cave anymore. Christ, he wasn't on Cain's End anymore.

'Is this...'

The sky was an ocean of deep, sick red washed with traces of yellow and orange. Purple clouds fragmented and writhed as they closed in on a fat, bloated sun. The ground was a dense, boiled sand, crashing away from him and toward the blinding horizon in waves and pillows of deep, burnt fire. The desert stretched for miles, as far as Kramer could see, and he whirled around, fear settling like a sickness in his belly. In the distance, a wall of red rock and clay rose up and carved out great swathes of the sky. Scattered about the place, dead trees curled into claws. Gnarled, coiling roots reared up from the sand and whipped about in the sway of a hot, rushing wind.

Things crawled under the sand, screeching as they ploughed great trails of red dust into the air. Kramer turned and raised his eyes, blinking up at the wall of light he'd passed through. It spread and throbbed, different here, somehow corrupted on this side, bloody and splashed with red and black. Narrow, shining tendrils broke into the sky like the veins of a flat, bloodshot eye -

'Where the fuck am I?' Kramer whispered.

He looked back to the horizon, staring up at the diseased sun. Sweat drizzled over his forehead, pooling around his throat as he pulled at his shirt. The overcoat

226

around his shoulders trapped a sheen of heat at his back and he grimaced, shifting his weight in the sand -

'Oh, shit,' he murmured.

Forty or fifty feet away, a man in a white forensics suit lie still in the sand. Blood spattered the canvas of his uniform, bright and sickening in the pale glow of the sun.

Slowly, the man looked up, raising his head from the burnt dust of the ground. Red streaks erupted over one side of his face. Kramer couldn't see clearly from here, but it looked as if his eye was gone. A dark, black hole in his face oozed.

'*Run...*' the man croaked.

Kramer stepped forward. Behind him, the light whispered. 'I'm coming!' he yelled. 'Hang on!'

'*No!*' the forensics guy shrieked, raising a hand.

Kramer froze.

The man's arm had been shredded. His hand was a mangled, black mess of blood and bone, shining in the sun. Blood streamed down into the sand. Kramer shook his head, staring, mouth open.

'*Run!*'

Suddenly the sand shifted. Something moved beneath Kramer and he fell, stumbling off to one side as something thick and winding broke free of the ground and coiled upward. The worm was a dozen feet long and its tail thrashed about in the sand, throwing great clouds of dust into the humid air. It hissed with a hook-filled

227

maw, wild, wet tongue whipping about in its mouth. The thing's eyes glared a sickening, fleshy white as it lunged for him, entire body convulsing as it launched a spike-encrusted head toward Kramer's throat -

Kramer ducked to the side and the worm smacked into the sand, burrowing deep, tail flicking gobs of sand and stone at him as it disappeared beneath the ground.

'*Run, you idiot! Fucking run!*'

Kramer ran.

The wall of light screamed purple and red as he thrashed toward it, sluggish in the heat and the sand. The thing was on him in less than a second and it coiled around his legs and dragged him tumbling to his knees. In moments it was wrapped around his waist in a curled mess of dark, slippery skin and gnashing barbs.

Kramer smacked a fist against the thing's side and cursed as a thick, armoured layer of bone smacked right back, pushing up from beneath the worm's rubbery flesh. He fumbled with his belt, grabbing at the taser clipped there. He had almost forgotten about the thing. Frantically he squeezed the trigger, aiming blind as the thing lashed out at him -

Bzzz

The worm screeched and reeled back, thrashing wildly as strings of fragmented blue light threw its body into a fit of convulsions. Just for a second its grip on Kramer's legs was lost and he leapt forward, reaching desperately for the light -

Cold passed over him as something dragged him through the shivering mess of light and Kramer tumbled onto his back. Branches and dead twigs snapped beneath him as he rolled over, panting heavily. The heat was gone, dampened by a thin, autumn wind that bit at his face. Eyes closed, Kramer caught his breath, chest rising and falling as he laid there. His heart pounded.

'Fuck me...' he breathed.

Suddenly, he sat bolt upright and opened his eyes. He had expected to pass back through into the cave, to be met by the familiar drip of water and the cold of the black cavern in which he'd found the wall of light.

He was outside.

'Oh, this isn't right...' Kramer whispered.

Trees rose up around him, thick trunks brittle with the biting wind and stripped of leaves. The ground was a maze of foliage and crumbled bones and deep, black earth. Slowly, Kramer stood up, stared into the dark.

Beyond the trees, lit in the glare of a full, bright moon, a crooked house loomed above him. Firelight crackled behind the windows.

Kramer turned around, narrowed his eyes at the light. It was calmer here, a little darker. Faded, perhaps. It whispered softly at him, *come back. Come home.*

Kramer took one last look at the crooked house and stepped through the light, disappearing into the rippling wall of white with barely a sound.

A few moments passed, and the light flickered and

disappeared.

The forest was silent.

4

The sky was dark when Kramer stumbled out of the cave.

He glanced up at the sky, stumbling awkwardly over the sand. His head was throbbing. Above him the moon had risen and it dangled behind slivers of thin, black cloud, full and glowing. White shivers of moonlight danced over the waves. The wind was stronger than it had been when he had first gone into the cave.

Kramer's mind was dull as he walked, numb to the bite of the air and the sound of the waves as they tore the shore apart.

Slowly, Kramer pulled himself up to the clifftop, staggering exhausted along the ramp with one hand on the face of the cliff. Once he'd reached the ledge he paused for breath, stepping over the blue tape that appeared grey in the moonlight. He fumbled in his coat for a rattling set of keys. The police car was still parked where he had left it, a little way from the edge of the cliff. The thing was a battered shell of painted metal and glass and it looked like a wreck in the dark. Kramer unlocked the car and slid into the driver's seat. The leather was cold.

For a while he sat there, head down, eyes forward.

What the fuck had he just seen?

Something buzzed in Kramer's pocket. His brow furrowed as he grabbed for his phone and opened it up. His eyes darted to the time at the top of the screen and he swore. It had gone seven.

Christ, *hours* had passed. How long had he been through there? It had felt like minutes, the other side of the shimmering barrier of light. Barely that. But it was like time had passed quicker this side of the cave. A whole lot quicker.

'Shit,' Kramer said.

Three missed calls from Deb. One from Charlie. A text message flickered up at him. *Where the fuck r u?*

Kramer opened the message to send a reply. For a minute, his thumb hovered above the screen. He locked the phone.

It was a difficult question to answer. Besides, he needed to get home. Charlie would be waiting for him. God, she would be shit-scared by now.

The engine shuddered into life and Kramer slid the car into first. He turned away from the cliff, pulling the old vehicle away from the cliff and towards the village. The car bumped over rough dirt and gravel as he drove, eyes dull and focused on the windscreen as the headlights threw beams of white over the track. Kramer's thoughts were a murk of white lights and glaring, bloated suns and he swallowed. Sweat drizzled down his brow. Quickly he rolled the car window down, letting the cool night air draw over his face.

Christ, he needed a drink.

He blinked, and in that half-second of darkness he saw red sand and twisted, dead trees. He saw the face of the guy in the forensics suit. Blood stained the man's teeth and splashed his haunted eyes. Kramer saw the thrashing, black-skinned worm's wet, grey mouth open to reveal rows and rows of curved, sharpened teeth as it reared up above him, trembling and quivering and shrieking wildly.

'Stop it,' Kramer hissed, blinking the image away. His heel tapped the footbed, leg shuddering uncontrollably. God, he *really* needed that drink.

Ahead of him the squat, grey buildings at the edge of the village rolled over ploughed fields and rough, green-brown tracks. The dirt road stretched and became a wide, flat strip of tarmac as Kramer slid the car into the village. On the corner of the high street, a little supermarket was closing down for the nights. Lights blinked off as Kramer passed, turning a corner onto his road. Slowly, he pulled to a stop outside the house.

The car's engine cut to a grinding halt and Kramer sat, hands on the wheel. His skin was blistered, he realised, from the heat of that place the other side of the shining gateway.

'Shouldn't have gone to that damn cave,' he whispered. 'Should have let it be.'

Kramer closed his eyes, breathed in. He inhaled

deeply, taking in the cool air and the tobacco smoke that wafted toward him from the direction of the Crow's Head. He considered, for a moment, going down to the pub. Christ knew he needed a drink.

'Should have let it be.'

Slowly Kramer looked up at the house, peering through the greasy windscreen of the old police car.

Charlotte's light was on. He saw a shadow moving about in there, pacing the room.

That drink would have to wait.

CHAPTER NINE
MONSTERS OF CAIN'S END

1
NOW

Hayley tilted her head back, lips parted a little. She ran her hands through her hair as hot water fell around her; steam rose in the shower and settled on the glass walls as it spattered the floor, running off the curves of her body in thin, clear sheets.

She thought, for a little while, about Emma. The young nurse was cooking something in the other room, and Hayley could smell it above the steam. It reminded her of something, some meal her mum used to make. Back when she lived with her parents, *way* back before she moved out here.

Emma had invited Hayley around for the second night in a row, and she had accepted. Usually, she would've worried about what people would say. They would talk, and *really* talk this time.

Tonight, Hayley had other things to worry about.

Before long any thought of Emma was lost beneath the wash of the water and the heat that surrounded her and Hayley's troubled mind was a haze of condensation-streaked images and messy, scribbled thoughts. Red spatters stained the sand. Hayley stepped forward, bare, soaked feet planted in the grass at the clifftop. Bile rose in her throat. Steam in her nostrils. She could smell the salt on the wind, the blood on the air...

Hayley gasped as the water scalded her, stumbling back out of the spray. She fumbled blindly with the shower controls, twisting a fat, metal-plated knob until the water calmed to a pleasant warmth. Hayley counted the seconds as she stood with her back against the tiled wall. *One. Two. Three.* She rested her hands on her bare thighs, bending double to catch her breath.

Hayley watched as strings of water ran down the glass door in front of her, racing each other in erratic zigzags to the shower tray. Her eyes froze, gaze locked on a swill of water in the basin. Red clouds gathered in the water, beads of crimson trailing up the glass and spreading...

Hayley clapped a hand over her mouth. 'No...'

She could still see them, lying there on the beach. Bodies torn and spread apart like discarded hunks of meat on a butcher's table. Lumps and knots of red muscle and flesh were strung together with pulled tendons and broken, cracked fragments of bone.

They looked up at her with blank, hollow eyes. The man smiled softly, his shredded jaw hanging loose from bloody, wet teeth. Slowly, the sand started to swallow him up, crawling over his torn skin and seeping between his exposed ribs.

'*No...*'

'You okay in there?' Emma called from the other room.

Hayley looked up, wincing as the water stung her eyes. Water smacked the shower tray around her, thundering against the glass walls of the shower. She felt exposed, suddenly, as though someone was watching her.

'I'm good,' she lied.

Hayley pressed her palms to the tiles behind her back and slid down the wall until she was sat in the warm swell of shower water in the tray. She had watched Emma lock the front door behind them. She had checked.

There was no way he could have followed them.

Still, there was no way he could have murdered those two kids, down at the beach. He had been locked up the whole night. They had him on tape. And yet...

Edward Drake wasn't like the other patients at Black River Asylum. They had tried to call him a psychopath, but it went deeper than that. Deeper than anything Hayley had ever seen before. It was like Eddie was so far removed from his inhibitions, from his emotions that he had lost the ability to feel altogether.

Like he had murdered the parts of his brain responsible for emotion and left the rest to keep on killing.

Hayley's head shot up. Something moved over the tiles. A shadow beyond the steam. A soft, near-silent footstep.

'Hello?'

Hayley looked toward the door, but couldn't see it beyond the mist and the water. Slowly, she stood up from the tray, the soft slap of her feet muffled by the pounding of the water. She stepped forward, reaching for the glass with a shaking hand. Cautiously she wiped a streak of condensation away with her palm. The glass cleared.

The door was ajar. Hayley's breath hitched in her throat.

He's in here.

Hayley's hand moved to her mouth and her eyes widened as she stepped back, almost skidding over in the water. A hand shot out behind her and she fumbled blindly for something to hold on to. *Oh god,* she thought, *he's in here with me.*

He's right here.

Footsteps on the tiles. Hayley's eyes darted toward the source of the noise but she couldn't see. Hayley searched frantically for the shower controls, hand trembling behind her back. She couldn't find them.

He can see me, she thought. *He's in here with me. God, he's...*

What if he was already in the shower with her?

Hayley gasped, turning wildly, searching every inch of the glass-walled cubicle. Hot, steaming water ran heavy with fog and something moved beyond the glass, something tall, something shaped like a person, like *him...*

Hayley opened her mouth to scream.

The shower door opened and she recoiled; the skin of her back smacked the wall and she sunk down to the floor, eyes round and wet. Tears streamed down her face as she sobbed, bunching her head up in her elbows.

Emma leaned across her, ignoring the spray of water that darkened her blouse as she reached for the controls and turned off the shower. She knelt down, laid her hand on Hayley's bare shoulder. Hayley flinched.

'It's okay,' Emma whispered. 'It's only me.'

Hayley nodded. 'I know,' she whimpered. Tears stung her eyes. 'I know. I thought... I know.'

'Let's get you dressed,' Emma said. 'I think you need to get into bed, get some rest.'

'I thought you were...' Hayley whispered.

'I know,' Emma said quietly. 'Come on, it's okay. He's not going to get you in here.'

Charlotte was halfway down the stairs by the time Kramer had opened the front door. Her face was dark as thunder and she stormed for him as he fumbled with the lock, flashed him a look that said *I am going to* smack *you.*

'What the *fuck* is going on?' the girl snapped. 'You think you're funny, disappearing after everything that's happened today? Debbie came down to the school, did you know that? Told us there's some *animal* on the loose or something, and then you just go and fucking...'

She trailed off as Kramer took a step forward and wrapped his arms around her. 'It's okay,' he whispered. 'I'm sorry, Charlie. It's all going to be okay.'

'Dad, what's going on?'

Kramer held her for a minute, eyes closed. He trembled a little beneath the grey overcoat that pulled at his shoulders. Sand had filtered into his shoes through the eyelets of his laces and it shifted beneath his soles as he stood, breathing shallow, waiting for his heart to slow. 'It's okay,' he said again.

Charlotte pulled away from him, looked him up and down. Kramr's face was dark, his eyes haunted by some unseen thing. Charlotte's eyes flickered to his knuckles; still red and peeling, but no worse than they had been last night. And she couldn't smell whiskey on his breath, not tonight. But there was something there, in his face...

he had seen something. Something terrible. Tenderly, Charlotte brushed her father's arm with a pale hand. 'Dad, I was worried about you...'

Kramer looked down at her, and his eyes changed. His face twisted into a weak, apologetic smile. 'I'm sorry,' he said. 'It's been a long day, love. I would've called you...'

'You *should* have called me,' Charlotte said. 'What the fuck have you been *doing?*'

Kramer frowned. 'Language,' he said quietly.

'Seriously? Dad, what's *happening?* I nearly called *Debbie,* that's how worried I was! Tell me what's going on or I swear I will call her right now and ask her to tell me what you won't.'

'Charlotte... let's go through to the kitchen, yeah?' Kramer said. His throat was dry and hoarse; despite the cold, he could still feel sweat running over his chest. 'Let me get some water, then I'll tell you everything.'

Maybe not everything, he thought.

Charlotte hesitated. 'Okay,' she nodded after a moment. She followed him into the kitchen, moving to the counter beside the sink. She pulled herself up onto the worktop and folded her arms, watching as Kramer took a glass and filled it from the sink, drained the water in one long swallow.

There was sand on the back of his wrist.

'So, are you going to talk to me?' Charlotte said.

Beside her, Kramer had turned the tap back on and

was holding the glass beneath it. Water splashed into the empty container and he watched it, half-dazed. His face was blank.

'Dad?'

Kramer looked up, turning off the tap. He moved to the counter beside her, setting the glass down. He laid a hand on the surface to steady himself; it was trembling, Charlotte noticed.

'I don't know what to tell you,' Kramer said quietly.

'What's that supposed to mean?'

Kramer looked into the girl's eyes and shook his head. 'I don't know where to *start*.'

'Start with the animal. What is it?'

'I don't know,' he said. 'I thought... I don't know. I thought it was a dog, or something. Some rich bastard's mental pet, let loose on the beach. Or... I don't know. Wouldn't be the first time someone's ditched an unwanted family member on the island and got straight back on the ferry.'

'But it's not a dog, is it?'

'I thought so. Then we spoke to Creed. You know, the mad old farmer down the road? His cows were... they... well, he saw the animal do it. He said it was bigger than any dog. Like a *wolf,* he said, except... not a wolf. And then...'

Kramer thought about the things beneath the sand in that other place, the place beyond the wall of light in the cave. What if something had come through? What if there were others - like the worms, maybe, but capable of moving *above* the sand, capable of getting through the gate. After all, if Kramer could stumble through it into whatever crippled place they came from... maybe something could follow him back.

Maybe...

'It's big,' he said finally. He nodded. 'It's big, and it's dangerous, and I can't tell you any more than that until I've seen it for myself. But I need you to stay here. No school tomorrow, Charlie. Okay? You stay inside until we've caught this thing.'

Charlotte paused. 'Okay.'

Kramer reached for the glass, took another drink.

'So you're not going to kill it?'

Kramer swallowed. 'I don't know, Charlie. It's... if it really is some wild animal, it's just doing what it does. It's new to the island, it's scared. I... I don't know how we deal with this, kid.'

'And if it wasn't an animal?' Charlotte said. 'Would you kill it then? You know, if it was a person?'

Kramer cocked an eyebrow. 'We'd *arrest* it then.'

'Fair point.' Charlotte said quietly.

Kramer looked at her, then, and for the first time since he'd stepped inside the house he *saw* her. 'Are you okay, Charlie? I'm sorry about today, I really am. If I could have called you, I would. You know that, yeah?'

Charlotte smiled. 'I know, dad. And I'm okay. I just... I worry.'

'You don't need to worry about me, love. That's my job.'

'You've got more than enough on your plate,' Charlotte said. 'Look, is there... is there anything else you need to tell me?'

Kramer frowned. Maybe Debbie had let something slip. Christ, maybe *he* had let something slip. 'Why do you ask?'

'You just... don't seem like you lately,' Charlotte said quietly. Her eyes fell to the floor as she swung her legs, heels bumping the cabinet beneath the counter. 'You're quiet. You... you've been drinking again.'

Kramer paused. 'I'm sorry,' he whispered.

She looked up at him, eyes deep and sad. 'You know I'm here,' Charlotte said.

'I know,' Kramer said, and he reached out an arm, laying his hand on the girl's back.

Charlotte let her head fall on his shoulder and gripped him tight and they held each other for a long time.

Kramer blinked away a salty tear and closed his eyes. 'I'm not going to let anything happen to you, Charlie.'

'I know, dad. But you look after yourself, too.'

Kramer nodded.

'I think Debbie might *adopt* me if you get eaten.'

Kramer laughed, pulled away from her. He reached for the glass of water and took a long sip, wincing as it peeled down his throat. 'Trust me,' he said, 'you'd be in much better hands. But there's no way I'm letting this thing get me, or her, or you, okay?'

'Okay.'

Kramer paused for a moment.

Charlotte frowned, scanning his face. 'What is it?'

'You know when you were little, you used to have those dreams?' Kramer said.

Charlotte swallowed.

'You know,' Kramer continued, 'when you were a kid. The dreams with the forest, and that house. You called it the crooked house. Do you remember?'

Charlotte nodded. 'Why?' she asked slowly.

'Do you think you could draw it, for me? I know you used to do little sketches, I need... I need to see it.'

'It's been a while,' Charlotte lied.

'Fair enough,' Kramer said. 'Just a thought.

'Is it to do with the monster?' Charlotte said quietly.

'I don't know,' Kramer said, shaking his head. 'But it could be.'

Charlotte nodded, sliding off the counter. 'I'll go see if I can find any of my old drawings.'

The girl moved silently into the hall, didn't make a sound till she had reached her bedroom. She shut the door behind her and exhaled deeply, eyes closed. She saw it, then, the old house in the woods, orange lights behind the windows. She shivered. Revisiting those nightmares when she was awake... it was enough to make her blood run cold.

But that wasn't the worst thing.

Kramer hadn't flinched when she had said *monster*. He hadn't even *blinked*.

3

There was no birdsong, when morning came.

Debbie Martin watched through her bedroom window as the moon sunk into a hazy blue horizon, replaced with a glaring sun and the makings of a tight, grey stormcloud. The wind hadn't let up all night, and the rain had been loud enough that, even with the covers pulled around her head, she hadn't slept more than a couple of hours. It was still raining now, although it had slowed a little.

Debbie moved back to her bed and knelt on the carpet, leaning her elbows on the mattress. Breathing deeply, the woman bowed her head, closing her eyes. 'Morning,' she said quietly, folding her fingers together in a tight knot. 'Me again. Just... checking in. If you're listening.'

She paused. Behind her head, rain pounded on the window. She fancied, for a moment, that she could hear another sound over the steady hammering, but it was quickly drowned out and she shook it off.

'Anyway...' Debbie said. 'I know I don't normally ask for things, but... I'm struggling down here. If you can hear me, I just don't know what to do. Me and Matt, we've got to find this thing, and... I don't know what we're looking for. Honestly, if you could just...'

Debbie started as something pounded on the door, louder than the rain. Somebody was knocking. She scrambled up from the floor and rushed downstairs, taking them two at a time. A silhouette through the frosted glass peered inside.

'One second!' Debbie called, moving to the door. She fumbled with the lock and yanked it open, shuddering as wind flushed her face and drifted over the material of her pyjamas. They were her favourites; they had magpies on them.

'Morning,' Kramer said.

Debbie blinked. 'Matt? What are you doing here?' Quickly, she ushered him in, standing aside as she held the door open.

Kramer stepped quickly into the hall, brushing droplets of grey water out of his hair. He had changed into a pale, off-white shirt and a blood-red tie, but the overcoat stayed. Debbie had seldom seen him out of it. 'I'm sorry,' Kramer said. 'I should have called ahead.'

'You should have answered my calls, you mean.'

'Sorry,' Kramer repeated.

Debbie closed the door behind him. 'Why are you here? It's six forty-five in the morning, Matt. I know we should be out there, but we've got nothing to go on. And I know you can run full steam on a couple of hours sleep, but I know what I'd be up against. It's not like we can comb the island when we don't even know what we're -'

She stopped, then. She saw it in his face. An urgency.

'Couldn't wait any longer,' Kramer said. 'There's something I need to show you, Deb.'

'And it couldn't have waited *just* the extra hour till I'd have come into the station?' Debbie said, beckoning Kramer into the kitchen and reaching for a tea towel. 'Dry yourself up, Matt. What's going on?'

Kramer nodded, taking the towel and dabbing at his forehead, pushing damp hair out of his eyes. A cool trickle of water shivered down the back of his neck.

Debbie walked a rusted, black kettle to her sink and held it under the tap. She poured water into the thing, flipping the lid closed as Kramer started to talk. With her back to him, she remembered she was still in her pyjamas. Fuck, she must have looked like such a child. *Well, if you will come to my house so early in the morning...*

'Remember when Jamie told us one of his forensics guys found something in the cave?' Kramer said.

Debbie nodded, switching on the kettle. She turned and folded her arms, leaning against the worktop. She looked Kramer over, one eyebrow raised; the man's eyes were bright, almost frenzied, but circled with the unmistakeable red rings of exhaustion.

'I remember,' Debbie said. 'And then you went to check it out, and you full-on disappeared for the rest of the day. Do you know how difficult it was to get anywhere with this damn wild animal thing without you here?'

Kramer swallowed. 'I'm sorry. Look, this thing in the cave...'

'Matt, don't change the subject. Where *were* you?'

'I'm trying to tell you,' Kramer said. An unmistakeable flash of frustration crossed his face.

Debbie winced.

'I'm sorry,' Kramer said quietly. 'It... I didn't mean to...'

'It's okay,' Debbie said. 'So tell me.'

'It was a door, Deb. In the cave. It was like... I don't know, it was like this big, white light. But it *opened.* Like a gateway.'

'Like a gateway,' Debbie said slowly. Behind her, the kettle started to whistle. She ignored it.

'I went through,' Kramer said. 'I didn't even mean to, but... I reached out and touched it, this light, and it kind of pulled me in. And there was... Christ, I sound mental. There was another place on the other side. Like a desert, except the sky was all wrong. Like the air was sick. And I swear, Deb, I was in there for *minutes.* Then it spat me back out in the cave and... I don't know, hours had passed.'

'Right,' Debbie said. 'And how much have you been drinking lately?'

Kramer frowned. 'What?'

'Matt,' Debbie sighed, setting down her mug, 'I know you've got a lot going on. It's Charlie's birthday tomorrow, and you have to tell her... you know. And now this creature... *I'd* drink, if I were you.'

'No, no, I'm not... you don't understand. I wouldn't just make this up, Debbie. And I'm not drunk, I swear to you. I know... I know how messed-up this sounds.'

'So why tell me?' Debbie shrugged. 'You can't have thought I'd believe any of this, Matt. Why bother? This story, it's ridiculous.'

'There were creatures through there, Debbie. Like nothing I've ever seen before. What if the thing that we're trying to find came from the other side?'

'Matt, you need to sleep,' Debbie said quietly, stepping forwards. She laid a hand on his arm, brushed his sleeve. 'Maybe we need to see about getting you some help. All this stress, and the drink... I think it's messing you up.'

'I'm not crazy,' Kramer said. 'I'm not drunk.'

'I don't think I can believe that.'

Kramer paused. 'Then let me show you.'

Debbie shook her head. 'Matt, I'm not going into that cave. Bright light or not, we've got bigger things to deal with than your overactive imagination.'

'No, not that,' Kramer said, 'let me show you I'm sober.'

'How?'

'Breathalyser,' Kramer said. 'In the car.'

'Matt, you don't need to...'

Debbie's eyes fell to Kramer's belt and she frowned, catching a glimpse of something half-obscured by the folds of his sodden overcoat. 'Where's your taser?' she said.

Kramer looked down, blinked. His eyes came up again and he paused.

'Where is it?' Debbie said.

'I dropped it,' Kramer said. 'Zapping a giant tapeworm.'

'You're ridiculous,' Debbie said. The hint of a smile brushed her lips. 'Go on,' she said, nodding to the front door as she turned to the kettle. 'Go get the breathalyser. If you pass, we'll go check the cave, alright? If only to prove you wrong.'

Kramer disappeared into the hall and Debbie listened to his footsteps fade. She poured steaming water into a mug and stirred in some coffee, wincing as the metal spoon scraped the rim of the cup. She took a long, deep drink as the front door opened and closed. The rain outside seemed to have faded to a light drizzle, but any respite would be short-lived.

She hoped Kramer didn't pass the test. Either he was pissed, or he was mad.

Debbie swallowed. The third option, she supposed, was worse. What if, somehow, he was telling the truth?

For the first time since she'd known him, Debbie wished Matthew Kramer was lying about being drunk.

250

4

Charlotte reached for the buzzing phone on her bedside cabinet, groaning loudly. Blinking sleep out of her eyes, she checked the time on the display before answering. Coming up to eight. *Far* too early.

'Hello?' Charlotte murmured, bringing the mobile to her ear as she slumped back down onto the pillow. Her sheets were freshly washed, and they smelled good. She was glad of a day off school, whatever the reason - a part of her wanted to be pissed at her dad for telling her to stay indoors, but another was relieved. A day without Mr Crawford and his narrow little weasel eyes. A day to catch up on some of the sleep she'd missed the last few days.

'Charlie? Have you forgotten?'

Charlotte frowned, grinding dust out of her right eye with the heel of her fist. She hadn't bothered to check the caller ID, but even in her hazy state of half-sleep, she recognised the voice. 'Forgotten what?' she said.

'The pier,' Darcy hissed. 'The arcade, remember? You said you'd think about it?'

'I did,' Charlotte nodded. 'I've thought about it, Darcy. I'm not going. Neither should you lot, not with this thing out there.'

'You're kidding, right? It's the *perfect* time. Everybody's hid up indoors, Charlie. School's off, so it's not like we'll be missed.'

'I'll tell you who is out there,' Charlotte said. 'My *dad.*'

'Oh, come on, Charlie. It's your sixteenth tomorrow, it's not like he can stay mad at you. Besides, we'll be sneaky.'

Charlotte sighed.

'We're outside the Crow's Head now,' Darcy continued. 'Some rabid dog isn't going to scare us off. Come on, look out your window!'

Charlotte stumbled out of bed, kicking the tangled sheets away from her ankles. Wearily she moved to the window and pulled pale, cactus-pattern curtains aside. She could see the whole street from here, and off to her left the main road that ran through the village. She caught a glimpse of movement outside the pub - the Crow's Head was right on the corner, and she had a direct line of sight on the face of the building.

Darcy waved up at her from the gravel drive of the pub, grinning like mad. Above her head, a wooden sign swung loftily in the breeze. The rain had slowed, but the dark-skinned girl had a hood pulled up over her hair. There were two other kids with her. The first was Liam Porter, Darcy's boyfriend, about a head taller than her and standing with his back to the window, talking to the second. Sparrow, as scrawny as he'd ever been, was wrapped in a thick, green puffa jacket. The two boys were laughing over something.

'What happened to the others?' Charlotte asked, waving back through the window.

'Same as you,' Darcy said. 'Chickened out. Thought I could count on you though, Charlie. Nice pyjamas, by the way.'

'Shut up,' Charlotte said, snapping the curtains shut. She turned back to the bed.

'So are you coming?'

Charlotte paused. There was something about the way her dad had been acting last night that made her afraid. But surely this thing couldn't really be a monster.

Darcy was right - why should they be scared of a dog? They knew it was out there. Already, they had an advantage over the two people that it had...

The two people it had killed.

'I can't,' Charlotte said. 'I'm sorry.'

'Seriously, Charlie? Come on,' Darcy said, 'be brave. Come do something *fun.*'

Charlotte didn't reply.

'I'm sorry,' Darcy said quietly. 'Look, you don't have to come. Just won't be as cool without you, is all.'

Charlotte shook her head. This was stupid.

God, this was so *stupid.*

'Give me ten minutes to get dressed,' she said. 'But I'm not coming out for long, okay? We go, we take a look, and if you want to hang around you do that. But I'm coming straight back.'

'Chicken,' Darcy said.

'Damn right.'

Charlotte hung up, pulled the curtains closed as she tossed the phone onto her bed. Quickly she moved to the wardrobe across the room and dug around for something to wear; yellow jumper and jeans would do just fine. She gathered them up in her arms and crossed to the hall, sidling past the banister towards the bathroom to get showered.

Her eyes caught a flash of white at the top of the banister and she paused.

There was a crisp, square slip of paper taped to the wood, where she'd be sure to see it. Charlotte reached down, took the note and read. She swallowed, hard, as a twist of guilt curled about in her belly.

Stay indoors, her dad had written. *Be safe. Will let you know when we catch this thing. See you later. Dad x*

Charlotte folded the note and stuffed it into the pocket of her pyjama bottoms. *Catch,* it said. Not *kill.*

'I'm sorry,' Charlotte whispered, and she opened the bathroom door and stepped inside.

5

'This is the first time I've ever been down here,' Debbie whispered, sweeping the beam of her flashlight about. '*Years* I've been on this island, and I never once thought to come check out the caves.' She crept along the wall, pushing the wide beam of a torch into the dark. Light passed over the bloody writing on the opposite wall and she shuddered.

'Just a little further,' Kramer said, nodding forward. He walked behind his partner, eyes on the ground as he stepped carefully in her tracks. His own torch was still down here somewhere. Hopefully, he thought, on *this* side of the wall. His eyes snapped up as they walked and he directed Debbie to the next cavern. This was where he'd first seen the tunnel.

'God, you bring me to the most romantic places,' Debbie murmured, glancing up at the ceiling. It was black and scarred and dripping; in places, the water had been running for so long that the rock appeared to have softened and it glowed an eerie, translucent silver in the torchlight.

'I do my best,' Kramer said. They stood for a moment in the first cavern, a vast chamber of shadows that swallowed the light of the torch before it could hit the bumpy walls. It was oddly silent in here, save for the steady drip of greywater - like the shadows had somehow eaten up any sound, too.

'Where now?' Debbie said. She shivered. 'This place gives me the creeps.'

'Turn off the torch for a second,' Kramer said.

'What?' Debbie whirled round, shot him a wide-eyed look. Her face glowed a deep orange as the beam flicked upward, and Kramer shook his head.

'Only for a second,' he reassured her. 'You'll see.'

Debbie paused. 'Fine,' she said, 'but for *one* second. Then it comes back on. And no sneaky business, mister.'

'Promise.'

With a *click,* the light died. The two of them were thrown into pitch-darkness. Above Debbie's head, something wet scuttled over the rocks.

Kramer waited for the purple spots to fade from his vision and looked around, searching for the opening of the tunnel. If the doorway was still there, its light would bleed out of the tunnel like it had before and guide them forwards.

'It's gone,' Kramer said.

'What do you mean? Matt, if you've dragged me out here for nothing...'

'Shh,' Kramer said, raising a finger.

Debbie opened her mouth to protest, but she said nothing. She watched as Kramer's silhouette moved in the dark, hand still raised as he listened.

'Can you hear it?' Kramer whispered. He looked back to where Debbie had been standing, but he couldn't see her face in the shadows. He waited, trying to locate the source of the sound. It was quieter than before; a subtle hiss in the air, like radio static. An electric tingle accompanied it.

Behind him, Debbie shook her head. 'Nothing,' she said. 'Can I turn this torch back on now?'

'It has to be here,' Kramer breathed. 'It has to be.' He

turned his head toward the noise, narrowing his eyes. Just for the tiniest fraction of a second, a pale light flickered in the shadows. 'There!' he said. Too loud. His voice echoed off the walls and he winced. 'Did you see it?'

The torch came back on and the cavern filled up with light. Kramer saw it, now that his eyes were pointed in the right direction; the tunnel entrance, a narrow sliver of black in the rock.

'I'll take your word for it,' Debbie said, scanning the place. 'Go on, then. Take me to it.'

Kramer paused, turning back to her. He remembered why they were here. He had been so focused on finding the light again, he realised, that he had almost forgotten what was on the other side of it. The horrors of that other place...

'Take my hand,' Kramer said, holding it out to her.

Debbie raised an eyebrow. 'You really don't think I can handle myself, do you?'

Kramer looked at her, tiny spots of light glowing in his eyes in a muted reflection of the torchlight. 'It's not that,' he said quietly.

Slowly, Debbie smiled, slid her hand into his. 'Are you...'

'Yes,' he said. 'Just in case I don't get to do it later.'

Debbie pulled him closer, letting the torch hang by her side. The outline of her face was bathed in a pale orange. 'Go on, then,' she whispered. 'Ask me.'

Kramer gripped the woman's hand and smiled weakly. 'Do you want to go for a drink when this is all over?'

'Of course not,' Debbie said, shaking her head. Her face wrinkled in disgust.

Kramer blinked.

'I'm kidding,' Debbie said quietly. She squeezed his hand. 'You better take me somewhere nice, though. No more caves.'

'Promise,' Kramer said. Slowly he leaned forward, moved his hands to Debbie's waist and kissed her deeply. 'Just in case,' he murmured against her lips as Debbie kissed him back. She smelled nice, he noticed, even in the damp of the cave, and the scent washed over him as Debbie reached up and slid her fingers into his tangled hair, pulling his face deeper into hers before she pulled away, taking a breath.

'Do you know how long I've been waiting for that?' Debbie whispered.

'Not as long as I have,' Kramer said.

Debbie smiled in the dark. 'You know this doesn't change anything, right? If there's no crazy wall of light through that tunnel, Matt, I'm taking you down to Black River for an evaluation.'

'Sounds fair.'

'Course it is,' Debbie said, and she kissed him again. 'Let's go,' she whispered.

Kramer held her hand tight as they moved through

the tunnel, sliding into the dark with the torch held high before them. The passageway was narrow and Debbie led the way, playing the beam over the shadows as they stepped through into the next cavern. It was bigger than the first, and even with the torch beam on full there was no way to gauge the size of the place. The walls were masked by shadow, the floor a rough patchwork of rock and granite.

The two of them stood for a moment, staring into the dark.

The cavern was empty.

'Maybe it closed,' Kramer said quietly. 'It was here, Deb, honestly. I can't...'

'Then let's wait,' Debbie said, shrugging. 'Maybe you're right.'

'But it can't have just gone,' Kramer said. 'It can't have.' He stepped forward, into the centre of the space, looked all around him. It was empty. His eyes settled on Debbie's face and his expression sagged. 'You don't believe me, do you?'

'Not in the slightest,' Debbie shook his head. 'But I know you're not crazy. And if you're not pissed... well, let's wait and see.'

Kramer stood where the wall of light had been, face dark with worry. He raised a hand - the same hand that he'd first pushed into the shimmering doorway - and held it before his face. Something tingled over his fingertips. The air still felt strange on his skin, humming with the same raw, bristling energy that he'd felt before. But the light had gone. The doorway had shut.

'Is that your torch?' Debbie said suddenly, nodding at a space on the ground a few feet away from where Kramer was standing.

Kramer followed her gaze, frowning. His gaze fell on the thing and he nodded. 'Yeah, that's mine. Must have rolled away from where I dropped it.' Quickly he stepped across to the torch, reaching down to grab it. 'Hopefully it's started working again,' he murmured, wrapping his fingers around the metal shaft. It was slippery beneath his palm, covered in a thick, clear mucus, and he reeled back from it. He glanced at his hand and his mouth opened. The stuff was dark and murky, riddled with bloody gobs and swirls of spittle. He looked back at the torch. The stuff was oozed all along the shaft, a coat of phlegm that stunk of meat and scorched wood.

He recognised that smell...

'Oh, shit,' Kramer breathed.

'What is it?' Debbie said behind him.

'Get out,' Kramer said, frozen to the spot. Slowly, hardly daring to make a sound, he wiped the mucus off onto his trousers.

'What?' Debbie frowned.

'You need to get out of the cave,' Kramer hissed. 'It's here.'

Debbie paused. 'The creature?' she whispered.

Kramer shook his head. 'Not the creature. Not *our* creature.'

'I don't understand,' Debbie said. 'What is...'

'The worm,' Kramer said. 'From the other side of the gate.'

'Matt...' Debbie started.

Kramer turned round. Opened his mouth to explain. In the dark above his head, something moved, slithering over the ceiling. Kramer's eyes flickered up and his jaw clamped shut.

'Matt?' Debbie said. 'What is it?'

'Run,' Kramer breathed. 'Debbie, turn around. Get out of here. You need to *run*.'

Debbie ignored him. Anchored in place, she frowned. Slowly, without a word, she lifted the beam of the torch to the ceiling, following the direction of Kramer's wild-eyed stare. Something stuck in her throat as the torch beam lit the roof of the cave. 'Oh my god...'

There were half a dozen of them, clinging to the curved rock of the ceiling. Their lumpen, twisted bodies were suckered to the rock somehow, holding them up there. Armoured, thick skin shimmered and glistened. A thick coat of grey-brown mucus drooled over them and formed great hanging trails in the dark. Each of the creatures was a foot wide and three or four metres tall and they curled and coiled over each other, hanging like slippery cocoons in the shadows. The quivered and pulsated with every breath, and a low whisper slipped out of their bloody mouths. Thick, bulbous tails drooped down from the ceiling, lined with barbed hooks and spines. Fat heads erupted into spirals of curved teeth.

'Are they... sleeping?' Debbie whispered.

'I think we'd be dead if they weren't,' Kramer murmured. 'Deb, we need to get out of here. Now.'

Debbie stepped backwards, moving towards the tunnel as quietly as she could. Her eyes were fixed on the shimmering worm-creatures hanging above her head. 'This can't be real,' she whispered. 'What the fuck are they?'

Kramer stepped towards her, sticking to the pale circles of light that the torch cast on the ground. 'I don't know, Deb, but I'm gonna need you to run.'

Debbie nodded, never taking her eyes off the ceiling. She took another step back.

Kramer's eyes widened. 'Careful!'

Debbie took another step backwards and her elbow crashed into the wall of the tunnel. She swore as the torch flew out of her hand, skittered over the ground. Crooked shafts of light danced wildly on the walls. 'Shit!'

Above them, something moved.

'*Run!*' Kramer yelled.

Debbie stumbled into the tunnel, staggering through the dark; she cried out as the passageway twisted off to one side and she grazed her shoulder on the rock, turning the corner. She whirled around, scanning the dark desperately for Kramer.

He stumbled forward and grabbed her arm, pulling her forwards. Behind them something rasped and a hot, stale vapour wafted through the air. There was a sound like a wet, damp squelching as the creatures started to drop from the ceiling, slapping their bodies against the rock in a thick, glistening mess of mucus.

Kramer and Debbie burst out into the next cavern and something *shrieked.* The sound echoed off the walls around them as they rushed toward the entrance to the cave, following a steady haze of daylight. The screaming grew louder and shadows writhed in the dark; the worms had woken up, and they were hungry.

Something snapped at Kramer's ankle and he cried out, stumbling onto his knees.

'Matt!' Debbie yelled, grabbing for his hand as he fell. She pulled him up quickly as the worm reared up, hissing with a red, raw mouth littered with spines and thin, grey teeth. The thing's mouth opened and a thrashing, veiny tongue coiled over its teeth. Hot, sticky spittle flew out of its maw as it snapped and sucked at the air, leering over Kramer and whipping its throbbing tail against the wall as it roared -

Something flashed white and red behind the worm's head and it shot around, glaring toward the tunnel. Kramer scrambled backwards and Debbie pulled him up off the ground as the thing hissed, distracted by the dazzling light. A smell like sulphur and burnt orange peel washed through the cave as the air hummed electric. The worm turned back to Kramer and opened its jaws wide, screaming wildly at him. Something called out to it from the cavern, wild, animal sounds echoing over the electric crackle of the gateway. The dark, snake-like body of the thing writhed and it dipped its head back through the tunnel and disappeared into the dark.

In moments, the shrieking of the worms had faded and all that was left was the high-pitched whine of the gateway and the pounding of Kramer's heart. Light filled the cavern, burning a fierce yellow as the worm-things slithered back through.

Kramer fell back against Debbie's leg, panting. 'Fuck,' he whispered.

'I guess the door opened again, huh?' Debbie said quietly.

Kramer looked up at her, out of breath. 'I guess so.'

'And you've been the other side of that?' Debbie said. 'Where those... *things* came from?'

Kramer nodded. 'Lot warmer through there,' he said. 'I guess... I guess they'd rather go back home than eat us two.'

'Bloody hell, Matt.'

He opened his mouth to reply, but he was cut off by a vibration in his pocket. He fumbled for his phone, answered it breathlessly.

'Kramer,' he said. 'Jamie, is that you? I meant to tell you, your guy in the cave -'

Kramer fell silent. His face froze.

'What is it?' Debbie said.

'We're on our way,' Kramer breathed. He swallowed. Already he was scrambling to his feet. 'It's Charlie,' he said, heading for the cave entrance. 'She's with some kids on the pier.'

'What?' Debbie said. 'I thought you said...'

'I did,' Kramer said. 'I told her to stay home. She went anyway.'

'So we take her home, yeah?'

'It's there, Deb.' He turned to her, eyes wild and afraid. 'It followed them. The creature. It's *there with them.*'

CHAPTER TEN
FOR LACK OF A SOUL

1
1995

Eddie ran, farther and faster than he had ever run before. Dead leaves and branches cracked under his bare feet as he scrambled around the old, hollowed trunks of long-crippled trees. The forest around him moved and shifted, every shadow a looming threat, every sound a terrible creature stumbling about in the darkness. In the distance, something crashed to the ground and sent shudders rippling through the soil. Narrow trees cascaded over each other, toppled and dragged up from the dirt by harsh winds and terrible storms.

The moon had all but faded, dipping beneath the horizon, and rivers of soft blue and grey coursed between the curled branches above Eddie's head. Still, it was dark, and a thin layer of mist rolled over the ground, dampening the boy's ankles as he ran.

'I'll find you, you little *shit!*' Nana hissed. Her voice was little more than a rasping whisper, but it carried on the mist and surrounded Eddie so that he couldn't tell which direction it was coming from.

Eddie waded through the fog, eyes on the hazy silhouettes of the trees ahead. Something moved behind him, back in the direction of the swamp, slithering between the crumbling, brittle skeletons of trees that burst up from the bog. Eddie turned his head, stumbling over twisted knots and roots as they tore up from the earth and tried to drag him down by his ankles.

'*Marco...*' Nana rasped. She sounded closer, somehow, but Eddie hadn't heard any footsteps.

Eddie swallowed, frowning as he ducked between two slanted, narrow trunks. Who was she calling after now? Was there someone else out here? Eddie broke into a tangle of thickets and tripped, steadied himself against the trunk of an old silver birch.

'Marco!' Nana called.

Eddie stopped. Something ached in his throat, like something was trying to force its way up into the cavity of his mouth. He opened his lips, just a little, and all of a sudden his tongue was pushing upward and before he could stop himself he was yelling, screaming. '*Polo!*' he shouted.

In the dark behind the trees, Nana laughed. She was playing with him. Toying with him. 'Marco!' she trilled.

Eddie clamped his jaws shut, grunting. He could feel the word trying to slip out of his lips like spittle and he screwed his eyes shut as his teeth tried to wrench themselves apart. The boy's hand shot up to his mouth, covered it, but he couldn't stop the word.

'Polo!'

The call was muffled a little by Eddie's palm, but he knew that she had heard it. Nana could speak through him, he knew - she had put words in his mouth before, forced him to spit them out - but she couldn't *move* him. If she could control his legs, as well as his tongue, she wouldn't follow him into the woods.

He could escape. It was possible. He just had to get far enough away...

'Marco!' Nana shrieked. She was close. Off to Eddie's left, now, separated only from him by a mess of narrow trees and a blanket of mist that had risen up into the air and filtered between the branches.

Eddie ducked to the right, out of breath as he staggered over broken foliage and crumbling, dry earth. Already his mouth was opening to reply, under the old witch's control, and he raised his arm again, lifting his hand to his lips -

Eddie bit down. He yelped as pain seared through his hand. Warmth spilled into his cheeks and he spat, crying out as blood drizzled over his torn palm and flecks of skin splashed the ground. '*Polo!*' he screamed, helpless as Nana forced her words out between his teeth.

'Aren't you having fun, child?' Nana called. 'Don't you like this game?'

A shadow lurched out of the dark and Eddie ducked beneath a lashing tongue, grunting as he fell to the ground. The giant worm recoiled and raised its head, lunging for the boy again. Eddie's eyes widened as he rolled off to the side, kicking upwards. His bare foot connected with the creature's horrible, grey sliver of a belly with a terrible smacking sound. The worm groaned and lashed out again, thrusting its head in the boy's direction.

'Get away from me!' Eddie yelled, staggering to his feet and dipping beneath the coils of the worm's body. His shoulder crashed into a thick, round trunk as he stumbled into a small, dark clearing. The boy looked around him, moving to the middle of the clearing. The trees around him rose up in a perfect circle, digging crooked paths up into the sky. Stars glittered above Eddie as his hands bunched into tight little fists. Hidden by the mist on the ground, his soles were bloody and swollen and they burned as he passed over thorns and fragments of stone.

It was quiet, here. The worm had given up; they tended to be most dangerous when surprised, but they rarely followed him once he had gotten away. He couldn't hear Nana, either. The only sound in the clearing was the eerie chirping of a frog hidden in the foliage.

Eddie turned his eyes down, looking forward. Ahead of him, at the edge of the glade, the trees bunched together and twisted around each other, forming a writhing archway of oak and ivy. The boy stumbled forward, crossing the clearing with ragged, fumbling steps. His breathing was heavy, heart pounding in his chest. He could feel Nana Death's cold, psychic fingers pushing about in his skull but he ignored them. If he kept his mind clear, she wouldn't be able to see where he was. He just needed to stay calm. Slowly, he pushed forward and ducked under the archway.

Cold passed over him as thickets and thorns curled up out of the ground. Eddie peeled them apart, getting down onto his knees and crawling through a wall of thistles. His hands plunged into the undergrowth and he turned, looking over his shoulder. Eddie couldn't see the clearing through the spiky, gathered branches of bushel behind him.

Nana wouldn't see *him.*

Slowly, Eddie ducked down, slid as far into the thickets as he could, curling his body into a ball. His hands moved to his head and he realised there was blood on his wrist. A warmth at his side where the thin scar around his torso had torn running.

After a moment, the boy's breathing slowed. He was safe here.

'Marco...' Nana hissed, somewhere on the other side of the clearing. Her disembodied voice echoed in the darkness; she was close. But she would abandon the search, as long as Eddie was absolutely, completely still.

As long as he didn't make a sound...

'*Polo,*' Eddie whispered.

Something burst through the thickets and a withered, leathery hand wrapped itself around Eddie's neck and yanked him free of the thorns and branches that tore and scratched at his skin. Pain rushed through his body and he screamed, kicking out at her, but it was useless.

'There you are, you bastard little fucker,' Nana hissed, and her crooked teeth glittered in the dark.

2

The door slammed behind Nana as she threw Eddie onto the floor, wiping her gnarled hands on the moth-eaten folds of her gown. Slowly, the old woman reached down, peeling tall, black heels from her feet. 'Sit up,' she hissed.

Eddie stayed where he was, panting heavily, blood sticky on his face and his arms. It oozed over the cuts in his feet and formed little red beads where thorns had dug holes in his skin.

Nana froze, her eyes locked on the boy. They narrowed into a vicious stare as she cocked an eyebrow. 'I said, *sit.*'

Eddie's spine coiled upwards, wrenching his upper

body off the floor. He yelped as some unknown weight pushed him forward until he was sitting, stomach twisted with fear. 'How are you doing that?' he whispered. 'You don't... you don't have...'

'I don't have *what,* boy?' Nana snapped, setting the shoes down and stepping past him. 'I don't have one of your wretched little hairs? You may as well tell a magician he can't perform without his wand, you little runt. Get up.'

Eddie's feet pushed him up and he stumbled, pressed his back to the wall. Behind him, he could hear the crackling fire in the living room. The white door was closed. 'Don't make me go in there...'

'No, child. Not in there,' Nana rasped. 'Upstairs.'

Eddie paused. He didn't dare move. 'To... my room?' he whispered.

'Upstairs. Now.'

She didn't need to tell him a third time. Eddie turned, moving to the staircase. The wood of the stairs sent splinters digging into his bare feet, but he barely noticed the pain. Blood trickled from his left nostril and slipped into his mouth and he swallowed it, head raised high as he lifted his arm to wipe away the crimson trails over his face.

Eddie stopped at the top of the stairs, eyes falling on the ground. A spider scuttled over his toes and he cried out.

'Keep walking,' Nana hissed.

Eddie pushed forward, one foot in front of the other. The landing was dark, and the wooden floor was warped and sagging. Shadows swooped out of the corners and drifted over the boards.

Nana snapped her fingers behind Eddie's head, and the boy winced. Gas lights flickered into life, jutting out of the walls and throwing damp, orange shapes over the landing. Cracked plaster rose up from fading, shredded carpet. One long, spiralling crack swam the length of the wall on Eddie's left, interrupted by two doors. Each was made of a knotted, ancient wood and stained dark with paint that had, a long time ago, been red. There was a third door to Eddie's right. His eyes flickered downward as something slipped beneath the wood; another spider, bigger than the first.

Eddie moved towards the first door. His room. Slowly, he lifted a hand to the knob.

'No,' Nana whispered behind him.

Eddie swallowed, turning his head. 'But...'

Slowly, the old witch stepped up beside him, laying a wrinkled palm on the boy's shoulder. She nodded towards another door, right at the end of the corridor. Buried in the shadows of the crooked house, it was narrower than the rest, scratched and faded. The frame was deep and red and splinters cut across the wood, like something had tried to break its way into the room beyond.

'In there?' Eddie whispered.

'In there.'

'You told me to never go in there,' Eddie protested. 'You said... you said there were *things* in there. That I could never see.'

Even as he spoke, Eddie found himself walking forwards. He didn't know if it was her, pushing him forward, willing him on, or if it was his own curiosity, but one foot in front of the next, he moved slowly and steadily along the hallway, closer to that door and that forbidden room...

'Tonight,' Nana said. 'You ran away from me, boy.'

'I didn't mean...'

'You tried to tell that *woman* to run, too, didn't you?' Nana said. 'The police officer, the one who brought you here. I'll tell you something, child. I've had enough of your *shit*.'

Eddie gulped, said nothing. The door seemed to burn with a heat like he'd never felt before, and the air shimmered and tingled as he came closer to it. It was humid, this far down the corridor, muggy, and the wood hummed with a sick electricity that sent shivers through Eddie's blood. Three bolts held the door locked, each one rusted and bent into place. The wall around the doorframe had cracked and crumbled away in places, and white powder sprinkled the floor.

'You want them back, don't you, Eddie?' Nana said behind him.

Slowly, the bolts started to slide across. Bent metal

ground over metal as the door started to open, squealing on its rusted hinges.

'Your parents,' Nana continued. 'My *daughter.* My pathetic son-in-law. You miss them, don't you? You wish, more than anything, that you could have them back.'

'Yes,' Eddie breathed.

The door stood open, and the landing fell silent. Beyond, Eddie saw darkness. But at the very back of the room, a light flickered in the shadows...

'All it takes is a wish,' Nana whispered. 'Wish for it, and they can come back.'

Eddie stepped into the room.

It was bigger than he'd imagined, bigger than seemed possible, and he couldn't see the farthest wall for a curtain of shadow split in half by that inexplicable light, a shivering, pulsing glow in the dark.

The walls were lined with shelves, crooked and sagging. On those shelves, faded and coated in dust, were dozens - *hundreds* - of little jars. Tiny glass containers and fat, sealed mason jars, lids screwed tight and clasped down. Bathed in the light of that flickering thing at the back of the room, things moved inside the jars, twisting and writhing in the shuddering glow. The jars were filled with shadows, black, curling shadows that hissed and sang and wept, thrashing against the walls of their tiny glass homes, *screaming* at him.

'What are they?' Eddie whispered.

'Currency,' Nana said quietly.

Eddie stepped forward, moving towards the light at the back of the room. It wasn't strong enough to fill the room, and the floor was bathed entirely in darkness. It moved and rippled, growing stronger with every step the boy took.

His foot hit something and he stopped.

Eddie's eyes dropped to the floor. At first, the thing was little more than a lumpen bulge in the shadows, but as Eddie's eyes adjusted to the darkness he saw what Nana Death had been hiding up here, what he hadn't been allowed to see. He cried out, stepping backward. Above his head, something shrieked from inside a crimson, clay jar. It sounded like it was laughing at him. Tentatively, Eddie took another look. Swallowed. 'Are they...'

'They're real,' Nana told him. 'And they can be *yours,* Edward. For a price...'

At his feet, Eddie's parents had been unceremoniously dumped on the floorboards. Elizabeth and Philip Drake were twisted around each other, carcasses curled and rotted. Their skin was dark and bruised, encrusted with dried, thickened blood. It pooled around Elizabeth's torn belly, splashed Philip's throat and his broken, scarred face. Shards of glass littered the floor. A shiver of bloody fur was caught inbetween the boards.

At the far end of the room, the wall of light threw out

a final burst of static and fizzled out to nothing. Eddie was left in darkness.

'All you have to do is say yes,' Nana told him. 'Say yes, and they will be yours again.'

'I'll die,' Eddie said quietly. 'I've seen it... I know what happens when people say yes.'

'They pay the cost.'

'And it *kills* them.'

'Nearly always,' Nana smiled.

Eddie turned. It smelled the same now as it did that night, even now the light had disappeared. Burnt rubber and smouldering, steaming blood. 'I'd be *free,*' he whispered. 'I'd never see you again.'

Nana grinned, and her eyes were dark. 'That's right,' she said. 'You'd be in a better place, child. And your parents would be *alive.*'

Eddie hesitated, bowing his head. He turned back to his parents and stepped across to his mother's side. His body crumpled and he knelt there, on the floor. Pressed a hand to her belly. The sliver of glass that had ruptured her gut was cold in his hand. Carefully, he pulled, and it came free. The blood that painted its tip was still warm, still wet.

The glass fell to the ground, and Eddie nodded. A tear dropped from his eye and mixed with the blood on the floorboards.

'Yes,' he said.

3

Something stung Eddie's gut as he opened his eyes. It barely registered as a sensation, or a feeling, but instinctively, a trembling hand moved to his navel and he clutched at the flesh there, laid his hand on the skin where Nana had cut him. The scar shivered beneath his palm, but for the first time since it had dug its way into his belly, it didn't hurt.

Nothing hurt. Eddie felt funny. Strange. His thoughts seemed... quieter, somehow. His heartbeat had faded.

Eddie sat up, blinking. He wondered if he was dead. He certainly didn't feel alive. If he was alive, it would hurt. He could *remember* the pain; the blood on his wrist, over the soles of his feet, in his crippled gut...

It was all gone.

He hadn't moved, though. A small part of him had expected bright lights, a soft singing. He thought he might have got to see his mother's face one more time. But he was still here, in the darkness of that room. A shiver of wood pierced the soft skin between Eddie's thumb and index finger as he set his hand on the floorboards. The splinter drew blood, but Eddie didn't notice.

'Hello?' he said. His throat was dry. His voice sounded rough. Lower. He could tell that it hurt to talk, but he didn't feel it. He tried again, pushed out the word with some effort: '*Hello?*'

No answer.

Slowly, the boy stood up. He caught a glimpse of the bloody soles of his feet, and his eyes travelled the network of scars across his skin. The only sensation was a dull, numbing ache at his ankles. The same soft tingling rang in his ears, peeling around the inside of his skull. Eddie stumbled for the door, reaching out to take the knob in his hand.

He froze.

His mind felt different. Like there was something new in there. Throbbing between his thoughts, trickling over every movement and impulse. No, it wasn't new.

It felt more like an *absence*, like a hole in his brain where something had been taken out. Like something was *missing*...

And something else, he noticed. He barely felt it, but it was there. A warmth beneath his chin. Slowly, Eddie's free hand moved to the skin of his throat and he felt around, massaging the flesh there.

Three long, bloody scars had drawn across his neck. They were still fresh. Wet and warm, a trio of jagged cuts torn out of him. Blood oozed down to his chest. Eddie remembered, then, a flash of black, a wrenching in his gut as something tore its way out of his skin, as it forced its way out, scratching and biting and *screaming*...

Eddie pulled on the doorknob.

It didn't open.

Eddie tried again, but the door was jammed. Locked from the outside. He was trapped, but he didn't feel afraid.

No, he didn't feel anything.

Eddie turned, looking into the middle of the room, searching for something. He could see more clearly now, even in the dark. The smell was gone, but his thoughts were unobstructed, transparent.

Eddie's parents were gone. There was something else, though, on the ground where Elizabeth and Philip Drake had been. A single, round-bellied mason jar.

Eddie paused. The jar was like the ones on the shelves around him, but there was no dust on the red-striped lid. No shallow scratch-marks on the glass, no smears where greasy thumbs had wiped away months and years' worth of grime.

This one was new.

Tentatively, Eddie stepped towards the jar. Something moved inside it. The thing was black and twisted, writhing and wriggling behind the glass, a burning, screaming shadow.

It looked so lost…

Something was written across the lid, scrawled in Nana's spidery, black handwriting. The ink was dry, faded. As if the old witch had written it a long time ago.

As if she had always known he would say yes.

Edward Drake, read the label. *Paid in full.*

Eddie had survived. Where so many had died,

screaming, he had *lived.* He remembered curling up in a ball in his bedroom, quivering as he listened to the sounds from the living room, as he listened to the wails and the shrieks and the terrible, deafening moans. He had been so terrified.

He wasn't afraid now.

The thing in the jar hissed suddenly, wriggling and coiling around itself in curls of mist and bloody strings of shadow, and crashed into the glass. The jar wobbled.

Let me out, the thing whispered, with a voice that seemed to transcend the air between them and sift directly into Eddie's mind. *Please... I'm so scared.*

Eddie stood where he was, transfixed. It had spoken to him. It *knew* him.

Out, said the thing in the jar. *Let me out. Please. Please let me out of here.*

Cautiously, Eddie knelt down before the little jar, laid his hand on the glass. It was cold, colder than he had imagined. Only now did he notice the tiny particles of ice that had gathered on the outside of the jar and formed a network of spider-web crystals over the glass. It should have hurt his hand, but he all he felt was a soft numbness on his palm.

Yes, the thing said. *Let me out… I'm so frightened.*

Eddie picked up the jar and peered inside. The thing seemed to smile out at him, tendrils of black smoke spitting drops of red onto the glass as it formed a jagged, writhing smile.

'No,' Eddie whispered, and he laid the jar on the ground.

The boy turned, moved back to the door. He gripped the knob and twisted.

No! the thing screamed, slamming itself against the glass. The jar toppled, rolled into the dark.

Eddie pulled the doorknob. This time, the door opened. The boy moved onto the landing, unfazed by the flickering light of the gas lamps. With one last look into that dark room and the swirling, black mass in the jam jar on the floor, he closed the door tight.

Let me out of here! it rasped, and Eddie turned away and headed for the stairs.

4
NOW

Hayley blinked, eyes scrambling over the sheet of paper in front of her. The clock on the office wall ticked loudly behind her head. The words swam in front of her face in a confusion of black type and scrawled, messy crimson. Absent-mindedly, she reached for a tab of aspirin on the corner of the desk and popped a couple, slipping them into her mouth. She swallowed. She hadn't slept for more than an hour, and the little time she had spent unconscious had been plagued with the image of that horrific scene on the beach.

The office was still as she worked, silent save for that relentless, rhythmic ticking. There was no movement aside from the slow rising and falling of Hayley's chest as she breathed. She hadn't bothered to dress up today; she was too tired, too frustrated. Too *distracted.* Instead she wore one of Emma's old t-shirts - it was black and emblazoned with the flat, white silhouette of a crow - and the same trousers she'd had on yesterday.

Hayley looked up as someone knocked on the door. 'Come in,' she said.

The door didn't open.

Hayley frowned. She watched the door for a moment. The paper trembled in her hand. 'Hello?'

Slowly, the door creaked open. A narrow slit of light poked into the office and she blinked, watched as a shadow slid over the gap -

'No,' Hayley breathed. 'You...'

Edward Drake stood in the doorway, smiling across the room at her. There was a knife in his hand. The blade was slick and wet with blood.

Suddenly Hayley couldn't move, couldn't even breathe. Her heart shivered weakly. Her mouth was dry. 'You're in your cell,' she said. 'You can't... you can't be here.'

'I'm here,' Eddie said. He lifted the knife, pushing the door further open. He stepped into the office, and Hayley saw splashes of red on his white t-shirt, on the fabric of his trousers. There was a little on his face, too, just beneath his lip. And there was something in his hand...

'Oh, god,' Hayley said. 'No...'

The head of the dead man looked up at her, eyes rolled up into his bloody skull. His jaw hung loose and fleshy, tongue drooping from behind his remaining teeth. Eddie gripped the thing by its hair, encrusted and stiff with saltwater.

The head blinked. Its eyes swivelled madly round the office and it screamed, strings of blood and sinew writhing from its jaw.

'Shh,' Eddie told the head, 'you're scaring her.'

'Get out,' Hayley breathed. 'Please, get out...' She screwed her eyes shut. She could hear the man's footsteps on the carpet as he moved towards her, feel his breath on her face - was it Eddie's, or the breath of the dead man? - and she bunched her hands into fists, dropping the papers on the desk.

Tick.

Hayley opened her eyes.

There was nothing there. The door was closed. She took a moment to gather herself, to let her breathing slow and soften. 'You're going crazy,' she said. 'You're seeing things. Stupid woman. *Stupid.*'

Tick.

'Stop,' Hayley whispered. 'Just... shh.' Quickly, she reached for the papers on the desk and held them up, narrowing her eyes to read. Perhaps she could distract herself.

...displays signs of what can only be called perfect psychopathy, whereby any emotional functions seem to have been entirely expunged...

Hayley's eyes darted up to the door. Still closed.

Shows a disturbing willingness to imitate the mood of those around him, as if latching onto their feelings and constructing an uncomfortable duplication of...

'No, not that,' Hayley murmured. She didn't want to read about that. She wanted details, about that night. She wanted to know what had happened. Impatiently, she turned the page over, skimming until she found a shortened version of the police report.

1995, she read. *23rd July.*

'This is it,' she breathed. 'This is the night.'

...murdered his adoptive guardian and grandmother. Having previously showed no signs of any mental disturbance, despite the accident in 1993...

'No,' Hayley said. 'Tell me how he did it. Tell me *why.*'

...two more victims found, although their identities have been redacted from the original reports. Both appear to have been killed by Drake, ten years old at the time.

Hayley frowned. *Two more victims.* She had seen the adoption papers; Eddie and his grandmother had lived alone. Perhaps somebody had walked in at just the wrong time. Perhaps...

Evidence suggests Drake was physically mistreated by his grandmother. Any emotional abuse could go some way to explaining the violent tendencies exhibited here and again, in 2003 (see below). Multiple lacerations on Drake's back, arms and legs, as well as bruising on his...

'So she hurt you,' Hayley whispered. 'That's why you did it.'

He killed his grandmother because she beat him. For a moment, Hayley was unconvinced. Surely, there must be more to it than that...

On her desk, the monitor whirred to life. Hayley jumped, breath hitching in her throat. The papers fluttered back to the desk and settled there and she caught sight of her reflection in the cracked screen.

The picture on the screen was the view into Edward Drake's cell. The camera display was black-and-white, hazy, but she recognised the room instantly.

'Weird,' Hayley whispered to herself. The display was supposed to cycle through randomly, unless she selected a certain camera.

Eddie sat on the edge of his mattress with his head bowed, black hair obscuring his face. His hands were clasped tight in his lap.

Cautiously, Hayley reached for a wheel at the base of the keyboard and scrolled up, zooming in on the image. Eddie's mouth was moving, lips parted a little. He was talking to himself.

Shame we can't get audio on this thing, Hayley thought. She moved closer, focusing on Eddie's face, on his lips, trying to read what he was saying -

A shadow flickered across the screen.

Hayley cried out, reeling from the monitor. 'You again...' she breathed. Behind her the clock was still ticking, but the sound faded into the background as she watched, eyes narrowed and still and unblinking as she waited...

There.

Quickly Hayley tapped *pause*. The screen was completely dark. She had caught the shape right at the moment it passed by the camera. It was nothing. Just a shapeless, black shadow. Maybe there was a fault with the camera. Or the whole system, if it was going to start booting itself up like that. *You're being paranoid,* Hayley thought.

Just a shadow.

Hayley tapped another button. Just out of curiosity. She wasn't expecting anything. But she played the image forward, just a single frame. Just one.

'Oh, my god...'

The shadow was gone, and Eddie hadn't moved from his place on the mattress.

But there was someone else in there with him.

The newcomer stood against one wall of the cell, leaning his back on the padded, white cushioning. His hands were buried in the pockets of an all-black suit.

His figure was blurred, out of focus, as though he was moving faster than the camera could pick up. His face was twisted and burned and discoloured somehow. His hair was black and wispy. One eye bulged like a nightmare.

Forward one more frame, and the man had disappeared.

Eddie was alone in the room, mouth open a little. His head was turned toward that spot on the wall, the space where, barely a fraction of a second before, the black-suited man had been standing.

Hayley was out of her chair and halfway across the room before the next frame showed.

5

'Show me,' Eddie said.

The yellow-faced man smiled at Edward Drake from across the room. Arms folded across his black-suited chest, the abomination leant against the wall, shoulders slumped a little. A thin string of golden pus trickled over his lips and down to his chin. After a moment he reached up with a yellow hand and wiped it away. A scrap of burned skin peeled away from his face and he flicked it onto the padded floor of Eddie's cell.

'I said *show me,*' Eddie repeated. He stood up from his place on the mattress, setting his bare feet on the floor. He could smell the yellow-faced man's odour from here, and he didn't step any further. It was repulsive, like the stench of an uncleaned stable; stale, dry grass and rotting wood mixed in with layer upon layer of old, hot shit. Beneath that, he smelled like smoke.

Yellow Face stood straight, sliding his hands into his pockets. Eddie could only imagine the amount of dead, discoloured skin that had gathered in the lining of that suit. He barely spared it a thought.

'Why?' said the nightmare man. Shadows flickered across his face, and for a moment his entire form shuddered and rippled. He solidified again, and one hand had shifted to his tie. Casually, he straightened it. 'Why do you want to see?'

'Curiosity,' Eddie replied simply.

'Don't lie to me, prick,' Yellow Face snapped.

'Excuse me?'

Yellow Face shook his head. Black hair drifted at the top of his scalp, floating over layers of sticky skin like he was underwater. 'You don't *feel* curiosity,' he said. He smirked, flashing rotten teeth. 'You don't feel *anything*.'

'You know I do.'

'I know you *can't*. Why do you think they put you here, you fucking idiot?'

'They think I'm insane,' Eddie said.

'They do,' Yellow Face agreed, shrugging a little. 'And we both know that's not true, don't we? You're not crazy. Well, not as half as crazy as the messed-up fuckers they keep locked up in this shithole.' He glanced up at the wall, face twisted with disgust. 'Honestly, this place *stinks*.'

Eddie said nothing.

Yellow Face stepped forward, smiling. 'Go on then,' he rasped. 'Why do you *really* want to see it?'

'I want to know what it's doing,' Eddie said.

'Why?'

'Because I can *sense* it. It's close, I know it is. It's getting closer. I want to know *how* close.'

'So look,' Yellow Face sighed.

Eddie frowned. 'What? I can't just...'

'You saw it before. When it killed. You felt its presence.'

'Because you showed me,' Eddie said slowly. 'You did your... voodoo thing. You let me see it.'

'I didn't do *shit,*' said the abomination. 'That was all you, kid. You can do it again. You just need to stop being such a *pussy*. Just focus. Concentrate, and you'll do it again.'

Eddie closed his eyes.

'That's it,' said Yellow Face, stepping forward. Drool hung in thick gobs from his teeth as he opened his mouth in a wide smile. His lips peeled back to reveal a twisted, shrivelled tongue. 'Look closer...'

Eddie's eyes snapped open. 'It's not working.'

'Try again.'

'I can't find it. It's not close enough.'

'Again!' Yellow Face yelled. His breath was hot and drops of spittle splashed Eddie's face. 'Or are you too fucking *weak,* Eddie?'

Slowly, Eddie closed his eyes again.

'I always knew you were an ignorant little shit,' Yellow Face hissed, 'but come *on,* kid. Grow a pair. Think, for once. All you've got left in that fucking deformed swede of yours is *thought.* Use it.'

Eddie lowered his head, focusing. He shut out the sound, the smell of that horrible, pus-skinned figure. Listened to the beating of his heart as it slowed, concentrated on that rhythmic, fatigued thumping.

Ba-dum.

'Pathetic,' Yellow Face snarled. 'You're a mess, kid. You were a mess when I dragged you out of that fucking wreck in ninety-three, you're even worse now.'

Ba-dum.

'You're a piece of shit, Eddie. You're *weak.* You're nothing but a fucking shell of a shithead and I can't believe I ever pulled you out of that car. Should have left you to fucking *die,* Eddie. I should have let you die.'

Ba-dum. 'I can see it...' Eddie whispered.

'There we go,' Yellow Face murmured. 'Wasn't so hard, was it?'

'I see... water,' Eddie said. 'It's down by the sea.'

'Good. You're seeing through its eyes, now, kid. That's step one. Now see if you can *talk* to it.

Communicate with it. You're linked, you've worked that much out. See how far that link goes. See if you can talk to it. Hell, see if you can *hurt* it.'

Eddie frowned. 'It's not at the beach,' he said. 'It's... looking *down* at the sea. Through... boards. Planks. Now it's looking up. Forward. Moving. It's walking towards... it's on the pier. The pier where the boat came in.'

Yellow Face sighed, turning back to the wall. 'Still focusing on *sight,* Ed. You could have so much more fun with this. Use your other senses. Feel what it feels.'

'How?' Eddie whispered.

Yellow Face shrugged. 'Figure it out.'

Eddie screwed his eyes shut and closed in. He saw shadows, at the end of the pier, silhouettes, moving like they were walking. Smaller than men.

Children.

They were moving towards the end of the pier, towards an old, battered building. Closed off. Broken.

'Wait...' Eddie said. He could smell something. Saltwater drifted on the wind. Manure, from the cattle farm the other side of the island. Clay and sand and driftwood and... blood. Thick and strong and *pounding.* He grimaced, raising a hand to his temple.

'What do you feel?'

'Pain,' Eddie breathed. 'Hunger and fear and *lust* and... pain. So much pain. Why is there so much *pain?*'

'Eddie?' came a voice from the doorway. It didn't

292

sound like the yellow-faced man.

Eddie's eyes snapped open.

Yellow Face stood in front of him, arms hanging by his sides, shoulders crooked. His round, bulging eye was on the cell door. The other drifted to the other corner of the room, lazy and narrowed and dark with crippled veins.

Slowly, Eddie turned his head towards the door. It was open.

'What is that thing?' Hayley whispered. Her voice trembled and cracked as she spoke. Her eyes were on the yellow-faced man, wild and terrified. Her mouth hung open a little.

Eddie shook his head. 'You should leave.'

'Eddie, tell me how it got in. Tell me how it's... god, what *is* it?'

'Get out,' Eddie said quietly.

Hayley stepped back from the door, shaking. Her hand went to her mouth. 'Oh, god...' she said.

'Get *out,*' Eddie repeated.

Hayley moaned something incomprehensible and took another step back, shaking her head. 'What *are* you?' she said, and she turned. Disappeared down the corridor.

Eddie stood there for a moment, staring out into the corridor.

Yellow Face stepped forward, standing just behind the man's shoulder. For a long moment they just stood, eyes on the open door, and then Yellow Face smiled grimly. 'She's seen me,' he said.

Eddie nodded.

'We can't be having that,' Yellow Face said, and the smile grew wider.

CHAPTER ELEVEN
ARCADIA

1
NOW

Sparrow took a step forward, ducking under a band of fluttering, white tape that barricaded the far end of the pier. The boards squealed under his feet, narrow and straining against the nails that held them together. In front of him, the arcade rose up from a mess of rotting planks and rusted scaffolding, a peeling wreck of a place.

Darcy reached out a hand, grabbed the back of Sparrow's bomber jacket before he could disappear round the side of the arcade. 'Hey, not yet,' the girl said, taking a step back and gesturing ceremoniously. 'This is a momentous occasion. *Look* at this place.'

Sparrow shrugged, scratching his head. Thick, dark curls shifted under his fingernails. 'It's just creepy,' he said.

Behind them, Charlotte nodded her agreement, arms folded over her chest. 'Let's just go inside, Darce. It's not like we brought any novelty scissors to cut open the police tape.'

'Sounds like a plan,' Liam nodded, laying his hand on Darcy's back. 'It's fucking freezing out here.'

Darcy shot a look in his direction.

'You think it's going to be any warmer in there?' Charlotte said, raising an eyebrow. Wind blew across the pier, throwing her hair in her face. She shook it away, moving forward to stand beside Darcy. 'Maybe we shouldn't do this,' she whispered.

'Chicken,' Darcy grinned.

Charlotte scowled. 'Fine. How do we get in, Sparrow?'

Sparrow winced. 'I told you guys to stop calling me that.'

'Oh, you prefer *Reginald*?' Liam retorted, lifting up the tape as Darcy stepped through, any aspirations of a grand ceremony forgotten.

Charlotte hesitated for a moment, turning her head to look back up at the island. The pier was about half a mile long, but now - with the wind howling about them and a light mist of rain seeping out of the grey sky - it seemed even farther. Beneath her, the sea crashed up against the thick, concrete pillars that held up the pier and she shivered.

'You coming?' Darcy called.

Charlotte turned back towards the arcade. 'Sure,' she said. She ducked under the tape and followed them around to the side of the building, avoiding the jagged holes in the pier where the boards had fallen away. Even where the floor was still solid, it hardly felt stable; the wooden slats were crooked, all pushed up against each other like they had no desire to be there.

Behind her, Liam held his phone out in front of his face, snapping a picture of the arcade. The phone flashed and he grinned as he slipped it back into his pocket, skipping over a wet patch on the floor to follow Sparrow around the corner.

'You better not get me in any of them,' Charlotte warned him, treading carefully over the boards.

'Wouldn't dream of it,' he called back. 'You'd shatter my camera.'

'Piss off.'

Ahead of her, Sparrow had disappeared; he was the shortest one of the group, only a little over five feet, and skinny enough that he could dip between two broken boards in the wooden wall of the arcade with no challenge.

'*This* is your way in?' Darcy snapped, incredulous. 'Bitch, how do you think I'm getting through there? Forget that, how do you think *Liam's* getting through there?'

'Hey!' Liam called, leaning against a white, peeling rail at the edge of the pier as he took a snapshot of the island with his mobile. 'Watch who you're calling fat, yeah?'

Darcy rolled her eyes. 'So *sensitive.*'

Inside the arcade, Charlotte could hear Sparrow moving about, every step on the crooked boards followed by the uneasy creak of rotting wood.

'Be careful in there!' Charlotte called. 'Can you even see?'

'Light from the windows!' Sparrow replied.

Charlotte's eyes darted up to the nearest window, a cracked, tired square of greasy glass. The frame had been painted a deep, blood red. A handful of dead flies laid in the flaking, dried crimson of the sill. Slowly, she stepped forward, peering through the glass -

'Boo!' Sparrow yelled, popping up behind the glass.

Charlotte's heart pounded and she stumbled, stepped back from the window. 'Jesus, dickhead! Don't do that!'

'Hey, guys, there's another opening round here!'

Charlotte turned her attention to the back of the building, watching as Liam disappeared around the corner, hopping over gaps in the woodwork.

Darcy followed him, grinning excitedly. 'Come on, Charlie!' she called, rounding the corner.

Charlotte walked slowly, keeping her hand on the railing. The arcade walls were thin and made of the same narrow, wooden slats of the boardwalk; the whole building seemed to sway a little in the wind.

From the front, the arcade was a nightmare on

crooked stilts; all the old neon signs had been dark for years and the bulbs that hadn't cracked had been stained black by a decade's worth of residue. The front doors had been boarded over with thick sheets of plywood and closed off with luminous, orange tape, and the red and green stripes that decorated the front wall had faded and cracked.

Around this side, the wood was plain and dull, and the eerie soul of the facade Charlotte had been greeted with was all but gone. She stepped over loose planks and sawn, littered debris, following Darcy around to the back of the building; here, the wall was nearly all torn away by the wind.

There was nobody there. For a moment Charlotte was alone, one hand on the peeling rain as the wind buffeted her face. 'Darcy?' Charlotte said. 'You still out here?'

'In here, dipshit!' Darcy called from inside the arcade. Charlotte stepped forward and saw it, dug out of the back of the building - a wide, gaping hole, black and shifting with shadows. She swallowed and moved towards it. Their voices grew louder as she came closer to the opening.

'I told you we should've come here alone,' Liam hissed from inside. 'This would've been a great place to _'

'Ew!' Darcy whispered. 'Shut up and go find Sparrow, will you?'

'Fine.'

Darcy sighed. Then, a little louder, 'Charlie? You coming or what?'

'On my way!' Charlotte said, crouching to squeeze through the hole. Something moved in front of her and she gasped, hand shooting to her mouth, as a shape appeared in the opening.

'Just me,' Liam whispered. His face was half-hidden in the shadows, but Charlotte could still see the childish grin plastered over it. Quickly he pointed to the hole, raising his phone. 'Just going back out to take some more pictures,' he hissed. 'Darcy's in there somewhere.'

He moved past her and Charlotte dipped through the hole, standing straight as the dark opened out above her head. She looked around, waiting for her eyes to adjust. Shadows consumed the place, but light broke in through the cracked windows and through the jagged holes in the floor.

The place was bigger inside than she had imagined, and it was crammed full of ancient-looking, battered machines that gleamed in the half-light.

'Sparrow?' Charlotte called, stepping forward. 'Darce? Where are you?'

Shadows moved in the dark. 'This is so cool!' Darcy called from a corner of the room. 'Charlie, did you bring any pennies?'

'The machines aren't going to work, are they?' Charlotte said. 'Not without electricity.'

'I've got some,' Sparrow said, voice swelling about the other side of the arcade. 'Hang on, let me just find them...'

Charlotte stepped across to the nearest window, pushing aside a ragged sheet of thin, black plastic that had been pinned over the glass. Light streamed in and she turned away, scanning the place. A machine in front of her was illuminated, bathed in the glow of the cracked window; *Black Dog Pinball,* read the faded blue letters across its metal top. A glass case covered peeled paint and rusted metal sliders. Howling, scruffy hounds raced up the sides of the machine. Charlotte grinned and raised a hand to the face of the machine.

Darkness fell over her for a fraction of a second as something moved past the window.

Charlotte's breath hitched in her throat and she turned back to the window, peering through the cracked glass. Outside, the white railings separated the fragile boards of the pier from the roaring ocean.

It had started to rain.

'Charlie?' Darcy said loudly. 'You coming, or what? Sparrow's got coins!'

'Coming...' Charlotte whispered. Slowly she moved closer to the window. She could have sworn...

A bloody hand slammed into the glass and Charlotte screamed, stumbling backwards. 'Liam?'

'Help me!' Liam yelled, hammering on the window with his fist. His face was a mess, orange-stained teeth showing through a tear in his jaw where the skin had been peeled away. One eye drooped, drizzling red down a shredded cheek. '*Fucking help me!*'

Suddenly Darcy was at Charlotte's side, screeching madly. 'Liam!' she yelled. 'What's happening? Sparrow, get out, help him!'

'The fuck do you want me to do?' Sparrow yelled.

Something smacked the back of the building, thumping the wood as if it were trying to get in. Liam disappeared in a smear of blood and howling agony. '*Help me!*'

Charlotte pressed her face against the window, scanning the pier desperately.

'Where did he go?' Darcy shrieked. 'Oh god where the *fuck* did he go?'

'I don't know...'

'*Help!*'

Bloody, red fingers scraped at the glass and Darcy screamed again, shrill and hoarse, throat strained. 'Fuck!' she yelled. 'Fuck, get him! *Help him!*'

'There's something out there with him...' Charlotte whispered.

'Liam!' Darcy screamed, recoiling from the window. Her hand went to her mouth. 'Oh, god, it's got him. It's got him Charlie, it...'

Suddenly Liam's face twisted and something yanked him away from the window. Charlotte could do nothing but watch as a dark blur threw him toward the railings.

'No!' Darcy yelled, but it was too late. Liam stumbled, leg caught on the rails as he fell backwards, and the thing turned, moved to the window. Darcy stumbled back and Charlotte was left, face pressed to the glass, staring into the eyes of the shadowy creature.

'Oh, my god...' she breathed.

Slowly, the creature raised a thick-skinned claw to its bloody lips and wiped them, flicking crimson onto the window in a sticky, flat spatter. It blinked, dark eyes narrowing as a narrow, splintered smile spread over its nightmare of a face, and Charlotte shook her head.

'You're not real...' she whispered. 'Shit, you can't be *real...*'

Hot, steaming breath misted over the glass and Charlotte screamed as the thing turned and started to slink towards the opening at the back of the arcade.

2

Kramer popped the glovebox open as the police car hurtled along a rough track at the top of the cliff. He fumbled about inside, rummaging amongst scraps of paper and receipts until his hand wrapped around something cold and metallic.

'The hell is that doing in here?' Debbie said, eyes flickering from the road to the thing in his hands as she drove. Her knuckles were white and strained at the top of the wheel. 'Christ, Matt, how long has that thing been out of your desk?'

Kramer released the pistol's magazine into his lap with a soft *click* and checked it, counting the bullets. Eight. A full round. Quickly, he slid the magazine back into its chamber and shoved the gun into his belt. 'Long enough,' he said.

Debbie slid the car round a tight bend, spinning the wheel wildly as she lifted her foot off the accelerator. The front tyre caught on a slab of rough, broken rock at the edge of the road and the car bumped madly over the gravel. Debbie ground the vehicle back on course and now they could see the pier, jutting out of the side of the island like a flat, skeletal arm reaching into the sea.

'Faster,' Kramer said.

They thundered along the track, winding down a rough slope of grass and rock that tore the clifftop down to another stretch of sand. Here, where the island bent around into the sea, the pier dug itself into the earth on tall, corroded stilts. The police car turned at the end of the track, skidding to a halt in a cloud of grey dust and sand.

Kramer was out of the car before it had stopped, crashing out of the passenger door and into the sand. His boots dug into the ground as he ran. The pier was thirty feet away and the arcade all the way along at the other end of it, but already he could hear it.

Screaming. A young girl.

Charlie...

Behind him, the car's engine cut out and the driver's door swung open. 'Matt!' Debbie yelled after him. 'You don't know what's in there!'

'My daughter's in there!' Kramer called back, scrambling up a set of crooked, wooden steps to the pier. Great, foaming swathes of ocean attacked the concrete pillars of the thing beneath Kramer and he ran faster. Wooden slats shuddered under his weight as his boots hit the ground; the grey overcoat flew at his knees, peeled back from his waist by the wind. A spatter of rain hit his forehead and suddenly it was a torrent that plastered his hair to his scalp and crashed against his chest. Kramer grimaced into the rain, kept running. His knees burned, sending shivers of hot, searing pain into his thighs and up his sides. His heart pounded.

'Charlie!' Kramer yelled, halfway along the pier. Another scream echoed from inside the old arcade, and he heard something thump against the wooden walls of the old building. It rose up before him in sheets of rotten wood and flaking paint, surrounded by blue tape and lashings of rain. Splashes of colour leered at the corner of his vision and he glanced toward the white rails at the edge of the pear. A long, dark smear of crimson washed over the paintwork.

Debbie called out behind him, but he couldn't hear her. She was trying to stop him going in there. He *had* to. Charlotte was inside the arcade, and so was that thing... what if it really had come from that place, where the worms had attacked him? What if it was *worse* than them, somehow? Bigger?

Kramer dipped under the tape and slammed his fist on the boarded front door of the arcade. 'Charlie!' he called again.

'Dad!' came a voice from inside. 'Help us! It's in here oh god it's *dad help us*,' the girl screamed, and then she was interrupted by a horrific snarl, a low, rumbling roar that sent vibrations along the wooden ground under Kramer's feet.

Kramer stood back, looking the door over. Thick, wide sheets of plywood had been tacked over the entrance, nailed all along their edges. The wood looked weakened, rotten, and if he could just -

'Get back from the door!' Kramer yelled.

'Help!' someone yelled from inside the arcade. A boy's voice, one Kramer didn't recognise. 'It ate Liam and it's in here and it's going to eat us please just *help us!*'

Kramer braced his shoulder and slammed into the door with all his weight. He felt it give, heard a thick, deep crunch beyond the wood.

It wasn't enough.

'Hang on!' Kramer yelled, backing up to try again. He rushed the door, crashing into it shoulder-first. Something moved beside him and he staggered back as Debbie kicked at the weak spot with her boot. Another crack shuddered across the surface of the door and

Kramer brought his knee up into the rotted wood and it *caved* -

Wide splinters broke away and fell back into the opening, swallowed up by the blackness of the old arcade. Pain shot up Kramer's leg and he grunted.

A figure staggered out through the jagged hole, scrambling past him. A boy. The kid sank to his knees a little way down the pier, clasping a bloody leg. Crimson drizzled through his fingers.

'Where is she?' Kramer said, grabbing the boy by his coat and lifting him to his feet. '*Where's Charlie?*'

The boy shook his head, stuttered. 'She's... they're in there. It ate Liam and then it came for us, and Darcy wasn't... I don't think she was fast enough, and now it's going after Charlie and it's *going to eat her...*'

Kramer dropped the boy and turned back to the door, reaching for the gun at his belt. 'Charlie!' he yelled.

Silence.

Debbie stepped forward, eyes wide. 'Matt, you can't...'

Kramer fumbled with the gun, face dark with anger and something worse, something terrible. Fear shattered the stony coolness in his eyes and Debbie saw it in his expression, far clearer than he would have wanted. Clearer than *she* wanted. She wasn't used to seeing him afraid.

'Matt...'

Kramer cocked the gun and stepped into the dark.

Shadows blurred and twisted and something crashed into the man in a mess of screaming and flailing limbs. Kramer stumbled backwards, crying out as the dark shape wrapped itself around his body and pushed him back. He steadied himself and reached out to grab the thing, to push it away -

'Charlie?'

Charlotte Kramer wrapped her arms tight around him, sobbing into his gut. Her face was red, her mouth bloody. There was a deep cut across her temple. The girl's clothes were ragged and torn. 'Oh my god, dad, you came, you're here...'

'Charlie...'

Suddenly the girl stood straight, whirled back around to face the arcade. 'Darcy...' she whispered.

'She's gone,' said the skinny kid, gripping his leg. 'It tore her apart...'

'No,' Charlotte said. She shook her head, looking up at Kramer. 'I saw her. She's still...'

Inside the arcade, something growled. Hot, wet tremors rippled in the air.

'Oh, god...' Charlotte said, eyes wet with tears as her hand moved to her mouth. 'If she's still alive...'

Kramer nodded. 'Get home,' he said. 'Run.'

Debbie shook her head, reaching out with her free hand. 'Give me the gun,' she said. 'Get your daughter safe. I'm going in.'

'Debbie, don't be stupid,' Kramer said. In the arcade,

something smacked against metal and thick, bony claws scraped out the shell of the place. The creature made a noise - low, leering - like some sick, maniacal laughter.

'Give me the gun!' Debbie snapped. 'Don't you dare send your daughter home while you go in there, you fucking *idiot!*'

Kramer shook his head. 'I'm not -'

'The *gun,* Matt! *Now!*'

'I'm going in, Debbie. You can -'

'Enough, Matt!' Debbie said, grabbing the gun out of his hand. 'Get the kids out of here!'

Kramer looked at her for a moment. A ragged moan from the arcade told him everything he needed to know. 'Save her,' he whispered.

Debbie nodded and turned towards the opening. In seconds, she had disappeared into the arcade.

'Charlie, you need to go,' Kramer said quietly. Rain splashed the boards around him and he reached up, pushing wet hair off his face. At his side, one hand curled into a tight, knotted fist.

'You're going after her, right?' Charlotte said.

'Absolutely,' Kramer said. 'Get to the doctor's. Get your friend's leg looked at. Don't come back down here, not for anything. Okay?'

'Okay,' Charlotte whispered.

Kramer gave her one last look, one last weak, faltering smile, and then he stepped towards the opening and ducked inside.

3

Debbie walked slowly, holding the gun with both hands. The metal was cold and stung her palms. Every step took her further into the derelict building and the darkness grew stronger with every second. The woman blinked, waiting for her eyes to adjust to the shadows. Pale shafts of grey light bounced off the waves below the peer and filtered through cracks in the floor. Debbie's breath formed a ragged wisp in front of her face, grey and shining in the half-light and thick with particles of dust.

The floor sloped downward as Debbie pressed on, sagging under the weight of the decades-old building. In places the wooden slats had completely fallen away and half-hearted attempts had been made to cover up the wreckage with boards and sheets of corrugated metal. Even these, with time, had come loose, torn away by the wind and the relentless beating of the waves.

Debbie paused, listening. Ahead of her she could hear it, padding slowly over the boards. Hot, ragged breaths echoed from the creature's chest. The arcade opened up as Debbie took another step and the black, hollow shell of the entrance fell away behind her as she moved through a red-painted archway. Round, cracked bulbs all over the thing were strung up with cobwebs and strings of thick, black gunk. Some of the bulbs were smeared with blood.

Debbie gripped the gun tight as she passed through the archway and into a massive room broken up with displays and glass cabinets and old slot machines. A long time ago the old arcade had been a glittering spectacle of colour and noise and lurid, neon light, and remnants of that glory were here in this room, strung up and plastered about the walls. Peeling, faded posters screamed the names of abandoned attractions and two-penny games. Fat, yellow letters heralded *Phantom Drive,* an old-school motorcycle racer which lay ten feet away, toppled and bleeding thick, coiled wires onto the ground. Another poster was printed on a gothic-looking background; in front of a crumbling, multi-storey building dripping with blood, a white string of text read *Can You Escape The ARCHANGEL HOTEL?*

Something moved in the dark and Debbie swung the gun around, heart pounding. An old, heavy-looking console stood in the shadows, all metal plating and battered, rusted nails. The lights that had once gleamed along its edges had long been switched off; a faint red glow crept in through the holes in the floorboards and slithered over the bulbs.

Debbie crept forward with the gun held high, listening closely. There was a new sound, above the creature's shallow breathing. Like a pig's snout slopping through the mess of a swill-filled trough as it sucked and slobbered over old, unwanted trails of meat. A new smell rose above the rust and the salt encrusted over the wooden floor and Debbie had to stop herself gagging on it. It was the same smell she had backed away from at the clifftop, tangy and metallic and stronger with silent step forward.

Debbie reached the machine and paused, taking a breath. She balked as a wash of blood rose up into her throat. The slippery, squelching sound was louder, closer to the machine. Coming from just behind the thing. Debbie pressed her back to the machine as a surge of fear washed over her. If not for the adrenaline pulsing beneath her skin she would have run. God, she had never been so frightened.

Debbie stepped around the machine, raising the gun high.

Her arm faltered, dropping to her side as her eyes widened, horrified. Debbie could barely see the creature in the shadows, but she could discern its grey outline in the dark, a curved, rough shape hunched over at the back of the room.

The thing's hide was covered in blood and ragged splinters of bone. Its hind legs were bent and it lowered its head beneath armoured, spiny shoulders. The creature's jaw was packed with long, thin spines. It nuzzled something soft and wet and raw on the ground, chewing almost delicately as it peeled flesh apart with its claws.

Intestines drooped over the floor in a pool of red that

looked, in this light, completely black. Darcy's dark-skinned hand lay by her side, palm upwards; it twitched as the creature dipped its snout into her opened belly. The girl's legs were open, torn from each other at the groin and hanging from her broken torso by red strings of tendon and trembling, black skin that quivered and tore with each terrible bite the creature took.

Slowly, Darcy looked up. She saw Debbie, saw the gun. One side of her face was scratched and bleeding. Beyond deep, bloody holes, the muscles of her cheek were torn and hanging loose from her skull. Her eyes were white and wild as she opened her mouth. '*Help me...*'

'Get away from her,' Debbie said, raising the gun. A tremor in her voice gave her away. The gun wobbled.

Slowly, the creature turned, looked up. Its bloody maw slid around a chunk of shining, purple organ that it had ruptured with its teeth; clear, thick juice made a mess of its lips and drooled down its chin. Thick, dark claws planted themselves on the floorboards and it narrowed its eyes. They glowed a little, Debbie noticed, a faint, burnt-out white. Thick, spiny armour rolled over its thighs and humped shoulders. Sharp bones crushed together and jutted out from broken skin at its elbows and the joints of its hind legs as it took a step away from the girl. A narrow, black-skinned back twisted horribly as it moved. Its spine was a sickening mess of black bumps and shivering, flattened spikes.

The creature looked Debbie up and down; its jaws peeled open, thin lips cracking and tearing back from bloody teeth. It smiled.

'What are you?' Debbie breathed.

The thing ignored her, turning back to where Darcy lay spread-eagled on the ground. The girl's head had rolled back against the wooden wall and the creature traced bony claws over her throat, cutting a slim, red path down to her torso. Debbie swallowed as the thing dug into the gaping, red hole in Darcy's belly, pulling out reels of intestine and translucent slivers of gut and pawing them into its open mouth.

'I said get *away* from her,' Debbie said. Her finger hovered over the trigger. Her eyes flickered from the creature's shuddering shoulders to Darcy's pleading, near-lifeless eyes, and she inhaled. The creature chewed, chunks of flesh littering the floor as they fell from its crashing teeth. 'Away,' Debbie said. 'Now.'

The thing paused, as if considering, and then it raised a bony, leathery hand. Debbie watched, frozen, as the claws flexed and twisted. A sickening crunch echoed about the arcade as bone shifted and slid over itself and the thing's claws began to lengthen, cracking and splintering. Shadows writhed about the creature's hand and thick, brown skin peeled as it stretched. Slowly, the creature turned its head, staring Debbie dead in the face as its skin reformed and healed around the cuticles of the claws that, now, were twice as long as a human finger.

'I don't...' Debbie started. 'What are you...'

Then the creature curled it claws into a tight hook and *plunged* them down into Darcy's throat. The flesh burst open in a spray of red and black and Debbie yelled in surprise. Her finger bent around the trigger and the gun crashed back into the palm of her hand -

Crack!

A bullet erupted from the end of the barrel and crashed into the creature's shoulder, bouncing off a plate of rough, rippling armour. Somewhere in the dark of the room, it ricocheted off the back of an old arcade machine and trickled to the floor.

The creature spun around, mouth open and red as it reared up, screeching and swiping forward with its dreadful claws. Debbie fired again as the creature bore down on her, but her aim was off and the bullet skewed off to the side, barely grazing the shadowy thing's rump and burying itself in the rotted wood of the wall.

'Fuck!' Debbie yelled, stumbling back. Her heel caught on the corner of the arcade machine and she fell, crying out as the creature swiped at the spot where her head had been only half a second before. Debbie rolled onto her front and scrambled to her feet and she caught sight of something glinting and silver on the ground; a wide square of corrugated metal, almost completely torn from the ground and rusted away, held in place by a single, rusted nail in one corner. It barely covered a ragged hole in the boards; white slivers of light gleamed at its edges. Below the arcade, waves crashed around the ancient pillars holding up the pier.

Debbie looked around her, swinging the gun around wildly. The creature had vanished into the shadows; she couldn't hear it anymore - the only sound was Darcy's tortured moaning, and even that was starting to fade into an uneasy, wet silence.

Something slashed at Debbie's calf and she howled, staggering forward as warmth spread over the back of her leg. She twisted her body around and raised the barrel of the gun into the dark -

Crack!

The bullet sheared the creature's arm as it swiped forward, passing straight through shadowy meat and bone in a mess of black, inky blood. The thing yelped, taking a crooked step back, but already the broken bone was reforming, twisting about and fusing together.

It was healing itself, even as Debbie watched.

'What the hell are you?' she whispered. She stepped back, ducking behind an old claw machine. Glass walls obscured her view as she slid around to the back of the machine, breathing heavily. Frantically, she peered out through a pile of stuffed teddies and cracked, plastic eggs, coated in dust and abandoned cobwebs.

The arcade was silent as Debbie squinted into the dark.

The glass crashed open and covered her in a shower

of clear, sharp dust and then the creature was on top of her, lashing out with its claws as its mouth opened wide and a hot, harsh screech burst out from behind rows of teeth. A thick tongue flickered and drool spattered Debbie's face as she raised the gun again -

'*Hey!*'

The thing turned, recoiling. The claw machine toppled to the ground with a crash as the creature moved toward the voice - Matt's voice - shivering shards of glass off its bloody back. A three-fingered, metallic claw dangled from the roof of the machine and bounced off the metal frame of the thing as old teddies spilled out of the shattered windows. Debbie stumbled to her feet, staring frantically into the dark.

The floorboards around the machine groaned; six feet from the space where it had fallen, the sheet of bent, corrugated metal strained with the weight of the thing.

Debbie turned her head to face the creature and lifted the gun.

The shadowy thing stood on its hind legs in the middle of the arcade, eyes glaring a dull yellow. Long, bony forelimbs hung at its side, claws dripping blood. Kramer stood six fet from the thing, hands bunched into fists, teeth gritted. The creature looked from him to Debbie and back again, assessing them.

Figuring out who to kill first.

'Matt, I told you to go,' Debbie whispered.

Kramer shot her a look. 'It was going to kill you,

Deb!'

The creature sniffed.

'I can handle myself!' Debbie hissed.

'I know!' Kramer said. 'Are we really doing this right now?'

Suddenly the creature moved, lunging for Kramer's throat. Debbie yelled, pointing the gun toward the back of the thing's skull and curling her finger tight around the trigger. The bullet plunged into a spot at the top of the creature's spine and it screeched, turning towards her as black blood spurted from its neck. It pounced, but already Kramer was rushing toward it, something long and heavy-looking in his hand. He slammed it into the top of the creature's head, grunting as something cracked. The pipe bent and he cried out. The creature fell, landing on the boards with a *thud*. For a moment it was still.

Kramer looked towards Debbie, eyes wide. 'Are you okay?' he said, out of breath.

Debbie nodded, eyes fixed on the pipe in his hand. 'Where the hell did you get that?'

'Lot of shit lying around.'

Debbie turned her attention back to the creature and her mouth opened. She froze. 'Matt...'

Kramer looked. 'Oh, shit.'

The creature was gone. The space where it had fallen was a bloody mess of splintered floorboards.

Kramer took a step towards Debbie, rusted pipe held

high.

The air in the old arcade seemed heavier now, colder. Thicker, as though a mist had risen up through the holes in the ground. 'We need to get out of here,' Kramer whispered, eyes wild as he looked into the dark. The creature was nowhere to be seen. 'Did you find Darcy?'

'Too late,' Debbie breathed.

'Shit,' Kramer said. 'Okay. So, let's just head for the -
'

The creature leapt out of the shadows, barrelling forward, teeth gnashing furiously in its bloody jaw as it swept one crooked arm into Kramer's shoulder, knocked him to the side. He tumbled and the pipe fell out of his hand, clattering across the floor. The creature roared, flecks of spittle pouring out from black, broken lips as it turned to Debbie and *lunged* -

Debbie lowered the gun and pointed to a spot between the creature's feet. Metal glinted up at her as she fired.

Crack!

The single nail was the only thing holding that rusted sheet of metal in place. It crumpled with the impact of the bullet and the sheet flew backwards, skittering over shivers of glass and crashing into the wall. Debbie stumbled back as a hole opened up in the ground opened up and the creature flailed, grabbing wildly at the boards as it fell. It shrieked as the ground swallowed it whole. A set of bony, bloody claws gripped the edge of the hole and the creature started to pull itself up -

'No!' Debbie yelled, kicking out with her boot. Her toe connected with the creature's wrist and the thing lost its grip, falling beneath the pier. It roared, disappearing through the hole in the ground.

'Out!' Kramer shouted, reaching for Debbie's hand. Below them, something crashed into the sea. A fine spray of saltwater burst up through the hole in the ground and Kramer pulled Debbie away.

For a second Debbie held onto him, gun shivering in her hand as she wrapped her arms around Kramer's back. 'Do you think it's dead?' she whispered.

Kramer shook its head. 'I think it's still learning,' he said. 'We just have to hope it hasn't learnt to *swim* yet.'

Debbie looked up at him. 'What do we do?'

'I don't know,' Kramer said. 'But we need to find out what this thing is.'

'You think he knows,' Debbie said. 'Edward Drake. You think he knows what the creature is.'

'Yeah,' Kramer said, turning his gaze to her. 'Yeah, I do. Let's go ask him, shall we?'

CHAPTER TWELVE
THE LONG NIGHT

1
1995

Brown meat slopped about in the saucepan, streaked with red and blue. Blood boiled in a thick, brown swill that sizzled over onto the stove. The stew smelled bitter and sulphurous; chunks of marrow floated to the top of the broth and bobbed in the blood and the foam.

Nana Death stirred with a splintered spoon, ignoring the flecks of stew that spattered the rim of the stove and splashed her dress. She inhaled the steam as it rose about her and her haggard face pulled inward. She smiled.

'Do you remember this dish, Lizzie?' Nana said slowly. Her voice was a ragged croak above the hissing in the pan.

'I remember,' came a voice from behind her. 'You used to cook it for me... when I was a little girl.'

Nana turned her head, smiling across at the woman sat at the kitchen table. 'That's right,' the old witch said. 'Clever girl.'

Elizabeth Drake's hands were folded in her lap. Her eyes were glazed and she stared blankly at the wall, like she was trying to remember what she'd come into the room for. She rocked a little on the stool, legs twisted around each other.

Nana's eyes flickered down to the dead woman's stomach. Half-hidden by the table, it was soaked a deep, dark red. The wound was still there, shining and wet, and something quivered beneath the open skin, shorn in half by the glass that had almost finished her off all those years ago. Splinters of glass poked out of Elizabeth's shoulders and narrow strings of crimson drizzled over her throat. Her hair was a ragged, red-stained mess.

'What's wrong, mother?' Elizabeth said slowly.

Nana smiled, turning back to the pan. 'Nothing, sweetie. Almost done.'

Elizabeth's wounds could be sewn up and healed, but it would be a while before the smell of decay washed out. The woman's skin was shrivelled and it peeled back, crispy and burnt, at the corners of her eyes. In places old bruises had risen and spread, brown and blue and lurid yellow. The walls of her scars were crusty and black, and at her neck and chin her flesh had pulled inward and wrapped tight around her windpipe.

There was a hole in her chest where something had pulled out her heart.

'So how are you feeling, dear?' Nana said.

Elizabeth Drake's eyes darted up suddenly and she smiled at the back of Nana's skull. The smile looked all wrong on that face - her lips were dark and dry and cracked and they sunk into a backdrop of pale, discoloured skin that pulled her face just a little off to one side. 'I'm better,' Elizabeth said. 'Mother, I don't remember... what happened to me? Where's Eddie?'

Anger flashed across Nana's face and she gritted her teeth as she looked down at the pan, stirring until all the bubbles had faded and disappeared beneath the swill. 'Edward left you, Lizzie,' she said. 'There was a terrible accident, and he went away. Edward isn't here anymore.'

'Oh,' Elizabeth said. 'Okay. And Philip?'

Nana paused. 'Philip's sitting next to you, dear.'

There was a low, sickening creak as Elizabeth turned her head and the bones in her neck ground against each other. 'Oh, there you are,' she said flatly. 'I didn't see you there, Philip.'

Philip blinked. One shoulder stuck up high above the other; his neck was bent so far that one ear pressed against his left shoulder. A fragment of his bent spine poked up through the side of his throat, pushing the skin outwards. His decay had been faster than Elizabeth's, for some reason, and his skin was a palette of brown and black and a sickening, yellow-green discolouration. Philip opened his mouth to speak, but a bloody, hideous gargle was all that came out of his lips. A trickle of red ran over his tongue as bubbles formed at the corner of his mouth.

'Something must have ruptured his windpipe in the crash,' Nana said, stepping across to the table and slopping stew onto a cracked, ceramic plate in front of Elizabeth. 'Shame.'

'Oh dear,' Elizabeth said, turning her eyes down toward the plate. 'Can you fix it?'

'No,' Nana lied. 'I'm afraid Philip isn't going to be doing much talking from now on.'

'Oh, okay,' Elizabeth said again. 'This looks delicious, mother.'

Nana smiled. 'It's good to have you home, Lizzie. Now tuck in. We don't want your stew to get cold, now, do we? It would be a shame to waste such good meat.'

Philip twitched in his stool.

'It tastes good, mother,' Elizabeth said as a forkful of flesh slid down her throat.

Nana leant back against the counter and folded her arms, smiling across the room as Elizabeth chewed. 'Best meat on an animal,' Nana said. 'The shins.'

Quickly Nana turned back to the worktop and slid something into the sink; the rusted blade of the hacksaw clattered against splintered ceramic and she turned on the taps. Red clouded the basin.

'Where did this meat come from?' Elizabeth asked. 'It's so... soft.'

Nana smiled, rinsing the hacksaw blade until all the red had scrubbed off.

Below the table, a single bead of blood dropped from the stump above Philip's knee and splashed the ground.

He said nothing.

'Now, Lizzie,' Nana said. 'You've been gone for a long time. How about we head through to the living room once you're finished and -'

Something moved upstairs.

Nana's eyes tracked up to the ceiling and her lips parted. A wisp of breath slipped out of her mouth. 'No...' she whispered. 'That's not possible...'

Elizabeth frowned. Red sauce dribbled over her chin. She didn't seem to notice. 'What is it, mother?'

'He was weak...' Nana breathed. 'He should be...'

Above her head, slow, soft footsteps carried him across the landing. The boy moved slowly, shuffling over the floorboards, and they squealed beneath him.

'You little shit...' Nana hissed.

'Mother?'

Nana smiled across at Elizabeth and shook her head. 'It's nothing. You eat up, dear. I'll be back in a second.' Calmly, the old woman wiped her palms on her dress and stepped out of the kitchen, crossing to the hallway. With a cold, grey look in her eyes, she turned her head toward the stairs.

Edward Drake stood at the top of the staircase, one hand on the banister. There was something missing from his expression. His face was still, stony; his eyes were empty. The boy looked down at her with an air of knowing, of understanding, but without feeling.

Without emotion.

'You should be *dead*,' Nana rasped.

Slowly, Eddie took the first step. 'You're afraid,' he whispered.

Nana backed away from the bottom of the stairs. 'You're alive.'

Eddie took another step. Blood seeped out from beneath his bare feet as the scarred soles pressed down on hard, solid wood. 'Did it work?'

'Child...'

'Did it work?' Eddie said again. He lowered his foot to the third step, sliding his hand along the banister as he walked. 'Are they here?'

Nana paused. After a moment, she nodded her head. 'Yes, boy. They're here.'

Eddie moved slowly, deliberately, tracking the stairs one at a time.

Nana moved backwards, towards the front door, but there was nowhere to go. 'It should have *killed* you...' she breathed.

Eddie said nothing as he reached the bottom of the stairs.

'How does it feel?' Nana said, staring down at him

with narrowed eyes. 'To be without it? To be *separated?*'

For a long time, Eddie was silent. When he spoke, his voice was cold. His eyes bored into the old witch's face and she shivered. 'I've been here two years,' Eddie said. 'I was ready to die. I *wanted* to die.'

'And now what?' Nana said. '*Now* what do you want?'

Eddie shook his head. 'Nothing,' he said. 'I want... nothing. I feel... *nothing.*'

Nana smiled. She leant forward, bending down. On the boy's level, she looked right into his eyes and she *saw* it - the hollow, empty blackness beyond them, the absence of that which had made him exactly who he was...

'Look at you,' Nana cooed. 'All grown up -'

Eddie thrust his hand towards the old woman and grabbed her throat, wrapped his fingers around the withered pipes of her neck. 'You're in my way,' he whispered, pressing his nails into her flesh, waiting for it to pop beneath his grip, to bulge between his fingers in that final moment -

Nana gasped as her throat caved in with a horrific squelch and a spray of thick, dark blood. Her eyes widened and she opened her mouth to tell him to stop, to *beg* him to stop, but Eddie kept squeezing, pressing the tips of his fingers into the crimson mess of her throat.

'I remember what you did to me,' Eddie whispered. Then he plunged his fingers deep into Nana's throat in a spray of blood, reaching in and grabbing something long and thin and slippery and pulling it forward -

Nana's spine broke free of her neck and her head cracked backwards. The old woman's body convulsed and tore into a horrible, violent fit and then she fell, limp, to the ground.

Eddie pulled back his hand and wiped it on his trousers. 'Don't get up,' he said, stepping over her body into the kitchen.

Elizabeth Drake turned her head as Eddie crossed the threshold. Something flickered over her face, but it wasn't love. Recognition, that was all. Familiarity. 'Eddie,' she said slowly. 'Mother said you went away.'

Eddie turned to her, looked into the woman's eyes. 'You're not my mum,' he said quietly.

Behind her, Philip gurgled, drooling onto his crooked throat.

Eddie moved over to the counter, eyes dropping to the blood-stained saw. He wrapped his fingers around the handle and lifted the thing; it was heavy, and the serrated blade was rusted so badly that it was almost completely brown. The teeth were blunt and bent.

It would do.

The boy turned, stepping across the kitchen to the old table.

'What are you doing, Eddie?' Elizabeth said, but she didn't blink, didn't move.

'You're not my mum,' Eddie said again. Turning to

328

Philip, 'You... you're not my dad. I can see it now. This... was a mistake.'

Elizabeth swallowed, and for the first time since she had come back from the dead something close to emotion visited her face. Something like relief. A single, wet tear gathered at the corner of one eye. 'Do you pity us?' she whispered. 'Will you set us free?'

Eddie hesitated. Pity...

'No,' he said. And it was true, he felt nothing. His bones were empty. But he could *remember* pity - what it was, what it meant...

Slowly, Eddie moved to Philip's side and laid the teeth of the saw against the resurrected man's jarred, bent neck. 'This will be slow,' Eddie warned him.

Philip's eyes flickered to his son's face and he blinked. '*Do...*' he gurgled. The next word never came, but Eddie knew what it would've been.

Quickly, without compassion, without pity, but with the memory of what they might've compelled him to do, Edward Drake began to slide the teeth of the saw over his father's throat. Philip Drake's screams sunk back into his lungs and blood bubbled over his lips as a shrill, ruptured gargle escaped his mouth.

A single teardrop formed at the corner of Elizabeth's eye and rolled down her corrupted face, and she nodded. 'Please...' she whispered. 'Set us free...'

2

For a long time the shadowy thing screamed, wracking the glass walls of its prison. The room was silent and dark and its bitter, agonised cries went unnoticed. It was cold. It *hurt.*

It had never been without Eddie before. It had always been... *tethered.* Attached to the boy. Now, for the first time since Edward Drake had been conceived, the thing in the jar was free. It was completely alone.

And god, it hurt so bad.

'There you are,' came a voice from outside the jar. It was a man's voice, but it wasn't like any voice the shadowy thing had ever heard before. It was low and gravelly and it hung on the air like lead.

The shadow reeled back from the glass, torn up in a mess of babbling, fragmented fear. A light flickered at the back of the room, stronger than before, filling the place with a wave of white. It was warm on the glass and it whispered, *turn around. Look.*

The shadow turned wildly, almost toppling the jar in its frantic effort to see the light.

It was wonderful. It filled the back of the room, tearing a hole in the darkness and spreading, throbbing, casting wiry tendrils of white into the shadows. It fizzled and cracked with some wild electricity and it called to the shadow, singing to it.

There was something else, in front of the light. A figure. A silhouette. The source of the voice. The shadow saw polished, black shoes. Black trousers. It saw a face, in the dark, and it recoiled.

The man in the black suit stood with his hands in his pockets, looking down at the jar. His breathing was ragged, like his throat had been cut up and stitched back together. The shadow could hear the newcomer's heartbeat...

'Are you ready?' the man said. He knelt down before the jar, laying a yellow-skinned hand on the lid. Lowering his head to the floor, he looked at the thing inside the jar and smiled. A bulging, bloodshot eye stared through the glass, twisted and warped by the curves of the shadow's cold container.

The thing in the jar shrieked. At the back of the room the light had grown stronger and it pulsed violently, humming all the while.

'Oh, but you are beautiful,' whispered the yellow-faced man. A grey tongue flickered over peeling, pus-stained lips. 'Shh,' he said quietly. 'I'm not going to hurt you. I'm here to *free* you.'

The shadow stopped screaming. *Free me?* it hissed.

The yellow-faced man nodded. His head turned back, towards the light, and he smiled. His throat stretched upward, thin flesh cracking as it pulled tight over a raw, red mess of muscle.

'It's time,' Yellow Face said, and he wrapped his fleshy fingers around the jar and lifted it off the ground. The thing inside crashed and skittered over the cold, thick glass, hungry with that cold, screaming lust to be free.

Slowly, they moved towards the wall of light. The man's footsteps were loud and heavy as they walked across the room. Around them, the jars on the shelves echoed with the cries and calls of agony and distress, but the yellow-faced man ignored them.

Where? came a voice from the jar in his hand.

Yellow Face glanced down, smiling at the writhing shadow within. 'Out,' he said, and they stepped into the light.

For a second, they were consumed by a dazzling surge of white, a prism of colours so vast and so brilliant that they rippled and swam and melted into each other. The whispering was louder in here and the light sang and bristled with an incredible, electric hum that was almost deafening.

Then the light was gone and they were somewhere else.

The dark, dank room was gone, and the walls had been replaced with a sweeping, burning sky. Flames licked the clouds as they trailed across a yellow sea of poisoned air. Through the curved glass, the shadow saw a blot of light on the horizon; a glowing, bloated sun. Plains and vistas of scorched, ashen sand rose and fell around them and great, twisted shapes moved and swam beneath the ground.

'Ugh,' Yellow Face said. 'Not here. This fucking

thing...'

He turned, black shoes digging into the sand, and they stepped back into the light.

Again, that prism of colour, and again the light flickered and disappeared as it pushed them through, chewing them up in a haze of white electricity and spitting them out into the dark.

For a moment, the thing in the jar thought they had gone back to that room, the room with the shelves and the floorboards, but it felt different here. The air, even through the glass, felt fresh and new. A cool wind brushed over the surface of the jar, heavy with salt and dew and the tingle of an oncoming storm.

Yellow Face smiled. Broken, darkened teeth flashed between those narrow lips. His bulging eye seemed to glow a pale, ashen white in the dark. Rock walls rose around them as they stepped forward; the cave was silent, save for the slow dripping of water. The nightmare man gripped the glass jar carefully as he passed through a low, black tunnel. Rough stone scratched his soles as he carried the jar over the floor of a high-ceilinged cavern towards the cave entrance.

Moonlight broached the dark and the stone turned to thick, damp sand.

Before them, the sand curled around the base of a cliff. The beach was narrow and pale and a black, crashing ocean tore it apart. The cliff drew a jagged path across the night towards a stretch of flat, pale wood that jutted out into the sea.

A boat curled around the edge of the pier, gleaming silver in the light of the crescent moon.

'Can you smell him?' Yellow Face said, nodding towards the boat.

He is different, the shadow mused, latching onto the smell. *He is... older.*

'He's *ready,*' Yellow Face said.

Suddenly the man looked up. 'Shh,' he warned, clasping his hand over the lid of the jar. 'Company.'

The shadow heard it, then - a voice at the top of the cliff. A man's voice. Not Eddie's.

This was someone new. He smelled... interesting. The thing could taste blood on the air, blood and alcohol and the strong, potent aroma of despair. It smelled sweat and drunkenness and heard heavy, laboured breathing. The man spoke:

'Nothing ever happens here. Ever. I wish...'

The man paused. A new smell: fear. Paranoia. Curious, the shadow watched from inside the jar as Matthew Kramer leaned forward and peered over the ledge of the cliff.

Yellow Face stepped back and pressed his body against the rock wall. Waited.

'Is that why you're angry, Matt?'

A second voice. Female. Muted by the wind.

The man at the top of the cliff turned his head, frowning. 'What?'

334

'Now,' Yellow Face whispered. His hand moved to the jar's red-striped lid. 'Have fun, kid.' Then a scarred, deformed hand twisted off the lid of the jar and the shadow flew out into the shadows at the bottom of the cliff.

CHAPTER THIRTEEN
THE RUNAWAY MADMAN

1
NOW

Sparrow hobbled out of the doctor's office, leaning heavily on a plastic crutch tucked into the crook of his arm. His knee was bandaged, the joint propped up by a thick, metal splint that was buckled to his ankle. Blood pooled around the edges of the fabric bands and thin, red rivers criss-crossed the boy's leg.

Charlotte stood up from her seat in the waiting room and moved towards him, smiling weakly as she looked Sparrow up and down. 'Here, sit down for a bit,' she said, helping Sparrow to a blue-cushioned bench by the wall. The room was small and dimly-lit and, aside from the two of them, empty. A pale light flickered beyond a deep, rectangular window in the wall, through which the pharmacy, too, was silent.

'What'd he say?' Charlotte asked, nodding toward

Sparrow's leg as the boy grimaced, sitting awkwardly on the blue-cushioned seat.

'Broken,' Sparrow said. His voice was slurred. His eyes roamed about the room, taking in the light. He looked half-baked. 'He said...'

Charlotte frowned. 'Are you on something?'

'Pain,' Sparrow said. 'Until... ferry.'

'Hey,' Charlotte snapped, grabbing the boy's shoulder. 'What are you talking about?'

Sparrow blinked, gazed across at her. 'He put me on *pain* medication. Until the ferry. They're sending me... to a hospital. On the mainland.' The boy smiled suddenly, as if he was daydreaming. 'It hurts,' he whispered through the smile, eyes on the wall.

'Sparrow?' Charlotte said. 'What else did the doctor say?'

'He said I was lucky not to lose my leg,' Sparrow murmured. 'Where's Darcy?'

'I don't know,' Charlotte said. 'We just have to wait for my dad to get here, alright? Then we'll know.'

Sparrow nodded. His mouth opened. The smile had gone; his eyes were wide. 'Buh...' he moaned.

'What?' Charlotte said, frowning. 'Christ, Sparrow, how *strong* is that stuff?'

He pointed. 'Buh...'

Charlotte turned her head, following the direction of his finger. There was a small, metal waste-paper bin across the room. Quickly she stood, grabbing the container and shoving it towards him. 'Here.'

Sparrow took the bin in his lap and bent double, thrusting his face into the bin as he hurled. Vomit and blood splashed against the metal walls of the bin, streaming from his nostrils and mouth. After a moment he stopped, breathing heavily. A wretched stink rose up from the bin and he pulled back his head, face screwed tight.

'You're disgusting,' Charlotte said.

Sparrow grinned up at her, wiping a string of vomit from his lips. 'Love you too,' he rasped. His eyes widened again and his cheeks swelled and Charlotte turned away as he pushed his face back into the bin.

'I'm gonna head outside for some air,' Charlotte said quietly. 'Stay here.'

She turned, walking toward a wide, glass door in the corner of the room. It slid open as she stepped forward, gliding back into the wall to let her through. Cool air brushed her face as she moved down a set of crazy-paved steps onto the lawn.

Charlotte breathed slowly, taking fresh air into her lungs. For a moment she stood there, back to the waiting room door, looking out at the grass and the gravel. Then she crumpled.

The girl's legs buckled beneath her and she knelt on the grass, breathing heavy, head pounding. Her heart beat fast - faster than it had in the arcade, when she'd seen the face of the thing through the glass, faster than it had when the creature had smashed through the wall behind her and lunged toward her face, faster than...

'Oh, shit,' Charlotte breathed.

Then her breath was gone, sucked out of her throat by something unseen and she looked up, eyes wide and round and open, pupils wide and black. She shuddered uncontrollably, trying to slow her breathing as her heartbeat grew louder and louder and *louder.* Gasping, Charlotte clutched at the ground, at the grass, tearing it free of the earth, trying to keep hold, to grasp it in her hands, but it just kept coming *loose* -

'It's okay,' said a low voice above her head.

She tried to look up, to slow her breathing, but her lungs wouldn't have it, couldn't take it, and she opened her mouth to scream -

'Charlie,' said the voice. A shadow moved in front of her. Hands laid softly on her shoulders. She knew those hands. The faint, moth-eaten odour of that old coat. 'It's okay,' said the voice. 'Breathe, Charlie. It's okay...'

'Dad...' Charlotte tried.

'Don't speak. *Breathe.*'

Charlotte squeezed her eyes shut and focused. A hazy, blurred image passed before her - a swiping, blackened claw dug into her heart and pulled and the creature reeled back into the shadows, and then the arcade wasn't the arcade anymore and Charlotte saw trees. Gravel. That crooked house.

Flickering, orange lights. An open door. And the old

woman, beckoning her forward.

'Breathe...'

Charlotte's eyes snapped open. She looked up.

Kramer's face was a mess of worry, his brows knitted into a curious frown.

'I'm okay,' Charlotte whispered, reaching up to wrap her hand around Kramer's arm. 'Sorry, I... I don't know what happened.'

'Has this happened to you before?' Kramer said quietly. He stood in the grass, pulling the girl to her feet.

'Couple of times,' Charlotte said, eyes on the ground. Her heartbeat had slowed and her chest felt lighter. Cooler. 'At school. Never this bad.'

'You should've told me, kid.'

'I didn't want... you've got your own stuff,' Charlotte said.

A pang of guilt slid up Kramer's gut and he swallowed. 'I'm sorry, Charlie. For the way I've been lately. The way I've treated you. I don't want you... I don't want you to feel like you can't *tell* me things. Especially if you're having - what was that, a panic attack?'

'I think so. I'm sorry, dad, I should have...'

'Don't apologise,' Kramer said. He raised a hand to Charlotte's chin, lifted until she was looking up at him. 'Don't you ever apologise to me for that, okay? I'm just sorry you felt like you couldn't just talk to me. Things are going to be better, Charlie. I promise.'

Charlotte nodded. 'Okay, dad.'

There it was again. The guilt. Kramer nodded. 'It's going to be okay. We'll get this sorted, kid, just as soon as we can. As soon as this thing's gone.' He paused, then, looked up. 'Where's your friend?'

'Inside,' Charlotte said. She was afraid to ask, but she couldn't stop herself. 'Darcy?'

Kramer said nothing.

A tear pushed at the corner of Charlotte's eye and her breath hitched in her throat. 'Oh, god...'

'I'm sorry.'

'She's dead.'

'Charlie, I'm so, so sorry.'

'Oh, my god,' Charlotte whispered. 'She's *dead*.'

'We did what we could,' Kramer said. 'This thing... it was too fast. She was too far gone.'

Charlotte raised her hand. 'Don't tell me. I don't want to know.'

Kramer nodded. 'Okay.'

She looked up at him, wiped tears from her eyes. Took a long, slow breath. 'Did you catch it?'

'That's not the plan anymore, Charlie,' Kramer said. Something in his voice had changed; it sounded different. Darker. 'Not now. We're going to kill it.'

Charlotte nodded. 'Good. How?'

'I don't know. But I don't need you to worry about that now, okay? I need you to go back inside and wait with your friend. I've asked someone from the station to come pick you up. Jamie, his name is. He'll take you home, keep an eye on you for a little while. Okay?'

'Dad, I don't need -'

'Charlie.'

She paused. 'Dad, the doctor's putting Sparrow on the next ferry off Cain's End. We could go with him. We could get away from here. It can't follow us off the island, right? We could leave, go back to the mainland. Bring Debbie with us. We don't have to *stay...*'

She trailed off. Her eyes met Kramer's and she understood.

Sand-brown hair flew about his face in the wind and he smiled sadly down at her, and Charlotte nodded.

'I've got you a ticket,' he said. 'You've got a place on the boat, Charlie. If you want it. You can go with Sparrow.'

'But not you?'

'Not me.'

'Then I'm not going.'

'Charlie...'

'Dad. You can't send me away. Not if you're staying. If I lose you...'

Suddenly she wrapped her arms around him, buried her face in the man's chest. 'Don't die,' she whispered, choking up in the folds of his coat. 'Please don't die.'

Kramer closed his eyes, filtering his fingers through her hair. 'I promise,' he said quietly. They held each other a little while longer and he closed his eyes. 'Go on, now. I'll see you soon.'

Charlotte pulled away from him and sniffed. 'You better.'

'Don't worry about me, Charlie. I can look after myself.'

'No, you can't,' Charlotte said. The tiniest hint of a smile crossed her face.

'I know,' Kramer nodded. He gestured towards the road, towards the police car parked there. Debbie was sat in the passenger's seat. Slowly, she lifted her hand in a gentle wave, smiled through the glass. 'That's why I've got her looking after me.'

Charlotte smiled. 'You should tell her, you know.'

'Tell her what?' Kramer said, turning back to the girl.

'You *know* what, dad. She probably knows, too. You're terrible at keeping secrets.'

Charlotte turned and headed for the glass doorway at the front of the doctor's surgery, and Kramer watched her go with a wrenching in his heart that he couldn't push down.

'I wish,' he murmured, and he turned and walked back to the car.

2

Cain's End seemed to have missed the worst of the storm. The rain had slowed to a low drizzle, and while a damp, earthy smell lingered above the sand, the clouds had parted. The tide had sunk to a low, pallid swell, no longer thrown about by the violent winds of the morning. Any traces of blood in the white sand of the beach had been washed away by the waves. The long, grey shadow of the cliff fell across the shore, breaking into fragments and shattered pieces as it crashed into the ocean.

For a moment, the beach was still. The sun had reached a high point in the sky and faint grey light shifted over the sand. The water was a dull reflection of that same grey, rising and falling like the belly of a great, wet beast.

A bony claw crashed up from the foam and tore down into the sand, clutching at white, powdery grains even as they sifted through its fingers. The silence was broken as the shadow dragged itself up and out of the water, clambering onto the beach with a surge of effort that tore its whole body into bloody, writhing convulsions.

The creature lay, for a while, at the shoreline, hind limbs trailing into the water. It panted wildly, crimson jaw hanging open. Its teeth shivered with every ragged breath. The cold of the ocean made it shudder - frozen, damp fingers pulled at its rump as it crawled forward, freeing itself of the sea's icy grasp.

The thing slunk quietly into the shadows at the bottom of the cliff and laid there, heavy. A slow, burning pain spread across its spine, curling up its neck and the back of its skull. The creature would heal, but not like this. Not while it was wasting so much energy in sustaining the complex form it had created. It was exhausted, and while the voices in its twisted mess of a brain had calmed almost to silence they would soon return. When they did, it would have to focus on keeping them quiet, keeping the hunger satiated and the endless, relentless pain stilled.

While it could, it had to concentrate on healing itself.

Quickly, the creature's armoured skin sank back and sunk into itself. Grey folds of muscle and shears of bone became a dark, lucid mist. In seconds the creature's shape was all but gone and it was nothing more than a shadow. It shifted in the air, coiling around itself, free of the confines of its skin.

The shadow pressed itself to the cliff and shut out the smell of the sand, the sound of the swaying ocean and the wind and the rain. It focused on the pain, the agony that made it twitch and shiver in the sand. Slowly, it repaired.

But not fully. No, it left little traces of hurt untouched, here and there. Reminders. There was a certain pleasure, it had found, in the sting or tingle of the leftover pain. In the burning afterglow.

When the shadow was finished, it opened up its senses again. It could smell *them*, on the wind...

The shadow moved, drifting up the clay and the rock face of the cliff. It latched onto the scent, curling over the ledge and shifting between the long grass and the trees. Little more than a whisper on the wind, it moved until it could see them, a little way along the road.

The police car had stopped. One window was cracked open.

The shadow stopped for a moment, exploring its surroundings. It hadn't been to this corner of the island before.

A low, square building lay off to the right. There was a glass door in the wall, red bricks and plaster. A sign above the door; the shadow knew that it could read, if it concentrated, but the letters were blurry, out of focus.

There, stood in the grass before the building, was the man from before. A long, grey coat flew around his waist. He smelled different; the bitter hint of alcohol had dried up; the blood on his clothes had been washed off.

There was someone else with him. A girl. One of the children from the asylum. Her eyes were wet. She was... *feeling* something.

The shadow pitied her. It knew feelings, better than it knew anything else.

It wasn't here for the girl. The shadow turned, moving towards the parked car, drifting silently over gravel and dirt until it could almost taste her. It was her scent the thing had followed, not the man in the grey coat. Not the little girl.

The bitch that had *shot* it.

She sat inside the car, her head laid back against the top of the passenger seat, eyes on the window. The thing could smell her sweat, her faded perfume. It snarled, and for just a fraction of a second its form twisted up and took the shape of a face, a nightmare of a face with gritted, splintered teeth and burning eyes.

The woman in the car frowned, turning her head. The shadow dipped beneath the car, losing its shape as it pressed its shadowy back up to the undercarriage. It wanted to growl, to roar with anger and fury and some deep, straining emotion that it wanted to call *rage*. This woman had tried to *kill* the shadow. She had shot out its throat and thrown it into the ocean.

She looked delicious...

The thing slid out from the belly of the car and moved silently towards the open window. Slowly, it slipped into the car through the crack in the glass; the car was warm, despite the cracked cold of the island, and the shadow sank into the backseat, exploring the leather folds of the seats and the particles of dust in the footwells.

Her scent was overpowering now, and the shadow was hungry. It listened - she was saying something. Her words meant little to the thing, but nevertheless it understood that she wasn't talking to herself, but to someone very far from this car and from the island.

'I know,' the woman was saying. She spoke quietly, as if she didn't really want to be heard. Her voice was breathy; her heartbeat was loud and the shadow struggled to tune the thumping out as it listened. 'Twice in one day, right? But I feel like...'

The woman paused. She looked out of the window, towards the man in the grey coat. There was a tear in her eye.

'I feel like you might not be hearing from me quite so much anymore,' Debbie whispered. 'I'm sorry. It's just... I know there's a plan, and I really believe that whatever it is you must be doing the right thing. You *must* be. But...'

Again, she stopped, and this time it lasted longer. The shadow was growing impatient. It watched as the woman closed her eyes, leaning back in the seat. Breathing heavy. Slowly it leered over her shoulder, reaching with a dark, shifting claw for her throat -

'How could you let this happen?' Debbie said suddenly. Louder, her voice tinged with anger. 'I stood by you while you let Matt suffer, I really did. And that was rough, I'll tell you what, because I had to *watch* him. I had to sit there while he drank and got angry and beat himself up over this whole thing, I had to tell him that things would get better because *you*... you just weren't there. And now where are you?'

She sighed, opening her eyes. The creature sunk back into the shadows, flattening itself against the fabric of the footwell.

'Because now we *all* need you, boss. This thing,

whatever it is... it's killing people. It's killing *kids*. And I have tried so, so hard to believe that you're watching, but honestly... I'm close to giving up.'

Debbie's mouth closed, then, and she swallowed. As if she was just realising what she'd been saying. Eyes on the glass, her hand moved to the cross around her throat and she toyed with it gingerly.

This was the chance it had been waiting for.

The shadow moved, trickling up the back of the passenger seat, gliding soundlessly over the leather. Splintered teeth formed in the darkness of the shadow's belly and it opened wide, moved towards her neck -

'Ready?'

The driver's side door opened and Kramer stepped into the car. The shadow recoiled, sunk back into the shadows of the back of the car.

It could wait.

'Let's go,' Debbie said.

The shadow listened to the tremor in her voice and it smiled.

3

Thick, red carpet muffled the padding of Edward Drake's bare feet as he moved down the corridor, so that his footsteps were near-silent. The folds of his white, cotton trousers and t-shirt drifted over him like shadows. The air in the corridor was stale; even his breathing was so slow and controlled that it was soundless.

Eddie stopped halfway along the corridor, listening. A faint whisper rose into the air from beyond one of the cell doors to his left. A slow, rhythmic chant. Eddie pressed his ear to the metal of the door. It was cold on his face, but he hardly noticed.

'*...saw it through the light and the dark and it was hungry, so hungry, always hungry...*'

Eddie stepped away from the door and kept walking.

Above him, a fluorescent light set into an old-fashioned, gothic bulb flickered gently. The man's shadow twisted and danced on the wall as he passed by the fixture and he ran his fingertips over the wall, tracing paths and trails along the plaster.

'Hayley...' Eddie whispered. His low voice trickled over the air like the haunting, eerie notes of a song. 'Where are you?'

The corridor narrowed before him, pointing him towards a glass-panelled door. The light was pale here, faded somehow. 'This way,' Eddie whispered to himself, stopping at the door and laying his hand on the frosted glass. He peered through, squinting into the next corridor. The glass distorted the square frames of doorways in the next corridor; white flares of light from the bulbs in the wall were twisted and warped.

Eddies eyes darted down to a small, metallic panel halfway up the wall, inset with numbered keys. A narrow display at the top of the panel flickered with digital lettering: *LOCKED.*

'Another way round, then,' Eddie murmured.

'No need,' came a voice from behind his shoulder.

Eddie didn't turn around. He knew that voice, knew that looking was unnecessary. The yellow-faced man had come to him so many times now, in dreams and hazy visions in the daylight, that he doubted there was a single detail on the nightmare figure's burned face that he couldn't recall.

Still, he had always thought he was the only one that could see Yellow Face. And then Hayley King had walked in on the two of them talking, and she had seen him too.

Eddie had to make sure that didn't happen again.

He kept his eyes on the control panel, watching as a thin, dark shadow passed over the keys. The digital display flickered after a second and died. A low, electronic whine signalled the death of the lock, and a soft *click* opened the door.

Eddie paused. Spoke to the thing behind him. 'You could've unlocked my door as soon as we got here,' he said quietly.

'You weren't ready, kid,' Yellow Face said behind him. Hot, wet breath traced a spiral over the back of Eddie's neck.

He ignored it.

'What are you waiting for?' said the voice. 'Find her.'

Eddie didn't bother to reply. Slowly, he passed through the door into the next corridor, closing it softly behind him. The control panel on the wall whirred back into life, humming quietly.

Eddie kept walking. Around him, the lights flickered as he moved. 'Hayley...' he said again, a little louder this time. 'I'm coming for you...'

There was a sound up ahead: heavy, shuffling footsteps. Eddie turned a corner at the end of the corridor, following the noise around to the left.

'You,' Eddie said.

Karl looked across at him. The barrel of a slick, black rifle poked up from behind his neck like a spike buried in his shoulder. He raised a hand, never taking his eyes off Eddie as he reached behind his back for the weapon strapped there. 'How did you...' he said.

Eddie looked the man calmly up and down. Karl was still dressed in the all-black guard's uniform, padded vest strapped to his chest. His belt shone. His hands were gloved. 'I guess the guards in this place aren't up to much,' Eddie said simply.

Karl grunted. 'Shut it, prick,' he hissed, and then he grabbed the rifle by the stock and swung it around to his front, hand moving to the trigger -

Eddie barrelled into the guard with all his weight, slamming his shoulder into Karl's chest. The guard stumbled, falling back against the wall, and Eddie threw his hand towards the strap at the man's shoulder, deftly working the clasp. The gun swung free and fell downwards, crashing into Karl's hip. A fist flew into Eddie's belly. He felt nothing.

'You think you're fast?' Karl spat, sending his knee crashing into Eddie's groin. 'You think you're *strong?*' His fist came swinging forward again, knuckles colliding with Eddie's jaw. He pushed forward and grabbed Eddie's shoulders, kicking out with a steel-capped boot that sunk deep into Eddie's shin.

Eddie looked at him, unmoving, unblinking. His eyes were cold.

Karl frowned. 'You think you're...'

His fist smashed into Eddie's throat.

Finally, Eddie blinked.

Karl raised his fist again but his face was red with exhaustion. He had put everything he had into those first few hits, expecting Eddie to crumple. He lashed out again, but his knuckles barely glanced across Eddie's jaw.

'What are you?' Karl breathed.

Eddie said nothing. Instead, he reached for Karl's belt and grabbed the baton clipped there, freeing it. He stepped back as Karl kicked upwards and the guard toppled forward, stumbling.

Eddie held the baton in one hand, balanced perfectly in his palm. His breathing was slow. Karl slammed his elbow into Eddie's chin but the pain hardly registered. Eddie was focused now, listening to the rhythm of his heart, getting into time with it. Slowly, he flexed his fingers over the sleek, black handle baton. 'You think you can hurt me?' he whispered.

Karl stepped back, shaking his head. His ankle crashed into the gun on the floor and his eyes widened as he turned around, reaching desperately for it -

The baton crashed into the back of Karl's skull with such force that he let out an involuntary squeal, tumbling into the wall. Bone cracked loudly under the impact of the thing and Eddie struck again, smashing the baton into Karl's head a second time, a third. Karl screeched, twitching as he tried to turn and face his attacker.

The baton struck the curve of his forehead. Eddie almost smiled as a deafening *crack* echoed about the corridor. Blood vessels burst inside Karl's left eye and his pupils rolled back into his skull and Eddie swung the baton again. Again. Karl's face sunk inwards in a meaty, sloppy mess of muscle and Eddie smashed the baton into the top of Karl's head with one more swing.

Crack!

Blood sprayed the wall as the baton sunk through flesh and bone and Karl's skull caved in.

It was another few seconds before the screaming stopped. A final, devastating swing sent chunks of brain onto the floor, spatters of grey and pink littering the crimson carpet.

The baton dropped from Eddie's hand and rolled. He

stood still for a minute, eyes on Karl's convulsing, rigid body, watching as the movements slowed. Stilled.

Karl stopped moving and Eddie reached up, absent-mindedly wiped a spatter of blood from his chin.

'I told you what would happen,' he said.

4

Hayley reached for the desk, leaning heavily on the wood. She clutched at her thigh with her free hand, massaging the aching flesh of her leg. Her chest was numb and she closed her eyes, panting as she tried to catch her breath.

She had run all the way here from Eddie's cell after she had seen that... *thing*, in there with him. She could still *see* it in the corner of his room, glaring across at her with a wild, bulging eye and its narrowed, roving partner...

Hayley moved awkwardly around her desk, sliding papers aside with shaky hands in a desperate search for her phone. A sheaf of yellow forms dropped from the desk and floated to the floor. Hayley cursed and bent down to pick them up, grimacing as her heart thumped in her ears. She gathered the papers into her arms and set them on a corner of the desk, almost bumping into the corner of the wood with her burning thigh. She stood for a moment, hands on the desk, veins throbbing in her wrists. Closed her eyes.

Breathe...

'Phone,' Hayley reminded herself, eyes snapping open. Quickly she lifted a book from the desk and slammed it down again - nothing. She groaned, shuffling brown manila folders and crisp white sheets over each other. Above her head, the clock ticked loudly.

There, at the corner of the desk, a glint of silver. Hayley leaned across the desk and grabbed the phone, fumbling with trembling thumbs to unlock it. If she could just call Emma, tell her what had happened...

'Calm down,' Hayley told herself. Her fingers hovered over the phone screen, pads illuminated by a soft, blue glow. 'Just *breathe...*'

Hayley opened up her contacts and found Emma's name. With her thumb, she tapped at the *Call* button. Missed. Tried again.

The phone rang for a moment and Hayley closed her eyes, finally letting out the breath that had been pushing up into her nose for the last thirty seconds. *Calm,* she thought. *Everything's going to be just -*

The phone stopped ringing abruptly, beeping up at her from the desk. Hayley opened her eyes and glanced down at the screen. 'Shit,' she whispered. *No signal.*

'It's okay,' she whispered. 'Just try again.'

Hayley tapped *Call* again. This time, the phone didn't even ring.

No signal.

The bars at the top of the screen were empty; a small, red cross had struck them out. Hayley's connection was gone.

'Shit!' she said again, stuffing the phone into her pocket as she turned for the door.

Hayley froze.

The screen of the computer monitor flickered in the corner of her vision. Hazy, black-and-white stripes filtered downwards as the machine hummed. Slowly, Hayley turned towards the screen and looked it over. 'Oh, *shit...*'

The door to Eddie's cell was open.

Hayley could remember standing in the doorway, staring into the cell as Eddie turned to look at her. She could remember the look in the yellow-faced man's eyes as he saw her standing there, remember the *hunger* in his face. She could remember turning and running away...

She couldn't remember closing the door.

'Oh, god,' Hayley whispered, eyes fixed on the screen. Quickly she laid her hand on the keyboard and zoomed in on the picture. 'Oh, fucking god...'

The cell was empty.

No yellow man. No flicker of shadow.

No Edward Drake.

Hayley backed away from the computer, shaking her head. Her eyes darted up to the office door. She'd left that open, too.

Quickly the woman moved back to the front of her desk, stumbling across the room. Hayley pushed through the door and stepped out into the corridor, looking left and right. Empty.

Why isn't the alarm going off?

Hayley reached for her phone, looked down at the screen. Still no connection. Hurriedly she turned and started to walk down the corridor, pushing forward on her aching leg. She must have pulled a muscle when she started running, twisted it somehow. *Does it matter now?* she thought. *Where's the damn alarm?*

More to the point, how could you leave the fucking door open?

Hayley reached the end of the corridor and checked her phone again. Still no good. Weird, the signal was never usually this bad anywhere in the asylum. *Today, of all days.* She turned a corner, shoving her phone back into her pocket. Outside, that was the only hope.

Hayley stopped walking. Her breath caught in her chest.

Forty feet down the corridor, one of the guards was laid, face-up, on the carpet. His arm was twisted behind him, still reaching for something, all bent up and twisted. The man's head had caved in completely and his face was unrecognisably mutilated. His eyes had sunk into his skull and pulled together, drawn in by the same force that had carved a deep, curved trench into his forehead.

Blood and brain had splashed the wall behind him. Bloody shards of bone scattered the floor around his head.

'What have I done?' Hayley whispered.

Edward Drake stood over the guard's body; his hands dangled by his sides. In one, he grasped a thick, black baton.

As Hayley watched, the weapon dropped to the ground with a *thud.* It rolled over the carpet and Eddie stepped back from the carcass, raising a hand to his lips to wipe the blood off his face.

He looked up. Turned his head.

'No...' Hayley whispered.

Eddie smiled as he saw her and started walking, stepping easily over Karl's body. He moved with purpose, eyes stony with determination. One hand clenched into a white-knuckled fist at his side. '*There* you are...' he said. 'We've been looking for you.'

Hayley ran.

Quickly she turned back the way she'd come, ran past her office without a glance behind her.

She didn't need to look to know he was following her.

Soft, slow footsteps on the carpet echoed in Hayley's ears, even above her panting and the throb of thick, warm blood in her veins. Her own ragged steps, uneven and erratic, scuffed the floor as she reached the end of the corridor and thumbed a code into the keypad on the wall. Her hand trembled.

The door opened and Hayley passed into the next corridor. Turned another corner. The lights flickered around her, throwing fluorescent shafts onto the walls. A shadow flickered across her shoulder and she cried out.

'Emma!' Hayley yelled, but it was no good. Even if the nurse was somewhere in the building, she wouldn't hear Hayley calling. Not through the soundproofed asylum walls.

Suddenly Hayley remembered she'd put her phone in her pocket, yanked it out as she ran.

'Shit!'

The mobile tumbled out of her hand and crashed onto the carpet. Hayley stumbled to a halt, bending down to pick it up. She scrambled for the device and it slipped out of her fingers and she lost her balance, crashed to her knees.

Ahead of her, something clicked.

Hayley froze on the floor, hand laid over the phone, watching with wide eyes as the door at the end of the corridor started to open.

Eddie knew the codes. Somehow, he had made his way around her and he knew the passcodes for the doors. *All* of them.

Hayley wrapped her fingers around the phone and staggered to her feet, dialling as she turned away from the door, running before she had straightened up.

'Emma!' she yelled into the phone. 'Emma, pick up!'

No signal.

Another *click*, off to her left.

How could he be there? How was he *moving* so fast?

Hayley kept running, ignoring the sound. On her right, something else clicked. One of the cell doors.

It can't be...

Metal doors on either side of her blurred into nothing as Hayley ran past. Something moved on her right. Hayley reached the end of the corridor and ducked as something passed over her head, a shadow flickering over the walls, curling across the ceiling -

Hayley stopped for breath, doubling over. Her leg *burned.* She turned her head as another door clicked, looking down the corridor. Her eyes caught a flash of movement and she watched as the shadow dipped and flitted about the corridor, moving like a ghost, like a wraith.

The shadow ducked, passing over a door at the end of the corridor.

Click.

A faint, electronic beep rang into the corridor and the shadow moved again, crossing the corridor. Hayley raised a hand to her mouth as it passed across the opposite door. Another beep. Another *click.*

The sound of a cell door unlocking.

'Oh, *fuck,*' Hayley whispered.

The shadow moved from one door to the next,

flickering and twisting, tracing cold whispers over the walls as it paused to kill the electronic control panels.

A slow, metallic grinding filled the corridor as a dozen bolts slid back, a dozen doors curled out into the corridor and opened wide...

'Eddie!' Hayley yelled. 'You need to stop this! However you're...'

Edward Drake stood at the end of the corridor, looking right at her.

There was still a drop of blood on his chin, a spatter of red across the scars on his throat. His eyes were empty.

Shadows moved at the open doors and Hayley backed away, turned, almost tripping and falling to the ground.

Footsteps sounded in the cells as inmates woke, stood from their beds. Slowly, cautious figures started to appear in the doorways, stepping out into the hallway.

Hayley's heart cracked against her chest and her leg throbbed as she ran. Behind her, a low, wild laughter rippled through the corridor.

5

The canteen was dark when Hayley stumbled through the door. One dim, orange bulb crackled above the hot counter, tingling with a low, metallic hum. The greasy half-light touched the backs of a row of plastic chairs along the wall. Slithers of yellow trickled over the edges of a fat vending machine in the corner of the room.

The door squealed to a close behind Hayley and she headed for the farthest wall, moving slowly in the dark. She held a hand in front of her chest, fumbling with tables and chairs as she passed. Her calf bumped something and the thing rattled. Hayley stepped aside, moving awkwardly past a low trolley littered with trays of cold, metal cutlery.

Hayley ducked between two circular tables as her eyes adjusted to the dark and she moved toward a third. Laying a hand on the table, Hayley looked back; a thin line of white flickered between the door and the frame, a glimpse of light from the corridor.

Hayley drew in a breath, half-expecting to see a shadow pass over the door. She knew what it was now, that shadow: it was *him*. The yellow man. The man she had seen in Edward Drake's room.

She didn't know which one of them she should be more afraid of.

Hayley kept moving. She pulled two chairs apart and knelt down, crawling between them until she was underneath the table. On her hands and knees she slid the chairs back together, wincing as they groaned loudly over the vinyl floor.

Huddled in a ball beneath the table, Hayley looked up at the door. She could just see it, beyond the trails of tablecloth that draped over her and hid her from view. Her eyes were wide as she watched. Waiting.

'Don't find me here,' she whispered, hanging her head. She caught sight of her hand, wrapped around the metal table leg - it was shivering. Her entire body was trembling like a leaf set to be torn from the branch of an old, rotting tree. 'Please, don't let him find me here...'

Hayley raised her eyes as something moved above her head.

The glowing band of light around the door flickered. Hayley covered her mouth with a clammy palm. '*No...*'

A grey shadow fluttered across the flickering line and Hayley held her breath, refusing to blink.

Turn around, she thought. *Please, just turn around and go. Don't come in here...*

The shadow disappeared.

Hayley waited, afraid to believe that it could really have been that easy. Perhaps he had just stepped aside. Maybe he was listening, waiting until he knew for sure that she was in here before he came in.

Seconds passed, and those seconds turned into a full minute. Nothing moved in the corridor. The door stayed closed.

He was gone.

Hayley let out a breath, shuddering uncontrollably as her hand fell from her mouth. Relief washed over her like a wave and she almost wanted to laugh. He was really gone. She had done it.

Hayley let her head sink, hair falling in front of her face, dangling in the dark. A tear poked at the corner of her eye as her breathing returned to her. *Oh, thank god. Thank god,* she thought. She had to resist the urge to smile, to break out laughing.

He was *gone.*

Hayley looked up, pushing her hair back from her eyes. She started to move, leaning back on her rump and preparing to sit up, to crawl out from under the table. In front of her face, the tablecloth flitted off to one side as she exhaled.

Hayley froze.

The canteen door was wide open.

Orange light poured into the room, tossing glowing blankets onto the tops of the tables closest to the door.

A heavy-set silhouette stood in the middle of the canteen, broad arms hanging by his sides. His head was tilted, just a little. Like he were sniffing the air.

Hayley's heart stopped.

The silhouette moved silently, with a disturbing kind of grace that shouldn't have been possible with his size. He stepped to the side of the room and Hayley swallowed. Another hot, stinging tear slid down her cheek. Salty and wet, it traced a slow, dangerous path over the curves of her face and dripped to the floor -

The silhouette stopped, twenty feet or so from where Hayley was hiding, half-obscured by the tablecloth. Slowly, Edward Drake reached out his hand to grab something.

Hayley followed the direction of the silhouette's outstretched arm and her eyes widened as she saw what he was grasping for.

The figure rummaged, for a second, in the contents of the cutlery trolley. Thick, long fingers brushed delicately over polished spoons and long, curved knives. They settled on something else.

Slowly, Eddie wrapped his hand around a fork and slid it out of its tray with a long, slow shearing of metal on metal.

Hayley took her chance and shuffled backwards, kicking out at the chair behind her. She shoved it aside, already on her feet and darting for the next table. Eyes on the door, she staggered over an upturned chair and bolted.

Eddie was behind her in less than a second and Hayley screamed as hot, heavy breaths danced over her neck and the back of her head. He was no longer concealing his footsteps and they were loud on the hard, smooth surface of the canteen floor. A chair clattered over the vinyl as the man shoved past it, coming for Hayley, fork shining a dim, dark orange in his hand.

Something tightened at Hayley's throat and she gasped as Eddie yanked her back by the collar of her blouse. 'Please!' she croaked, but it was no use. Eddie's eyes burned with a calm, collected emptiness that Hayley knew she couldn't bargain with, couldn't reason with.

There was no compassion in those eyes, no feeling at all.

Calmly, Edward Drake turned the doctor around, facing her. His face was empty.

'I don't need to kill you,' Eddie said quietly. His voice was almost a whisper. 'But you saw him. You understand, something has to be done about that.'

Hayley struggled against the man's grip, kicking out with her aching limb. A river of pain shot up from the twisted muscle into her stomach and she cried out in agony. She shook her head, grabbing at the man's arm, but she couldn't force his hand away from her throat, couldn't wriggle out of his grasp.

Hayley's eyes moved to the fork in Eddie's hand. The prongs glinted silver in the light that streamed in from the corridor.

'Something has to be done,' Eddie said again.

CHAPTER FOURTEEN
BLIND

1
NOW

Charlotte slid a bolt across the front door, locking it tight. She turned and kicked off her shoes, moving toward the stairs. She felt patches of warmth at her neck, at her belly, and she reached a hand to her neck. When she looked at her fingers, they were streaked with red.

It wasn't her blood.

The creature had been coming straight for her when it saw Darcy, eyes wide in the dark of the arcade. The shadowy thing had turned, opening its jaws as it lunged towards her -

Before Charlotte could blink, the blood had splashed her face and her shoes and she was stumbling back, away from the creature as it buried its jaws in her friend's gut. She had slipped, fallen -

Charlotte shook off the image, gripping the banister

to pull her up the stairs. A long, hot shower, that was all she needed. She would wash the blood off her skin, the sweat and the fear out of her pores.

Then she would feel better.

Quickly, Charlotte crossed from the top of the stairs to the bathroom and flicked on the light. The tiled floor was cold through her socks and she stepped onto a dark, blue bathmat, reaching across to turn on the shower.

Charlotte paused. Perhaps a bath would be better. She could take as long as she liked, lay in the water and let it soak her as steam filled the room and misted up the mirrors. She could close her eyes and forget everything that had happened as the blood drifted off her skin and disappeared into the water.

But the creature would still be out there...

Charlotte turned on the taps and stepped out of the bathroom as a surge of water splashed the ceramic floor of the bath. A vein at the back of neck throbbed and trembled as she crossed the hall to her room, stepped through the door. She could feel the stress returning to the base of her skull, feel the headache coming on and the panic that came with it and she moved to the window, leaned on the sill with her eyes closed.

'It's okay,' Charlotte told herself. 'It can't get me in here.'

It got Darcy. It got Liam...

'It can't get me. The door's locked,' she whispered. 'It doesn't know where you live.'

What if it does?

'They'll find it,' Charlotte said. 'They'll kill it.'

The girl could feel her breaths quickening. Her heart fluttered madly in her chest. She opened her mouth to say something else, but the headache had already started to push at the backs of her eyes, black spots dancing before her face. There was nothing she could say to stop it now. All Charlotte could do was ride it out, like she had at school all those times. Like she did when the nightmares came and she woke up, throat closed up and burning, nails dug so deep into the mattress that her wrists ached.

All she could do was *breathe...*

Charlotte opened her eyes. Looked out the window.

Parked on the street in an old police car, her dad's friend sat in a pale shirt and tie, face half-hidden by a hazy rectangle of light on the glass. Charlotte could see the phone in his hand; Jamie had been trying to reach someone when he had picked her and Sparrow up from the doctor's - one of his forensics team. The man had gone missing, apparently. No word from anyone, no sign of him anywhere on the island.

Charlotte wondered if he'd been eaten. Or thrown into the sea, like Liam. She wondered if he'd ever show up, washed up on the beach, dismembered and bloody and...

'Breathe,' Charlotte whispered. Quickly, she turned back and headed for the bathroom. Perhaps if she kept moving, kept herself distracted, the attack would pass.

Charlotte crossed the bathroom again and dipped a hand into the bathwater. It was hot, so hot it stung, and she pulled her hand out, ramming the cold tap on full. She stood back from the tub and undressed, wincing as a shot of pain washed over the top of her head. The headache was getting worse.

Charlotte whirled round and opened up a mirrored cabinet above the sink. She fumbled about amongst the pill bottles and toiletries, searching for a tab of paracetamol.

If she could quell the headache, the migraine would never have a chance to fully set in.

In her haste, Charlotte knocked an empty flask off the shelf and it clattered to the tiled floor with a metallic rattle. The girl swore, reaching out to close the cabinet door as she bent down. Her hand froze on the glass handle as she caught sight of the bottles at the back of the cabinet, stashed away where she wouldn't find them.

Recent.

'Oh, dad...' Charlotte whispered. Her heart slowed, just a little. Her breathing slipped back under her control. A new feeling washed over her, overpowering the others for a moment.

Disappointment.

Then the headache slammed into the front of her skull in a fury of thundering, crushing pain and Charlotte cried out, losing her grip on the handle. She fell against the sink, grabbed at the edge of the basin, but already her legs had crumpled beneath her and she was on the floor. Her forehead crashed into the funnel of the sink as she fell but she had blacked out before the pain could ring in her ears.

Everything was cold.

In the very last second before Charlotte fainted, she saw it. Hidden beyond the trees, bathed in the light of a full, bloated moon, the crooked house stood decrepit and waiting.

Orange firelight soaked the windows.

The door opened and an old, black-clad woman stood in the opening, beckoning her forward with an old, withered hand...

Then everything went black, and Charlotte Kramer was asleep.

2

Chunks of gravel bit and scratched at the tyres of the old police car as it wound through the forest. Mid-afternoon light filtered through the tops of the dying trees and threw patches of gold and white onto Kramer's face as he drove, eyes narrowed and focused on the dirt track ahead. Before long the trees split and a tall, iron-barred gate rose up at the end of the track.

There it was, crowned by the forest as it crashed up from the ground in slivers of stone and brick and dull, grey turrets.

Black River Asylum.

All the windows were small and square and barred, dark in the shadow of a shallow, slanting roof. There was only one way in, one way out: a wide, heavy-set door set into the face of the building.

Kramer pulled up to the gate and slid his foot onto the brake, peering through the bars. The engine rumbled patiently.

Just beyond the gate, half-obscured by a crumbling brick wall topped with barbed wire, a guard tower leaned on criss-crossed metal stilts. At the top of the structure, a small, glass-walled room was flanked by floodlights. One blinked incessantly, emitting a dull, damp glow every couple of seconds. The bulb in the other had died altogether.

'Should there be someone in there?' Kramer said quietly, pulling up to the gate.

'There was yesterday,' Debbie murmured, peering through the windscreen. 'Maybe he's taking a break.'

'Maybe...' Kramer said.

'I'd be more worried about *that*, right now,' Debbie said, pointing forward.

'Shit,' Kramer said, turning his head back toward the windscreen. He hadn't noticed it before, but now that they were a little closer he could see it clearly.

The front door was wide open.

An electronic panel set into the wall had gone dark.

As Kramer watched the door swung back, pushed by the wind, and a shaft of light widened around the jamb. The door hung open for a second and Kramer blinked.

He could've sworn, in that second, that something flashed across the empty hallway, like a shadow...

The door slammed shut and Kramer winced.

'Do you think something's happened?' Debbie said.

'I've got a feeling,' Kramer murmured.

Debbie said nothing. She felt it too. There was something in the air around this place. Something thick and heavy and cold, even this far from the asylum. It had felt the same just before the storm.

A jerking, fragmented movement caught Debbie's eye and she glanced down, looking toward Kramer's hands. One was still resting on the wheel, shivering just a little with the rumble of the engine. Still running. The other, in his lap, curled into a tight fist. The sores on his knuckles were wet and cracked.

The fist twitched wildly as Debbie watched, veins throbbing over the back of Kramer's hand.

'Matt...' Debbie said.

Kramer looked down, caught himself. His fist unclenched and he exhaled softly. He blinked, sliding his hand beneath his leg as if to trap it there. 'Been a while since I had a drink,' he said, as if that explained the convulsions.

'We should go,' Debbie told him quietly. 'Get help. Someone from the station. Right?'

374

'Station's empty, Deb,' Kramer said, but he wasn't even looking at her. 'There's nobody there.'

The detective's eyes had darkened, Debbie noticed, half-hidden by the thick strands of hair that had fallen loose of his fringe. He looked exhausted. Neither of them had eaten, Debbie realised, for a long time. Kramer didn't look as if he'd slept in a week. Even as she watched, his hand started to tremble again.

A tiny bead of blood drizzled over his knuckles, freed from the scab that had peeled open on the back of his hand.

'Matt, we should *go.*'

Slowly, Kramer unclipped his seatbelt, moved to open the door.

'Matt! Listen to me,' Debbie tried again, grabbing his arm. 'Look at me. You're not in any state to go charging in there. Let me just call someone...'

Kramer looked into her eyes for a moment, silent. Then he nodded. 'Alright.'

'Good choice,' Debbie said, throwing him a weary smile. She grabbed her phone and flipped it open. 'Bollocks.'

'What is it?'

'No signal,' Debbie shook her head. 'Pissing *trees* everywhere, maybe I can get a connection if I just -'

Kramer opened the car door and stepped outside.

'Matt!'

Kramer ignored her, closing the door behind him. He

stepped across to the gate, overcoat flapping about his legs in the wind. A drop of rain hit his forehead and he grimaced, looking up.

Above the asylum, the sky was darkening again. Thin wisps of shimmering, white cloud seemed to shift and change as he watched. On the horizon, wide slants of rain peeled down to the horizon.

'Matt!' Debbie yelled, stepping out of the car behind him. 'We don't know what's going on in here! We should at least go somewhere we can call -'

'It's him,' Kramer said.

'Drake?' Debbie said, stepping up beside him. 'Matt, just because his name was on that wall -'

'Do you know the code?' Kramer cut in, nodding toward a control panel by the gate.

Illuminated a soft, pale green, the display upon it read: *LOCKED*. Whoever had opened the front door to the asylum didn't want anyone getting out into the forest.

Debbie shook her head. 'Hayley opened it for me,' she said. 'When we came yesterday. I didn't get a chance to see...'

'Then we need to find another way in,' Kramer said, stepping back. He looked up, blinking as another raindrop splashed his eyeball. His eyes drew over the barbed wire at the top of the wall, and he sighed. 'Maybe there's another gate, or a back entrance -'

'Matt,' Debbie said quietly.

'There's got to be a service door, or, I don't know, maybe there's a staff entrance somewhere...'

'*Matt,*' Debbie repeated.

Kramer turned. 'What is it?'

Debbie nodded toward the gate. 'Look,' she whispered. Kramer whirled around, turned his attention to the iron bars -

A tall, broad-built man stood just the other side, dressed all in white. His face was square and shaven, eyes set beneath a thick, slanting brow. His black hair was matted and twisted back from his forehead. A white t-shirt clung to him, spattered with damp, grey spots as a low drizzle started to cover him. Baggy, white cotton flapped about his legs. His feet were bare.

His face was expressionless.

'This him?' Kramer said.

Debbie nodded behind him. 'That's him.'

Kramer stepped forward. Inches from the gate, he looked into Edward Drake's eyes. 'Who *are* you?' he whispered.

Slowly, Eddie moved closer to the bars.

'Matt, be careful...' Debbie said.

Eddie blinked. A trickle of rain ran down his face.

Damp strands of brown fell into Kramer's eyes. He gritted his teeth. 'I asked you something,' he said quietly.

Eddie was silent. His face didn't change, didn't move. His eyes were a dark kind of hollow that was

377

disconcerting, somehow. Analytical, without being curious. Cold, without being angry.

'Who are you?' Kramer asked again.

A thin, dark smile peeled across Eddie's face. There was no emotion in that smile, no kindness. 'Who are *you?*' he said.

'Don't play games with me,' Kramer hissed. 'What do you want?'

'I want you to let me out,' Eddie said.

'I'm not going to do that.'

'Matt...' Debbie said.

Kramer looked down and his eyes fell upon Eddie's clenched fist, hanging stiff by the man's side. Flecks of blood dotted his wrist, his exposed forearm, curls of red tracing thin lines over his muscular flesh. Beads hung off of the hairs on his arm like dew clinging to blades and stalks of grass. Crimson seeped between his fingers.

There was a bloody fork in his hand.

'Debbie, go back to the station,' Kramer said. 'Get help.'

'I'm not leaving you...' Debbie protested.

Slowly, Edward Drake wiped his bloody palm on the waist of his trousers, never taking his eyes off the man the other side of the bars.

'Now, Deb,' Kramer said, as calmly as he could manage. 'Get someone down here *now.*'

Behind him, the car door opened and shut. The engine cut into life and revved wildly.

'Are you sure that's a good decision?' Eddie whispered.

Rain lashed Kramer's face as he frowned. 'What?'

The car spun around, tyres grinding into the gravel as the skies roared above Black River Asylum. Dirt and flecks of stone flew upward as it pulled away.

'You brought it here,' Eddie said. 'The one thing I want. The one thing I would *tear down these gates* to reach.'

'What are you talking about?' Kramer said, moving closer to the bars. 'What do you *want?*'

'You brought it here,' Eddie repeated, and now his eyes were on the car. 'And then you sent it away.'

Kramer turned around, eyes locking on the car as it moved away, rolling fast over the dirt track, bumping wildly as it slid into the depths of the forest.

'Oh, shit,' Kramer said.

Through the rear window, barely visible in the dark of the trees and the woods, a twisted, writhing shadow rose up in the backseat of the car and *grinned,* flashing splintered, blood-stained teeth as it raised a set of thick, bony claws.

3

The phone screen was cracked, broken into dozens of sharp, shattered pieces by a jagged spider's web of scars. Hayley fumbled for the mobile in the dark of the canteen, laying her palm on the screen. It had fallen out of her pocket when Eddie had come for her and crashed onto the vinyl.

Shards of glass and plastic littered the floor.

Everything was black.

'Emma,' Hayley gasped, moaning as a sharp, dark pain shot through the front of her skull. Eyes screwed shut, she traced paths over the screen with shaking fingers, wincing as the cracked glass dragged blood out of the pad of her thumb.

She couldn't see. God, she couldn't *see...*

Hayley found the splintered home button and held it in for a second. Two seconds. One more second, and the voice activation would kick in -

The phone vibrated softly in her hand. A dull, electronic voice greeted her, crackling through the damaged speaker. 'How can I help you?'

'Call Emma,' Hayley moaned. She lifted a hand to her eyes, covering them, leaning her head against the leg of the table behind her. 'Fuck, it *hurts...*'

'I'm sorry,' the phone said. The simulated voice sounded unnatural, sounded *wrong* through that speaker. 'I don't recognise that request.'

'Call *Emma,* damn it!' Hayley snapped. Pain shot up the side of her face to her temple.

Hayley waited a few moments, lamenting the silence, afraid to open her eyes. She could feel a warmth on the back of her eyelids, trickling down her cheeks, and she shook her head. God, it *hurt...*

A soft, muted beep rang out from the phone. 'No signal,' it said, in that same damning monotone.

'*Fuck!*' Hayley yelled. 'Fuck, fuck, fucking *fuck!*' She threw the phone to the ground, listened as it clattered onto the vinyl. Darkness swam in front of her vision and she kept her eyes shut tight. Loud in the emptiness of the canteen, the mobile skidded across the floor, crashing into a toppled chair.

'No signal,' it repeated.

'*Fuck you!*' Hayley screamed. Slowly, she lowered her head. The pain rippled all over the front of her face, spreading from her eyes. It was soft, now, warm...

'You can do it,' Hayley whispered. 'You just need to open your eyes.' She peeled open one eyelid and screeched, slamming it shut again. Hot needles pierced her temple.

Behind her, the door opened.

'No!' Hayley cried. 'No, get out! Get out! Leave me alone, you've done enough, you've done *enough just go* _'

A hand on her shoulder. 'Hayley, it's me.'

Soft voice. Female. Hot, sweet breath on Hayley's skin. And a familiar smell. *Emma.*

'It's okay,' Emma whispered. She sounded close, but Hayley couldn't pinpoint the sound, couldn't tell if the nurse was standing off to one side or right in front of her. 'I came to find you, Hayley. In your office? And I saw... I saw what happened. On the cameras. Please, love, open your eyes for me.'

Hayley shook her head. 'I can't,' she moaned. 'Please, I can't...'

She reached out into the dark. Black shapes swam before her. She grasped at something, fingers wrapping around empty, cold air. 'Emma...'

'You have to open your eyes, Hayley,' Emma said. Her voice was hazy, displaced. Something pounded in Hayley's ears.

'It hurts...'

'I know,' Emma said, 'but I need you to do this for me. Open your eyes, Hayley. Please. Let me see...'

Slowly, Hayley tilted her head back. 'I can't do it,' she moaned. 'I can't...'

Emma made no reply.

'Emma?' Hayley whispered. 'Emma, are you... I can't see you. I can't...'

Fighting the urge to scream as agony flashed through her skull, Hayley took a breath. Slowly, she forced her eyes open.

The blackness didn't go away.

'Oh, Hayley,' Emma breathed. She laid a hand on Hayley's arm. The other moved to her mouth as she choked back a sob. 'I am so, so sorry...'

'Please,' Hayley rasped. 'I can't see... How bad is it?'

Emma shook her head, taking a step back. 'Oh, my love...'

Deep, red dots surrounded Hayley's eye-sockets, dug into the flesh where Eddie had jabbed the fork into her face. Her eyeballs had been shredded, twisted about the prongs of the fork, punctured and gouged and torn to nothing. All that was left of each was a scrap of wet, white fluid, glistening like egg yolk in the bloody remains of her face.

'How bad is it?' Hayley repeated. 'Tell me...'

'I am so sorry,' Emma said. 'Oh, my love, I am so, so *sorry*.'

'They're gone, aren't they?' Hayley said, shaking her head. She reached out, grabbed Emma's arm. 'My eyes... he took them from me. My eyes are gone, aren't they?'

Emma said nothing.

Hayley sobbed, crimson tears streaming down her face as the last slivers of her eyeballs seeped out of their sockets in a bloody, gelatinous mess.

'Emma, *did he take my eyes?*'

CHAPTER FIFTEEN
CHARLOTTE KRAMER

1
NOW

Debbie's grip tightened on the wheel as she pushed into the forest, slipping into second and punching her toes down on the accelerator. The engine spat loudly and gravel churned beneath the spinning tyres as the trees thickened and twisted around the police car. A sliver of guilt had buried itself in Debbie's gut; she shouldn't have left Kramer on his own. She should have stayed. Easing off on the pedals, Debbie glanced up into the rearview mirror to catch a glimpse of the asylum -

'Fuck!' Debbie yelled, ducking her head as the shadow swiped at her with a bony, bloody claw. The thing lunged forward and the tyres squealed as Debbie slammed her foot onto the brake pedal, grinding it into the floor. She cried out as the creature tumbled into the front of the car, and within half a second it had turned to face her and it pulled back a knotted, stone-coloured fist, set to slam it into her face. Debbie fell back against the door and shoved it open, tumbling out of the driver's seat. The ground bit at her shoulder and she rolled, covering her head as the car skidded to an uneasy halt on the other side of the road. Above her, the trees cast curled shadows on the track.

'Where the fuck did you come from?' she cried, heart pounding as she scrambled to her feet. She turned her head toward the car, clutching her shoulder. It might have been dislocated, but there was no time to worry about that now.

The car's nose was buried in the shadows at the edge of the road, inches from a crooked tree. A thin plume of smoke crept up from the exhaust. The engine had stalled and the silence was eerie. Slowly, Debbie took a step back.

In the passenger's seat, dark shapes moved and twisted and Debbie watched as the creature tilted its head upward, opening its jaws as wide as they would go. There was a loud crack as the thing's jagged teeth lengthened, pushing upward out of thin, shadowy gums until they were inches long. Strings of muscle snapped together and pulled tight across plates of armour and mucus-covered skin. A low, deafening rumble erupted from the pit of the creature's belly and the windscreen splintered.

'How the hell...' Debbie breathed. She moved

towards the car, taking slow steps, hand outstretched. If she could close the door, if she could just trap the thing in there...

The creature turned its head, looking at her through the open driver's door. Its eyes smouldered with a deep, hot orange as it caught sight of her. Teeth crashed together in a hungry smile.

It lunged.

'No, you don't!' Debbie yelled, rushing forward and slamming the driver's side door closed.

The creature crashed into the door and the window cracked. A thin crevice opened up along the glass and the shadow lowered its head, ramming the top of its skull into the window. The crack widened and Debbie shook her head. 'This is fucking insane,' she whispered as the creature slammed its face into the glass. The crack opened up and spread and blood smeared the window.

It looked her in the eyes and buried its bony fist in the window. It shattered and shards of glass showered the road. Debbie backed away as the creature forced its head out of the window, screeching and shrieking, mouth open and dark and crammed with teeth.

Debbie turned and ran.

A harsh wind rippled along the road, funnelled by the tunnel of the tree trunks around her. The breeze passed over her face as she tore along the gravel. Above, it had started to rain again, but she was sheltered by a canopy of thick, dying leaves.

Behind her, there was a sickening, metallic crunch. Stones flew over each other as the creature slithered out onto the road, and then it was running after her, breathing hard and hot, claws pounding the dirt as it leapt for her -

Debbie ducked to one side, stumbling as the solid ground beneath her crumbled away and broke into loose earth and clumps of sand and dead, broken foliage. She pushed on through the trees, panting heavily, clutching at her side as a splitting pain pulled her muscles in on themselves. On the road behind her the creature was following her, turning around in the road. It moved like nothing she had ever seen.

Running back towards the asylum, Debbie saw movement in the trees ahead. A flash of grey. The creature was behind her, gaining fast. She could almost smell the blood on its claws. But there was something else, in the forest with her.

'Deb!' Kramer yelled, crashing through the woods up ahead. He hadn't seen her, not yet.

'Here!' Debbie called, running towards him, plunging deeper into the trees.

Thick claws dug into her ankle and she screamed, falling forward. Her skull crashed into a tree and scraps of bark flew out from the trunk, carving deep scratches in the skin of her face.

A glint of silver through the trees, glowing as she

fell, as the ground came rushing up to meet her, and she turned onto her back, looked up as the creature bore down on her, snapping its teeth like something possessed -

Bang!

The gunshot echoed and Debbie screwed her eyes shut, yelling as the creature fell back, disappeared. She stumbled up to her feet, ducked under the shadow's slashing limb as it tore another swipe at her face.

'Matt!' she yelled, staggering through the dirt and the broken leaves. 'It's here, it's in the trees!'

Then she saw him, panting as he burst through the trees, gun raised. A thin trail of cold, grey smoke rose from the barrel. He looked across at her, eyes widening. 'Debbie!'

She moved towards him, shaking. Blood thumped loudly in her ears. Shadows swelled around her and she ran, throat dry, side split with pain. Something moved behind her and she quickened her pace. 'Matt, it's here!' she yelled.

He stepped forward, lifting the gun high. 'Debbie, get down!' he shouted, eyes narrowing as he saw it, twisted and brutal and bloody. 'Get *down!*'

Debbie moved to one side, ducking her head. Kramer pulled the trigger and a bullet soared from the end of the old pistol, smacked the creature square in the mouth. It passed through the back of the thing's head and the shadow screamed.

A spurt of black blood trailed out of its skull and drifted, upwards, into the air.

The creature turned towards Kramer, roaring, and suddenly it was moving faster than Debbie had imagined it could, a blur of grey rippling between the trees. Kramer cried out, stepped aside, and the thing barrelled out onto the road, tearing up gravel as it dug its claws into the ground and stopped itself. It turned, lunged, and Kramer staggered back, finger on the trigger -

'Run!' Debbie screamed, but it was too late.

A grey fist crashed into Kramer's arm and the gun fell to the ground, sliding into the dirt at the edge of the trees. Kramer turned, moved to reach for the gun, and for just a second his eyes caught Debbie's and she could see it there, in the bloodshot whites that surrounded his dulled irises, in the lines of his face.

He wasn't afraid, not now. He wasn't thinking about what could happen to him. All he saw was her, and she was the only reason he'd run after the car, the only reason he had left Edward Drake alone and free beyond the gate -

The creature grabbed at Kramer's shin and he went down, tumbled onto his face. Kramer lashed out behind him with a fist, bringing up a cloud of earth with the movement, but he missed and the creature opened its mouth, pinning its victim to the ground with its forelimbs as its face peeled apart and thick, translucent strings of drool flew from its teeth.

'Hey!' Debbie yelled, standing at the edge of the road. The creature's head snapped up and it snarled, burnt eyes narrowing. 'Over here!'

Then it was on her, before she could move, before she could run, and she screamed as its jagged teeth clamped down on her arm and tore at her flesh. Warmth spewed over her hand and splashed the ground and pain shot up to her shoulder and the creature pulled away a chunk of her skin, spat it to the ground. Debbie fell back, legs crumpling as she grabbed at her broken limb, knees crashing into the gravel.

The creature smiled. 'Oh, shit,' Debbie gasped, and the thing snapped its jaws and moved in for the kill.

2

Kramer lunged for the gun, crawling into the dirt and the mess of leaves at the edge of the forest. He wrapped his fingers around the cold, metal barrel of the thing and flipped it into his palm, glancing up as he pointed.

Ahead of him, Debbie screamed. A shower of red rained over the gravel as the creature tore into her arm and Kramer's heart pounded. 'No!'

He aimed, narrowing his eyes along the barrel of the gun, squinting at the back of the creature's head. It moved in a blur of black and grey, a twisted wraith with armoured, wet skin and spines shearing its rump and its crooked spine. And for just a moment, just long enough, it *stopped* moving, and one last time, Kramer squeezed the cold trigger of the gun -

Click.

Kramer froze.

'Shit,' he moaned, pressing the trigger again. Nothing. Damn thing was jammed. Or empty. He scrambled to his feet, dropping the gun.

Debbie grabbed at her bloody arm as the creature circled her, digging shallow trenches in the dirt with every wretched step. 'Matt, go!' she yelled. 'It's too late, just *go!*'

Kramer turned his head. The car lay at the side of the road, empty and silent. One of the front tyres rested precariously on the edge of the track; the other hovered two inches above the ground. The driver's door had been torn off and lay in the shadows further along the road. Glass littered the ground.

Before he could stop himself Kramer was staggering towards the car, lurching up onto the road. He turned his head. 'Hey!' he barked. 'Leave her alone!'

Debbie froze as the creature moved. 'No...' she started, but it wasn't going for her.

The thing growled, looking over at the car.

'Leave her!' Kramer yelled again, waving his arms. He looked across at Debbie, arm hanging limp and bloody at her side as she tried to crawl onto her front in the dirt. He smiled.

It was a smile that said far too much all at once, but Debbie understood.

Kramer slid into the driver's seat and turned the key in the ignition. The engine sputtered into life and he shoved the car into reverse, forced it back into the road. He spun the wheel, facing the old vehicle back in the direction of the asylum.

The creature growled, lurching over Debbie's body onto the road.

'Chase this,' Kramer murmured. The engine spat and roared ferociously and he jammed his foot down on the accelerator. The tyres spun as he sped up the track and Kramer glanced up into the rearview, expecting to see a blur of shadow pursuing him along the road.

Nothing. He frowned, turning his eyes back to the windscreen -

The creature reared up before him, screeching as it crashed onto the front of the car. It slashed at the glass windscreen, crumpling the bonnet as it roared and pounded bony claws on the metal. The engine protested violently and the creature smacked its skull into the windscreen, hurling great gobs of red spittle onto the glass.

Kramer fought with the wheel and the car swerved off to one side - the creature grabbed at the frame of the vehicle and its claws scraped the metal loudly as it tumbled onto the ground. Kramer gritted his teeth as something burst the front tyre with a loud bang and righted the car, heading for the asylum.

Already the iron gates were looming up before him and Kramer forced the accelerator into the floor. He gripped the wheel tight and his eyes turned to the rearview mirror. He watched as the creature came after him, bounding over the gravel in great, bloody strides.

'I'm sorry, Charlie,' Kramer said. 'I did what I had to do...'

Behind him the creature leapt forward, pouncing onto the back of the car and grappling with the bumper as it smashed in the back window with its bony, bloody heels.

'I'm sorry,' Kramer said again. His eyes turned back to the gates ahead of him and he ground the accelerator as far into the ground as he could, bracing himself against the wheel.

Above his head, something crashed over the ceiling of the car, crippling the roof. White knuckles burned as the peeling blisters over Kramer's hands cracked open and bled. 'You deserved more than this, Charlie. You deserved a better dad. God, you deserved a fucking *dad*...'

Kramer closed his eyes.

The bonnet of the car crumpled as it crashed into the gates. The engine screamed as the iron bars tore deep, open wounds into the grille and the bonnet. Sparks flew and a twisted mess of metal and glass tore around the front of the car.

Wheels still spinning, the police car fell silent and died.

Kramer's head fell forward and smacked the steering wheel and his vision disappeared as a deep, warm throbbing consumed him.

Behind him, the creature leapt over the roof of the car and crashed into the mangled gates, howling as its hind legs stomped down the windscreen and a thick, deep crack spread over the glass.

Smoke rose up from the bonnet, and a stream of blood trailed over Kramer's bruised skull.

4
2003

The street was quiet, save for the low hum of a police car parked on the side of the road. The night was dark, and the tarmac was lit by a row of fizzling streetlights.

'I should fucking kill you,' Kramer hissed, spittle flying from his lips.

Shadows fell over his face as he curled his bloody palm into a fist and threw it forward, catching the younger man's jaw with a *crack* that sent him staggering backward.

'Stop…' Stone whispered, but Kramer wasn't going to stop, not until he was finished.

The detective was young, broad-built. His face was narrow, his hair tangled and unruly. His uniform was a patchwork of blue and white; dark blazer, pale shirt. Crumpled, red tie. Kramer grabbed Niles Stone by the collar and yanked him forward, throwing a knee up into his groin.

Stone grunted, moaning as his hand moved to his belly. '*Stop…*'

Kramer let Stone go.

The man stumbled backwards, legs crumpling. He fell. His knees smacked the ground and he raised a hand, shaking. 'Please…'

'Is that what she said?' Kramer spat. The young detective thrust his fingers into the Stone's hair, thick and knotted and greasy. 'Is that what she said to you?'

Niles Stone looked up at him with pleading, wild eyes, blood drizzling from his cracked gums. 'Why are you… I don't…'

Kramer's fist barrelled into the man's face again. Warmth spread over his knuckles, but he barely noticed. He yanked Stone's head backward, punched him again. The kid's jaw cracked. Spiny bristles lined his chin and upper lip, glinting white in the half-light. Kramer tossed a fist into that ugly mouth again, almost smiling as teeth cracked in Stone's gums. Again. *Again…*

'You know what you did!' Kramer yelled. He kicked out, slamming the toe of his boot into Stone's gut.

The younger man groaned, hands splayed on the ground. Doubled over, he spat blood into the gutter. Grit and tarmac rolled over his palms.

Kramer's knee rose up to meet the kid's throat and Stone's skull flew back. He squealed, bleating like an animal. 'Stop! I didn't...'

'You're nothing,' Kramer snarled, stepping back. He

reached up, wiping spit from his mouth with the back of his hand. 'You understand? You are *nothing*.'

'I didn't do anything…' Stone shook his head, eyes on the floor. He tried to stand, but his leg gave way and he fell forward.

'Don't you dare,' Kramer whispered. 'Oh, don't you dare try that one with me.'

Stone looked up. He spluttered, steadied himself. Kramer moved forward, pulled back his fist –

Niles Stone was smiling.

'You think this is funny?'

Kramer's knuckles crashed into the kid's teeth and Stone fell back, head bouncing off the concrete. Blood flowed from his nostrils, streamed over his face and into his eyes. He reached out, laying a hand on the ground, and Kramer stamped down, hard, crushing the bones of the man's fingers.

Stone shrieked.

Kramer turned away from the younger man, taking a moment to catch his breath. Quickly, he shrugged off the cobalt blazer of his detective's uniform, let it float to the ground as he started to roll up his sleeves. A badge glimmered gold at his belt.

'You know they'll suspend you for this,' Stone rasped from the ground, clutching at his gut. 'My uncle's police, down in Weeping. I know what *happens* to cops like you…'

'I know,' Kramer said. He lowered his head a little, closing his eyes. The image flashed before him, the same image that had haunted him for weeks now. Mercy Kramer tilted her head back and moaned, unable to stop herself. She knew that her husband had come home, that he could see her, but she was too far gone to care. He saw it all again, in that moment; the drab, plain office of the divorce lawyer, the endless reams of crisp, white paper bound in brown folders, waiting for his signature.

'I know,' he repeated, turning back to face the younger man. 'I just don't care.'

Stone was curled up on the ground, clutching at his jaw, blood streaming between his fingers. 'Please...' the kid begged. 'I didn't do *shit*.'

Kramer saw something else. Niles Stone, with his belt undone and his hands around the throat of a twelve-year-old girl as he forced her to the ground. He heard the girl scream, her terrified cries echoing all along the alley as Stone pinned her down. He saw her face, contorted with agony and pure, childlike fear. He saw nothing but relentless, indiscriminate shades of crimson.

'They'll fire you. I'll have you *arrested*,' Stone said. 'Police brutality, that's what this is. You can't just... you can't come to my street and start beating on me, you know that. You know you're going to lose everything...'

Kramer looked at the kid, and his face was dark. His eyes flashed. 'I told you, I don't care.'

'You...' Stone trailed off. Swallowed. 'You can't...'

Kramer reached for something tucked into the back of his belt. His hand rested on cold metal. He unclipped the thing and held it in his palm. Perfectly balanced.

Stone's eyes widened. 'You wouldn't...'

Kramer pointed the gun at the younger man's forehead, narrowed his eyes. His arm was steady, steadier than it had ever been.

'You can't kill me,' Stone said. 'You won't do it. You

don't have the *right*.'

Kramer barely heard him. 'You know, when my wife left me, she told me something. You want to know what she said?'

Stone raised his hands. Blood trickled from his nose. 'If it means you won't kill me.'

'She said I didn't deserve her,' Kramer said. He laughed. The gun trembled in his hand, just for a second, and he tightened his grip on the butt of the thing. 'She told me she was going to take it all, in the divorce. My house, my savings... my fucking *salary...*'

'Please,' Stone said. 'You don't need to do this. I didn't do anything. That little girl, she was lying. I'm not... I'm not into that. I wouldn't...'

'Shut your mouth,' Kramer said, thumbing the hammer. 'See, Mercy told me I didn't deserve that house. She fucked another man in my bed, kid, and she told me I didn't deserve *her.* You don't deserve a *damn thing,* that's what she said.'

'Why are you telling me this?' Stone said.

Kramer paused. 'Tell me why you deserve to live,' he said quietly.

Stone started talking, but Kramer couldn't hear him.

He saw the little girl, wide-eyed, afraid. Sobbing, even with Stone's hands forcing the air out of her lungs. Kramer saw her kick back at the man with a bruised, purple leg, saw Stone push her face to the ground and yank her back, into him.

Kramer's finger brushed the trigger and he breathed, in, out.

In...

Slowly, he lowered the gun.

'She was right,' he whispered. 'I don't deserve a fucking thing.'

Stone didn't, either. There was nothing the kid could say that would convince Kramer not to pull that trigger. But this wasn't his choice.

This should never have been his choice.

'If you ever touch a child again,' Kramer said, 'I will kill you.'

Stone shook his head. 'You're crazy. I didn't do anything.'

Kramer smashed the butt of the gun into Stone's head and the kid's jaw cracked. Slowly, the detective turned away, sliding the gun back into his belt.

'You'll lose everything over this!' Stone called out behind him. Kramer shook his head.

'Too late,' he whispered, and he walked back to his car. But the kid was right. He couldn't stay here. Mercy was going to win the house, that was certain. He'd have to find a new job before he could lose this one. Somewhere far away. Somewhere isolated.

Somewhere nobody would ever know what he'd done.

5

Kramer stumbled into his bedroom, smacking the light switch with his elbow. He strung off the belt at his waist, looping it around the doorhandle as he pushed it closed. He unclipped the detective's badge and it dropped to the floor. The gun lay cold in his hand and he turned, tossing it onto the bed.

The gun landed next to a faded, brown folder, open

so that a sheaf of documents spilled onto the stained mattress. Kramer glared at the folder, stepping past the bed. He had kept his boots on, but as he crossed the room he reached up and unfastened the tie around his neck, slinging it over the bedpost.

For a long time Kramer stood at the window, hands in his pockets, scowling out at the night beyond the glass. Terraced houses looked grey and cold in the moonlight, roads and pavements were great swathes of black. Past it all, stretching out to the horizon, vast fields of wheat and tall grass swayed and rippled in the wind. The moon dangled in an inkblot sky, full and fat and gloating.

'Bastard,' Kramer murmured. He could see the police station from here; a low, squat building set behind a low, brick wall. Soft blue lights glowed around the perimeter of the station, rigged on tall, grey poles.

Oh, Stone had been right. Suspension was the very least of his worries. If they found out what he'd done, they'd fire him. Or worse.

Maybe he could transfer. Find a police department in some sleepy little town, way out in the country, where they'd never find him. Maybe his days as a detective were over. He could get a job as a caretaker, somewhere. Security guard, if he was extraordinarily lucky.

But what if that wasn't enough?

I should have killed him, Kramer thought. He bowed his head, closing his eyes. His breathing had slowed, to the point where he no longer had to fight to control it, but his heart was pounding.

Even drink wouldn't dull that.

'Shut up,' Kramer hissed. The hammering in his chest

400

was in competition, now, with the voices in his head, all screaming and shrieking to be heard, and the worst, the loudest, was her voice, Mercy's voice. Scornful and riddled with hatred and anger and so happy to be there, in the blank space behind his eyes. *I'm going to take everything,* the bitch kept saying. *It's mine.*

Kramer staggered back, shuddering as his calves hit the mattress. He sunk down, perched on the edge of the bed, and he raised his trembling hands until they were on the top of his head, pushing sand-brown hair out of his face. His face flushed and he looked up to the ceiling and he *sobbed*. Doubling over until his guts hurt, he pressed his face to his knees and let the tears fall. His breath hitched in his throat as it all broke down and the room shifted and swayed.

'I can't do it anymore,' Kramer moaned hoarsely. 'Oh Christ, I can't...'

He lowered his hands, clenched them into fists at his sides.

'I can't do it anymore,' he repeated.

After a few minutes, Kramer's hands stopped shaking. Everything stilled. Finally, his heartbeat slowed. The tears stopped coming, and the young detective raised his head and *breathed*.

'I don't have to,' he said, calmer than he'd been all night. He looked up at the moon through the greasy glass of the window and shook his head. 'You can't make me.'

Kramer reached behind him, fumbling for the gun. Cold metal brushed against his fingers. He wrapped his hand around the weapon and brought it to his lap, gripping it tight with both hands.

'Oh, god.'

Kramer thumbed the hammer of the old gun and lifted it to his face. His eyes travelled the barrel of the thing, taking in every detail, every rusted edge, every curve. 'I can't do it. Not without her... god, what have I done?'

It didn't matter.

Kramer pushed the gun into his mouth and squeezed the trigger.

6

The man's head was bowed and shadows fell over his face. Thick-fingered hands hung in his lap; his back was pressed against the cell wall, rump perched carefully on a low, concrete bench. He could only have been eighteen years old, nineteen at best, but he was broad-shouldered and muscular. Long, black hair hung from his scalp in rough, matted coils, curling around the scarred flesh of his throat. The iron bars of the cell cast slanted shadows over a tattered plaid shirt and mud-stained jeans. A rough, black beard covered the lower half of the man's face, sticky with spittle and filth.

'How could you do it?' Sergeant Mills hissed, stepping up to the bars. He stared into the cell, arms folded across his chest, half-obscuring the badge pinned to his armoured, black vest. Light passed over his face as he shook his head. 'I never understand this,' he continued, voice low and quiet. 'How could you be so... *evil?*'

Slowly, Eddie looked up.

There was no expression on his face. A smear of mud

tracked from his right temple into the thick of his beard. There was a thin line of red in the brown and the black, a bead of blood caught in the dirt. He stank, Mills noticed, smelled of the forest and the swamp and something else, something rotten and wicked and decaying.

'We found the bodies, Drake,' Mills said. 'All of them. Buried around that house, where my boys found you. You've been a busy boy, haven't you?'

Edward Drake said nothing. His eyes flashed a deep, hollow dark and the fingers of his left hand rapped on the edge of the bench, tapping out a rhythm Mills couldn't recognise.

The sergeant seethed. Slowly, he moved towards the bars, one fist bunched at his side. 'You *sicken* me,' he said. 'People like you. How long have you been living in those woods, Drake?'

No answer.

'We came to the house, you know. So many times, these last few years. Looking to see if you'd come back. When you disappeared, after... after you killed your fucking grandmother... we kept checking, just in case.'

Nothing.

'You never fucking *left,* did you?'

Again, there was no reply. Eddie's fingers shifted, patting his knee softly. The rhythm played a little faster now, a ragged beat that echoed in the corners of the old cell. Rough, bitten-down nails tapped on the harsh stone surface of the bench and Mills snarled through the bars, narrowing his eyes.

'And every time we came by, the ground out in those old woods seemed just a little fresher. As if it had been dug up and turned. We never thought... Christ, Drake, I can't imagine the fucked-up mess inside your head.'

'They came for the witch,' Eddie said. His voice was coarse, as if he hadn't spoken for days. Weeks, even. 'I told them she was gone, that she couldn't help them. They wouldn't listen to me.'

'And you killed them. Just like you killed her. How could you *do* it?'

Eddie sat back, leaning his head against the cold, stone wall of the cell.

Mills sighed, glanced back toward the station. The holding cells were empty, save for this one. There were no other officers around. If he could get just a *minute* inside that cell, if he could show Edward Drake just what happened to bastards like him, to sick, *broken* bastards like him...

'Do it,' Eddie said.

Mills frowned, turning back to the cell. 'Excuse me?'

'Open the bars,' Eddie rasped. 'Come join me. You saw what happened to those people, in the woods. You know what'll happen to you.'

'You're sick, Drake. There's something wrong with you. You know that?'

Eddie didn't reply. A glimmer of white flashed across his eyes, a reflection from the lights above Mills' head. Slowly, the bearded man stood up from his bench. He moved forward, every step slow and laboured. He had all the time in the world.

'Don't come any closer,' Mills said, when Eddie was halfway across the cell.

Eddie kept walking.

'I said -'

'I know,' Eddie said. He stepped up to the bars. Pressed his forehead to the cold, harsh metal. 'I heard you.'

'Then take a step back,' Mills said. 'I'm warning you, Drake -'

He stopped. There was something in the black-haired man's face, something that he hadn't seen before, hadn't wanted to see. A cold, grey emotionlessness, but more than that, worse than that.

It was like Edward Drake's heart had stopped beating and he was walking around without it.

'How could you do it?' Mills said again, quieter. 'All those people... your own *family*... it's like...'

Eddie raised an eyebrow. 'Yes?'

'It's like you don't have a *soul,*' Mills said.

Eddie took a step back. The shadows danced wildly over his bearded face.

And for just the tiniest fraction of a second, Mills could have sworn that he saw the man smile.

7

Click.

Kramer yanked the gun out of his jaw and closed one eye, pressing the other to the end of the barrel. Jammed. He could see the tip of the bullet, glinting silver all the way down the tunnel. It hadn't moved.

'Fuck,' he hissed. He threw the gun to the ground, watched as it skittered over the floor. '*Fuck!*'

Kramer stood, moving to the window. His bloody knuckles peeled open as he gripped the base of the frame, grunting as he pushed upward. The window opened and he took a step back, pushed away from the opening as a gust of wind pressed against his chest, against his face. Kramer steadied himself, laying his hands on the sill. Slowly, he dipped his head beneath the frame and looked out, looked down.

It was high enough. Just one step...

Kramer exhaled. His breath appeared before him in a cloud of fine, grey mist and he closed his eyes, listening to the wind and the sounds of the night. Somewhere, deep within the city, a glass shattered. Car horns bleated, people yelled and fought and screamed at each other, and above it all he could hear her voice, telling him to *go, do it. You'd be doing us all a favour -*

Kramer raised his leg and lifted his foot onto the sill, gripping the window frame tight. *Do it,* said the voice in his head. *It was never going to be a gun, not for you.*

Kramer's breathing was slow, ragged. This was it. He was really going to do it.

It was the only way...

In the distance, a baby wailed.

Kramer's eyes snapped open. Vertigo slammed the back of his skull and his vision swam and he moaned, steadying himself. His front garden was a mess, overgrown and rotting, strewn with dead leaves and wilted flowers and the writhing coils of weeds that he'd tramped down until even they were near dying out. But there was something new, something he hadn't seen before.

Something on the doorstep...

'Oh, fucking hell.'

Kramer's foot slipped off the sill and he took a step back, looking up. Before him, the street laid flat, dark

406

in the shadows of the buildings on the other side.

There was someone there. A figure dressed all in black, walking away from the house. As Kramer watched, the black-suited man passed under a flickering streetlight on the other side of the road.

Kramer's eyes darted to the thing on the doorstep, then back to the thin silhouette in the street. 'Hey!' he yelled. 'Get back here! You can't...'

He trailed off. 'Oh, fuck.'

Then he was turning away from the window and stumbling out into the hallway, shoving past the bedroom door. He turned down the stairs and took them two at a time, breathing fast. Kramer winced as his palm ground over a rough patch on the banister, splinters digging into his hand. His heart was pounding again, beating hard and hot in his ears as he reached the front door, yanked it open.

'Shit!'

Kramer stumbled over the thing on the doorstep, staggered through the overgrown grass of his front lawn. He called out as he passed through the front gate and onto the street.

Kramer stopped, in the middle of the road, bathed in the glow of the streetlights. '*Hey!*'

The black-suited figure stopped walking.

He was tall, Kramer noticed, impossibly tall. Going on seven feet, taller even. Long, slender arms hung at his sides. He stood a little crooked, shoulders slanted so that he didn't seem *natural*, so that he looked out of place.

'You can't leave that here!' Kramer called, fist shaking at his side. 'Not now, not tonight! Who the *fuck* do you think you are?'

Slowly, the figure turned his head.

Kramer took a step back, mouth open. 'I... what are you?' he whispered.

The man smiled. A thin, black line opened in his face. His skin was peeled and raw, his eyes bulging.

His flesh was a lurid, repulsive yellow.

'Come back,' Kramer said, but he wanted the man with the yellow face to keep walking, to turn back around and disappear forever. He felt something, in the pit of his stomach, writhing and twisting inside him. Fear, stronger than any he'd felt before. 'You can't...'

'Take her,' said the yellow-faced man. His voice was wrong, all gravel and blood and hot, burned coal.

Kramer shivered. 'I can't.'

The grim smile grew wider. 'You will,' said the man.

Kramer looked back toward the doorway.

The baby's tormented cries had grown louder. She lay, wrapped in a bundle of stained, white rags, face red and puffy as she bawled.

'I can't...' Kramer whispered.

When he looked back toward the road, the yellow-faced man had gone.

Kramer stepped back through the gate and moved slowly to the doorstep. He glanced up, for a second, at the open window on the second floor. This was wrong. This was so wrong. He blinked, but he couldn't get rid of the image of that man's face, all discoloured and burned and broken...

He looked down and a tiny, round face looked up at him.

'Bollocks,' Kramer said, and he knelt down and

408

wrapped the baby in his arms.

CHAPTER SIXTEEN
LEVIATHAN

1
NOW

Kramer groaned, peeling open his eyelids. Red smears filled his vision, ink-blot splashes of crimson obscuring the dashboard before him as he blinked rapidly. The world swam around him and for a second he felt as though he was falling, crashing down towards the steering wheel and the blood-spattered dash. Kramer realised his head was drooping and it shot up, weightless and numb.

Grunting, he ground the blood out of his eyes and blinked away clouds of purple afterglow. Darkness coated the dashboard like mist and red stars glowed beyond, blinking dully up at him.

There was no sound. Kramer panicked; *oh god, I'm deaf.* The crash had taken away his hearing. Somehow, it had deafened him.

Surely he should be able to hear the rain...

Slowly, Kramer leaned forward to look out the windscreen. He laid his hand on the wheel, grimacing as a thick pool of warmth seeped between his fingers. He yanked the hand back and glanced down, grunting.

'I'm not deaf,' he realised, shaking his head. He could hear himself breathe, hear himself talk. God, he could hear the *thumping* in his ears. But the rain had stopped.

How long have I been out?

Kramer peered out the shattered windscreen. The glass had fallen inward, cracked with the impact of ramming the asylum gates, and a limp film of plastic supported the remaining shards like a flimsy, transparent spider's web. Beyond the windscreen, the twisted iron bars gleamed silver in the moonlight.

Moonlight. He'd been out for hours.

Kramer leaned back and peeled himself away from the wheel. He looked up into the rearview mirror, gingerly touching his forehead with bloody fingers. A jagged wound had opened up at his temple and it was still dark and wet. Blood drizzled down into his eye and he blinked it away, watched as a bead of red poked out from between his eyelids and slid down his face. Christ, his head was *pounding.*

'Eddie,' he remembered, grabbing for the doorhandle. His fingers brushed cold air and he frowned, turning his head.

'Right,' he said, looking out into the trees through the

hole in the car's side. He could feel the cold now, blowing in through the empty frame where the creature had forced the door off its hinges. Kramer shivered.

He moved to step out the car, cried out as a deep, burning pain shot up his leg. His shin was stuck in place, and he tried to pull it free, wincing as warmth spread around his ankle. It had twisted, caught around one of the pedals. Probably the only thing that had stopped him flying straight through the windscreen when he'd crashed.

'Shit,' Kramer murmured. He grabbed his thigh, wrenching it back. His bent ankle protested, tied around the pedal in a thick, crooked knot. 'Come on...'

Kramer's leg came free and he stumbled out of the car, ducking beneath the crumpled doorframe. Hot, bloody pain burst up his shin as he stood straight, catching his breath.

The car was a wreck. The frame of the windscreen was a battered, caved-in scaffold of bent, scarred metal. The smoke rising from the bonnet had dissipated and a dusting of soot covered the dented plates at the front of the car. The headlights had died.

Kramer turned away from the car and walked towards the gates, gripping his thigh with one hand as he reached for the gun at his belt with the other. His ankle burned with every step and he swore.

'You still out here?' he called. The gates had cracked and twisted open, torn apart by the force of the impact.

The wreckage of the bars formed a thick, iron spiral that dug into the front of the car, bending the grille into a sharp, shining *V.*

'Edward!' Kramer yelled. 'Edward Drake, can you hear me?'

Nothing.

'And what about you?' Kramer said, a little more quietly. '*Whatever* you are. Are you out here somewhere?'

Kramer paused, suddenly remembering something. He fought with the casing of the gun and it opened up with a *click.* Empty.

'Bastard thing,' Kramer grunted, hobbling around to the passenger door of the car. He forced it open, tossing the empty gun onto the seat. Hands trembling from the cold and the pain that shot up his side in throbbing rivers, he fumbled about in the glovebox and wrapped his fingers around a full magazine. He picked up the gun and popped the spent case free, clicked the new one into place. His eyes caught sight of something glittering in the back of the glovebox and he paused.

The flask was half empty. Half was all he needed.

'Not now,' Kramer hissed, slamming the glovebox closed and turning back toward the gates. He stood for a minute, gripping the pistol tight in his palm, eyes locked on the front door of the asylum.

It was closed. Kramer's eyes darted up to the guard tower. Empty. Nothing moved. Nothing *breathed.*

'I'm coming for you,' Kramer whispered, and he limped through the wreckage of the gates and towards Black River Asylum.

2

Red lights flashed in the dark as Kramer approached the asylum. Small, red bulbs set into the walls pulsed and glowed, throwing dull shadows over the grass and the gravel. There should have been sirens, Kramer realised, making his way along the long, snaking driveway towards the front door. If the bulbs had been triggered, there should have been some kind of alarm.

Nothing. The building was swamped by a thick, heavy silence. Even the wind struggled to reach him here, pushed back by the tall brick walls around the perimeter.

He gripped the gun with both hands as he crept over the path, eyes focused on the door. Stones crunched under his boots and ground beneath his dragging, twisted heel. No sound, other than the thundering of his heart.

'You had to come to the creepiest fucking place on the island, didn't you?' Kramer hissed. 'Couldn't just stay in the fucking sea and drown like a reasonable... thing.'

He reached the door and paused, looked around him. For a moment the gun dropped to his side as he glanced

414

down at his ankle, inspected the damage in the throbbing red light. Nothing visible. He lifted up the hem of his trouser leg, winced as he saw a ring of fat, purple bruises around the base of his shin. The same cracking, aching pain tore up his ribs. He might've cracked a couple; a shearing at the muscles around his chest told him he could be right.

The door cracked open behind him and Kramer whirled round, lifting the gun as it squealed at its rusted hinges.

Nothing. The red-carpet hallway was empty.

'I told you,' he said, 'I'm not playing fucking games.'

No reply.

Cautiously, Kramer stepped forward, pushing the door wide with his free hand as he held the gun forward with the other. The hallway lights had been shut down and the same red glow that half-illuminated the face of the building threw jagged shadows over the walls.

'Hello?' Kramer said, moving along the corridor with trepidation. 'Eddie, you here? Hayley?'

He glanced up at the walls as he moved, inspecting a row of framed, black-and-white photographs. The shapes within the frames were hazy in the dark, but in the first he could just about make out an aerial shot of the island, carving a jagged, saw-toothed knot in the ocean. The next photograph presented him with an image of the asylum, back in the sixties; the small, barred windows were completely bricked up; the

415

shadows crawling over the walls were shorter, thinner, as though even in the sixty years since it had been taken the trees had doubled in size.

The third image wasn't a photograph, Kramer realised, halfway along the entrance hallway, but a framed drawing; an old, black ink sketch of a man tied to a tall, jagged stake, feet bound beneath him, dangling into blotchy, spattered flames that hadn't yet reached his ankles. Behind him, a group of tall, faceless men and women raised their fists as the man started to burn. He was screaming.

'Right,' Kramer muttered, continuing along the corridor. It widened out into a tasteless, hotel-lobby reception, decorated with more pictures and the same high, plain walls. A couple of the lights through here were still functioning, and patches of white flickered among the pulsing, swaying red. A horseshoe-shaped desk was empty at the back of the room. A plaque across the front of the counter read *All Visitors.*

Kramer looked around him; a corridor led off from the reception through to the east wing of the building, on his left, and to the west on his right. He moved left, hobbling along the carpet, gun hanging by his side. Kramer stepped quietly, wary of the shadows around him as they rose and fell in the eerie swing of the lights.

His toe hit something on the ground and Kramer paused. The lights were paler along this corridor and he could hardly see in front of him. The floor was little more than a strip of shadow stretching out to the end of the hall. Quickly, he reached with his free hand for the flashlight at his belt, wiping the worm-gunk onto his coat. He flicked it on.

Light burst into the corridor and Kramer took a step back as he saw what he'd stepped into.

Bodies littered the hall, strung about the floor, thrown against the walls like ragdolls. A dozen of them at least, maybe more. The red carpet was a little darker here, splashed and soaked with blood, and rivers of it ran up the walls, smeared and spread like paint. Kramer's eyes flickered up to the ceiling as he raised the torch beam - there was blood there, too, in places, drops of it slowly pooling into the plaster.

'Looks like I'm going the right way, then,' Kramer breathed, stepping over the first body. A thin, scrawny-looking man in the white shirt and trousers of an inmate. Tattoos covered his left arm. His right had been separated from his body and lay six feet down the corridor.

All the doors along here were open, Kramer realised as he moved. He reached out, elbowed the closest all the way ajar, holding the gun steady as he peered through into the cell. It was open. A thick, red trail of blood spread from the centre of the room into the hall. The creature had dragged its victim out here to be with the rest, it seemed. It had left them out to be found. It had *wanted* them to be found.

Kramer winced as a smell rose up to meet his nose, suddenly shocked that he hadn't noticed it before. Blood mixed in with detergent and stale, dry plaster, dead and decaying meat dripping into the carpet.

The first body had been one of the lucky ones, apparently. Kramer saw a corpse a little further along with a deep, wide gash opened up in her dark-skinned throat. Her legs had been torn off. Kramer couldn't see them anywhere. Blood pooled down from the stringy stumps beneath the woman's hips as she sat up against the wall, spine torn half out of her back and dripping onto the carpet.

Another broken carcass was so twisted up and defiled that Kramer couldn't tell if it had been a man or a woman; arms and legs knotted up behind a shredded back; the thing's face had been mashed up and smashed in until it was nothing more than a thick, red pulp. One eyeball rolled up in a mushy socket, pointed right at him.

Kramer shook his head. His eyes fell on a corpse that couldn't have been any older than twenty, her red hair torn out and her scalp peeled back from her skull. The bone had been cracked open and her brain slithered out in a flood of pink. At the end of the corridor, a fat, wide-armed man laid with his head against the wall and his belly opened up, entrails and coils of gut spilling from him. Chunks of meat had been torn out of his sides and his fleshy throat. His mouth hung open; his tongue was missing.

Something moved at Kramer's feet. He swung the flashlight down, pointed his pistol toward the source of the movement. The man sat with his back against the wall, bald, scarred head tilted back. His guts had been ripped out in much the same way as the wide-built man's; his skin was the colour of burnt caramel, his neck tattooed with a black, twisted dragon that spun around the base of his skull and spread its wings up his jaw and across his left shoulder.

'Kill me,' the Haitian man croaked. Kramer knelt before him, in the blood and the entrails on the carpet, and he lowered the gun.

'I'm sorry.'

The man's stomach was torn apart, the folds of his skin laying across his hips like a fleshy chocolate wrapper - except the chocolate was his insides, and now they were all outside. Slivers and trails of purple and red broke free of the bottom of his ribcage and tumbled out into his lap. Long, deep scratches mutilated his chest and the gristly remains of his arms. Slowly, he lifted a hand, pointed.

'Shoot me,' said the Haitian. 'Right in the head. Put me out...'

Kramer pulled the gun away from him. 'I need you to tell me,' he said quietly. 'Did you see it? The creature?'

The Haitian man nodded, just a little. A blood vessel

had broken in his right eye and clouds of red broke into his iris. 'The shadow...'

'Where did it go?' Kramer said.

The dying man's pointed finger slid off toward the end of the corridor, shaking. Blood dripped off the end of the twisted digit and Kramer stood straight. 'Thank you.'

'Kill me,' said the Haitian. 'I need... do it. Please...'

Kramer looked at the gun, then back toward the dying man's face. 'I'm sorry,' he whispered. 'I need all the bullets I can spare.'

The Haitian's eyes widened. 'No...'

'I'm sorry,' Kramer said. He stood, started walking away, limping through the carnage and the bodies on the floor. The gun hung at his side like an extension of his arm, heavy and cold in his hand.

'No!' the Haitian screamed behind him. 'Kill me! Kill me! *Kill me!*'

Kramer kept walking, swallowing down the guilt and the bile that rose up into his throat.

'*Beware the yellow man!*' the Haitian yelled, his voice hoarse and bloody.

Kramer froze.

He turned, eyes dark. 'What did you say?'

'The man with the yellow face...' the Haitian whispered. 'He is not all he seems to be. He moves like one of us, he... *talks* like one of us... he is more than that. More than you could know.'

Kramer raised the gun, pointed it at the Haitian man's head. 'Tell me who he is,' he said. 'Tell me how you know about him.'

'Not who,' said the man. '*What.* He is more than a man, more than a monster. He is a god in this world. He is the darkness, the storm that wakes you up and brings you out of your bed. *He is the rope that pulls you to the gallows.*'

'Tell me his name,' Kramer said. His finger brushed against the trigger as his teeth gritted in a stone-set jaw.

'His name is Death,' said the Haitian, 'and he is the first of three. When the third comes to Cain's End, the Beast will wake. Humanity's screams will wake the oldest gods as the Beast feeds on our souls and brings about the final days of our time.'

Kramer frowned. 'What Beast? What are you talking about?'

The Haitian grinned. Blood-stained teeth flashed red and white in a wet, dripping mouth.

'*Leviathan.*'

The gunshot echoed about the walls of the corridor as a bullet cracked the Haitian's skull and his head fell back against the plaster, mouth still wide and grinning as a stream of crimson trailed down his face.

Somewhere deep in the asylum, something roared. Kramer turned, pistol still smoking in his hand, and limped towards the sound, grimacing as he stepped over a discarded, punctured lung on the carpet.

3

The canteen door was locked shut. Behind the frosted glass window, twisted shapes moved in the soft, red glow of the corridor.

Emma Green knelt before Hayley on the vinyl floor, one hand on the older woman's arm, the other cupping Hayley's bloody cheek. 'It's going to be okay,' the nurse whispered. Hayley nodded frantically, eyelids closed tight. Her neck was smeared and caked with red, her clothes spattered with it.

'We need to get out of here,' Emma said quietly, glancing over at the door. 'Can you get up?'

'He's out there,' Hayley said. 'He'll kill us both.'

'He can't get out,' Emma said. 'Please, Hayley, we can get past him. If we're clever, if we're fast. We can get past him, get you out of this place. We need to take you to a hospital, get you off the island -'

'I can't see,' Hayley moaned. 'You'd be fast without me. I'll slow you down...'

'No,' Emma snapped. 'Stop this. I've got you, okay? I'll get you out of here. If we stick together -'

'He'll catch us,' Hayley nodded. 'Emma, you can't let me slow you down. You have to run.'

'I'm not leaving you here.'

'You have to.'

'*No,*' Emma said again. She paused. Gingerly, she

brushed fading, brown-grey hair out of Hayley's face, rubbed the woman's wet cheek with her thumb. 'I love you.'

Hayley opened her mouth. Closed it.

'Now come on,' Emma insisted. She stood, wiped blood off her blouse. 'We need to go.'

'You said...'

'I know,' Emma said.

'You've never said it before,' Hayley whispered.

'I know,' Emma said. 'I should have.' She reached down, took Hayley's hand in hers and pulled the woman up off the floor. They stood, for a moment, in the dark of the empty canteen, and Emma swallowed as a visible wave of pain moved over Hayley's face.

'Come on,' said the nurse, guiding Hayley across the room, leading them between chairs and overturned, plastic tables. They reached the door and she raised her free hand to tap in the passcode -

'What's that?' Hayley hissed. Her face was twisted into a frown, eyes screwed tight, head tilted up.

'I don't hear anything,' Emma said, shaking her head. Her hand hovered over the keypad.

'Out there,' Hayley said. 'In the corridor.'

Emma turned, peered through the frosted glass window into the dark. 'I don't -'

Something slammed against the glass and she cried out, stepped back. Behind her, Hayley stumbled as her rump knocked the edge of a table and Emma grabbed for the woman's arm, steadied her. A fist hammered on the glass.

'Let us in!' someone screamed, voice muffled by the door. He pounded on the glass with both fists, thumping the door with desperate abandon. 'Please, you have to let us in!'

There was someone else now, at the door, a third fist crashing against the glass. *'It's coming!'* yelled a woman. *'Oh god, it's here!'*

Emma moved to the door, looked through the glass. She ducked back as the faded, hazy silhouette of a fist flew towards her face and a thin, hairpin splinter cracked across the surface of the glass.

Further down the corridor, a second woman screamed.

'How many of them are there?' Hayley whispered.

'I can't see,' Emma said, close to the glass. 'Six? Seven?'

'There has to be another way out...'

'Let us in!' the first voice screeched. 'Please, it's going to *kill us all!'*

Hayley flinched as a gunshot rang out from the other end of the building, stepped back from the door, fumbling behind her with a shaking hand. She found the edge of the table and steadied herself. Her legs trembled.

'How many?'

'You have to let us in!'

424

'*Open the fucking door, bitch!*'

Emma shook her head, turned away from the door. 'We can't open it,' she said. 'We can't... we can't get out. Not while they're out there.'

'Why are they here?' Hayley breathed. 'They could get out. If they're out of their cells, they can get out of the building. Why are they still here?'

'*It's here!*' the woman outside screamed. The hammering on the door was deafening, frantic and panicked and terrified. The crack was wider now, longer, and it spread into a network of jagged scars as it reached the corner of the window.

Another scream. Thundering footsteps, as though something were bounding down the corridor, and then a terrible slashing sound as long, bony claws tore through flesh and severed cartilage and strings of tendon -

'*Open the door! Open the fucking door!*'

The hammering stopped. Emma's hands moved to her mouth to stifle a sob as a terrified, agonised screaming filled the corridor. Something roared, growling with a low, guttural hatred as it wrenched the frightened inmates' bodies apart.

'It's killing them...' Emma said.

'It's going to get through that door,' Hayley whispered. 'What do we do?'

Emma said nothing.

'God, what do we *do?*'

425

The screaming stopped. Something thumped against the corridor wall and slid down to the floor. The only sound was a heavy, low breathing that rattled through jagged teeth as it rolled over a slither of fat, grey tongue.

'I don't know,' Emma's voice rocked with tremors.

'Emma, what do we do?'

Something moved to the door and the glass fogged up with a dark, black mist. Claws tapped on the wood and Emma cringed as the creature pressed its face against the window.

'God, what is that thing?' she whispered.

'What do we do?'

Emma shook her head. Her eyes were locked on the shadowy face behind the glass, narrow, burning eyes set into a spiny, fractured skull. 'We hide,' she whispered.

Outside, the thing dragged its claws over the surface of the door and smiled. Slowly, it stepped back from the window, lowered its head, and Emma watched as the blurry silhouette of the thing reeled back, ready to strike -

'Hey!'

Something moved, at the very end of the corridor. Behind Emma, Hayley gasped. 'I know that voice...'

The creature turned away from the door and Emma stepped forward, pressed her face to the cracked glass. 'It's a man,' she said. 'Long coat. He's got a gun...'

As she watched, the man raised the gun and aimed it at the creature's head. The thing stepped towards him, shoulders bunched into a thick arch, hind legs taut and ready to propel it forwards.

'There you are,' Matthew Kramer breathed.

Emma shook her head, peering through the window. 'He's going to die,' she whispered.

Slowly, the man in the long overcoat stepped forward. The pistol was steady in his hand, raised high and proud. He narrowed his eyes. 'Christ, you are *ugly* up close,' he said, and the creature roared as it barrelled towards him.

4

Charlotte moved to the window, eyes half-closed. It was dark outside, she noticed, pulling back the curtains, and a fat, silver moon had risen above the village. The Crow's Head was empty tonight; no lights on inside the old pub, nobody outside. Nothing moved. Everyone had heard by now - there was a wild animal loose on the island. The threat was real, now. It was dangerous. It was frightening.

Charlotte's eyes fell to the pavement outside her house. The old police car was still there. Jamie sat behind the wheel, his head tilted forward, eyes closed. His mobile had fallen into his lap. The screen was still lit. Charlotte wondered if he'd given up trying to get hold of his friend. Perhaps she should go out there, offer him a drink. Coffee, or something.

The girl sighed, turning away from the window. She had cleared up the bathroom - a splash of hot water on her leg had woken her and she'd realised that the tap had been running while she was unconscious; minutes more and the bathroom would have started to flood. But once she'd emptied the bath and dried the tiled floor, she hadn't felt much like taking a bath. As soon as her head had hit the pillow on her bed, she had been asleep again. Apparently, fear was exhausting.

Charlotte moved down the stairs wearily, grinding sleep dust out of her eyes with the heel of her fist. She was still in her clothes, still damp in places with blood, although most of it had dried and flaked off onto the floor as she headed down. Slowly, she moved to the front door.

Outside, glass shattered.

Charlotte froze.

She waited, listened. It had been too loud for crockery, too close for a window across the street.

She turned, stepped through a doorway in the hall and moved across the kitchen. The room was dark and she fumbled about, sliding her hand over the marble counter as she crossed to the sink. Cautiously she reached across, wincing as the cold metal of an overhanging tap brushed against her wrist. A low, wide set of curtains hung above the sink, white, laced net just thick enough to obscure whatever was going on outside.

Charlotte lifted up a corner of the net curtain and

peered through.

The police car was still there, but the driver's side door had imploded. Blood trailed over the sharp mess of the frame, smeared down the door. It dripped onto the tarmac of the road, dark and thick and oozing.

Jamie was gone. In the passenger seat, his phone lay overturned, light seeping out from beneath it and rolling over the leather.

Charlotte stepped back from the window and the curtain fell back into place. Quickly, she moved back into the hall, resisting the urge to cry out as she stubbed her toe on something in the dark. Hurrying back up the stairs, she stepped into her room and shut the door. After a moment's thought, she locked it, sliding a narrow bolt into the frame.

'You're seeing things,' Charlotte told herself. 'It's been a long day, and you're tired, and you're scared. Or it's a dream. You're still asleep. This *isn't happening*.'

Charlotte moved to the window and whipped back her curtain.

From above, she could see the entire road.

Jamie was laid on the tarmac, spine stretched across the faded white marks that ran down the middle of the street. He moaned quietly, bubbles of red filling his mouth as he looked up at his attacker with wide, frightened eyes. For a moment his pupils shifted and he looked up, to the window, looked right at Charlotte and she gasped.

A man in a wrinkled black suit stood over Jamie, flicked glass off a shadowy lapel. His hands were yellow. His face was hidden, but Charlotte could see that the skin stretched across his skull was yellow too, slick with pus and blistered and cracked at the top of his neck. Slowly, he turned his head, followed Jamie's gaze.

'No...' she whispered. The yellow-faced man smiled up at her and raised a hand, tossed her a friendly wave.

Then he turned back to Jamie and knelt in the road.

'No,' Charlotte said again, but she was helpless. '*No!*'

Yellow Face ignored her. He leant over Jamie's body as the man shook his head, urgency on his face, raising his hands to fend off the black-suited demon. Then he was screaming, gargling on blood as Yellow Face shoved his fingers into Jamie's mouth and wrenched his tongue out of his throat in a spray of red. The tongue flopped to the ground, wriggling for a second in a pool of spit and blood, then it lay still. Jamie's hands went to his mouth but the yellow man had moved down to Jamie's belly. As Charlotte watched, the nightmare figure leaned back, rolling up his sleeve. His eyes flickered up to the window and the smile was gone, a pair of thin, wet lips parted in a grim scowl.

Without looking down at the man sprawled in the road, Yellow Face plunged his hand into Jamie's belly and grabbed for his spine. Charlotte backed away from the window as yellow fingers wrapped around bloody cords and nerves and yanked them free of Jamie's twitching body, tearing his backbone out of him with a sickening *crack.*

'Oh, my god...'

Yellow Face dropped the spine next to Jamie's corpse and wiped his bloody hands on black, velvet trousers. Slowly, he stood straight. With a long, yellow finger, he pointed up at the window. Charlotte shook her head.

The yellow man smiled and, without even a glance at the man he had just killed, he started to walk towards the front door of Charlotte's house.

5

Red lights pulsed around Eddie as he stood in the corridor, head bowed. He was completely still, silent. Listening.

In his hand, the fork was perfectly steady, shining, red prongs pointed down at the floor. Slowly, a single drop of blood slid down the edge of the fork and formed a glistening bead before falling to the carpet.

He moved down the hall, passing an open door on his left. Someone breathed heavily, fearfully in the cell beyond, and he pushed forward. He could hear screaming, somewhere in the building. Somewhere close.

Not close enough.

Eddie narrowed his eyes. There was another sound, among the agonised, animalistic howls that filled his ears, a deeper sound. His grip on the fork tightened.

'Show me,' he whispered, closing his eyes.

For a moment, he saw nothing but the dark behind his eyelids. The screaming faded as he concentrated on that darkness, pushed himself forward into it. All he could hear was his own breathing, slow and shallow within his chest. His heart slowed as he focused, pulse softening until he could barely sense it at all. Even the floor beneath his feet seemed to slip away and the corridor disappeared.

He was somewhere else. Eddie watched, through eyes that weren't his own, and he shuddered. Another corridor, deeper inside the asylum. He saw a door, wet with blood and scratched. Darkness beyond a cracked, frosted-glass window.

'The canteen,' he whispered. He had been there before. Maybe the creature had been following some sort of trail, tracking Eddie's footsteps.

A noise behind him sent Eddie whirling around, raising the fork as his eyes snapped open. He frowned. Nothing there. The corridor was empty. He focused again, brought himself back to that dark, empty place, threw his mind into the depths of that shadow and waited...

Matthew Kramer stood at the end of the hall, gun raised in his hand. Eddie heard a snarl, realised it was coming from his own mouth. Then he was tearing forward, claws smacking the ground as he ran for the detective, drooling, heart pounding six times faster than possible, blood throbbing hot and thick and angry as he opened his mouth and *roared* -

Eddie opened his eyes. There were no claws, no long, muscular legs dripping with mucus and shadow. He was on his own. But he knew where to go.

'I see you,' Eddie whispered, and he started walking.

6

The gun jerked up in Kramer's hand as he pulled the trigger, stepping back as a loud *crack!* thundered along the corridor. His heel hit the wall behind him and the bullet flew forward, seared the edge of the creature's skull as it lunged towards him. It barely drew blood, sunk into the canteen door at the end of the hall with a flat, wooden crunch.

The creature was still coming for him, undeterred by the gunshot, jaws open wide as it swung its head wildly, eyes glowing a fierce, brilliant yellow. It leapt forward, shadows drifting over its skin as its claws came up, rough and grey like stone and swiping at Kramer's face -

He ducked aside, diving to the ground and rolling off to the left as the creature smacked into the wall. Plaster cracked and caved in as the shadowy creature's body slid down to the carpet and it turned, snarling, contorting and twisting as Kramer staggered to his feet.

'What the fuck are you?' he breathed. The creature grinned. Long, bony teeth unsheathed from its black gums and its jaw dislocated, hanging loose as its mouth opened wider. The top of its head slid back and all Kramer saw was that terrible pit of a mouth, rings of fangs surrounding a sliver of tongue, spiralling in towards the bloody, black cavern of its throat. It roared and spittle flew on its hot breath, spattered the floor.

'Eat this,' Kramer grunted, firing again.

The bullet smacked the shadow creature square in the mouth and it howled, raising its head. Its jaws twisted and shrunk back into a horrific, bleeding skull and for a second its entire form shifted, writhing like black, stringy putty in the wet, phlegm-covered hands of a toddler.

Then it lowered its head and the muscles over its back solidified as it arched its spine and moved towards Kramer with death burning in its mouth. A thick coat of dark, black blood rolled off its tongue as it slobbered.

'Guns don't work, then,' Kramer murmured, and he turned and ran.

The thing roared behind him as he raced down the next corridor, pivoting round a corner, grey coat fluttering behind him as his boots thundered over the carpet. The shadow followed him, clambering up the walls, body twisting around the corners of the corridor as it moved, digging its claws into the ceiling and crawling with powerful, muscular legs. Kramer glanced

434

up, lifted the gun above his head, fired blind as he ran. A howl brought the creature crashing down to the ground behind him but it was up in less than a second and thick, dark claws grabbed for his head -

Kramer sent an elbow flying up into the creature's throat, grunted as a shiver of pain shot up from his twisted ankle. He ducked beneath the thing's swinging arms and stumbled forward, turned another corner. The shadow creature barrelled forward, missed the turn, pulled itself back around, snarling as it reached for him.

The door at the end of the corridor was locked. Kramer looked desperately behind him, clocked the beast as it lunged, cried out as a warm, sticky wetness lashed his face. Blood pooled in his mouth.

'Fuck you!' Kramer yelled, slamming his body into the door. He tore at the handle, jerking it wildly, trying to force it open. No good. He took a step back, screaming as claws slashed at his twisted ankle. He lifted the gun, aimed it toward the door handle -

A shadow passed over the door and the control panel on the wall flickered. Kramer didn't have time to frown - he ducked underneath another sweeping claw and squeezed through the door into the dark beyond, slammed it behind him. Quickly he turned, jammed the handle, made sure it was locked. Slowly, he took a step back, eyes on the door...

Behind the wood, the creature howled, crashed into the door. The whole thing shuddered as it pounded and bit and scratched at the door and Kramer raised the gun again, breathing heavy, wiped blood from his face with a tattered sleeve.

'Come on then, bitch,' Kramer whispered.

Behind him, something moved in the shadows of the corridor.

'Who are you?'

Kramer jumped, turned around, holding the gun high. In a moment, his eyes had adjusted to the dark, and he saw them. Half a dozen at least, seven or eight maybe. Men and women, all dressed in the inmates' uniform. White t-shirts clung to scrawny bodies and they looked at him, quizzical and suspicious and angry.

'What are you doing here?' one of them asked. A thick, broken accent dripped off the man's words as he stepped out of the shadows, eyes dark and black. His hair was shaved, buzzed close to his skull, and his jaw was burned and bubbling.

Behind the buzzcut man, a woman raised her head - the woman who had first spoken, eyes wild and round and insane. Her skin was wrinled and pulled back over a tight, shrivelled skull. Her hands clasped in front of her, fingers twisted in a cat's cradle of tight knuckles and thin, pale skin, she smiled. 'Have you come to take us home?'

A big, black woman at the end of the corridor pointed a beefy finger at the gun in Kramer's hand and her eyes narrowed. 'He's come to kill us,' she said.

436

Another of the inmates nodded. 'We should kill him first.'

'Sounds good,' said the buzzcut man. 'Who wants him?'

Kramer swallowed. Behind him, there was another heavy, splintering crash at the door.

'Oh, shit.'

7

Eddie watched as the shadow creature snarled and snapped at the door, face empty of emotion. His hands hung by his sides, shoulders hunched just a little. The muscles of his neck and chest rippled. Slowly, he raised a hand to his throat, brushed the scars there with his fingertips. Something in him felt different, this close to the beast. Stronger, somehow.

It crashed its skull into the door in a desperate attempt to bring it down, and something splintered deep within the wood. A few more hits like that, and it would be through. The creature bowed its head to strike again, drool swinging from its jaws -

It stopped.

'That's it,' Eddie whispered. 'Guess who?'

In his hand, the bloody fork twitched.

The creature stood there for a second, ragged breaths convulsing along its body. It shivered, lowered its head. A slit of yellow peered back over its spiny shoulder, narrowed and furious. Eddie saw so much, then, in that single eye, so much that he had missed. He saw hatred, pure, *raw* hatred, saw pain and suffering and sorrow and gorgeous, beautiful hunger. He saw anger and rage and greed and everything else he couldn't feel and somehow, in the twisted nothing inside his head, he felt *sorry* for the monster.

'Look what you've done to me,' Eddie breathed. 'I'm... feeling.'

Slowly, the creature turned around. The pads of its claws flattened on the carpet as it stood, panting, looking Eddie up and down. He could see the shivers of its heartbeat as they racked a horrible, deformed chest, as every bone rippled and tremored. Its spine twisted and cracked in its back as it took a single, slow step forward.

'No closer,' Eddie shook his head. 'Not yet. Let me look at you...'

The creature stopped moving, stood still for a moment. Its breathing had slowed and its eyes dulled, the fiery glow in them dampening and smouldering as it calmed. The armoured plates over its skin slid back and disappeared beneath layers of muscle and shadow and slowly it stood up on its hind legs, long, crooked claws dangling by its side. It waited. Long, slender arms dropped from bent shoulders and dripping talons curled and uncurled as the thundering heartbeats that had rocked its chest slowed to a gentle, quiet rhythm.

Something new stirred in Eddie, an appreciation that he hadn't realised, until now, had been missing from him. It had been years, now, since he had felt anything like that, since he had felt anything at all. Perhaps it was because the creature was so close, or...

Eddie paused. There was another feeling, buried at the back of his skull, mirrored in aa dark, twisted pain in his gut. Beneath the admiration of this thing, the unearthly desire to be at one with it again, to be *whole* again, he felt... sorrow. Loss. Guilt. He remembered, all those years ago, digging his fingers into Nana's throat and tearing out her windpipe. He remembered raising the rusted hacksaw to his father's broken neck and sawing away at his flesh, remembered turning the same saw on his undead mother once Philip Drake's head had hit the ground.

He remembered the car crash, the yellow-faced man in the road, that beautiful, white-streaked deer laying bloody and broken on the tarmac. He remembered the worst thing he had ever felt, trapped in the backseat of that car, remembered it so clearly.

Fear.

Eddie shook his head, closed his eyes for a moment. These weren't his feelings, weren't his memories. They belonged to the shadow, to the sick carnage that it called a mind. They belonged in that bloody soup of a heart that the shadow had learned to form in its chest.

'You're beautiful,' Eddie whispered, eyes on the

thing. 'I've waited so long...'

He gestured the creature towards him and it moved, sinking onto its front legs and stalking forward on all fours, head dipped to the ground. Shadows drifted about its face.

'That's it,' Eddie said, fingers wrapped tight around the shining, silver fork.

The creature paused, eyes dropping to the bloody thing. Eddie felt that fear again, felt it rise up in his chest and propel his heart into a spinning, clapping blade that juddered against his ribs.

Eddie shook his head. 'I'm not going to hurt you,' he said. 'Not you.'

The fear sunk back and Eddie's heart slowed. Cautiously, the creature looked up at him.

'Never,' Eddie said, and the creature's lips pulled back from vicious, jagged teeth and it *grinned*.

8

Debbie crumpled to her knees at the edge of the forest, clutching her savaged arm. She gritted her teeth as a hot, searing agony tore up her arm and throbbed over her chest. Gasping, she glanced down at the wound, clamping a hand over her mouth to suppress the scream that was trying to force its way out of her throat. Once this new wave of pain had subsided, the hand moved to her shirt and she tugged it down to her waist, grunted as she tore the material. She bit her lip and wrapped the shredded fabric around the torn flesh of her wrist. The pain worsened as she pulled it tight, tied it awkwardly with her good hand. She couldn't help but cry out, stumbled to her feet. The wind blew harsh and bitter at her face, scratched at her newly-exposed side.

'Get help,' she murmured, walking forward. The pain crippled her thoughts and she blinked wildly into the wind, heart pounding muffled and dull in her ears. Her ankles twisted over each other and she fell, scuffed her cheek in the gravel.

Debbie propped herself up on her good arm, panting. She was tempted to stay there, now, to give up and wait for some kind of pain-induced fatigue to swallow her up and drag her into unconsciousness. The cold washed over her body and she pressed her nose to the dirt, braced herself. 'You have to get up,' she whispered. 'You have to get... to the station.'

She pulled herself back onto her knees, swayed a little. A drunken haze came over her and she laid her hand on the crudely-bandaged arm, squeezed a little as if the pain would be released, somehow, by the pressure.

'Feet,' she mumbled, and she stood up. Unsteady, she moved forward, staggering along the path. As she turned away from the forest and began heading up the slant of the island towards the village, the road before her sunk under orange streetlights, flickering in the dark. A low mist had rolled in off the ocean and it laid over the ground like a shifting, swirling blanket, slipping over blades of grass and filtering over the foliage that had blown out of the forest and cluttered the hills.

Debbie turned her head as she walked, looked back into the trees. Usually, even through the thick of the woods, she would be able to see the asylum from here, or at least the glare of the floodlights that surrounded it, but not tonight,

Black River Asylum had gone dark.

Debbie swallowed and kept moving. Her arm dangled, heavy, at her side. Blood pooled over the bandage, seeping thick and wet through the folds of the torn material. Her shoulder was numb and it felt as though the blood flowing from her chest out to that side of her body had slowed and gone cold.

'There you are,' she whispered, reaching the crest of the path. Before her, the village was a distant smudge toward the end of the island, a haze of black rises and yellow lights that drove up out of the mist like a thick, jagged scratch across the landscape of an oil painting. And there, halfway between her and the village - almost exactly halfway between the two ends of the island - was the police station. A handful of cars parked out front told her there should be somebody there. A couple of officers, at least. The building was a low, squat thing, a dull structure of brick and glass set into a wide, tarmac compound. Moonlight dripped off the slanted roof and slid over the windows.

Debbie kept walking.

As she reached the station, dirt turned to concrete and her feet found solid ground. Her arm throbbed. A few more rough, shaky steps and she was in the compound, good hand resting on the gatepost as she turned. She paused for a minute, caught her breath as the wind whipped around her.

Debbie pushed forward, stumbled to the front door. Her good hand slid into her belt and she yanked out the keys, jammed them into the lock. The door opened and she fell into the hallway, leant against the wall as she caught her breath. She kept her shoulder to the wall as she stumbled forward, forced open the door and stepped into the office. There was a first aid box on a desk past the door and she spent a minute struggling with the lid, grabbed a roll of gauze and taped up her arm as best as she could manage.

Debbie turned, flicked on the lights. The station was empty.

'Hello?' she called, moving forward into the office. Desks littered with paper and coffee-stained were abandoned, computer screens flickering, mugs still steaming. 'Anyone here?'

No reply.

Debbie moved to her desk, fumbled with the top drawer. She grabbed her gun, slid it into her belt, searched the desk for her car keys. No sign. She had left them just *here...*

Debbie's eyes flickered up to her computer screen. She frowned. She was certain she had turned the computer off yesterday afternoon, but a word document was open, some ramble of unfinished paperwork half-typed on the display. She reached out to turn the thing off -

Debbie froze.

As she watched, new letters appeared on the screen, a string of type bursting rapidly across the document in a blur of black-and-white. Debbie glanced down at the keyboard. Nothing moved. When she turned her eyes back to the screen the message had been written out so many times that it had formed half a page of text

he is coming he is coming he is coming he is coming he is coming

and she took a step back from the screen, turned to move around to Kramer's desk. The same message flickered on his computer, typed in grim red font over a black screen.

He is coming.

Debbie swallowed, pored over the papers on Kramer's desk. There had to be something here, a number or a spare set of keys or...

Debbie stopped moving, held her breath as a faint, eerie scratching sounded behind her head. She turned her head, eyes moving up to the wall behind her. Her breath hitched in her throat.

The letters had been dug into the plaster, carved into the wall with the tip of a sharp, serrated blade.

HE IS COMING.

CHAPTER SEVENTEEN
ENDGAME

1
NOW

Kramer raised his hands, stepped forward into the corridor. Behind him, the banging had stopped. Perhaps the creature was finding another way around. It had displayed more intelligence than he had imagined possible, even in whatever screaming mess of a brain threw it into the wild rages that had nearly killed him and Debbie.

That had nearly killed Charlotte.

'I don't want to shoot anyone,' Kramer said. His eyes darted from one hungry face to another and he winced. Buzzcut narrowed his eyes while the crazy-eyed lady moved forward, knuckles still twisted together as she played her hands in front of her stomach. 'I'm police,' Kramer continued. 'There's something loose in this building. An animal. A creature. It's dangerous. I'm not here to hurt any of you.'

'No,' buzzcut growled, 'just to stuff us back in our cages, am I right?'

Kramer shook his head. The gun trembled in his hand and he tried to remember how many shots he'd fired so far. Two? Three? Meaning he had a maximum of five bullets left.

There were seven of them, gathered in a bunch in the corridor. Behind them, shafts of pale, red light sifted through the gaps in the open cell doors. 'I don't want to hurt anyone,' Kramer said again. 'And I don't want to force you back in your cells. What I want is for you to let me do what I have to do, okay? This creature needs to be stopped. It needs to be killed.'

'He's lying,' someone hissed. A red-haired man at the end of the corridor, arms folded over his chest.

The broad, black woman nodded. 'You're not here to stop any creature.'

'Didn't you see it?' Kramer tried, desperate. He pointed his gun at the door, gesturing wildly. Blood trickled out of the cuts over his face and he moved forward again, leaning heavily on his good ankle. 'Look, I'll leave you all alone. I don't want to cause any trouble with you. I just... if anyone knows a way through, or...'

'We should kill him before he kills us,' said the wild-haired lady.

'Aren't you listening to me?' Kramer cried. 'I just...'

'Stop talking,' the buzzcut man said quietly. Kramer

turned to him, looked into the man's eyes. He had taken a step forward, and his face was bathed in the throbbing, red light from a cracked bulb above his head. 'We've heard enough.'

'Kill him,' said the black woman.

Kramer shook his head. Slowly, he pointed the gun at the buzzcut man's chest. 'Listen to me,' he said. 'Just let me through, and I won't hurt anyone. There's no need for this.'

Buzzcut stepped forward again. His hands bunched into fists. 'How about you give me the gun, then?' he said.

'I need this. The creature...'

Buzzcut held out his hand. 'The gun.'

'Kill him!' the black woman cried again.

Behind her, the red-haired man pointed a shaking finger. 'He's not here for any creature! He wants to kill us all!'

'Is that true?' buzzcut said. 'Do you want to kill us all, detective?'

Kramer looked into the man's eyes and shook his head. 'You know I don't,' he said. 'Please.'

Buzzcut took one more step and smiled.

'Oh, don't make me do this,' Kramer said.

Another step. 'I will tear that gun from your hands and rip out your throat, son,' buzzcut snarled.

'Please,' Kramer said.

At the end of the corridor, inmates cheered the

buzzcut man on. 'Kill him!' yelled the black woman.

Buzzcut took another step and grinned.

Kramer angled the gun and squeezed the trigger. Buzzcut yelled as the bullet sheared his kneecap and blood spurted out of the top of his shin as the bone splintered and shattered, passing out the back of his leg. He toppled, fell back against the wall clutching at his bloody knee.

'Anyone want the next one?' Kramer yelled.

'Monster!' screeched the wild-haired lady. She lunged forward, swinging a twisted hand towards him as he swung the gun about, aimed at her foot -

The gun tumbled from his hand as the old lady knocked his arm and skittered over the carpet, spinning beneath a white-trainered foot and disappearing in the shadows. Suddenly the lady's hands were on his face, her thumbs bent and digging into his eyeballs, and Kramer brought his knee crashing into her belly, sending her sprawling backwards. Someone reached for the gun, grabbing at it with a withered, vein-stricken hand, but his arm was kicked away by another inmate as a third - the big black woman - slammed a meaty fist into his face. The red-haired man seized his moment and leapt for the gun and now buzzcut was scrambling to his feet, leaning back on his good leg, screaming as he launched a fist towards Kramer's nose -

Crack!

Buzzcut's bald head exploded in a fine, red mist as

the bullet smacked the back of his skull and sunk into his brain. His eyeball bulged out of its socket and rolled back into his head and bone erupted, crumbling away as the bullet passed through and coils of brain and blood splashed the wall.

The corridor went silent as the inmates stopped, watched in horror as buzzcut stumbled. For a moment he stood there, fist still raised, one eye staring straight forward as blood pooled over his iris and the top of his face caved in, strings of flesh dropping over his cheek and drizzling thin, red lines of blood down over his lips and his throat. He crumpled, shattered knee giving way first, fell onto his face.

The gun fell and the red-haired man stepped back. 'I...'

'Enough,' Kramer said. 'Give me the gun.'

After a second, there was movement. The wild-haired lady with the twisted hands bent down, grabbed it. She hesitated, finger hovering over the trigger, eyes darting from buzzcut's drooling brains to Kramer's face.

'Give it to me,' Kramer said. 'Now.'

Slowly, she handed it over.

Kramer opened up the chamber and looked over the magazine. Three bullets left. Three shots. Clicking the magazine back into place, he slid the gun into his belt and looked up. 'You all better hope that's enough,' he said.

He turned, reached for the door handle. It was

jammed shut. He waited, a second, for whatever shadow had opened it before to return and do the same again. Nothing.

Whatever had let him through, it didn't want him to go back. It was trying to keep him away from the creature, he realised. That could only be a good thing. Kramer turned, back to the door. 'Now someone, tell me. Is there another way around?'

Silence. Then the black woman stepped forward, nodded her head. She pointed to the far end of the corridor. 'Round to the left. Keep turning left and it'll bring you back around.'

Kramer walked through their midst, stepping over buzzcut's bloody corpse. He nodded at the red-haired man as he passed, the man who had shot buzzcut's head open. 'Thank you.'

'I missed,' the man whispered, and Kramer kept walking, hobbling on his torn ankle, hand hovering over the gun at his belt.

2

Charlotte pressed her forehead against the panelling of the front door, eyes locked on the bolt. A shadow passed across the frosted window above her head and a tear seeped out of her eye as she clamped a hand over her mouth. Yellow Face stood on the doorstep, rasping breaths throwing cold, grey mist onto the glass.

'Aren't you going to let me in?' he said, and Charlotte whimpered. His voice was grainy and coarse but it dripped with malice and seemed to slip straight through the keyhole like wind. 'You should be more accommodating, you little bitch. You filthy, putrid little _'

'Shut up!' Charlotte yelled. 'Just shut up!'

The yellow man was silent. Charlotte took a step back from the door. His tall, slender silhouette was still there, behind the window, balding skull prominent in the moonlight. His shoulders were crooked.

'Leave me alone,' Charlotte whispered, brushing a tear off her cheek, smearing it over her skin. 'Please. Just go.'

'You don't remember me,' said the nightmare-faced figure. 'He never told you, did he?'

'That's enough,' Charlotte said. 'Leave me alone.'

'He never told you who I am... who *you* are...'

Charlotte frowned. Outside, hazy beyond the little window, the yellow man tilted his head. The corners of his silhouetted skull pulled up as he smiled.

'Daddy never told you about ol' Yellow Face, *did* he?'

'Shut up!' Charlotte roared, pounding her fist against the door. 'Shut up about my dad! You don't know anything, you... you *twat!* You're just some freak of nature, some twisted *fuck*, you get away from my house right now!'

A yellow hand pressed against the window and

452

Charlotte stumbled back, eyes wide. 'Leave me alone...'

'Oh, I'm so much more than twisted,' Yellow Face rasped, and his voice filled Charlotte's head like a disease, made her numb. 'I'm a deranged bastard, you know. But I am so much more than you know...'

'What are you?' Charlotte whispered.

'I am the end,' Yellow Face said, smiling with rotten, wet teeth. Then he disappeared.

Charlotte blinked. The silhouette on the doorstep had vanished, faded into the dark of the night. She moved forward, peered out through the window - nothing. The doorstep was empty.

Something moved in the back garden and Charlotte whirled around. 'Back door,' she breathed, and she was running, staggering awkwardly past the stairs and dipping through the laundry room, making her way to the back of the house. She reached for the lock, slid a heavy, flat bolt across, breathed a sigh of relief. She turned, moved back into the hall -

The front door hung open. Moonlight poured in over the doorstep, slanted over the carpet in the hallway. The wind bit at Charlotte's face as she shook her head. 'No...'

He was in the house. Somehow, the man with the yellow face had unlocked the front door and got in and now she was in here with him, *alone* in here with him...

Charlotte rushed toward the front door and slammed it shut. Maybe he wasn't in here. Maybe the wind had opened the door, somehow, or...

'There's my little girl,' Yellow Face said behind her, and Charlotte screamed as a wrinkled, pus-covered hand covered her mouth and hot breath shivered over the back of her head.

3

The creature looked Eddie up and down, licking its blood-flecked teeth with a slippery, bumpy tongue. Its eyes were a hot, smouldering black, like cooling coals left in the ashes of a burnt-out fire. Tiny flakes of glowing amber seemed to float in the shadow around the thing's face, like embers drifting to the ground.

Eddie paused. 'All this time,' Eddie said, 'I waited. You know, I didn't think it would take this long.'

A bead of blood drooled over the prongs of the fork in his hand. He remembered thrusting the fork into Hayley's eyeball, remembered scooping it out of her face in a mess of goop and blood, and he felt... *remorse*.

'Is it you?' he said. 'Ae you doing this to me?'

The creature said nothing. A trickle of low, quiet rumbling emanated from its throat as it blinked. Eddie could feel the thing's heartbeat echo around him, feel the warmth of its breath as it seeped out into the corridor. He felt pain, at the band of scarred flesh around his belly, at the scars across his own throat.

'I haven't felt pain in years,' he said. He had missed it.

Slowly, the creature took a step forward. It was barely six feet from him now, and Eddie swallowed. It was inexplicable, he realised, that he would be afraid of this thing, but he couldn't push it down, couldn't quell the fear.

'How does this work, then?' Eddie said. 'How do I... how do I get you back?'

The creature didn't reply, tilted its head. Sniffed the air. Slippery, grey-brown skin shifted and rippled over its back as its coiled spine clicked and moved.

'Tell me,' Eddie said. 'Tell me how to be whole again.'

He looked behind him, as if the yellow-faced man might appear suddenly and guide him forwards. The nightmare figure had helped him out, helped him find the creature... where was he now?

'I wanted you back,' Eddie said slowly, turning back to face the thing. 'You know, all those years, I never wanted a damn thing, but I wanted you back. Now you're here, and I... I don't know what to do.'

The creature smiled.

Slowly, it reared up onto its hind legs and closed its eyes. Shadows started to curl and twist around its limbs, around its caved-in belly, around its shoulders and throat until it was all but consumed by darkness, by a thin, dark mist that Eddie couldn't help but recognise from all those years ago. The same dark mist that had been trapped in that jar upstairs at Nana's, the very same that he had abandoned over twenty years ago and

455

wanted back ever since...

Then the darkness cleared, and the creature's form shifted, changing. Bones twisted into knots and forced themselves up through its grey skin and its limbs peeled back, shrank into its spiny shoulders as it convulsed, head lowered, throat closing in. A horrific cracking sound rang out in the corridor as the thing found a new form, a far more human form, about the same height and weight as Eddie except it still had that same mucus-covered, grey-brown skin and its spine was all twisted up to the left so that it stood awkwardly, head tilted to one side. Its face was gone and its grey, shadowy skull was blank and expressionless. It stepped forward.

'No,' Eddie said. 'That's not how we're doing this. Show me what you really look like. No more pretence, alright? No more made-up nightmare faces. No more claws. Show me *you*.'

The faceless figure clenched its fists and shadows pooled over its skin and one more time it began to change. Muscles sprouted and spread over cracking, fusing bones and tendons snapped between scraps of grey flesh that were slowly gaining colour, and its face twisted up and tore itself into shape and the thing screamed as pink skin wrapped around it, coloured with blood and fear.

The thing's transformation was complete.

Eddie blinked. 'So that's how we're playing this, is it?'

456

The thing smiled. It looked exactly like him.

For a moment, the two Eddies stared into each other's eyes, faces blank and emotionless, black, tangled hair matted and bloody. The thing had mirrored him, right down to the white t-shirt and the fork in his hand, except it was covered in blood; crimson trails ran over its face, seeped from its eyes. Dark, wet pools spread over its shadowy clothes.

'You want me back,' it said, speaking with Eddie's mouth for the first time; the words seemed jumbled, messed up, coming off of that borrowed tongue, and it rasped and spat as it spoke. 'You know what to do.'

Eddie shook his head. 'Honestly, I never thought this far ahead.'

The second Edward Drake grinned, blood-stained teeth glinting in the pulsing lights of the corridor. Its eyes glared a fiery, crackling orange.

'Remember how you gave me away,' it hissed. 'Just say *yes.*'

4

The creature moved forward in Eddie's skin, a bloody replica of the man. Its entire body shifted and pulsed in a coil of shadow, and it left dark, bloody footprints in the carpet. 'Just say yes,' the thing repeated, and Eddie cringed at the sound of his own voice, hollowed out and stripped of whatever cadence and speech patterns he usually carried and replacing them with a low, near-inaudible hiss that sifted over every word. 'Let me back in, Edward, and we can be one again. We can be *me* again.'

Eddie gritted his teeth, held firm. He opened his mouth to reply. Surely it couldn't be that easy. The single word that had damned him to a hollow existence for the last twenty-four years couldn't be the one to free him again.

'This is it, then,' Eddie whispered. The creature smiled with his bloody lips, showing off those spattered teeth again. Its eyes flashed golden yellow and it nodded.

'Say it...'

Something moved at the end of the corridor. 'Whatever the fuck you are,' came a voice from behind Eddie's shoulder, 'get away from him now.'

Eddie sighed, turning his head. 'You again?'

Matthew Kramer stood with the gun in his hand, looking from one Eddie to the other. The pistol wavered as something faltered in his expression; he wasn't sure what he was looking at. Eddie supposed he couldn't blame the man.

'Which one is... for fuck's sake,' Kramer shook his head, steadying the gun, aiming at the real Eddie's head. 'Which one is Edward Drake?'

Eddie smiled. 'We both are,' he said.

Kramer frowned, turned the gun on the replica. The

second Eddie gave him the same smile, the *exact* same expression, but his lips were red and dripping. His eyes were the giveaway.

'How does it do that?' Kramer said, keeping his gun trained on the monster.

'We don't have time for this,' Eddie said quietly. 'You need to leave, detective. Take the gun and go. There are bigger things on the way. It would be a shame for you to die tonight, wouldn't it?'

'It's killed,' Kramer said, eyes never leaving the monster's not-quite-human face. 'You know that, don't you? You know that it's killed people on this island.'

'I do.'

'And you know I can't let that slide.'

'Bigger things -'

'Enough!' Kramer shouted. 'Bigger things, I know!' He flipped the gun back on Eddie, pointed the barrel right between the man's eyes. 'Leviathan, right? And the yellow man. I know. But right now I'm looking at a psychopath and his monster buddy and I know I've got enough bullets for both of you.'

Eddie shook his head. 'You should leave,' he said. 'Now. Before we... before I let *him* kill you.'

'Then at least tell me first,' Kramer said. The gun switched hands and he trained it on the creature's false face, watched as blood oozed from the corners of the second Eddie's eyes. 'Tell me what it is. What it's doing here. What the hell this all has to do with you. Tell me who the man with the yellow face is and why the *fuck* he gave me a child to look after.'

Eddie tilted his head. 'You don't know who he is,' he said, and for a second he almost sounded curious. 'Yet, you took the girl.'

'I didn't have a choice,' Kramer said. 'And I don't regret a damn thing.'

Eddie smiled. 'You will,' he said. 'Once you find out what she is. What she's capable of.'

'I don't know what you're talking about,' Kramer said.

Suddenly the Edward Drake replica stepped forward. 'You waste our time,' it said, voice a shallow reflection of the one it had copied. 'Run.'

'I would do as he says, if I were you,' Eddie said.

Kramer swallowed. 'Answers,' he said. 'Now.'

'*No,*' Eddie hissed, and then the replica was lurching forwards, blood-soaked skin twisting and peeling as bony, grey claws burst out of the flesh of its palms and long, slender forelimbs tore out of the shredded skin and muscle of its arms. The second Eddie's face was ripped apart by a gaping, jagged-toothed maw and the creature lunged, barrelling towards Kramer as it changed. Ragged bones punctured its body and threw it into a spiralling convulsion as its spine cracked and bent and *writhed.*

It raised its claws, tearing up the wall and twisting around the ceiling until it was right on top of Kramer

460

and it opened its mouth wide and screamed spit and blood. Kramer pointed the gun upward and fired and a bullet smacked the creature in its nightmare face, and as it fell to the ground it shifted again, pulling shadows from the corners of the corridor as it found a new, humanoid form, one taller than the first, one Kramer recognised.

He stumbled back as the creature snarled, lips pulling back as its face shrunk and broke into something more human, something terrible. Kramer shook his head. 'No,' he breathed.

The creature stood on two legs, one ankle twisted and bloody, face scarred and red. A long, grey overcoat hung about its knees and it looked at Kramer, smiling wickedly with the detective's own face.

'Like looking into a mirror,' it said with his voice, spitting out the words like they were poison. Kramer watched as the creature licked its lips - *his* lips - and the smile grew wider. Burnt, yellow eyes narrowed.

'You know what I've just realised,' Kramer said, breathless. The gun hung, limp, in his hand.

The creature cocked an eyebrow. 'What's that?'

'I need to shave,' Kramer said, nodding towards the thing's borrowed face, and he raised the gun and pointed it at his doppelganger's skull.

5

Edward Drake watched as the detective and his blood-soaked replica fought, eyes locked on them as they moved. His thoughts were dulled, numbed by some throbbing pain at the top of his skull and he frowned, laid a hand at his temple. The pain was warm and fuzzy and Eddie blinked, tried to will it away. It was relentless.

In front of him, the creature lunged for Kramer's throat, biting and snapping with jagged, bony teeth as its mouth tore open its copied face. The detective ducked beneath the snapping jaws and slammed an elbow into his doppelganger's groin and the fake-Kramer lashed out with a fist, knocked it square into the real version's jaw. Blood flew and the fist split, bloody knuckles cracking open as a grey set of long, vicious claws broke free of the human skin.

'That's cheating!' Kramer yelled, grabbing the creature's wrist, holding the curled claws millimetres from his face.

Eddie turned away, clutched at his chest as a surge of adrenaline rushed to his heart. He had felt something like this before, when the creature had killed those two on the beach. Not as strong as this, but recognisable. He felt what it felt. He hurt when it hurt. The pain in his head...

Eddie closed his eyes, thought back. Kramer had

shot the thing in the head. Now Eddie's temple *burned*. Whatever connection he and the thing shared, it was stronger now that they were together. Now that they were so close. All he had to do was say yes.

Eddie looked back toward the creature, watched as it broke free of Kramer's skin, wriggling out of the bloody, flesh-bound cage it had made for itself in a confusion of grey and black and shining, haunted yellow. It plunged its claws into Kramer's thigh and grinned as spines rippled on its back, thicker and darker than before, lengthening even as Eddie watched. Kramer screamed, falling to his knees, jabbing the gun into the creature's belly.

Eddie opened his mouth. All it would take was a word...

Eddie, someone whispered. He whirled around, half-expecting to see her at the other end of the corridor. There was no one there.

'Mother...' he whispered. He closed his eyes again and he saw her, trapped in the passenger seat of an overturned car, blood pouring down from her belly to her throat as a sliver of shining, wet glass poked out of her gut.

My Eddie.

Eddie swallowed. For a moment, he was just a little boy. Just a scared little boy trapped in the backseat of a broken wreck, praying that somebody would come save him. He *remembered...*

'No,' he murmured. A surge of pain shot up his ankle and he grimaced.

Eddie turned, one last time, and his eyes snapped open.

His grip tightened on the handle of the bloody fork.

6

Kramer gritted his teeth as the creature sunk its claws into his leg, collapsed as he shoved the gun upwards. 'Fuck you!' he yelled. 'Whatever the fuck you are, *fuck* you!'

The creature grinned, twisting its claws, a savage kind of satisfaction spreading over its face. Kramer shrieked as the muscles in his leg shredded and a tendon snapped, springing back and sending a cold, electric pain shooting up to his hip. The barrel of the gun slammed into the creature's gut and his finger hovered over the trigger as the thing leered down at him. Its face changed and contorted - one second it was a snarling, animal mask of horror, the next it was Edward Drake. The next, a bloody reflection of his own. The creature's body twisted and convulsed as it threw itself between forms, and Kramer pulled back, aiming carefully as his target changed and morphed and writhed in a shroud of shadow.

'Be me,' Kramer whispered, and the creature froze in his shape, grinning wildly. It reached up with a mangled hand and wiped blood from its lips, stepped forward.

'Fitting,' the creature hissed through Kramer's mouth, 'that you would die at your own hands.'

'No,' Kramer shook his head, lowering the gun. 'I just know my own weak points.'

He fired and the bullet tore through the replica's twisted ankle, shearing bone and severing the tendons at the back of its scarred, already-torn Achilles' heel. The thing roared, slipping back into some primal, shadowy form as the pain dragged it to the ground. It fought against the pain and lunged and Kramer stumbled back, pressing his back to the wall.

The creature snatched at Kramer's throat and wrapped cold, rough claws around his neck and squeezed and Kramer launched his fist into the thing's gut, kicking out and sending his boot into its groin. It barely flinched and Kramer retched as the air seeped out of his throat and his head throbbed as the thing crushed his neck with those long, serrated claws and his lungs threatened to burst in his chest -

Kramer jabbed the barrel of the gun up into the creature's chest and fired his last bullet.

The thing's ribs shattered as its skin tore back in an explosion of black and grey and brown, mucus and blood splashing the walls as it staggered back, letting go of Kramer's throat and dropping him to the ground. Its chest caved in and Kramer glanced up, watched as the thing's heart beat once, twice, dripping and pulsing and shrivelling as the bullet buried itself in the twisted organ, shining and black in that mess of a cavity. The creature fell to one knee, clutching at the air with its claws as it screamed -

The screaming stopped. The creature stood on its hind legs, glanced down at its ruptured chest, then its eyes moved back to Kramer's and it smiled.

'Nice try,' it hissed.

As Kramer watched, the thing's broken ribs started to burst outward and fuse together and the bullet wriggled free of its blackened heart, dropped to the carpet. In seconds, the skin had sealed over and any evidence of a bullet wound had disappeared altogether.

'Oh, fuck,' Kramer said. He pointed, squeezed the trigger -

Click.

'No!' he screamed as the creature bore towards him, reaching out as it grinned with that horrible, splintered mouth. He pressed the trigger again, harder -

Click.

Click click click click click click -

'Enough,' the creature rasped, grabbing Kramer by the hair and dragging him up to his feet. 'I'm done with you.'

Kramer dropped the gun and his eyes widened as the creature's bloody jaw dislocated and its teeth rattled with some unearthly hunger. In one last, futile act of defiance Kramer slammed the toe of his boot into the creature's gut, twisted ankle screaming at him as his shoe connected with thick, armoured flesh. Hot breath tore at his face as the creature's maw opened wider, black and bloody and *greedy* -

Then it screamed and the claws around Kramer's throat moved to its own, clutching at its jugular. Kramer fell to the ground, crumpled onto his back, and his head thumped the wall. He watched as the creature collapsed, black mist tearing out of a rupture in its neck, drifting up into the air as it screamed and twisted and its body was thrown into fits. Its eyes widened and dulled and its form was tossed about in a wild mess of limbs and shadowy, broken skin and it reached one last time for Kramer's heart -

The thing collapsed and laid still.

Slowly, Kramer turned his head, panting.

Edward Drake was on his knees on the carpet, blood spurting from a puncture in his throat. The prongs of the fork were buried deep in his jugular and deep, strong rivers of crimson flowed from the wound and spattered the walls.

'No...' Kramer whispered.

Eddie's eyes dropped, met his. 'I wanted... to be whole,' he said, blood bubbling out of his lips. 'For so long, I wanted to be... *whole.*'

'What have you done?'

'If I'd let it in...' Eddie gargled, eyes rolling up in his head, 'I would have been...'

He fell, face smacking the ground as the fork throbbed in his neck. Blood pooled into the carpet. 'I would have been like *you...*' he hissed.

'I don't understand,' Kramer grunted. He stood, clutching at his bloody leg. His face burned with blood. 'What was that thing?'

'Don't you *get* it?' Eddie hissed. His eyes moved up and he breathed heavy, dribbling blood. 'It was *me.*'

Eddie's eyes closed and Kramer stood over the man's body, watched as the last breath shuddered out of his lips.

Kramer looked toward the creature, eyes fixed on the black, jagged puncture wound in its throat. His eyes moved back to Eddie and he watched as the fork quivered in the side of Eddie's neck.

Kramer slid down the wall, sat for a while between the two corpses, closed his eyes. Tears slid down his face, mixed with the blood and slithered into his mouth as he sobbed wildly, uncontrollably. He should have felt relief, he knew. He should have felt *something.*

Edward Drake was dead. The creature - whatever it had been - was gone.

Kramer exhaled, listened as his thumping heart slowed.

It was all over.

CHAPTER EIGHTEEN
THE MAN WITH THE YELLOW FACE

1
NOW

Kramer grimaced as he staggered down the corridor. The pain in his torn ankle burned as fresh as it had when the creature's claws had first swiped through the flesh, and a knot of deep, red holes pooled with warmth at the top of his leg. His face was just as badly scarred, and his throat was bruised and coarse, but every step sent a brand new wave of pain up his leg. He would barely make it home, if he didn't get it bandaged up soon.

He glanced down the corridor before him, swallowing hard. It was littered with bodies. Torn apart in the soft, red lights that lit the place, bones wrenched from sockets and torn aside, bloody limbs ripped and shredded. He knelt down by the first body, screwed his eyes shut as he reached down and pulled the tight, bloody t-shirt off of the corpse. It resisted and he yanked it over a limp, lolling head, tore the shirt into a crude bandage. Leaning back against the wall, Kramer tied the fabric in a tight bunch around his ankle, stuffing the ends of the knot into his boot. With the rest of the shirt he wrapped up his bloody thigh, covering the numb wounds, holding the leaking fluid at bay. He sat there for a while, panting heavily, chest rising and falling as the pressure around his leg cut deep into his torn muscles.

With a trembling hand, Kramer reached inside his coat, pulled out his phone. He had one bar of signal – not much, but it would do. Quickly, he found Charlotte's name in his contacts and rang.

No answer.

'Come on…' he whispered. What if something had happened to her? Christ knew how long he'd been down here now. What if something had found her? He tried calling again. The phone rang out. A soft dial tone echoed in his ears.

'Debbie,' he whispered, finding her number quickly and thumbing the faded, green button. He waited as the phone rang, closed his eyes, set the phone to speaker as his hand fell into his lap. 'Pick up,' he murmured. 'Just pick up…'

Nothing.

'Debbie,' Kramer breathed, once the tone had rang out. 'When you get this, call me. It's done. Everything's… it's all over. Just let me know you're safe. Let me know you're okay.'

Kramer hung up, cut the message short. He slid the phone back into his pocket and looked up. The corridor was dark, shadows hanging over everything even in the dim glow of the red bulbs. Corpses littered the floor. Awkwardly he stumbled up, shifted his weight onto his good ankle, hobbling down the hallway. He turned a corner and limped into the reception. The front door was still open.

'Going to be a hell of a walk home,' Kramer grunted, moving towards the door with one hand on the wall to steady himself. His fingertips smeared a sticky trail of red over the plaster as he walked. Blood soaked his shirt, warmed his belly. He ignored the pain, gritting his teeth as he stepped out the front door. Red lights flickered over his face. His eyes fell onto the bonnet of the battered police car and he sighed, heading for the mangled iron gates. There wasn't a chance the thing would start, not with its engine shredded so badly. Even if, by some miracle, the ignition threw the whole thing into some sort of life, it wouldn't get him home.

Kramer winced as he squeezed through the gates, laying a hand on the bonnet of the car. 'I'll be back to fix you up,' he whispered, patting the hood. 'You did good today.'

Kramer tried the phone again, as he walked through the forest, moving slowly, face twisting into a painful scowl every time he stepped on his bad ankle. Charlotte wasn't picking up. Her phone could be out of battery, or she could be asleep…

Or something had happened. Something terrible.

Kramer glanced up at the sky – the moon hung high above his head, fat and shrouded in dark, black clouds. It was late. Charlotte was okay. Just sleeping. That was the only reason she wasn't answering.

Still, he kept trying her until he'd reached the edge of the forest and the village threw itself out of the shadows, thumbing the button every few minutes to see if there was any change. 'It's fine,' he told himself. 'She's fine. You're worrying about nothing.'

His gut twisted up as he hobbled down the main street, dragging his ankle over the tarmac. Streetlights welcomed him home, throwing shadows over the bloody trail he left in the road, bathing his scarred face in crackling, orange light. He turned, past the Crow's Head, limped down the street until he was standing in front of his house.

The light was off in Charlotte's window.

'It's late,' Kramer reminded himself. 'She's asleep. She's fine.'

He drew in a long, deep breath and stumbled up the garden path, reaching for the keys in his overcoat. They fell out of his shaking hand and he bent down to pick them up, almost crying out as a wave of numbness burned his skull. He steadied himself, jammed the keys into the front door. Twisted.

'I'm going to tell her,' Kramer whispered suddenly. He couldn't put it off any longer. He closed his eyes, breathed heavy, fingers shaking as he gripped the key, held it tight in the lock. He should tell her tonight. No more waiting. She was ready. And after tonight…

The door opened.

Kramer lifted his torn ankle over the doorstep and stepped inside, closing the door behind him. 'Charlie?' he called. 'Are you here? Are you okay? Listen, I've got something to…'

Something moved upstairs. Shuffling in the dark.

Kramer frowned. 'Charlie? Are you…'

He trailed off. There was something in the hallway, standing by the stairs. Taller than Charlotte. Slender, long-armed and bent up, as though if it stood perfectly straight its head would bump the ceiling.

'Charlie!' Kramer yelled.

The yellow-faced man stepped forward and Kramer saw the kitchen knife in his hand, too late. A sliver of metal flashed in the dark and he heard Charlotte screaming, somewhere in the house, but the blade of the knife had already plunged into his chest and it slid between his ribs and *twisted* –

'You,' Kramer gargled, and Yellow Face smiled as he pulled the knife free of Kramer's chest and shoved the blade deep into his belly, drawing it up in a jagged, vertical line until the blade caught on the bottom of Kramer's sternum and then the yellow-skinned man

473

thrust it deeper, deeper, until the tip of the knife pierced Kramer's lung and warmth flowed down into his guts.

Something moved in the shadows. Charlotte. Yellow Face turned, yanked the knife out of Kramer's torso, shearing his intestines with a wide, curved sweep.

Red filled Kramer's vision and he fell back, skull smacking the door as blood shot out of his guts and splashed the floor. He grabbed at the mess of his torso but it was too late.

The damage was done.

Matthew Kramer shook his head, swaying as he spoke. 'I had something to tell you...' he rasped. His eyes moved to Charlotte as she threw herself forward, grabbing at the lapels of his jacket. She was screaming something at him, her eyes wide and tearful, face flushed. Kramer looked up at Yellow Face and back to his daughter and he toppled out of her hands, dropped to the ground with a *thud*.

'*Run...*' he whispered.

Everything went black.

2

Hayley held Emma tight in the darkness of the asylum canteen, sobbing into the nurse's shoulder. Outside, the noise had stopped. The building was silent. Slowly, Emma pulled away, turned her head. Hayley shook her head as shapes shifted in the dark.

'Don't leave me,' she whispered. 'Please, please don't go.'

Emma gripped her shoulders tight, tilted her head forward until their foreheads were pressed together. 'I'm not going anywhere,' she said quietly. 'Hayley, I don't know what's going on out there, but you and me are going to be okay, alright?'

She glanced over toward the locked door and exhaled.

'I think they're gone,' Emma said. 'And that… creature. Whatever it was. I think they're gone.'

'What do we do?' Hayley asked. Her eyelids were glued tight, lip quivering as she spoke. Everything seemed louder in the dark; her heartbeat, frantic and fluttering, Emma's breaths on her cheek, the soft, rhythmic tick of a clock on the wall behind her. 'I can't see. We can't stay in here…'

Emma shook her head. 'Not for much longer. We have to get out of the building. I'm going to go to the door, okay? I'm just going to open it and see what's going on out there. See if the coast is clear.'

'Don't leave me,' Hayley said again. 'Please…'

Emma stood up, winced as Hayley gripped her arm. 'I have to see,' Emma said. 'We have to know what's happening. We have to get out if we can.'

The nurse pulled away, stepped back, and Hayley clutched at the air where her hand had been a moment before. 'Please!' she called, face torn up in desperation as Emma's footsteps grew quieter.

'I'll only be a second,' Emma said. 'I promise.'

Hayley listened as Emma tapped digits into the keypad by the door, bowed her head as it clicked open. 'Please…' she whispered.

'I'm coming back,' Emma said. 'Just give me a second…'

Emma stepped outside, and the door closed.

Hayley knelt in the dark for a long time, swaying a little, one hand wrapped around the leg of a plastic table behind her head. The ticking of the clock seemed faster now, louder. A minute passed.

Then another.

'Emma?' Hayley called. Silence. The shadows in the room closed in and Hayley swallowed, heartbeat quickening. 'Emma!'

Blindly, she stood up, holding her hands in front of her as shaky legs carried her forward. She moved slowly around the tables, heading away from the clock behind her head. Emma had gone this way, she was sure…

Hayley's hand hit the wall and she laid it flat on the plaster, walked slowly, carefully along towards the corner of the room. 'Emma!' she said, louder. The shadows stroked the back of her head and she whimpered, one foot crossing the other as she tracked a path along the wall.

Cold metal. The door handle. Hayley wrapped her

fingers around the metal shaft, pulled –

Something slammed into the door and she screamed, stumbled back as it fell open. Something warm and wet slumped over her feet. She crumpled, fumbling with both hands, feeling at the lumpen shape. Her palms moved over a slim, wet throat, shook as she traced the lines of a narrow face, cupped warm cheeks.

'Emma…' she whispered. Two fingers moved to the woman's throat as Hayley felt for a pulse.

Nothing.

'No!' Hayley cried. She clutched at Emma's blouse, cradled the nurse in her lap. '*No!*'

Footsteps, a little way down the hall.

Hayley froze. 'Who's there?' she yelled. 'Did you do this? Did you *kill her?*'

The footsteps stopped. Cold washed over Hayley's face as the darkness swamped her and she whimpered, shrinking back into the shadows.

'Who's there?' she whispered.

'You know who I am,' someone hissed in the dark, and Hayley screamed.

3

1998

The clearing was empty. The trees stood in a perfect circle, crooked, clawed fingers digging up out of the earth and scratching at a full-bellied moon. The forest was alive with cracks and moans and the eerie, rasping whispers of the creatures that roamed the broken foliage in the dark and even the rain that lashed the sky couldn't drown them out. Twisted bodies slithered over cracked bones and branches. The whole forest shifted and morbid, black shapes moved in the shadows and coiled around the trees.

There was no warning. The air in the middle of the clearing bristled with electricity and a narrow, shimmering wall of light tore open the dark, shooting tendrils of white, glistening electricity into the edges of the clearing. The light glowed and swelled and spat something out, a damp, bedraggled silhouette, ankles wet with saltwater. There was something in the little girl's arms, something long and heavy. Blood dripped into the dirt as she stumbled, fell to her knees.

She knelt for a while, panting in the light of the rippling doorway, and the lumpen shape rolled onto the ground. The girl laid a hand on its chest to stop it falling away from her, and after a minute she collapsed, her head falling onto its bloody gut.

The things in the forest watched as she stood, grunting as she dragged the hefty shape up with her. The girl was stronger than she looked, but still, she could go no more than twenty feet before collapsing again, dragging the thing down with her.

It was more than half an hour before Charlotte Kramer reached the edge of the forest. She didn't know

478

what had brought her here, but it had been calling for a long time. In her dreams, in every waking nightmare she had had.

This was the place.

Charlotte stumbled across the gravel driveway, moaning as her shoulders strained under the weight of the thing in her arms. She almost dropped it, halfway to the porch, but she was too close now, too near to fall down.

She was always heading here. She knew that now.

The door opened before Charlotte reached the porch. Orange light threw itself into the dark and a crooked, narrow silhouette stood in the doorway, looked out at the girl with narrow eyes.

'Help me...' Charlotte moaned, falling to her knees.

Matthew Kramer's body fell out of her arms and lay sprawled in the gravel, blood pooling around the jagged cuts in his belly and the twisted, savage hole in his chest. His face was torn to pieces, the bandages over his broken legs red and slick and heavy. His eyes were closed.

'He is dead,' the old woman whispered, standing above the wreckage of Kramer's body.

Charlotte sobbed into the dirt and the stone and nodded. 'Please...' she said.

'There is a cost.' The old woman's voice was cold. 'Are you prepared to pay that cost in full?'

Charlotte Kramer looked up, eyes round and wet and

full of fear. 'I just want him back,' she whispered.

The old woman smiled, her withered face sharp and broken in the moonlight. Her eyes glistened. Her hair was tight and grey, her skin taut over hallowed cheeks. Her throat was bruised, half-covered by the scruff of a tight, black dress that fell down to her ankles so that her long, slender frame seemed to melt into the shadows. 'I'll see what I can do,' she said. Something deep in the forest howled.

'Come,' the woman said, teeth flashing white in the dark. 'Bring him inside.'

'You can help him?' Charlotte said. Thunder rumbled above the forest and the crooked house seemed to moan above them, as if in protest at the oncoming storm.

Nana Death smiled. 'I'll do everything in my power,' she said, and she reached out a withered hand.

Printed in Great Britain
by Amazon